"I am feeling regret for love lost," she said.

He touched his forefinger to her lips. "Do not speak of love," he said. "We have used that word too freely in the past, and it is debased currency between us."

"Is it? I would like to think that we could find some ... affection ... for each other."

He lifted one of her luxuriant curls. "It is a beguiling fantasy that you offer," he said, his voice thickening. "A new start to our lives, the past unwritten, the stained and blotted pages of our marriage wiped clean. But then you have always been the mistress of beguilement, have you not?" He bent his head and covered her mouth in a hard, aggressive kiss.

For a moment—a wild, passionate moment—Robyn felt herself respond to the powerful physical demand of his embrace.

Was it a memory? Or was it a premonition ... ?

Timeless

BUY TWO TOPAZ BOOKS AND GET ONE FREE ROMANCE NOVEL!

With just two purchases of Topaz books, you'll be able to receive one romance novel free from the list below. Just send us two proofs of purchase* along with the coupon below, and the romance of your choice will be on its way to you! (subject to availability/**offer good only in the United States, its territories and Canada**)

Check title you wish to receive:

☐ **WILD WINDS CALLING**
June Lund Shiplett
0-451-12953-9/$4.99($5.99 in Can.)

☐ **A HEART POSSESSED**
Katherine Sutcliffe
0-451-15310-3/$4.50($5.99 in Can.)

☐ **THE DIABOLICAL BARON**
Mary Jo Putney
0-451-15042-2/$3.99($4.99 in Can.)

☐ **THE WOULD-BE WIDOW**
Mary Jo Putney
0-451-15581-5/$3.99($4.99 in Can.)

☐ **TO LOVE A ROGUE**
Valerie Sherwood
0-451-40177-8/$4.95($5.95 in Can.)

☐ **THE TURQUOISE TRAIL**
Susannah Leigh
0-451-40252-9/$4.99($5.99 in Can.)

☐ **SO BRIGHT A FLAME**
Robin Leanne Wiete
0-451-40281-2/$4.99($5.99 in Can.)

☐ **REBEL DREAMS**
Patricia Rice
0-451-40272-3/$4.99($5.99 in Can.)

☐ **THE RECKLESS WAGER**
April Kihlstrom
0-451-17090-3/$3.99($4.99 in Can.)

☐ **LADY OF FIRE**
Anita Mills
0-451-40044-5/$4.99($5.99 in Can.)

☐ **THE CONTENTIOUS COUNTESS**
Irene Saunders
0-451-17276-0/$3.99($4.99 in Can.)

*Send in coupons, proof of purchase (register receipt & photocopy of UPC code from books) plus $1.50 postage and handling to:

TOPAZ ⬥ GIVEAWAY
Penguin USA, 375 Hudson Street, New York, NY 10014

NAME_____

ADDRESS_____ APT. #_____

CITY_____STATE_____ ZIP_____

TIMELESS

by

Jasmine Cresswell

A TOPAZ BOOK

To Alexander and Caitlin
with fondest love

TOPAZ
Published by the Penguin Group
Penguin Books USA Inc., 375 Hudson Street,
New York, New York 10014, U.S.A.
Penguin Books Ltd, 27 Wrights Lane,
London W8 5TZ, England
Penguin Books Australia Ltd, Ringwood,
Victoria, Australia
Penguin Books Canada Ltd, 10 Alcorn Avenue,
Toronto, Ontario, Canada M4V 3B2
Penguin Books (N.Z.) Ltd, 182-190 Wairau Road,
Auckland 10, New Zealand

Penguin Books Ltd, Registered Offices:
Harmondsworth, Middlesex, England

First published by Topaz, an imprint of Dutton Signet,
a division of Penguin Books USA Inc.

First Printing, April, 1994
10 9 8 7 6 5 4 3 2 1

Topaz is a trademark of New American Library,
a division of Penguin Books USA Inc.

Printed in the United States of America

PUBLISHER'S NOTE
This is a work of fiction. Names, characters, places, and incidents either are the product of the author's imagination or are used fictitiously, and any resemblance to actual
persons, living or dead, events, or locales is entirely coincidental.

BOOKS ARE AVAILABLE AT QUANTITY DISCOUNTS WHEN USED TO PROMOTE PRODUCTS OR SER-
VICES. FOR INFORMATION PLEASE WRITE TO PREMIUM MARKETING DIVISION, PENGUIN BOOKS
USA INC., 375 HUDSON STREET, NEW YORK, NEW YORK 10014.

The illustrious House of Hanover and Protestant Succession
By these I lustily will swear—while they can keep possession.
And in that faith and loyaltie I never more will falter.
Great George my King shall ever be—unless the times do alter.

—Eighteenth-Century Folk Rhyme

Prologue

Dorset, England, August 1746

FOR days, William had been waiting to hear that troops had arrived in the village. When he saw the gatekeeper's son running toward him, shirttails flapping in the early morning breeze, he braced himself to receive the news.

"Me lord, soldiers!" The boy was so out of breath, he could barely speak. "A score or more, and they be riding this way. Heading straight for the house, they be."

So, they were come. After days of tense anticipation, William almost welcomed their arrival. His brother's hotheaded and oft-proclaimed devotion to the Stuart cause rendered the entire family suspect, and spies had no doubt reported seeing Zachary in the thick of Charles Stuart's ragtag rebel army. With the Duke of Cumberland's troops determined to chase down every last, pitiful survivor of the Culloden massacre, William knew his estates were seriously at risk. Damn Zachary for the reckless, romantic fool that he was!

William conquered the urge to lash out, to fight back against fate, to cry out his rage and frustration. He reined in his horse and swung around to face the gatekeeper's son.

"Thank you for carrying the message, Tom." The baron spoke mildly, as always, and Tom was rather disappointed by his master's languid response to the great news. It wasn't every day that a backwater village like Starke played host to a troop of redcoats, and Tom would have enjoyed the importance of provoking his lordship to some greater display of emotion. But then, William Bowleigh, third Baron of Starke, was known throughout the county for his placid manners and lack of interest in politics. All he cared about was farming, and new ways to grow turnips, Tom thought with a touch of disdain.

Still, he felt obliged to offer a final warning. "They soldiers bain't far off, me lord. They'll be here right soon."

"I understand." The austere lines of the baron's mouth relaxed into a fleeting smile. "If you go to the kitchen, you may tell Mrs. Moffet that she is to give you a slice of pippin pie. You may have cream, too, if you wish. You did well to let me know of the soldiers' arrival."

"Thankee, me lord, thankee kindly." Tom tugged the scrag of hair hanging over his forehead and forgave his lordship for being a milksop. Pippin pie with cream was almost as exciting as seeing a troop of redcoats. Feet flying over the long grass of the park, he ran to the house in search of his promised treat.

William returned to the stables at a leisurely canter, chatted with his groom and his farrier, then strolled back to the house without any appearance of undue haste. His heart sank when he saw Arabella waiting for him at the door. She greeted him with a perfunctory curtsy, her cheeks white, her beautiful face ravaged by weeks of anxiety and fear.

"Have you heard the news?" she demanded. "Cumberland has sent his butchering monsters into the village. They are riding straight toward this house!"

William stripped off his gloves and handed them to the footman, together with his hat. "I had heard something of the sort, but I confess I do not understand your alarm, my dear—"

"Are you mad?" she demanded, not allowing him to finish his sentence. "They will search the house! They will demand that we turn Zachary over to their mercy—"

William raised an inquiring eyebrow. "I fail to understand your concern, my lady. We have neither of us seen my brother in many months, so we can provide no information likely to lead to his capture."

"And what has that to say to anything? My nerves are in shreds simply thinking about talking to these monsters! Dear God, I swear your heart is carved out of marble! How can you remain so unmoved? Does it not concern you that your own brother may at any moment be captured and hanged as a traitor?"

"What concerns me," he said coldly, "is that the rest of my family should not march to the scaffold alongside Zachary. He chose to throw in his lot with the traitorous Stuart princeling, and now he must pay the consequences."

"How can you speak thus indifferently of your brother's fate?"

He shrugged. "Calm yourself, my lady, I beg. Your tears do nothing to improve your beauty and they surely are of little help to my brother."

"You could at least show grief for the desperate straits in which he finds himself."

"Believe me, my lady, nobody could regret the enormity of my brother's folly more than I." William gestured toward the door of the withdrawing room, and the footman immediately flung it open. Arabella stalked into the pleasantly sunny room, her slender body shaking with the force of her agitation.

"Bring tea for her ladyship," William directed the footman, who bowed in silent acknowledgment and left.

"How can you order tea!" Arabella exclaimed. "At a moment of crisis like this!"

She seemed to have no inkling of how indiscreet her conversation had been, no idea that she put not only herself but also innocent servants at risk when she rattled on about Zachary. William did not attempt to explain. "I ordered tea in the hope that you would find it refreshing. This hysteria must soon cease, my lady, or the servants will come to believe that you have my brother hidden in your dressing closet."

"Would to God that I did!"

"Thank God that you do not."

"At moments like this, I feel that I will go mad. I cannot imagine why I married a man so totally lacking in sensibility!" Arabella exclaimed.

He gave a wintry smile. "I believe the size of my fortune seemed extremely attractive at the time you accepted my proposals."

She swung around in a whirl of satin skirts and imported French lace. Without any trace of emotion, or sexual response, he thought how beautiful she was. She clasped her hands to her bosom. "Dear God, if your brother could hear how you treat me, he would run you through with his sword!"

"Then I am doubly grateful that he is not here to observe the wretched state of my behavior toward you."

"Can you never give me a serious answer?" she asked, her voice thick with bitterness. "Must you respond to everything I say with your same odious sarcasm?"

"Yes," William said after the slightest of pauses. "I fear that perhaps I must."

The banging of the great iron door knocker silenced whatever fresh accusation Arabella had intended to hurl at him. She sank onto a chair, her cheeks whiter than before. "The soldiers," she breathed. "They are come!"

"I hear them," William said, sounding bored. "It is most fortunate, is it not, that we have nothing to hide?"

"I cannot bear the cruelty of your indifference to Zachary's plight!"

"My dear, you have passion enough for both of us. However, next time you take a lover, I beg that you will choose a good, solid Hanoverian. These Jacobites, you know, are a totally lost cause."

She cast him a look of such utter loathing that for a moment, the armor of his indifference was pierced. He recovered himself almost immediately, and went to stand in front of the empty fireplace, resting his spurred and booted foot on the hearth guard with every appearance of casual unconcern.

A lackey flung open the door. "My lord, Captain Bretton, of the Fourth Dragoons, wishes to speak with you."

"Captain Bretton!" Arabella looked ready to faint.

It was no more than a second or two before William recovered. "Show him in," he said, his voice as remote and cool as ever. "We have no reason to keep him waiting."

Chapter 1

AFTER twenty-nine years of prudent hard work and sober living, Robyn Delaney met Zach Bowleigh and fell instantly and recklessly in love. Zach was interviewing her for a job at the time and gave not the slightest hint of reciprocating her feelings. Robyn surrendered her heart anyway.

If Zach gave no hint of being bowled over by her cute Irish looks and bubbling personality, he did at least seem impressed by her professional qualifications, which included a master's degree in fine arts from Columbia and a year's internship at the Victoria and Albert Museum in London. Fifteen minutes into the interview, he offered her a job as junior buyer in the English furniture department of the Bowleigh Gallery, his family-owned firm. Robyn, with reckless disregard for her emotional health, accepted.

Now, six months later and still hopelessly in love, Robyn wondered how in the world she had ever been so foolhardy. Her infatuation hadn't faded with daily exposure to Zach; if anything it had grown worse. She had learned during the past few months that unrequited love was not only ridiculous, it was physically painful. When she looked at Zach, her entire body ached with longing. If it weren't for the fact that she loved her job almost as much as she loved Zach, she would have quit and crawled home to Virginia weeks ago.

But she hadn't quit, and here she was, watching Zach and his current arm decoration—otherwise known as Miss Cosmos 1993—work the crowd. Tickets for tonight's reception had cost a thousand dollars a pop, a hefty price even though the proceeds were going to benefit New York's homeless. Zach was obviously determined to see that his guests got their money's worth and he was turning on the charm full

blast. Even buried in her obscure corner, Robyn felt
scorched.

She speared a chilled shrimp from the tray of a passing
waiter and ate it morosely. The Gallery's main showroom
had been turned into an approximation of the reception
rooms in an eighteenth-century French château. Against a
backdrop of silk-covered walls, gilt-framed mirrors, and un-
limited supplies of champagne, five hundred of Manhattan's
most glittering glitterati were admiring the Louis Sixteenth
chairs, the rococo cabinets, the exquisite collection of snuff-
boxes, and the even more valuable collection of *singeries,*
those intriguing tapestries depicting monkeys in human
dress, pursuing human activities.

Guests who tired of viewing antique furniture could retreat into one of the smaller salons, where musicians performed Mozart on authentic period instruments, and dancers
in powdered wigs and panniered satin gowns performed
lively minuets and gavottes.

The concept of the gala exhibit was chiefly Zach's, and as
usual, it was a huge success. Male guests were impressed by
Zach's impeccable taste and subtle showmanship. The
women split their admiration equally between the museum-
quality trinkets and Zach's spectacular body.

Watching his female guests strut and preen, Robyn
cheered up a little. Whenever she felt too humiliated by her
wayward hormones, she could comfort herself with the
knowledge that she wasn't the only intelligent woman to
succumb to Zach's blond good looks and smoldering sexuality. Sophisticated New Yorkers, some of them dedicated
feminists, tumbled over themselves in order to bask in the
blaze of Zach's high-voltage smiles. Gossip about his sensitive, powerful performance in bed circulated in the same
tones of hushed awe as gossip about his skill in discovering
fabulous antiques in the most unlikely places.

A cultured British voice murmured into her ear. "Darling,
don't pant, it's terminally vulgar."

Robyn dragged her gaze away from Zach and turned to
smile at the head of her department, Gerry Taunton. "Hi,
boss, I didn't realize you were still here."

Gerry rolled his eyes. "Now isn't that a surprise? Why
would you notice me, or trivial people like our clients for

that matter, when you haven't taken your eyes off Zach and his popsicle since the moment you arrived."

Robyn had given up trying to hide her unrequited passion from Gerry, whose nose for office romance was infallible, but she refused to dignify her obsession by gossiping about Zach. "I did speak to a couple of customers," she protested. "But most of my clients aren't here tonight."

Gerry sniffed. "They have better taste."

She chuckled. "I guess that's a polite way of saying they're too poor."

"Darling, your clients aren't poor, they simply recognize value. Did you see that hideous baroque armoire Simon Brescht bought for his penthouse? Twenty thousand dollars' worth of gold leaf, and two hundred bucks—maybe—of craftmanship. If he'd ever looked at a piece of Hepplewhite or Adam he'd know better."

"You don't think you're just the tiniest bit prejudiced? You are English, after all."

Gerry pretended to consider. "No," he said, with absolute conviction. "Eighteenth-century English furniture is the most elegant that was ever produced anywhere."

Robyn laughed at his fervor, but they both knew she agreed with him. From the corner of her eye, she noticed that Zach had cleared his arm of Miss Cosmos, and was heading straight for the alcove where she and Gerry stood talking. He arrived in front of them before she could escape. He nodded to her, then grinned at Gerry.

"Take that supercilious sneer off your face, my friend. We all know what you think of French furniture but there's no need to frighten away the customers. Besides, some of it's quite handsome. I chose it myself."

"All of us make mistakes," Gerry said.

Zach laughed. "I can see I need to do major penance. Any suggestions as to how I can get myself back into your good graces?"

"Give the English department an exhibition," Gerry said promptly. "With a couple of months lead time, Kevin and I could mount a really fine show of English country house furniture. We already have at least a dozen splendid Regency and early Victorian pieces in house, and we've just acquired some 1920 Chippendale reproductions that are works of art in themselves. Best of all, we're inventorying a shipment of early Wedgwood pottery that would make the perfect focal point for a show."

Zach swung around to look at Robyn. "You discovered that cache of Wedgwood, didn't you? How did you hear of it?"

As always, the full blast of his attention reduced Robyn's brain to jelly. "It's ... um ..." She cleared her throat. "The pieces belonged to the Wade family in Virginia. Mr. Wade is a great-uncle to my sister-in-law, which is how I got involved."

"They offered it to you for sale?"

"No, at first they simply wanted a rough valuation. They hadn't a clue as to how much it was worth, so they asked me to take a look."

"Why did they change their minds and decide to sell?"

"They're childless, in their eighties, and they want to move into a retirement community. I told them they could get a lot more money if they found private buyers for individual pieces, but they just wanted fast cash, and no hassle. They had several unmatched bowls and platters, and some wonderful decorative pieces. The best is a jasper-ware vase designed by John Flaxman that dates from 1785."

She ground to an unsteady halt, aware that she sounded breathless and overeager. Suddenly furious with her idiotic infatuation, she frowned and turned away.

"What did you pay them?" Zach asked.

"Thirty thousand. The Gallery paid for packaging and freight, which came to another couple of thousand, with the insurance."

"What does Stella say about it?"

Stella Bartolomeo was the Gallery's pricing expert, and made Scrooge look generous. "She thinks we'll be able to sell the pieces for at least sixty thousand. I believe we can get more if we approach the right buyers." She lifted her chin slightly. "Because of my personal involvement with the Wade family, I checked with Gerry and Kevin before I made an offer. I didn't want to cheat anyone, the Wades or the Gallery."

"There's no need to sound apologetic," Zach said mildly. "If it weren't for your personal connection, we would never have heard of the collection in the first place. And early Wedgwood doesn't often come on the market, certainly not John Flaxman jasper ware. Well done."

Despite her best efforts, she felt her face turn pink with pleasure. "It was an exciting discovery for me."

"Gerry and I have been talking about you," Zach said. "We're both impressed with how fast you've learned the ropes."

"Th-thank you. Everyone here has been very helpful."

"Glad to hear it." He pulled out a slim leather pocket diary and consulted it briefly. "Could you have dinner with me tomorrow night? I know it's Friday, the start of the weekend, and so on, but I'm tied up all day in meetings, and I'd like to take some time to outline a special project I have in mind for you. It's something Gerry and I both think you're ready to tackle."

Her regular Friday night routine consisted of a session at the health club, followed by a late-night stint in front of her VCR, watching a rented movie. "I believe I can juggle my schedule around and make that," she said, trying to sound like a woman sacrificing her busy social life for the sake of her career. "What time, and where would you like us to meet?"

Zach scribbled a note in his diary. "Seven-thirty sound okay? My secretary will fill you in on the details. She has a system for keeping all the maître d's around town bullied into giving her the best table, so I go wherever she sends me."

"Fine. I'll expect Shirley's call tomorrow morning."

"Great." He gave Gerry a hearty clap on the shoulder, nodded his head briskly toward Robyn, and left to reclaim Miss Cosmos, who was wiggling her silicone-enhanced assets at a small group of fascinated reporters.

Watching Zach weave his way through the crowds, Robyn realized her mouth was hanging open and hurriedly snapped it shut.

Gerry patted her on the arm, his gaze annoyingly sympathetic. "Darling, don't pant," he said. "It's terminally vulgar."

* * *

Robyn woke up on Friday morning, determined that this day would mark a change in her attitude toward Zach. Six months was long enough to spend in a state of sophomoric sexual obsession. At their dinner tonight she would behave with brisk, professional courtesy. She would not allow herself to explode into bursts of nervous chatter. She would not spill the salt, or drop her napkin, or get distracted by the twinkle in Zach's dark blue eyes. She would not wonder if he'd noticed her freckles. She would absolutely and definitely not wonder if he by any chance happened to find freckles cute. By the end of the evening, if she stuck to her plan, she would have taken a giant step toward transforming six months of unproductive sexual fantasy into an efficient business relationship.

Her optimistic mood survived a typically frantic Friday at the office and a frustrating half hour in front of the ladies' room mirror during which she confirmed the sad truth that a woman who is five feet three inches tall and has red curly hair cannot make herself look aloof and businesslike even when she is wearing an austere forest-green suit and no jewelry. Having spent most of her adult life convincing fusty professors and sexist museum curators that a woman with curls and dimples could also have brains, Robyn knew she ought to appreciate the strict professionalism of Zach's attitude. Unfortunately, love was not a very rational emotion and she wished—just once—that he would look at her as if he registered the fact that she was a functioning, anatomically correct female.

Quelling an absurd impulse to try the effect of the suit with no blouse under the jacket, and a dangling pair of rhinestone earrings, she dusted another layer of powder over her freckles, wiped off most of her lipstick, and left the ladies' room satisfied there was nothing more she could do to increase the businesslike severity of her appearance.

The afternoon's drizzling rain had turned into a full-blown downpour by the time Robyn left the office for La Grenouille on Fifty-second Street, but by some marvel she got a taxi without much difficulty and was paying the cabbie outside the restaurant at precisely seven-thirty. She considered this punctuality a good omen. From now on, even the traffic jams of Manhattan would give way to her supercompetent han-

dling of life. She was a dedicated career woman, with no time
for the inefficiency of a one-sided love affair. Confident in
the power of her new and improved self, she strode into the
restaurant's pink-lit interior—and stopped dead in her tracks
at the sight of Zach chatting amiably with the maître d'.

He glanced up and saw her, his smile faintly quizzical, his
blond hair a slash of brightness against the sober dark gray
of his suit. Even at a distance of fifteen feet, he radiated a
lethal combination of wealth, power, and sexuality. By the
time they were two feet apart, Robyn was shaking. She drew
in a deep, calming breath, reminding herself that she was
now a woman with a Plan. Resisting the cowardly urge to
replace her new and improved self with the old infatuated
and wimpish model, she gave Zach her best imitation of a
cool and dignified smile.

"Good evening, Zach. I hope I didn't keep you waiting?"

His answering smile was warm, friendly, and open. But
then, Robyn thought gloomily, he had no adolescent infatuation to hide. "Your timing's great," he said, taking her coat
and handing it to the attendant. "I was a couple of minutes
early. It's getting cold out there, isn't it?"

She had no idea what the temperature was, had been much
too flushed with bravado and excitement to notice, but the
new Robyn was not going to be thrown off track by a simple
remark about the weather. She treated him to another of her
brisk, professional smiles. "Yes, it's really cold. Maybe it's
going to snow."

"That would make a change. It's years since we had a
proper winter in New York." Zach guided her through the ta-
bles in the wake of the maître d'. "Have you eaten here before? It's one of my favorite places, partly because it's close
to my apartment, but mostly because the food is great."

"No, I've never been here before." She kept her answers
clipped and short, because that seemed better than the alternative. It was either monosyllables, or gushers of verbiage
when she was around Zach.

A waiter materialized at their table. "Would you care to
order a drink before dinner?"

"We'll need a few minutes to choose our meals," Zach
said, taking the menus from the waiter. "Robyn, what would
you like to drink?"

She ordered a diet Coke, since the last thing she needed at this point was a muzzy head. He nodded to the waiter. "Make that two, please."

As soon as the waiter left, Zach turned back to Robyn. "Thanks for agreeing to meet with me on a Friday night when I know you must have a hundred more exciting things to do. You've put in a lot of overtime these last few weeks, and I want you to know your hard work's been noticed and appreciated."

"I enjoy my work," she said. "I've always wanted to make a career in the antique trade, so my job at the Bowleigh Gallery is a dream come true for me."

"It's good to hear you say that. To be honest, I wasn't sure we should take you on. Gerry's had two assistants in the past four years who simply weren't up to the job even though their qualifications looked terrific on paper. When I interviewed you, I was almost to the point of deciding we needed someone with hands-on, practical experience and no fine arts background. But Gerry said you were the right person for the job and I'm certainly glad that I took his advice."

Robyn flushed with pleasure. "Thank you. It's great to put all my academic training to practical use at last."

"And that brings me to the reason for this meeting," Zach said. "It's time for you to expand your scope, Robyn. You need to get out in the field and do some actual buying. Some distant relatives of mine in England are planning to offer part of their family collection of porcelain and silverware for sale and they've offered me the chance to make a first bid. English bone china is your major area of expertise, and I want you to come with me. My opinion may be tainted by the family connection, so I'd like you to share the responsibility for deciding whether the Gallery should bid for the collection."

She was astonished and thrilled by his offer. "I'm delighted by your confidence in my judgment," she said. "But has Gerry told you that I've never placed a bid on behalf of the Gallery without his prior approval?"

"Gerry agrees with me that it's time for you to put your theoretical knowledge to the test. On paper, you have more qualifications than any other buyer. In reality, you've had almost no experience of handling buys under pressure. On the other hand, I have plenty of buying experience, but I know next to nothing about the output of the English potteries. I hope we can improve each other's skills."

The possibility of her being able to teach Zach Bowleigh anything about antiques was absurd enough to make Robyn chuckle. "What's so amusing?" Zach asked.

"I'd love to go to England with you, it would be a fabulous learning experience for me. But the idea of giving you lessons on this business is literally laughable. You've forgotten more than I could learn in the next ten years."

He frowned. "You're wrong," he said quietly. "My expertise and my success tend to be exaggerated. In more ways than one."

"I've seen no evidence of that. Your reputation seems well deserved, in every way."

"Superficially, maybe, but you don't know me very well, do you?"

She wondered exactly what it was they were talking about, and she was determined not to leap to foolish conclusions. "You're my boss, the president of the most successful antique company in the country. I know you're an excellent employer."

He sighed. "Yes, I'm very much aware of the fact that I'm your boss." He paused for a moment, then shrugged, almost visibly deciding to change the subject. "Let's order dinner, then we can talk about the trip to England without being interrupted."

Robyn indulged herself browsing through the menu before choosing a safe filet mignon topped with truffles. Zach ordered something in swift, colloquial French, which she had a horrible suspicion might be stewed frogs' legs. Despite a year in London and two brief visits to Europe, Robyn's choice of food remained strictly American heartland. When their meals arrived, Zach's plate was covered in a creamy sauce. Robyn breathed a sigh of relief that if he was tucking into a reptile of the type she had dismembered in biology class, at least she didn't know for sure.

When their waiter left with a final flourish of his napkin, Zach inquired politely if the meal was to her satisfaction, and they discussed cuisines of the world in a desultory fashion for a few minutes before Zach returned to business.

"The Bowleigh family is anxious to complete the sale as soon as possible," he said. "I'm leaving for Paris on Tuesday night, and I plan to fly from there to London sometime on Friday afternoon. I realize this is short notice, but could you meet me in Starke on Saturday morning? That would be a week from tomorrow. The family is quite willing for us to view the collection over the weekend."

Robyn's work schedule for the next couple of weeks was already tight, but the chance to accompany Zach on a buying trip was much too exciting to turn down. "I'll have to juggle a few appointments," she said. "But I can work things out."

"Great. I'll ask Shirley to make a reservation for you at the Starke Manor Hotel, which was once the family home of the Bowleighs. They turned it into a hotel twenty years ago, when the inheritance taxes got too steep for them. Rental car is the easiest way to get from the airport to Starke. How do you feel about driving on the left-hand side of the road?"

"I drove around quite a lot when I was working in England, so it shouldn't be a problem. Is Starke far from Heathrow Airport?"

"Seventy miles or so. It's in Dorset, a very picturesque little village, about ten miles from the coast."

She pulled a face. "If I don't turn up for breakfast on Saturday, you'd better send out a posse. I'm a world champion at getting lost on English country roads."

He laughed. "The village pub is called the Dog and Kettle, and it's been going strong for three hundred years. After spending a year in England, you should know that if you need directions, pubs are the only sure landmarks."

She grinned. "I'll keep that in mind. Do you have any written material describing the Bowleighs' porcelain collection?"

"Not as much as I'd like. I can give you some excellent photos and a few notes made for the insurance company. I have the file with me, so perhaps you could glance at it over the weekend. I'd like your impression of the overall quality of the collection."

"I'll do my best, but to make an accurate assessment, I need to see the actual pieces."

He smiled. "I know. That's why I asked you to come with

me. I'm not asking for an official valuation, just an initial
impression."

Neither of them ordered dessert, but they lingered over
coffee and chocolate truffles, talking about the differences
between early European and English porcelain, and the recent upsurge in prices for nineteenth-century Japanese Imari
ware. Robyn found the conversation so interesting that she
was able to ignore the current of sexual awareness that never
went away when she was near Zach. She wondered if perhaps her infatuation had flourished during the past few
months because, until tonight, she had never had the chance
to get to know Zach the Man, instead of Zach the Sexual
Fantasy. With an upsurge of hope, Robyn decided that the
trip to Starke, and two or three solid days of Zach's company, might be all she needed to complete the cure.

Zach took a final sip of his coffee and leaned back in his
chair. "You look mighty pleased with yourself," he said.
"Was your meal that good?"

"I was thinking about the trip to England," she replied,
glad that she could tell at least a partial truth. "I'm looking
forward to working with you."

"I'm looking forward to that, too." Zach was silent for a
moment or two, staring at his steepled fingers. "Tell me
something, Robyn, if you were a dealer who wanted to palm
off an expensive fake on one of the Gallery buyers, how
would you set about doing it?"

"I wouldn't bother to try." Robyn answered without needing to stop and consider. The question of fakes and fraud
was always fascinating to insiders in the antique business, in
part because so many more fakes were offered for sale than
genuine articles.

"Why wouldn't you try?" he asked.

"For the obvious reasons. It would be much too risky,
with the high standard of documentation we require, and all
the in-house experts we have available. We're tougher to deceive than most museums."

"But let's suppose this mythical dealer wants to sell a
museum-quality piece, something that's going to fetch thousands of dollars if it's accepted as genuine. Where can he go
if not to us? There aren't that many commercial outlets operating in his price range."

"True, but let's be realistic about our industry, Zach. There are dozens of ways for a crooked dealer to make money on fakes without trying to outwit the Bowleigh Gallery. There's a huge demand for nineteenth-century Americana, for example, and we both know there are dozens of factories in Taiwan turning out instant antiques to meet that demand. Why risk jail trying to sell one elaborate piece for a few hundred thousand bucks, when you can make a million selling 'hundred-year-old' desks for a thousand dollars each?"

"But what if you could come up with a scheme for circumventing the experts and the documentation at the Gallery?" Zach asked. "Then you might be able to rake in mega-bucks on a consistent basis. Wouldn't that be worth taking a few risks for? Wouldn't it be worth trying to crack our systems?"

He sat slouched in his chair, the picture of a man engaged in idle chitchat with a fellow professional. And yet something about his manner set Robyn's antennae twitching. She leaned across the table, meeting his gaze head-on. "What are we talking about, Zach? Are we indulging in idle speculation at the end of a pleasant meal, or are we having a serious conversation about fakes reaching the floor of the Bowleigh Gallery?"

For a moment she thought he wasn't going to answer. "I'm not sure," he said finally. "You know as well as I do that this trade is riddled with fraud and dubious deals. You're a relative newcomer to the company, so you look at our authentication systems with a more open mind than the rest of us. Can you see any way somebody knowledgeable—and clever—could consistently manipulate a crack in our system?"

She shook her head. "I'd say it's impossible. We use the latest technology to run sophisticated tests on all the important pieces, and we have trained experts exercising their professional judgment to assess authenticity. It's tough to deceive machines *and* human experts."

"Well, I'm relieved to hear you say that. It's always good to be reassured that our systems work."

"Why were you worried, Zach? There must have been a specific incident to trigger your concerns."

"An insurance company approached me about a seventeenth-century *pietra-dura* cabinet that had been bought from our Gallery about four years ago. The owner recently died, and the heirs were trying to sell. A routine X ray of the joints revealed that the piece was a fake."

"But the original cabinet had been out of our hands for years," Robyn protested. "You can't assume we were negligent in our original authentication. There are dozens of reasons why the owner might have substituted a modern replica for the genuine piece he bought from us."

"That's what I told the insurance company," Zach said, getting to his feet. "The man in question had been losing money, but needed to keep up appearances to prevent a run on his business, so it wouldn't be surprising if he quietly sold the genuine article and bought himself a nice little replica from a factory in the Far East."

"This is a fascinating business, isn't it?" Robyn said as they walked back toward the lobby. "I love the unique combination of creative genius, ancient splendor, and high tech that keeps the whole industry afloat."

Zach smiled. "And the best part is, some of the creative genius is even legal."

She laughed, happy with the success of the evening, happy with the new sense of relaxation she felt around Zach. All in all, she felt confident that she had taken a giant step toward overcoming her infatuation. The entire evening, in fact, had followed the outline of her new Master Plan with gratifying precision. And their trip to London would complete her transformation into a new woman, she was sure of it.

When they reclaimed their coats, Zach handed Robyn a slim portfolio containing about a hundred pages of photographs. "As soon as you've had a chance to look these over, tell me what you think about the Starke inventory," he said, walking her toward the door. "I'm going to be in the office all day on Monday and Tuesday until early afternoon."

"I'll call Shirley first thing and fix a meeting time."

"Do that."

The maître d' hurried up to them. "I 'ope everything was to your satisfaction, Mr. Bowleigh?"

"Wonderful as always, Jean-Pierre. Now all we need to make the evening perfect is a cab."

"I can call for one if you wish. But it is no longer raining, and probably you will 'ave more success if you just walk up to Fifth Avenue."

"That's what we'll do," Zach said. "Unless you're still cold, Robyn?"

"No, I'm fine."

Once outside, they found that the gutters ran with dirty rainwater, but the sidewalks had dried off except for the occasional puddle. The skies had cleared, revealing an ethereally beautiful moon and a brilliant scattering of stars. Pausing on the corner of Fifty-second, Zach scanned Fifth Avenue in search of an empty cab.

The traffic roared past, including dozens of yellow cabs, all occupied. Zach sighed. "At moments like this I wonder why the hell I don't buy a house in the suburbs so that I could own a car and drive myself where I want to go like a normal American."

She burrowed her chin into her upturned collar. "It's the challenge," she said. "The feeling that if you can make life bearable in New York City, you could do it anywhere."

He laughed. "You're probably right, although I always kid myself I stay in the city because of the fascinating people and the great cultural—"

He suddenly lunged toward her, pulling her close against his chest and throwing her bodily to the pavement. Only the fact that he kept his arm around her neck prevented her from cracking the back of her skull against the concrete. Vaguely, in the distance, she was aware of the sound of a car backfiring.

They landed in a doorway, a tangle of legs and arms, with her face squashed against the buttons of Zach's shirt, her nose tickled by the smell of Fendi cologne, her vision obscured by the hanging flaps of his overcoat. For thirty seconds, he lay on top of her, panting, his body rigid with tension. When he lifted his head slightly, she was able to move just enough to see his face.

He was staring toward Fifth Avenue, his expression tight with fury. He looked pale and mud-splattered, but otherwise sane enough. On the other hand, she hadn't met too many

crazy people and was no expert at identifying them. She
tried to wriggle out of Zach's grasp, wincing as her bruised
haunches scraped over the cement.

"Get down," he commanded, straddling her with his knee
and thrusting her—none too gently—back into the recesses
of the doorway where they had landed. "Don't move until
I'm sure they're gone."

"Until who has gone? Zach, what happened? What frightened you?"

He ignored her, but she obeyed him anyway, largely because she had no choice. Zach remained spread-eagled on
top of her, effectively blocking her view of the street, and he
was a foot taller and sixty pounds heavier than she was.

She moved her legs, which were getting pins and needles.
Cold, gritty rainwater sloshed against her calves and the
back of her knees. A couple walked by, averting their gaze,
and she realized just what a spectacle she and Zach were
making of themselves. A surge of irritation replaced her bewilderment, propelling her into action.

"Zach, get off me. This is ridiculous."

He stood up, pulling her with him. He'd thrown her into
a puddle, she realized, as icy rivulets of dirty water trickled
off her hair and into her face, but she didn't feel the cold because her fury was keeping her warm. She picked up her
purse and the portfolio with the catalogs. Fortunately nothing had spilled, although the photos were wet.

"What the blazes was that all about?" she demanded, using the sodden sleeve of her coat in an effort to stop the water dripping from her hair into her mouth.

"I . . . thought someone was shooting at us."

"Shooting at us?" Robyn looked around the peaceful
street scene and swallowed hard. Zach's nerves must be
shredded, she thought sadly. She could imagine her mother
or her sister-in-law finding the blank-faced, scurrying New
Yorkers somewhat menacing, but for a city-dweller there
was nothing threatening about the brightly lit street, or the
people in it. "Zach, we're fine, honestly."

He kept her pinned close to his side and scanned the sidewalks as if he expected an assassin to leap out from behind
a lamppost at any minute. He finally seemed satisfied that
they weren't in imminent danger, and he dragged his gaze

around to hers with visible effort. "I'm sorry. Are you all right?" he asked.

"No, of course I'm not all right! I'm freezing cold, my clothes are ruined, and your attitude is making me very nervous. But you didn't manage to break any of my bones, if that's what you mean."

"I'm sorry," he said again. He sounded remote, impersonal. "I thought you were in danger and I reacted without thinking."

"Yeah, well those he-man reflexes could get you into a lot of trouble. Miss Cosmos probably likes hitting wet cement even less than I do."

He didn't crack even the ghost of a smile. Instead, he took her arm and started hustling her uptown. "Come on, we need to get out of here. I'll take you back to my apartment. Walk as fast as you can, please. It's not safe — You'll catch cold if you don't get out of those wet clothes."

Robyn didn't relish the prospect of a wet and muddy cab ride back to Queens, but the prospect of going to Zach's apartment was even less appealing. She didn't think she had ever seen a man who looked closer to the brink of a major explosion, and she had no desire to be around when the explosion occurred. "It's late, so I'd prefer to go straight home," she said.

He hesitated. "You're soaking wet."

"My coat's wet. The rest of me is pretty dry."

Her shoes were discernibly ruined and her hair still dripped mud, but he accepted her lie without protest. She had the sudden feeling that his mood had changed and he was now as anxious to be rid of her as she was to be home in the safety of her own apartment.

"You must send me the dry-cleaning bill," Zach said. "That way, I might feel a bit less stupid about the way I—overreacted."

The pause before his final word was almost imperceptible, but Robyn had spent too many months obsessing about Zach not to notice it. He didn't really believe he'd overreacted, she was sure of it. In fact, she realized with a flash of insight, he was determined to send her home so that she'd be out of what he considered the danger zone. She looked up at him, worried by the carefully expressionless lines of his face, and the tight-drawn grimness of his mouth.

"Zach, what is it? What's bothering you?" she asked.

"Good heavens, do you need to ask? I behaved like an idiot." He gave a chuckle that sounded charmingly embarrassed and apologetic. She noticed that his eyes were still scanning the sidewalks and wasn't deceived. "Look, there's a cab," he said, stepping out into the street to hail it. "Are you quite sure you don't want to stop off at my place to clean up?"

"I'm sure. Do you need a ride home?"

"No thanks. My place is only five blocks from here and I prefer to walk."

Surprisingly, the taxi stopped, despite their bedraggled appearance. The cabbie stuck his head out of the window. "Where d'ya wanna go?"

"Queens," Robyn said, giving her address.

"You've gotta be kidding." The cabbie rolled his eyes with as much exasperation as if she'd asked to be driven across the Atlantic Ocean. He launched into a storm of protest, which Zach silenced by the surefire method of stuffing several large-denomination bills into his hand.

"Make sure you wait to see the lady safely inside her building."

"Yeah, yeah." The cabbie took a hearty drag on his cigarette, indifferent to the sign that proclaimed smoking in city cabs to be illegal.

Zach wasn't so far gone in craziness that he risked commenting on the cigarette. He leaned down to say good-bye to Robyn. "I'll see you in the office on Monday. Look, I'm really sorry about the way this evening ended."

"You have nothing to apologize for, Zach. In this city, we all get jumpy at times."

"I guess we do. But I'd have preferred not to make a total ass of myself in front of a woman I admire as much as you."

"Time to go, folks!" The cabbie put the car in gear. Zach just had time to slam the passenger door before the cabbie drove off in an impatient squeal of tires. Robyn looked back and saw that Zach was already striding purposefully downtown, coat collar turned up, hands shoved into his pockets.

She was so disoriented by Zach's strange behavior that

she was back home, standing under a hot shower, before she realized a final oddity: Zach's purposeful strides had been carrying him in precisely the opposite direction from his apartment.

Robyn wondered where he'd been going. And why.

Chapter 2

ZACH keyed in his personal code to turn off the laser-activated alarm system, then walked into the deserted showroom. He couldn't be sure all the staff had gone home, but he figured he was likely to arouse less suspicion at this hour of the evening than if he came back to the Gallery at midnight. His presence in the showroom would be photographed by automatic cameras and noted, even if only by a guard, since the security system was set up to record who shut it off and when. Fortunately he always took a personal interest in the Gallery's major acquisitions, so his scrutiny of the Farleigh cabinet wasn't likely to raise questions. With a price tag of fifty thousand dollars, the cabinet represented an important piece of inventory, important enough to justify some curiosity on the part of the company president.

His first step was to check the documents showing provenance, to see if there was anything in the record of previous sales that he could possibly have missed. The cabinet had been built around 1740 for Richard Farleigh, a merchant who had retired from profitable London commerce to the more genteel life of a country squire during the reign of King George II. After World War I, taxes and death duties had forced the impoverished Farleigh descendants to sell some of their accumulated treasures, and eventually the elaborate marquetry cabinet, complete with its gold-leaf stand, had been shipped to the States. Sold to a Wall Street broker during the high-flying eighties, the broker had been forced to sell in the more somber economic climate of the 1990s. Detailed descriptions and bills of sale were enclosed for every transaction, including the original sale by Richard Farleigh's descendants in 1919. In short, the provenance appeared impeccable.

The visual impact was impeccable, too. The cabinet stood on an elaborately carved and gilded stand depicting intertwined cherubs, flowers, and lush vines, giving the piece an overall height in excess of six feet. The doors of the cabinet were painted with scenes of Oriental horsemen, galloping across the black lacquer surface, their colored banners flying with formalized abandon.

To modern taste, it seemed strange to mix classical and Christian myths with imagined scenes from a romanticized Orient, but eighteenth-century craftsmen had enjoyed letting their imaginations roam free. Englishmen who had rarely traveled fifty miles from their homes liked to buy furniture decorated with pictures of mysterious beasts like elephants, or exotic emperors, or alluring Chinese maidens. In most cases, neither seller nor purchaser had any firm idea what elephants or emperors looked like, so everyone was quite happy with whatever fanciful image the artist dreamed up. The demand for authenticity, neat categories, and coherent decorative themes was strictly twentieth century. A too accurate picture of a wild animal, for example, was often a sure clue that an antique had been faked.

Zach opened the outer doors of the cabinet and revealed a typical inner display of exquisitely painted drawers and storage space, each sandalwood-lined section showing some detail of the larger picture portrayed on the doors.

Zach read the provenance notes again, frowning as he ran his fingertips lightly across one of the cabinet's joints. There was absolutely nothing wrong with this piece that he could see, not a single detail that suggested the cabinet was anything other than what it purported to be: a valuable two-hundred-year-old antique, built and decorated by master craftsmen.

Unfortunately, in this case seeing was not believing, since the X rays he'd ordered last week proved conclusively that the cabinet was a fake, albeit a superbly executed one. To add to Zach's frustrations, a check he'd conducted suggested that the broker who'd been listed as the owner in the 1930s had never existed.

Zach heard the sound of hurrying footsteps behind him, and recognized at once who was coming. Damn! Of all the people he didn't want to encounter right now, Robyn

Delaney headed the list. He should never have brought up the subject of that fake *pietra-dura* cabinet on Friday night, but Robyn had such a crazy effect on his libido that his brain rarely functioned at more than half speed when she was around—even when he wasn't worried that at any moment a scandal might break that would sink the Gallery.

He straightened slowly, giving himself a couple of seconds to control the inevitable rush of desire. Much as he relished the thought, this would probably not be a good moment to drag Robyn into his arms and beg her to go to bed with him. After the fiasco of Friday night, he'd better put on a damn good show of looking calm, rational, and businesslike, or she'd be sending for the men in white coats.

"Zach!" Robyn hesitated in the doorway of the showroom, her eyes darkening with surprise from green to amber. "I saw the lights were on and wondered who was in here."

"I'm leaving town tomorrow," Zach said, hoping like hell his smile looked more casual than it felt. "That's my excuse for working late, but what's yours?"

"Paperwork. Boring stuff. Is there a problem with the Farleigh cabinet?"

He trotted out the excuse he'd prepared for the security guards, aware that it was inadequate for someone as well informed as Robyn. "Kevin wasn't too happy with a repair that's been done on one of the cherub's wings. Do you want to take a look and tell me what you think?"

"I certainly would. I'm surprised Kevin didn't mention anything to me."

Too late, Zach realized he'd made a major error. In his effort to appear unconcerned, he'd invited Robyn to inspect a flawless repair which would inevitably increase her suspicion that he was either covering something up, or else teetering on the brink of a mental breakdown. Thinking with his hormones, he decided ruefully, was infinitely less efficient than thinking with his brain.

He watched as she walked across the room, wondering if she had any idea how perfectly her tailored navy-blue suit and starched white blouse emphasized the seductive curve of her breasts and the flamboyant color of her hair. Probably not, or she would be wearing a khaki smock and dun-colored knee socks. Short of pinning a label across her forehead say-

ing *Back Off,* Robyn couldn't have made her position about
mixing work and personal relationships more clear. The hell
of it was, he completely agreed with her attitude. In theory.

"Where exactly is the repair Kevin's bothered about?"
Robyn asked, holding out her hand for the file.

"Upper left-hand corner of the stand." He didn't have the
file open to the cabinet's repair record, because of course
that wasn't what he'd been checking. He handed her a magnifying glass, and bent down to point out the repair. Her hair
brushed against his chin as she zeroed in on the cherub's
wing, and for several tantalizing seconds she didn't move
away. Zach indulged in a wistful fantasy in which Robyn
looked up from the gilded cherubs and actually noticed that
he was a fully equipped, heterosexual male.

Robyn stood up. "The repair's fine," she said curtly. As
he'd expected, she gave no sign whatsoever that she'd noticed he was a man and not a robot, but he did detect a
flicker of anger in the depths of her eyes. Robyn was insulted by his clumsy lies, as she had every right to be.

She handed him back the magnifying glass, making no effort to pretend she believed his story. "It's late, and I have
an early start tomorrow morning. Good night, Zach."

She was almost to the showroom door before he said anything, and a second before he spoke he had no idea what he
was going to say. "Have dinner with me," he blurted out.

He was breaking every one of his personal rules about
dating an employee. Worse, he knew he had no right to draw
Robyn into the dangerous mess his life had become. He
should never have invited her to dinner—but he didn't regret
the invitation for an instant.

Robyn answered him without turning around. "Is this a request for another business meeting, Zach?"

"No, this is strictly personal. We could go back to my
apartment. I'd like to show you my grandmother's collection
of French fans. Or my etchings, if you happen to be in the
mood for etchings."

She still didn't turn around. "I'm not good at decoding
subliminal messages," she said, and her voice sounded as
cool and crisp as ever. "Is this an invitation to sleep with
you, Zach?"

Her ramrod-straight spine suggested that she viewed the

prospect of having sex with him about as favorably as she viewed the prospect of starting an affair with a tarantula. He thought he might just possibly possess sufficient self-control to take her home and refrain from throwing her on his bed and making love to her until they were both comatose from multiple orgasms.

"This is an invitation to dinner," he said huskily. "Nothing more, and nothing less."

"Then I accept."

He let out a long, slow breath. "Do I have to talk to the back of your neck for the rest of the evening, or is a view of your face included as part of the deal?"

She turned around, but she didn't come any closer, and she didn't say anything. Zach tried to think of some warm, witty remark that would put them both at their ease. Nothing came to mind. All he could think of was that his life right now was an irredeemable screwup, and he had no right to invite Robyn into it.

"I have to get my coat," she said.

"Me, too. I'll meet you in the lobby."

"Give me five minutes."

When he came downstairs, she was already waiting, wearing the dove-gray woolen coat she'd worn to La Grenouille. Zach didn't want to remind her of Friday's fiasco, but courtesy required him to mention the cleaning bill.

"I see you managed to get your coat cleaned," he said. "They seem to have done an excellent job."

"My local cleaner is pretty efficient. He has same day service even on weekends."

"I wish you'd send me the bill. It's the least that I owe you."

"Zach, forget it, please."

He saw that to press the issue only made her uncomfortable, so he changed the subject. "I've called for a limo. It's raining again, so we can't walk." He didn't admit that since Friday he'd stopped walking anywhere in Manhattan.

"Shall we wait by the door so that we can see when the car arrives?" she suggested.

"Good idea. It shouldn't be more than a couple of minutes; the driver's on call for me." Zach put his hand under her elbow to guide her to the front of the lobby. The gesture was instinctive, nothing more than a courtesy taught since childhood. The moment he touched her, they both jumped back as if they'd been jolted by live electric cables.

"Sorry," Robyn muttered.

Zach's self-control snapped. "Dammit all, this is ridiculous," he said. "Robyn, you're driving me totally crazy." He swung around, pulled her into his arms, and brought his mouth down on hers in a hard, demanding kiss.

God knew what he'd expected her reaction to be, but it certainly wasn't a momentary stillness, followed by a passionate acquiescence that heated his blood to the boiling point in about ten seconds flat. He'd always known he found her desirable, but he hadn't known that desire could be this crazy mixture of hot, sharp need and aching tenderness.

They broke apart, flushed and panting. "The limo's here," Zach said, but he didn't move.

Robyn didn't move either. "Where were you going on Friday night?" she asked.

His brain was still blurred with desire, so the question seemed less out of left field than it should have done. "On Friday night?" he repeated, confused.

"Yes. When we came out of the restaurant, we were on Fifth Avenue at Fifty-second. We walked up to Fifty-fifth before you flagged a cab. When the cabbie drove off, you turned around and started walking downtown, away from your apartment. Where were you going?"

He never could think worth a damn when Robyn was near, and right now, his functional IQ level was about twenty-six and sinking fast. So he told her the truth. "I was going back to the corner where we were shot at," he said. "I was looking for spent bullets."

"I see." Robyn's voice was carefully neutral. "And did you find any bullets, Zach?"

"Just one," he said. "But that was enough."

He felt her body tense, heard the tiny catch of her indrawn breath. If he hadn't been holding her, he would never have realized how strongly his words affected her. Robyn's face was in some ways so transparently expressive, he'd never considered how good she might be at concealing her deepest, most important feelings. She spoke quietly.

"You mean someone really was shooting at us? The noise I heard wasn't just a car backfiring?"

"Someone was shooting at *me*," he corrected. "And apparently they didn't care if you were in the line of fire. It's the second time this month that someone's taken a shot at me."

"Good grief, how can you sound so calm! Thank God they missed!"

He grimaced. "I'm not sure whether that's my good luck, or whether the gunman intended to miss."

"You're making no sense. Why would he shoot to miss?"

"A warning, maybe. The bullet I found was embedded in the doorpost almost seven feet above the ground. Way over both of our heads even if I hadn't sent you diving for the pavement."

Robyn finally moved out of his arms. She looked up at him, her eyes stormy, her expression troubled. "Zach, don't you think it's time you told me what's going on?"

He didn't say anything for a very long time. "Yes," he said finally, feeling relief wash over him in a deep, slow wave. Until this moment, he hadn't realized how badly he wanted to confide in her. "Come back to my apartment and I'll tell you what's happening."

Zach's apartment occupied the entire penthouse floor of a building near the corner of Park and Sixtieth. Robyn couldn't find much to talk about during the short limo ride uptown from the Gallery, and even when they stepped out of the mahogany-paneled elevator into Zach's private foyer, she wasn't sure what she was doing there, or why she'd agreed to have dinner with him. Her common sense warned that just because he'd given her a kiss that sent her hormones spiraling into maximum overdrive, she couldn't assume their attraction was mutual. One thing Robyn knew for sure. Her Master Plan was demonstrating a significant failure to cope with Zach's sudden transformation from fantasy sex object to flesh-and-blood man. A man, moreover, with problems he wanted to share.

His apartment was impressive enough to distract her momentarily from the wreckage of her Plan. For an antiques dealer, Zach's home was as intoxicating as a distillery for an alcoholic. Scarcely knowing where to look first, Robyn drank in the rich scarlet design of the Persian carpet, the elegant, almost flirtatious craftsmanship of an ormolu side table, and the earthy splendor of a Delacroix painting of a peasant woman, lazily scratching the throat of her parrot.

"This is magnificent," she said. "It looks like a very grand townhouse in nineteenth-century Paris."

Zach grinned. "My mother claims it looks like an upscale brothel, but I've loved the place ever since I was a kid." Zach loosened his tie and tossed his suit jacket onto a chair. "But you ain't seen nothin' yet, kid. Come on inside."

She followed him into an inner vestibule, peering upward to admire the elaborate plaster moldings on the twelve-foot ceiling. Amused rather than envious, she reckoned that her entire apartment would fit into less space than Zach's entrance hall and foyer.

"Why didn't your mother change the decor if she doesn't like it?" Robyn asked.

He chuckled. "She'd have given her eye teeth for the chance. My mother spent the past thirty years mentally redecorating from the walls out, but this apartment belonged to my grandparents. Grandma Bowleigh was French and my mother is strictly New England Puritan, so they consumed a great deal of time and energy inventing ways to drive each other crazy. My mother loathes Manhattan, and would hate to live here, but she was furious on principle when Grandma Bowleigh died and left this place to me."

He flicked a switch and the living room flooded with light. "I haven't changed much since I inherited the place, although I added a couple of comfortable sofas." He smiled, and Robyn could see he was remembering someone well loved. "Grandma Bowleigh believed that straight spines and upright morals went together. Her chairs were what you might call *uncompromising*."

Robyn chuckled. "People didn't sprawl about in the good old days, did they? However many times I look at one of those steel and whalebone corsets I can never quite believe that human beings voluntarily strapped themselves inside such instruments of torture. No wonder they sat up straight!"

"It's the shoes that get me," Zach said. "I guess they must have been more comfortable than they look or our ancestors would all have been cripples."

"Nothing will convince me the shoes or the corsets were comfortable!" Robyn stopped to admire a selection of painted fans displayed in a cleverly back-lit cabinet. "Are these the fans your grandmother collected?"

"Yes. She refused to let my father or grandfather help her with any of the purchases, and as you can see she had superb taste."

"It's hard to believe she had no professional training," Robyn said, admiring an exquisite confection in ivory and painted kidskin. "How long did your grandparents live here?" she asked.

"More than fifty years. Back in the thirties, normal middle-class families could actually afford to live in central Manhattan. Even so, my grandfather only managed to scrounge up enough money to buy this building because the stock market crash in '29 had reduced real estate prices so much. He considered he'd acquired a major bargain."

"And he was certainly right."

"Long-term, as it turned out. But during the Depression, rent income barely covered the expenses of upkeep. And business at the Gallery was so bad that this building was mortgaged to the hilt in order to meet Gallery payrolls. He and my grandmother came close to losing everything on a couple of occasions, but Grandpa Bowleigh was a wily old bird, and he hung on through World War II until the boom years in the fifties and sixties made him rich."

Zach was standing in front of the fireplace at one end of the long living room. Moving to join him, Robyn's gaze was caught by the portrait of a blond, blue-eyed woman holding a tiny, lace-gowned and bonneted baby. Hung in a commanding central position, with the rest of the wall left empty, the painting had a powerful impact on the entire room.

"What a stunning portrait," she said, crossing to Zach's side for a better view. She studied it in silence for several minutes. "Is it a Gainsborough?" she asked finally. "From the woman's dress, the dates would be about right."

"Yes, it's a Gainsborough, one of his earliest portraits."

"You're lucky that it's in such a good state of preservation."

"This seems to be one of his few early paintings where he

didn't experiment with paints or techniques. Fortunately for us."

"She looks a little bit like you," Robyn said. "I think it's the shape and color of her eyes. Is she an ancestor?"

"Yes. Her name is Lady Arabella Bowleigh, and she was married to William Bowleigh, the third Baron of Starke."

"I'm impressed. Does that mean you have a real British lord for an ancestor?"

Zach grinned. "Our blue blood turned normal Yankee red several generations ago."

"The Bowleighs—your relatives—are the people in England who offered you the chance to buy their porcelain collection, aren't they?"

"Yes, the current baron is more interested in prize Guernsey cows than in old china. He's a nice, down-to-earth kind of guy, who can't imagine why anyone would pay several thousand pounds for a vase that's too valuable to put flowers in, when you could buy a vial of prize bull semen instead."

She chuckled. "Sounds as if he should be living in Texas."

"As a matter of fact, his son is studying agriculture at Texas A and M."

"When did the American branch of the family split off?"

"Arabella and William had several children and one of the excess sons was shipped off to America to make his fortune. That son was my several times great-grandfather, and he brought this portrait with him."

"Is he the baby in the picture?"

"We believe so. A letter has survived that suggests the baby is my ancestor, the Honorable Zachary."

"You were named after him?"

"Along with a slew of relatives in each generation. It's a Bowleigh tradition to name sons William or Zachary."

"Doesn't that make for major confusion at family reunions?"

"Not really. We use a lot of nicknames. My brother is called Will, and my grandfather was Bill. Fortunately, my grandmother insisted on giving all her children French names, so the family had a break from tradition for an entire generation. My father, much to his disgust, is called Piers."

Robyn looked at the possessive curve of Lady Arabella's arm around her baby. "How sad she must have been when her son grew up and left for America. Imagine knowing you're never going to see your child again."

"Actually, Arabella never knew what happened to him. She was already dead by then."

Robyn grimaced. "That's better for her, I guess, but rough on the Honorable Zachary. Life must have been hell on the emotions in those days."

"Don't you think they must have trained themselves to accept death and separation more easily than we do? They didn't focus their emotional energy on the nuclear family as strongly as we do today. Extended family connections were more important."

"You may be right. On the other hand, I don't believe basic feelings like maternal love can change from generation to generation. Look closely at Lady Arabella. Her smile may be warm, but you can see in her eyes that she's not entirely happy." Robyn paused for a moment. "She looks as if she's hiding secrets."

Zach smiled. "Is that what you see? Personally, I've always felt the painting reeks of subdued eroticism. I look at Arabella and I wonder who her lover is. I doubt if the poor old third Baron of Starke was actually the father of that baby she's clasping with such fond attention. That's probably why the kid was banished to the colonies. A convenient way to get rid of the cuckoo in the nest."

"Good heavens, Zach, you're too cynical by half. How in the world can you conclude Lady Arabella was an adulteress just because her smile is enigmatic?"

"I didn't do all my leaping to conclusions on the basis of this portrait alone. Lady Arabella is something of a mystery woman. You can see how compelling she appears in this portrait, how intelligent her expression is, how sparkling her eyes are. And yet the English branch of the family has several other portraits of her, and in those she seems a uniformly cold and shallow woman. I'll show you her other pictures when we're in Starke."

"That's probably a testament to Gainsborough's skill as an artist rather than a commentary on Arabella's character."

"Could be. But the composition of this whole painting is rather odd when you think about it. We know Arabella already had three older children at this time, twin sons and a daughter, and yet none of them was included in the picture. Why not?"

"I agree, that *is* strange." Robyn stared at the painting, intrigued by the minor mystery. One of the reasons she loved working with antiques was the way they could sometimes open a tiny window onto the vanished past. "I'm no expert on Gainsborough, but that must be one of the youngest babies he ever painted."

"It's definitely the youngest, so the portrait has a unique curiosity value, quite apart from the sentimental value to our family."

"Baby Zachary looks surprisingly human."

"He does, doesn't he? Most people nowadays don't realize how unusual that is. The baby probably isn't more than three or four weeks old, and yet, if you look at his hands and mouth, you can see Gainsborough has taken the time and trouble to individualize him. We've no idea why he bothered. In those days, infants less than six months old were barely considered human, let alone unique individuals."

Robyn frowned, feeling curiously sad. "I guess that ties back to what you said earlier. You can understand why parents kept their emotional distance when you remember that more than half the newborns died before their first birthday."

Zach shook his head. "Nowadays, it's hard to grasp the full impact of statistics like that."

"Thank heavens." Robyn was beginning to find the portrait oddly disturbing, and she turned away. Her nipples had tightened and her breasts tingled as she looked at the rosy-cheeked baby with his unusually large hands and puckered, hungry mouth. It was an extraordinary sensation, and she hugged her arms around her waist in an attempt to make the tingling go away.

Zach reached out, then allowed his hand to fall without actually touching her. "It's late, we should think about dinner," he said. "Come into the kitchen and tell me what you'd like to eat."

She followed him out of the living room, happy to be away from the disquieting portrait. Zach held out his hand, and after a tiny hesitation, she took it. She smiled up at him. "Are you one of those intimidating men who can whip up a gourmet meal in between nailing down the business deal of the century and running five-minute miles at the health club?"

He laughed, pushing open the swing doors that led into the kitchen. "Nope. It takes me six minutes to run a mile and my cooking skills are what you might call sub-basic. I can grill steaks and I'm terrific at dialing out for pizza."

"Great, now I feel superior because I can cook at least three more recipes than you. What gourmet selection are you making for us tonight? Pizza or steak?"

"You're the guest. You choose."

Somehow his arm had curled around her waist and her head was resting on his shoulder. Robyn liked the casual feeling of intimacy. Too much, in fact, but she didn't move away. "If you broiled steaks, I could impress you with my tossed green salad."

"Is that one of your three recipes?" he asked.

She smiled. "The best of the three."

He turned on the indoor grill and reached into the freezer. "You've got yourself a deal. Steak à la Zachary coming up."

Zach poured more burgundy into her wineglass and Robyn sighed with pleasure as she took a sip. "You broil a mean steak, Zach."

He bowed. "If you're a one-note player, you'd better make it a damn good note. Your salad was great, too."

"Thanks. Someday I'll invite you over to my place and treat you to all three of my specialties at once: chicken paprika, tossed Caesar salad, and Irish coffee with sweetened whipped cream."

"How about the weekend after we get back from London?" he said, and the bantering note vanished from his voice. He leaned across the table and took her hands into his. "I want to spend time with you, any time you're willing to give me. I . . . care . . . about you, Robyn."

She'd worked all night long to keep her fantasies in check, and her common sense operating at maximum voltage. It was depressing to realize that Zach could dissolve her common sense with one softly spoken comment. The infatuated part of her was ready to say her life was his to command. Twenty-nine years of prudence warned her not to be such a fool.

Prudence won out. Temporarily. Robyn pushed her chair away from the table and carried their empty plates over to stack in the sink. Then she drew in a deep breath and swung around to confront him.

"You have a beautiful apartment, you cooked a great meal, and you've been a terrific dinner companion, but you haven't told me why we were shot at last Friday, and you haven't told me why you were sneaking around the showroom after hours checking out the Farleigh cabinet. I need to know what's going on, Zach."

He gave a mock sigh. "You really want to talk about this? Couldn't we just go to bed and have great sex instead?"

She wondered if he had any idea how tempting she found his suggestion. With difficulty, she produced a smile. "The offer's almost irresistible, but right now, I'd really like to hear who's taking potshots at you."

"How depressing," he said. "But you're right, as always. You need to know what's going on."

Robyn repressed a groan. Good grief, she was a total hypocrite! She kept telling herself that she didn't want to go to bed with Zach, but what she really meant was that she wanted him to do all the chasing. She wanted him to sweep her off her feet, to smother her in passionate kisses and hustle her into his bed. What she wanted, in fact, was the pleasure of his lovemaking without any of the responsibility. It was a disturbing insight into her own behavior.

Zach paced the kitchen. "I don't know where to begin, because there's so much I still don't know."

"You could begin with who shot at us."

"I don't know who, but I have an idea why."

"Then explain the *why*."

"For the past two months, I've been investigating the likelihood that someone is using the Bowleigh Gallery as a cover to pass expensive, high-end fakes into the antiques market. I believe the shots on Friday night were a way of warning me to back off from my investigations."

She'd been expecting him to say just that, and yet hearing the actual words was still a shock. "Good Lord, Zach, have you told the police?"

"You know I can't do that. A whisper in the marketplace

that the Gallery was having a problem identifying fakes and we'd be out of business."

"Better to be out of business than dead."

"The Gallery is a four-generation enterprise for my family. We have a hundred full-time employees, and the admiration of an entire industry." He smiled grimly. "I'm damn sure Grandfather Bowleigh would have faced a firing squad before he did anything to put the business at risk."

"Your grandfather's stubbornness isn't a good reason for you to put *your* life on the line."

He spoke a touch wearily. "I'm not a hero. If I could be sure I was in danger, I'd go to the police. But like I told you, I'm not convinced those attacks were intended to hurt me."

Robyn saw no reason to share his confidence. The shots on Friday night had presumably been fired from a passing car. The fact that a bullet landed seven feet up in a doorway didn't prove anything about where it had been aimed. "Tell me how you first suspected the Gallery might be selling fakes," she said.

"Within the space of a couple of weeks, I had calls from an insurance company and from Lascelles in Paris telling me that pieces bought from the Gallery had turned out to be fakes."

"Was that *pietra-dura* cabinet you mentioned at dinner on Friday one of the questionable pieces?"

"Yes, the first. The insurance company accepted my explanation that the buyer must have made the substitution, but the whole incident bothered me and when Lascelles reported an identical situation, I started doing some checking, casually at first and then with a great deal more intensity. We sold the *pietra-dura* cabinet to a banker in Chicago in June of 1988. I discovered that a virtually identical piece was sold to a land development corporation in Florida in May of the same year. By calling in a lot of favors, I managed to get the cabinet in Florida examined, appraised, and x-rayed. It checked out as genuine, beyond any reasonable possibility of doubt. It also checked out as a perfect, exact duplicate of the piece we sold to Chicago. Same provenance, same history, except for the last two sales."

"Even supposing the Gallery's piece was a fake, how could a factory turn out such a perfect reproduction?"

"Computers are useful tools for crooks as well as for honest people. Someone is using a highly sophisticated computer program to reproduce designs with an accuracy that comes within a hundredth of an inch."

In the face of such evidence, Robyn knew it was ridiculous to hope there might have been some sort of innocent error. "Who made the last two sales on the Florida cabinet?" she asked.

"Agnelli in Milan, and Greg Jones in New Orleans."

Robyn gulped. Zach could scarcely have named two more reputable houses. "Where did our cabinet come from?"

"A finder."

Zach didn't need to say anything more. Every major antiques dealer relied on the services of finders who worked on commission, turning up treasures in unlikely places. Most finders were honest, most of the time, but the temptation to "discover" a fake was enormous, and the profit potential high. Acquisitions from finders were always scrutinized with extra special care.

"Now you understand why I'm worried," Zach said. "I've tried every scenario I can think of to explain what happened, but there's only one that works: the cabinet we sold was a fake. A superb imitation, but still not the real thing."

She scowled in frustration. "Zach, it can't have been. A fake simply couldn't make it through the authentication procedures at the Gallery. What about the X-ray certificates? The paint analyses? Computers can't fake that."

"They don't need to," he said, his voice clipped. "Stop thinking honestly and start thinking crooked. All it takes is someone on the inside working with the finder."

"No," she protested. "For God's sake, Zach, even an insider couldn't get the fake past Gerry or Kevin, or any of the other head buyers. Those guys are simply too good at their jobs to be deceived."

"I agree." Zach's face settled into hard, bleak lines. "And since it's impossible to get a fake past my head buyers, the logical conclusion is that one of them is working the scam."

He spoke coldly, but Robyn knew that he wasn't feeling in the least cold. Most of the buyers had worked at the Gallery for years. All of them were valued authorities in their area of speciality. Mr. Chen Liu, the longest-serving employee, had been a buyer for the Asian Department since 1953 and was an icon in the New York art world. Gerry, Kevin, and the European buyers had similar reputations. To suspect such people of fraud undercut the entire foundation of trust and mutual respect that kept the Gallery functioning.

"You should tell the police." She repeated her previous advice chiefly because she couldn't come up with a better suggestion.

Zach spoke impatiently. "I've been searching company records for two months, trying to decide who could be responsible, trying to decide if anyone had both the means and the motive. I've gotten precisely nowhere. Each suspect piece of furniture was acquired by a different buyer, so there's no pattern. If I can't identify the villain, you can be damn sure a police detective isn't going to do it."

A buzz on the intercom startled them both. Zach switched on the speaker. "Yes?"

"Mr. Taunton is here to see you, sir."

Robyn was so impressed that the building managers had found a New Yorker willing to address a tenant as *sir* that she almost forgot to be curious about Gerry's late-night visit. Zach, however, sounded surprised.

"Mr. Taunton's here? In the building?"

Gerry's voice cut in. "Zach, I know it's late, but I need to speak with you urgently. Something's come up and you must decide right away what action you're going to take. I hope I didn't wake you?"

"No, I'm wide awake. Come on up."

Zach released the intercom switch and Robyn spoke hurriedly. "I'll leave, Zach. It's midnight, way past time for me to get back to Queens."

He turned around to look at her. "Please don't go."

"I must. You don't want gossip circulating in the office and if Gerry finds me here at this hour, he'll get the wrong impression—"

"Will he?" Zach asked.

The laugh she gave sounded forced. "Well, you know how Gerry loves gossip and he might not understand that I came here to talk about a problem at the Gallery—"

"That isn't why you came," Zach said. "That's just the excuse we gave ourselves. We could have talked about the

Gallery's problems at any one of a hundred different restaurants."

"That's not true! This is a confidential matter, and we needed to be somewhere with guaranteed privacy—"

"I asked you here because I want like hell to go to bed with you."

His words uncoiled a hot thread of desire inside her, and she felt her blood surge hard and fast through her veins. "Zach, I'm flattered—"

"I don't want you to be flattered, for God's sake. I want you to feel the same way I do."

Robyn clung to her fast-disappearing control. "I'm attracted to you, Zach, there's no point in pretending otherwise, but we have to be practical. Why screw up a good friendship and a great working relationship for the sake of sex that might not be so great? It's not smart for the two of us to get involved."

"Smart isn't the issue," Zach said. "It's already way too late for us to be smart." He put his arm around her shoulders and pulled her close. "We blew the chance to keep our relationship platonic the moment you walked into this apartment tonight, maybe the moment you walked into my office six months ago and interviewed for a job at the Gallery."

He looked down at her, his gaze serious. He touched her lips in a fleeting caress and despite her best efforts, Robyn's nerve endings thrummed in instant response. He felt the involuntary quiver of her reaction and his eyes darkened. "God, I want you," he murmured.

She wasn't sure who moved first, but suddenly she was in Zach's arms, his mouth was all over hers, and he was kissing her as if both their lives depended on it. His hands reached inside the sensible, white starched front of her blouse and unclipped her bra. Her breath drew in sharply, then squeezed out again in a soft, low moan when his thumb brushed over her nipples. She closed her eyes, feeling every ounce of hard-won common sense drain out of her as she concentrated on the wonderful, incredible feelings coursing through her body.

The buzzing of an electric bell seemed a barbaric intrusion into the warm, throbbing haze of her desire. With considerable difficulty, she formed the thought that Gerry

Taunton had arrived upstairs and that Zach was paying no attention whatsoever. She opened her mouth to point out that the doorbell was buzzing, but he took advantage of her parted lips to deepen the kiss. His arms tightened around her waist, his tongue thrust against hers, and she clung to him, her body melting in response to the pressure of his leg between her thighs.

The doorbell rang again, pressed on and off in an impatient tattoo. She spoke against Zach's mouth. "Zach, stop. Gerry's here."

"Who?" With a sharp intake of breath, Zach lifted his head. "Right. Gerry. Gerry's here."

He still showed no signs of going to open the door, and Robyn reluctantly drew away from him. "Gerry needs to talk with you about something important." She smoothed her hair and looked around for her purse. "I should put on some lipstick."

"Sure. Good idea. Put on some lipstick." Zach blinked, then finally started walking toward the front door. He was halfway across the room when he swung around again. "I guess you might want to put this on, too." He held out his hand. Her blouse dangled between his fingers.

Crimson with embarrassment, Robyn almost snatched the blouse. "This is insane," she muttered, fumbling with the buttons. "Totally insane."

"No," Zach said tautly. "This is desire."

Chapter 3

GERRY followed Zach into the living room. He stopped abruptly when he saw Robyn standing by the fireplace, his expression so critical that Robyn wondered if her blouse was still unfastened. Her hand crept over her buttons, making sure they were all closed. Of course, Gerry's quick eye caught the surreptitious movement and his censure shaded to outright contempt. With justification, Robyn thought miserably. She ought not to be fraternizing with the company president, and she sure as heck ought not to be hovering right on the verge of making love to him. Damn! She should have made her getaway by the service entrance as soon as the doorman announced the arrival of her immediate boss.

She said hello to Gerry, her voice squeaky with embarrassment, and he nodded an acknowledgment that was barely civil. His gaze narrowed as he turned toward Zach. "Sorry, old boy, I didn't mean to interrupt anything." As always when he was annoyed, his British accent thickened.

"That's okay," Zach answered easily. "I'm sure you wouldn't have come around so late unless you had something important to discuss."

"You're right," Gerry said. "It's important, and it's private."

Robyn flushed at the barb, although she didn't blame Gerry one bit for his blatant disapproval. "Zach, I should leave you two to get on with your business." She spoke with all the dignity she could muster. "It's a long ride home to Queens and I need to make an early start in the morning—"

"I still have a couple of things I need to discuss with you," Zach said. "There's a TV in the kitchen and plenty of magazines in my study. Please don't leave until we've had a chance to finish our—conversation."

It was utterly ridiculous to stay, but the truth was Robyn had no desire to leave. Common sense told her that she ought to call a cab and run while she had the chance. Her idiotic hormones told her that she wouldn't survive the night if she and Zach didn't make love sometime very soon.

"I'll be in the kitchen brewing a pot of coffee," she said, moving toward the door. "Let me know if either of you decides you'd like a cup." She gave both men a bright smile and spoke extra briskly to make up for the stupidity of her errant hormones.

Gerry watched her leave the room, then turned back to Zach. "I won't keep you long, old chap, but something's come up in regard to the Farleigh cabinet. We have a real problem. Bad news, I'm afraid."

He spoke softly, but a quirk of acoustics sent his voice floating through the doorway. Robyn skidded to a halt in the hall. "Good Lord, did you say there's a problem with the Farleigh cabinet?" she exclaimed, poking her head back into the living room.

Gerry gave her a look that was cold enough to freeze hot barbecue coals. "Why does that interest you so much?"

"Because that's what Robyn and I have been talking about most of the evening," Zach said. "The so-called Farleigh cabinet in the Gallery's main showroom."

" 'So-called'?" Gerry's eyes widened. "My God, are you going to tell me you already know it's a fake?"

"We already know it's a fake," Zach agreed. He glanced across the room and gave Robyn a rueful grin. "You may as well come back and join us, if Gerry wouldn't mind. You'll get a crick in your neck if you keep poking your head around the door like that."

Gerry shrugged. "Since she already knows about the cabinet, there's no point in banishing her to the kitchen."

Robyn came back into the living room, looking at Gerry in sincere admiration. "I'm so impressed that you spotted a problem with the cabinet, Gerry. Every time I think I'm getting better at my job, I realize I'm a complete novice in comparison to you two guys. Even when Zach told me the cabinet was a fake, it still looked perfect to me."

"It *is* perfect." Gerry sprang up from the sofa and paced the room, the intensity of his emotions too great to allow him to remain seated. "The truth is, I didn't spot a single thing wrong with the Farleigh cabinet. Can you believe that? I never had a twinge of warning that the damned piece wasn't genuine. I had to be *told* there was a problem before I noticed anything wrong, and that's sticking in my craw."

"You shouldn't berate yourself," Zach said. "It's probably the most perfect reproduction I've ever seen. A masterpiece of fakery."

"It would have to be perfect to fool me." Gerry spoke without bravado, because they all knew his claim was justified. His feel for antiques bordered on the uncanny, and he could usually identify fakes long before technical or mechanical tests confirmed his intuitive judgment. He plopped himself down on the sofa, rubbing his forehead wearily. "How the devil did you find out it was a fake?" he asked Zach. "Nothing will console me if you spotted something out of kilter that I didn't notice."

"Don't worry, your reputation's safe," Zach said. "The piece deceived me, too. Completely."

"That makes me feel a little better. So how did you find out it wasn't genuine?"

"Almost by chance. The insurance company requested a routine X ray of a repair done by our workroom, and the pictures happened to include a section of one joint that looked suspicious. So I ordered a complete survey of all the joints and the report that came back was unequivocal. The cabinet was manufactured within the last few years, probably within the last year."

"A couple of the other tests don't hold up either," Gerry said. "I've spent the past two days reworking them and going over the provenance documentation. As soon as I was certain of my conclusion, I came straight over to tell you. What I want to know is how the hell the cabinet passed the first set of tests we ordered. How did three different testing companies screw up and certify the piece as genuine?"

"Those are good questions," Zach said. "Any answers?"

Gerry shook his head. "The more I think about it, the less I understand what happened. The tests are all run by experts with impeccable reputations."

"The Gallery's reputation is impeccable, too," Robyn

pointed out. "And yet we've come within a hairbreadth of selling a fake."

Gerry scowled. "Are you saying the experts made mistakes, or that they were bought off?"

Robyn lifted her hands. "It could be either, couldn't it? Or a combination of both."

Zach and Gerry fell silent for a moment contemplating the unpleasant implications of her comment.

"Right now, we shouldn't get sidetracked," Zach said. "I guess the most important task for the Gallery over the next couple of weeks is to make sure this can't happen again. We need to go over our systems and see where the weak points are in our verification process. What made you suspicious of the cabinet, Gerry? You said you couldn't spot anything wrong with the feel of the piece, so what tipped you off?"

"Coincidence, I'm afraid, even more so than in your case. The fact is, I had dinner with Will on Saturday night." Gerry stopped and glanced toward Robyn, shuffling his feet uneasily.

"Go on." Zach walked to the small bar in the corner of the room and searched for a bottle of Scotch. "You had dinner with my brother, although what he has to do with the Farleigh cabinet I can't begin to imagine. He hates antiques, genuine or fake."

"But he knows a lot about them," Gerry said. He cleared his throat. "If you're planning to open that bottle of Scotch sometime soon, I would appreciate a drink, Zach."

"Coming right up." Zach poured a shot into a crystal tumbler and added ice. "Robyn, would you like something?"

"No, thanks." She joined him at the bar and spoke quietly. "Zach, Gerry seems uncomfortable talking about this. Are you sure your conversation wouldn't be easier if I weren't here?"

"Not for me." He turned his back on Gerry and looked down at her, vivid blue eyes dark with emotion. "I want you to stay," he said, and she knew he was asking her to remain not just for Gerry's visit, but for the entire night. His voice husky, he murmured, "Robyn, I need you."

She had spent twenty-nine years wondering why people made fools of themselves when they fell in love. Now she knew. She gazed up at him, helpless to hide her feelings. "Of course I'll stay."

He smiled, and she felt the warmth of his relief and pleasure right down into her toes. "Thanks, honey." He took the Scotch and carried it over to Gerry. "After what happened on Friday night, Robyn deserves to know everything about this situation that you and I do."

Gerry's ears almost visibly pricked. "What happened on Friday? You two had dinner together, didn't you?"

"Yes," Zach said. "And when we left the restaurant, someone took a potshot at us."

"My God!" Gerry choked on his Scotch. "Where? When? You weren't hurt, were you?"

"On Fifth Avenue, right by La Grenouille. And fortunately, as you can see, the bullets missed us."

"Thank God for that." Gerry's face was pale. "Good Lord, did you tell the police?"

"No, what would be the point?"

"None, I suppose," Gerry admitted, taking a calming sip of his drink. "With their workload, unless you're injured or dead, they won't do much more than file a report. But I certainly hope you've arranged for security guards from a private firm?"

"Yes, I did," Zach said. "They're already on duty."

Gerry frowned. "This is terrible news, Zach. I'm sorry you and Robyn had such a nasty experience. Let's just hope it was a case of being in the wrong place at the wrong time."

Zach smiled grimly. "Yeah. I can think of better ways to impress my date than having her sprayed with bullets."

Gerry swirled his ice around his glass. "But Robyn wasn't exactly a date, was she? I mean, that was a business meeting for the two of you, wasn't it?"

"It started out that way," Zach said. He didn't elaborate, nor did he mention that the shooting on Friday night wasn't the first time he'd been shot at. Robyn wondered why.

Gerry set down his glass. "Of course, there's no reason whatever to connect the shooting on Friday with the fact that the Farleigh cabinet is a fake. On the contrary. The sort of artist who could produce a reproduction as perfect as that cabinet isn't likely to cruise the streets spraying bullets. I mean, why on earth would he? What would he achieve?"

"I assume he was warning me off," Zach said.

"Warning you off what precisely?"

"My investigation into the provenance of the cabinet."

"Hmm, I suppose that's a possibility. But why attack you with Robyn there?"

Zach leaned forward in his chair. "Maybe he knew that Robyn is very important to me."

Gerry glanced from Robyn to Zach, then took a long sip of Scotch. "Yes, well, this speculation is all very interesting, but we're leaping to rather a lot of unfounded conclusions. If you think about it, old chap, this is New York City. It's much more likely that you were the victim of a random shooting than anything else."

"Why do you say that?" Zach asked.

"Well, God knows, New York has plenty of random shootings—"

"Not many of them occur on the corner of Fifth and Fifty-Fifth."

"True." Gerry shrugged. "But drug deals don't only go wrong in the South Bronx, you know. And besides, if the gunman was aiming at you, he must have known you would be eating at La Grenouille that night—"

"I agree, but so what?"

"Very few people knew where you planned to eat on Friday," Gerry protested. "In fact, probably nobody except Robyn and your secretary."

"But almost everyone who works at the Gallery could find out where I planned to eat," Zach said. "The reservation was entered on Shirley's desk calendar, so literally anyone who walked into her office could have seen the notation."

"But that means the person who shot at you was put up to it by a Gallery employee!"

Zach's eyes turned a hard, bright blue. "Who else? Come on, Gerry, let's inject a note of reality into this discussion. Our verification systems are superb. They can only be defeated by an insider. That means the Farleigh cabinet was introduced into the Gallery by a senior employee—someone we all trust. You know that, and so do I."

"I suppose so." Gerry looked gray with misery. "My God, I can't quite get a handle on all this. Last week, everything at the Gallery seemed to be going so smoothly it was almost boring. Now—"

His voice trailed away, and Zach picked up. "Now we have some problems to solve. And we need to pool all of our information if we're going to solve them quickly. Tell me about your dinner with my brother last weekend. How in the world did he manage to tip you off to the fact that there was a problem with the Farleigh cabinet?"

Gerry drained the last of his Scotch. "Okay, here goes. As you know, Will was in the Gallery a couple of weeks ago and I showed him around."

"Yes, you told me. Will has shares in the family trust and he always pays a token visit to the Gallery once a year."

"He stayed longer than usual this year. He may not like antiques very much, but he's an artist. He appreciates beauty and he was fascinated by the Farleigh cabinet."

"It's a very striking piece," Zach said. "The painting on the doors is of unusually high quality."

"Right, and it was the painting that fascinated Will. We chatted about the artist's depiction of the elephants for several minutes. Then Will left to catch his flight for L.A. and I never gave his visit another moment's thought."

Gerry fell silent and Zach prompted him. "But he called you?"

"Yes. While he was in L.A., Will happened to visit a very rich friend of your father's who was considering buying one of Will's paintings. And there, sitting in pride of place in this very rich friend's living room, was the exact duplicate of the Farleigh cabinet. The friend had bought it from Goodwin and Child's in Boston and he naturally insisted it was the genuine article. Will called me the minute he got back to New York, and I started to check into things right away."

Zach's fingers drummed on the table. "That's an amazing coincidence."

Gerry smiled tightly. "Amazing coincidences happen all the time in the antiques trade. The fact is, we're an incestuous business and anyone who knows enough about high-class antiques to produce a perfect duplicate of the Farleigh cabinet ought to know that you can't get away with passing exact duplicates into the marketplace. The circle of potential buyers is too small and you'll be found out sooner rather than later."

"When did Will call you?"

"Over a week ago."

"Why didn't you tell me earlier that you had suspicions about the Farleigh cabinet?"

Gerry shrugged. "Probably for the same reason you didn't share your doubts with me. This is an explosive accusation, and I wanted to be damn sure I wasn't getting worked up about nothing. Will's no expert on antiques, and frankly, I expected the whole brouhaha to turn out to be a storm in a teacup. But by the time I'd rerun the tests and rechecked the details of the provenance papers, I knew we were in trouble. This isn't a false alarm, it's a major, full-blown crisis. I came over here to consult with you as soon as I finished running the last test and getting all the documentation together."

"Any suggestions as to how we should handle this?" Zach asked.

"The first step has to be to notify the departmental heads at the Gallery to reexamine their inventory for fakes," Gerry said.

"I agree, but I don't want this story to break while I'm in Europe. Can you keep this to yourself until I get back?"

"It might be better if you canceled your trip," Gerry suggested. "At the very least, we'll have to pull the Farleigh cabinet from the sales floor and people will wonder why."

"Don't pull it. Announce that it's been sold," Zach said. "Say I've bought it to give to a relative who's getting married."

For some reason, Gerry's cheeks flushed scarlet. He coughed. "We could do that," he agreed. He seemed to feel a need to change the subject. "And while you're in Europe, I can personally double-check on every significant piece in the Gallery to make sure we don't pass on any fakes. Can you imagine what would have happened to our reputation if we'd actually sold a copy and passed it off as a genuine eighteenth-century piece?" Gerry's forehead broke out in a sweat, and he mopped it with the silk handkerchief tucked in his breast pocket.

"That's one major disaster averted," Zach agreed.

Robyn looked up, then quickly looked away, wondering

again why Zach had chosen not to mention the other fakes that the Gallery might already have sold. Surely—it just didn't seem possible—surely he didn't suspect Gerry of playing any part in the scam?

Gerry yawned. "Sorry, I didn't realize how tired I was until I got that pile of garbage off my chest." He stood up. "I'll be on my way, unless you have any other instructions you need to pass on, Zach?"

"None," Zach said. "I do have a question, though."

"Fire ahead, old boy."

"Why did Will call you with his news about the Farleigh cabinet and not me?"

Gerry gave a broad, insincere smile. "I don't think you should read any deep significance into that, Zach. Will and I chat almost every week. I was the person who'd shown him the Farleigh cabinet in our Gallery showrooms. I suppose it was natural for him to contact me—"

"I'm the president and general manager," Zach interrupted. "Will has always respected my professional judgment, just as I respect his artistic ability. We may have a pretty screwed-up relationship, but mutual professional respect is the one area we always had straightened out. He knew I was the logical person to call, so why didn't he? He's been avoiding me for the past three months, and I'd like to know why. Something's going on."

Gerry paced nervously. "Look, I feel very much caught in the middle here, but I've already told Will it's ridiculous of him not to let you know what's happening. The truth is, he's planning to get married."

Zach's face broke into a huge smile. "That's great news! Why the hell is he keeping it secret?"

Gerry looked up at the ceiling, then down at his shoes. "He's ... um ... planning to marry Claire."

Robyn's head jerked up, and Zach's smile froze. "Claire?" he repeated. "My ex-wife? Jesus H. Christ! Are you telling me my brother is planning to marry my ex-wife!"

"Er ... yes. That's what I'm telling you."

"He can't do that!" Zach yelled. If he had previously appeared the model of brotherly affection, he now appeared the model of Neanderthal jealousy and sibling rivalry. "What the

hell is he thinking about? For God's sake, they'll drive each
other crazy within a month."

Gerry seemed more at ease now that he'd broken his
bombshell. "Actually, I don't think they'll drive each other
crazy at all. They seem head over heels in love."

Zach walked over to the bar, poured himself a Scotch,
threw in a couple of ice cubes, and drank it neat. When he
put the glass down on the counter, he seemed more in control, although Robyn suspected a stewpot of emotions bubbled just beneath the surface calm. "Will should have told
me," he said curtly.

"Sometimes you can be a pretty intimidating man," Gerry
said. "Anyway, Will's news is out now, so you can handle it
however you think best." He shrugged into his overcoat, obviously anxious to get away. "It's one o'clock," he said. "I
need to get home. My sister's paying a flying visit from England and she'll be wondering what's happened to me."

"Your sister?" Zach asked.

"Yes, you remember Gloria, don't you? The two of you
met once before, a couple of years ago. She teaches at a
school in Dorset, not too far from Starke as a matter of fact."

"Of course, I remember now. We spent a weekend together at your place in the Hamptons. Give her my best.
Next time she's in New York, we must get together for dinner."

"She'd like that, I'm sure." Gerry walked toward the exit
and gave Robyn a friendly smile. "I'll see you in the morning, my dear. Don't let Zach keep you up too late. I have a
lot of work waiting for you tomorrow."

"I'll be in the office by nine on the dot," Robyn said.

Zach escorted Gerry to the door. When he came back into
the living room, he grimaced apologetically. "I'm sorry, I set
you up for that parting shot of his."

He looked exhausted, as well as apologetic, and Robyn
moved instinctively to offer reassurance. It seemed so natural to slip her arms around his waist and lean her head
against the rock-hard wall of his chest that she didn't stop to
consider all that was implied by her offer of comfort.

He wove his fingers through her hair, stroking gently, and
she nestled against him. "Why didn't you tell Gerry about
the other fakes and the other attack on you?" she asked.

"For the obvious reasons," he said tiredly. "Gerry is one of six or seven people working with me who have the expertise, the position, and the contacts to pull off a scam like this."

"But you can't seriously suspect Gerry," she protested. "That's absurd."

"On the contrary," he corrected tersely. "I have to suspect Gerry, along with every other senior buyer at the Gallery."

Robyn grimaced, unable to dispute his logic however uncomfortable it made her feel. "Where do we go from here, Zach?"

"I'm leaving for Paris tomorrow night, and then I'm going on to Starke. I can't do a damn thing until we get back from England. Maybe a few days of breathing space will bring some fresh ideas."

"Maybe Gerry was right. Perhaps we shouldn't go to Starke."

He tightened his arms around her waist, rubbing his cheek against her hair. "We have to go," he said softly. "Right now, the thought of you and me alone in a quaint English hotel is about all that's keeping me sane. I'm counting on having two very long nights to put my campaign into action."

"What campaign is that?"

He tilted her head backward and lowered his head slowly toward her mouth. "My campaign to seduce you."

Her body flushed with heat, and her mouth went dry with longing, but she resisted the foolish urge to close her eyes, drown in his kisses, and count the world well lost for love. She spoke with all the firmness she could muster.

"Zach, let's be sensible. An affair between the two of us would never work. I can't let you seduce me. You're my boss, the president of the company I work for. Right now, with the situation at the Gallery, you can't afford to show even a hint of favoritism—"

He silenced her protests by the simple expedient of covering her mouth in a passionate, seeking kiss. The kiss continued for several mind-blowing minutes. When they finally came up for air, Robyn discovered that she was lying on the sofa, with Zach on top of her, and her white blouse draped over the antique fire screen, along with his tie. When she was around Zach, she seemed to experience real difficulty in keeping her clothes on.

Zach eased his weight away from her, but he showed no sign of getting off the sofa. His thumbs brushed lazily across her breasts, wreaking erotic havoc. She was still wearing her bra, but she was sure he could feel the way her nipples stiffened and her body shuddered every time his fingers feathered across her skin. Desire, when you were half-naked, was rather difficult to conceal.

Zach, of course, made no effort to behave like a gentleman and pretend he hadn't noticed the effect he was having on her. He dropped a quick kiss on her swollen lips and smiled with infuriating satisfaction. "Are you sure my seduction campaign is doomed to failure?" he asked. "Somehow, I get the feeling you would enjoy our lovemaking as much as I would."

"No, I wouldn't," she insisted feebly. She quivered as he trailed a path of kisses across her shoulders, making nonsense of her claim.

"What a shame," he whispered, his kisses moving lower.

Robyn stifled a groan of pleasure. "Zach, we need to forget about the past few days and get our relationship back on a sound working basis—"

"My side of the relationship is already working overtime." Zach drew her hand down his body until her palm rested against the unmistakable hardness of his erection. When she didn't take her hand away, he wrapped her in his arms, holding her tight against the length of his body. His voice was husky and no longer teasing when he spoke again. "Robyn, stay here with me tonight. I want like hell to make love to you."

Her Master Plan was very specific on the subject of Zach Bowleigh and sex. There was to be none. Sexual fantasies were outlawed. Real-life, honest-to-God sex wasn't even to be considered. Robyn realized that a moment of choice had arrived: she could stick to her Master Plan, or she could blow her long-term strategy and succumb to the short-term pleasure of Zach's lovemaking.

With only a tiny twinge of guilt, Robyn consigned her Master Plan to oblivion. She linked her hands behind Zach's head and drew him down until his mouth hovered a tantalizing few inches away from hers. Some lingering, half-buried spark of sanity caused her to make a final, token protest. "Sexual relationships between a boss and an employee never work out," she mumbled.

"You're right. You're fired," he said, eyes gleaming with laughter. His hand stroked caressingly over her stomach and circled toward her thighs. "See how easily I take care of your ethical problems?"

"I sure do. Boy, you certainly know how to sweet-talk a woman into your bed."

"Never trust a man in the throes of sexual passion, he'll promise anything. Tonight you're fired, but tomorrow I'll expect you back at work, just as if nothing had happened. That's the way of the world."

"Zach, I should warn you, I'm not very good at sexual flings and casual relationships—"

"You're the one who keeps talking about casual relationships," he said softly. "Personally, I was thinking more along the lines of happily-ever-after, kids, dogs, a house in the country . . ." His fingers slipped between her legs, and her hips arched off the couch, pushing against him. "My God, Robyn," he whispered. "You feel so wonderful. Let's make this last a long, long time."

They climaxed together about a minute later. The second time, they managed to hold off long enough to shed all their clothes. The third time, they made it as far as Zach's bedroom.

"Great strategic planning," Robyn mumbled drowsily, collapsing against the pillows, weak with exhaustion and pleasure. "We can die comfortably in bed."

Zach didn't answer. He was already asleep.

The overnight flight from New York into London's Heathrow Airport was only a few minutes late, and the Customs and Immigration procedures went smoothly, so it was no more than ten-thirty on Friday morning when Robyn drove her Ford Escort out of the rental agency lot. Tired, and a little disoriented after sitting for eight hours in a plane, she circled the airport three times before finding the correct exit.

Despite this less than promising start to her journey, once she got onto the main road the feel of driving on the left soon came back to her, and she entered the motorway feeling reasonably confident. By noon, a light drizzle started to fall, making the pavement slick, but otherwise the drive to Starke proved uneventful.

Her first glimpse of the hotel swept away some of her lingering fatigue. Built on a small rise, its graceful origins as the home of an English aristocrat were clearly evident. As she drew nearer, Robyn could see the mullioned windows glinting in the fitful light of the rainy November afternoon. To the south, a thick copse of bare-branched trees protected the mellow stone facade from the assault of sea breezes. To the west, evergreens, shimmering with raindrops, added a splash of dark color. Although clearly visible for at least a mile, instead of dominating the landscape, the sprawling house melded in with the soft grays and browns of the autumn countryside, woven by time into the woof and warp of its surroundings. The drizzle of rain added a silver veil that gave the old manor a final touch of magic.

Robyn nearly always found English country houses beautiful; Starke Manor struck her as so perfect that her stomach lurched in a reaction that felt akin to recognition. She had the oddest sensation of coming home.

A dozen cars already took up most of the available parking space, but Robyn managed to squeeze in between a Jaguar sports coupe and the stone arches that marked the entrance to the hotel. The cobbled, hedged parking lot must once have been the forecourt of the old manor house, and it hadn't been very well adapted to modern traffic, but Robyn could understand why the hotel's owners had been reluctant to tamper with the quaint inefficiency of the layout. Breathing in air that smelled of rain and wet grass, with a tantalizing hint of salty ocean, Robyn could almost hear the sound of pawing horses' hoofs and jingling carriage harnesses. The English countryside often suggested an intimate connection between past and present, and Starke Manor seemed an especially fine example of historical continuity. She hoped the interior of the hotel would live up to the promise of its exterior, and not turn out to be an ugly pastiche of Victorian chintz and red flowered carpets. The English seemed to have an enduring passion for flowered carpets.

A blue car over to the left of the courtyard backed out of

its parking space, and the noise of its revving engine broke Robyn's daydream. So far, the departing car was the only sign of activity she'd observed since turning into the court-yard. Yawning, she reached into the rental car for her gar-ment bag. With luck, her room would be made up and ready for occupancy. After fourteen hours of travel, the thought of a hot bath and a cozy bed was infinitely appealing. Much as she was looking forward to seeing Zach, she hoped he hadn't yet arrived from Paris. If she could take a quick nap before meeting up with him, she would be able to do full justice to their reunion.

The thought of the night ahead was enough to curve her mouth into a smile. The past four days had seemed long and lonely, but this weekend was going to be *fun*.

Energized by the prospect of seeing Zach, she slung her garment bag over her shoulder and pushed the car door shut with her foot. The dark blue car she had noticed earlier stopped by the arched exit and the driver, a middle-aged woman with unlikely black hair and thick glasses, leaned out of the window. "Excuse me, but are you Robyn Delaney?" she asked, her manner polite.

"Why, yes, I am." Robyn rested her garment bag on the hood of her rental car, wondering how in the world the woman knew her name.

"Good." The woman raised her hands.

Gun. God Almighty, the woman was holding a gun.

There was no time for thought, but some primal instinct of self-preservation made Robyn throw herself forward, which was the only direction she could move between the two cars hemming her in on either side. She heard the soft, muffled pop almost in the same instant as she leapt.

There was a silencer on the gun.

Heat ripped in a thin, sharp line across the top of her head, tearing away flesh, tearing away her breath. She heard shouts, a man's voice. Zach's voice?

"Zach, help me!"

A car engine gunned, then raced away, tires squealing.

Pain exploded inside her skull and tightened around her lungs.

It hurt to breathe. Hurt so much that she knew she would soon have to stop breathing.

Rain. Cool rain washed blood onto the cobblestones, spreading in a pink puddle around her head.

She closed her eyes.

Purple, blood-filled darkness.

Nothing.

The pain in her head was unendurable. She screamed with the agony of it, but the scream made no sound. She didn't dare to move. If she moved, she knew that the pain would only grow worse, so she lay utterly still, tricking the pain, trying to hide from it.

Her face was wet, and she remembered it had been raining. *Starke Manor. Evergreens, misted with raindrops.*

It hurt to remember, it hurt to think, and so she retreated back into the darkness.

But he would not let her stay there in the warm safety of oblivion. She heard his voice, whispering softly in her ear, refusing to let her drift away. "Come, Arabella, you do not want to die here in this filthy, freezing mud. Show us all that you have too much spirit to allow your life to end this way."

Zach? Was it Zach talking to her?

Who is Arabella? she asked, but he didn't reply.

Another male voice spoke. A man, but not Zach. "Come, my lord, you must get up from that icy mud. You will do your children no service if you contract an inflammation of the lungs. If they lose you as well as their mother, then they would be orphans indeed."

"I tell you that she is breathing." The first man's voice was flat, but unmistakably commanding. "We must carry her back to the house. Aaron, Jake, fetch a trestle from the stables."

Don't move me, Zach, my head hurts.

"My lord, I am most sorry indeed for the loss with which you have been afflicted, but you must accept the fact that the Lady Arabella is dead, and the child, too. I detected no signs of life for several minutes before you got here. I have seen many head injuries during my years as a physician. Trust me, my lord, and believe that God has been merciful in taking her swiftly to heaven. With a blow to the head such as she has sustained, those who live are condemned to a miserable existence replete with madness and suffering."

"Dr. Perrick, if you would but bend your ear to her bosom, you would hear the beat of her heart, even as I do. Now, kindly stop worrying about dirtying your breeches in the mud and show my servants how they may lift Lady Arabella onto the trestle in a way that causes her the least injury and the least pain. Here, take my jacket to make a cushion for her head."

Dr. Perrick. Thank goodness a doctor had finally arrived. The darkness was fading, leaving her nowhere to hide from the pain. She remembered now that she was Robyn Delaney and that she had been shot. She drew in a deep lungful of rain-wet air and forced herself to confront the reality of her pain.

The aches and bruises covering her body were insignificant in comparison to the agonized throbbing inside her head. Her stomach roiled with nausea as the paramedics lifted her out of Zach's cradling arms, and she couldn't help moaning as they placed her on the stretcher.

"Dear God in heaven, she is truly alive!"

"Indeed she is. I am relieved to find that we are finally in agreement, Dr. Perrick."

"Our merciful Savior has returned her to us, so we must not delay in getting her to a warm bed! The onset of labor is virtually assured. Aaron and Jake, and you two stable lads, take the corners of the trestle. Easy, now! Move her limbs as little as possible. We must carry her home as speedily as we may, but it is essential that we do not jostle her wits. Do not run, or you will rattle her brain into certain madness!"

Robyn was too absorbed in her own pain to think about much else, but she did know that she wanted Zach to come with her to the hospital. The clasp of his hand around hers was too comforting to relinquish. She would have to make the effort to ask him to stay with her. Clenching her teeth against the pain, she opened her eyes.

The man standing next to her was tall and broad-shouldered, with blue eyes, and blond hair drawn back and tied at the nape of his neck in a floppy bow of thick black ribbon. His features were vaguely, irritatingly familiar. He was handsome in an aloof, aristocratic sort of way—and she had never seen him before in her entire life.

He smiled at her, a beautiful smile that dissipated the grimness of his expression. "Arabella, how do you feel, my dear? Can you tell us where it pains you most? Is the babe still moving?"

Arabella? Why was he calling her Arabella? And where was Zach? Her voice didn't seem capable of uttering any of the questions seething in her brain, perhaps because her throat was so dry and swollen. For several seconds she managed no more than grunts before she finally managed to shape a single coherent word.

"Zach?" she rasped.

The man's smile didn't fade, and his grip on her hand remained gentle, but she felt the incredible blaze of white-hot anger that shot through him. "No, my lady," he said, and she could feel in her own sinews and muscles just how much it cost him in self-control to keep his voice sounding mild and pleasant. "I'm afraid Zachary could not be with us this evening."

She licked her lips, and this time her words came out a little more easily. "Wh-who are you? What happened to me?"

He looked down at her, and the flickering light of the lantern made his expression appear shadowed and indescribably bleak. "I am William," he said. "Your husband. Your horse bolted and you fell from your carriage just outside the gates of Starke, but we are taking you back to the house, where you can rest until you are well and strong again."

"I don't have a horse," she said. "I don't have a husband. I was shot." She thought for a moment. "Why isn't Zach here? Is he in Paris?"

"We have no idea where Zachary is." The man called William spoke even more coolly than before. "My lady, have a care. Remember that my brother has been declared a traitor, an enemy of our King."

"Zach? A traitor?" Belatedly, she realized what nonsense the stranger was talking. "Besides, we don't have a king. We have . . . we have . . ." Her words died away. With a surge of panic, she realized that she couldn't remember the name of her country, or what sort of government she lived under. She had come to Starke Manor to be with Zach, but she didn't know why.

Robyn struggled to sit up, but the pain exploded with such

vicious force against the back of her eyes that her vision dimmed and she collapsed against the makeshift stretcher, gasping in agony.

William placed his hand very lightly on her forehead. A long time ago, Zach had told her something important about William, but she couldn't recall what. The blond man spoke to the doctor, and his voice sounded marginally less cold than it had done earlier. "Clearly, my wife is raving. Do you think she has contracted a fever?"

"It is more than possible, my lord. If I may make so bold as to suggest? I cannot hold out much hope for the child, but it would be better if you did not encourage the Lady Arabella to speak until she is safely in bed and her head is cushioned against a pillow. Any exertion of the brain is dangerous at this point. We must not risk rupturing the delicate threads that anchor her mind to her body."

"I am not Arabella," Robyn muttered. From some hidden reserve of strength, she dragged up the willpower to raise herself on one elbow and stare at the motley crew of men who had appointed themselves her rescuers. "I am Robyn Delaney, do all of you hear that? I am *Robyn Delaney* and I want to be taken to the nearest hospital."

"Ah, my lord, I warned you—"

The doctor didn't finish his sentence. William took her hand again and stroked it soothingly. "Certainly we hear you, my dear, and we understand perfectly. You are Robin de Lane. Rest now, and do not trouble yourself with these difficult matters until you are strong again."

She would have been angry at his patronizing tone if she hadn't been so tired. As it was, she had barely sufficient energy to convey the really important message. "You have to find Zach and take me to him." She tightened her grasp on William's hand. "Promise me," she pleaded. "Promise that you will find Zach and bring him to me."

William disengaged his hand from her clasp. His voice once again was a cold stream, flowing over ice. "I promise, my lady, that I will do everything in my power to make you happy."

"Then you will find Zach." Robyn sank back against the pillows. "Don't leave me, William. Not tonight."

She had no idea why she made such a strange request but

she knew she felt oddly comforted when William's fingers brushed lightly, almost hesitantly, across her cheek. "No, my lady," he said softly. "I shall not leave you. I have given you my word."

Chapter 4

THE paramedics seemed to carry her for miles on the uncomfortable wooden stretcher, jolting and jarring every inch of her protesting body. Robyn wondered why they had parked their ambulance so far away, and why they didn't give her a shot of something to ease the excruciating pain pounding behind her eyes. Perhaps they couldn't medicate her because of the wound to her head. Could you give painkillers to someone who had a concussion? She couldn't remember.

She turned to William. "Painkillers . . ." she whispered, hoping against hope. "I need some painkillers . . ."

William stroked her hand, his touch reassuring, but impersonal. "The pain will not kill you, Arabella. I know it is hard, but try to endure the discomfort for another little while. You are being wonderfully brave."

She wondered why he kept calling her Arabella, but it was too much effort to ask. The hospital would sort out the mistake eventually. If she kept her eyes closed, the nausea wasn't quite as bad, so she tried to lie still, relaxing and letting her body move with the sway of the stretcher. The pain in her head became marginally less horrible and she was content to lie passive, not thinking, just savoring the drizzle of rain misting her face. There was no wind, and the rain felt soft and comforting, a touch of coolness against her hot cheeks, anchoring her to reality each time she started to drift away into the dark mist of unconsciousness.

She could hear the doctor and the paramedics murmuring to each other but the individual words were hard to distinguish and she gave up straining to understand the broad English accents. Their voices floated over her, wisps of sound that she felt too exhausted to unravel. She was jolted back into awareness when her entire body convulsed with a sudden excruciating pain.

"Have a care! Do not allow her to fall." William spoke sharply. Robyn found his accent easier to understand than any of the others, although what he said often seemed to make little sense. Like now. "Dr. Perrick, what say you? Do you think my wife's birth pangs have begun?"

"I fear so, my lord, I fear so. And I regret it is my solemn duty to warn you that her ladyship is in such a weakened state that I cannot predict a favorable outcome to the labor, either for her or for the babe."

"Perhaps you are unduly pessimistic. Her other children have been delivered without mishap."

"That is so, my lord. But on previous occasions, her ladyship entered her travails in a state of robust health and strength. Childbirth is a dangerous enterprise even under the most favorable of circumstances, and her ladyship's head injury is severe."

"Bloody, certainly, but the wound seems to me to be relatively superficial."

"Infection and fever are almost inevitable, my lord." Dr. Perrick cleared his throat. "If I may make so bold, my lord, I would suggest that you send for the vicar. We may have double need of his services before the night is out."

"Let the vicar eat his dinner in peace. There will be time enough to fetch him to the Manor later this evening if his presence seems necessary. First we need to get my wife home and safely into her bed. Our most necessary task must be to see that she is made warm and dry and that her wounds are cleaned—and stitched if need be."

The individual words William spoke were definitely some sort of English, but his conversation made no sense, Robyn decided. Was she being taken to this arrogant William person's home? Why was he ordering everyone about like some feudal lord of the manor, and why were the doctor and paramedics listening? Robyn felt a spurt of rage. What was wrong with the doctor that he wasn't insisting she should be driven to a hospital? Good grief, she was in agony, she'd probably lost a ton of blood, and so far nobody had done anything except load her onto a stretcher and jounce her over miles of wet countryside.

"Hospital," she rasped. "Where's the hospital?"

William spoke again, his voice soothing, as if addressing an idiot. "The hospital is in the village, my dear. Do you remember that your own father endowed the funds for the building?"

She blinked, trying to focus her eyes, trying to understand. "My father? But he's never been to England!"

"My lord, her ladyship must be kept quiet—"

William's hand rested for a moment on her forehead. "Do not trouble yourself with these matters, my dear, we shall soon have you home and in your own bed. Then you will feel quite yourself again."

"I want to go to the hospital!"

"And you shall, my dear, as soon as you are well enough."

When she was well enough! The man was totally crazy, Robyn realized with a shudder of fear. Crazy—or deliberately cruel. She remembered in a sudden flash of coherence that she had left New York late at night and flown to England, arriving early in the morning. She had driven to Starke Manor Hotel, where she had been shot by a woman in the parking lot. Perhaps this William person was one of the woman's fellow conspirators. Perhaps his failure to seek medical care was a deliberate ploy, intended to cause her harm.

"Take me to the hospital," she pleaded, striving with all her might to speak clearly, despite her dry, swollen throat and painfully cracked lips. "Oh, God, why won't you take me to the hospital?"

William's hand tightened around hers in a comforting squeeze. "Of course you shall go there if you wish, my dear, you have my word on it. Now lie still, and do not trouble yourself further."

His voice was so calm and reassuring that Robyn felt herself relax, despite her realization that he was almost certainly lying. She tried to remember why she had come to England, and why she had arranged to meet Zach at Starke Manor. She wished Zach would come. Where was he? The gloomy November afternoon had already given way to dusk, so several hours must have elapsed since her accident. Why hadn't he come to take care of her? To protect her from these half-crazed locals.

She didn't understand why the usual sort of emergency medical procedures hadn't swung into immediate action after her accident. England, after all, was an advanced, civilized country. Was it possible that in this sleepy, rural part of the country people were so unused to guns and violence that they didn't know how to react medically to a drive-by shooting?

"Drip," she muttered. "I need a drip. A blood transfusion. Saline solution. Something. Take me to the hospital, dammit, and stop screwing around."

"What be 'er saying, my lord? 'Er ladyship be saying 'er words all jumbled up like. Why does 'er keep on and on about th'ospital? And did 'er say blood?"

"I'm not certain, Jake, but I am sure this strange talk is but a temporary condition. Her ladyship will be better once the babe has arrived and when she is recovered, we shall all be able to understand her once again."

What babe? That was the second or third time these weird people had mentioned the imminent arrival of a baby. Robyn didn't even want to consider what that extraordinary comment might mean. She tried to turn her head toward the William person, whose arrogant commands seemed to be at the root of all her troubles, but the wave of pain made her feel so sick she quickly abandoned the attempt.

"We're here!" William's voice contained unmistakable relief. "Be careful, lads, as you carry her up the stairs."

A murmuring swell of female voices was added to the male chorus surrounding Robyn. She forced her eyes open, and found herself staring into the worried features of a youngish woman, hair tucked into the strangest nurse's cap Robyn had ever seen.

"Am I in the hospital?" she asked.

"No, my lady—"

"Yes, indeed, my dear. You have been carried to the hospital."

William's voice. She didn't believe him, but she was too weak to protest. Tears of helpless anger and frustration welled up and poured over her cheeks.

"There, there, my lady, 'twill all come right in the end,"

the woman murmured. "Don't you fret, we'll see that your babe is borned safely."

"I—am—not—pregnant," Robyn said between sobs. Her tears vanished in a sudden hysterical urge to giggle. Good Lord, couldn't these yokels tell the difference between a woman with a gunshot wound and a woman in the early stages of labor? She would have laughed out loud, but her breath was swallowed up in a wave of pain so intense that it seemed to start at her toes and grind excruciatingly through her abdomen, culminating in an explosion of darkness inside her head. The pain left her body limp, her mind blank.

Their awkward, bumpy procession had barely reached the head of the stairs—there seemed to be no elevators in this place, although the building was huge—when the pain came again, grinding through the pit of Robyn's stomach, peaking in an excruciating knot right below her navel.

"Her pangs are but minutes apart, my lord. I fear she has been thrown straight into hard labor." Robyn heard the doctor's voice through a red mist of agony.

"Perhaps that is not an ill thing. It may be better if her strength is not drained by hours and hours of preliminary effort that achieves little save to exhaust her."

"Let us pray that your optimism is justified, my lord."

The darkness was washing over her in longer and longer waves. Robyn was distantly aware that she had been carried into a high-ceilinged room, dimly lit, and oppressively airless after the freshness of the rain-swept night. The close, cloying atmosphere left her gasping for oxygen, and when the pain swept over her at the same moment as she tried to draw breath, her gasp emerged as a frightened scream.

"Try to stay calm, Arabella. We shall soon have you out of these wet clothes and then you may rest a little in the comfort of your own bed."

"How can I rest?" Robyn asked, succumbing to panic. Tears clogged her throat, choking her, washing out to cascade down her cheeks. "I want Zach to be here," she sobbed. "Why won't you take me to him? He'd drive me to the hospital in a minute."

"My brother Zachary has not been seen since the Battle of Culloden," William said, removing his hand from hers.

Robyn hadn't noticed how tightly she'd been holding his hand until that moment, and she felt a renewed surge of panic when she realized he was walking away.

"Don't go!" she called out. "You promised you wouldn't leave me."

William stopped and turned around. There was weariness in his voice when he spoke again. "You cannot wish me to stay, my lady. Not for the birth of a child. You know how much you dislike me to see you when you are not properly dressed and painted."

"I'm not having a baby," she said, unwilling to let the absurd myth that she was in labor continue. "Don't be ridiculous. How can I have a baby when I'm not even pregnant!"

The room was shadowy, almost dark, but she thought she saw him smile, just for an instant. "It seems, my lady, that one or the other of us is going to be very surprised a few hours from now."

"It won't be me," Robyn said, furious with him, and yet oddly reassured by the glimpse of his smile. "Don't go," she repeated, although she had no idea why she wanted his presence. Nothing William had done or said suggested that he was a useful person to have around in a sick room. On the contrary, he seemed unaware of even the fundamentals of first aid.

Before she could say anything more, another pain convulsed her body and Robyn felt herself float away into a twilight half world where she dreamed she was trapped on a football field, and all the players were running over her, pulling her brutally from side to side as they searched for the ball that was hidden under her hips. After a while, she hurt so much that she stopped feeling the individual blows of huge, heavy feet stomping on her stomach in careless search for the football. Her body was so tormented and weakened by the buffets inflicted on it that she knew she was going to die, and she sank deeper into the darkness, mentally digging a little pit in the ground where she was safe from the rush of the footballers' heavy feet and their mad scramble for possession of the ball.

She would have stayed safely hidden in her cozy little hole except for William's nagging. She might have guessed that the annoying man wouldn't leave her alone to die peacefully. She felt a cool, lemon-scented dampness stroke over her forehead and across her cheeks, and the waves of her nightmare receded—receded enough to hear William's voice speaking softly and urgently in her ear.

"Come, Arabella, gather your courage one last time. Dr. Perrick assures me the babe is nearly here."

"I'm playing football," she said crossly. "Leave me alone. I've dug a pit and it's stopped hurting."

William drew in a short, sharp breath. "Thank God, you have heard me, have you not? Arabella, do not slip away again, I beg. I have so much admired your courage this night."

Robyn frowned. "I like it better in the pit." She screamed as her body ripped itself open and she pushed downward in an instinctive effort to force the pain out of her.

" 'Tis another miracle, my lord. God Himself is blessing this labor! Your lady wife has recovered her strength sufficiently to assist in the birth of her own babe."

"How long?" William asked tersely. "Miracle or no, she cannot endure much more of this agony. Dear God, I had never imagined that the birth of a child could cause such incredible torment."

" 'Tis the curse of Eve, my lord, and women do not feel the pain in the same way as you or I would feel it. Women are resigned to the fate God has assigned them, and accept the pain which is their just punishment for Eve's sin."

"Just tell me how much longer my wife must endure *her* punishment."

"I can see the babe's head, my lord. A few minutes more, two or three strong birth pangs, and we shall know if God has blessed you with another son."

Robyn wanted to interrupt this farrago of nonsense, but the breath was squeezed out of her lungs as she succumbed again to the overwhelming urge to push and bear downward. She only realized that she had drifted into unconsciousness again when William jolted her back into semi-awareness of her surroundings.

"Once more," he commanded urgently. "One more push, my dear, and your travails will be over."

She realized then that she must be dreaming. In the bizarre world of dreamland it was probably no more strange to

imagine herself giving birth than to imagine herself immobilized on the center of a football field with two opposing
teams scrimmaging over her inert body.

She was so tired she wished both nightmares would go
away, but William was holding her hand, bathing her forehead with the cool scented towels, and somehow she
couldn't manage to slip away from him into the peaceful
blackness of oblivion. Another pain, followed by a sharp,
high-pitched cry, and then a grunt of satisfaction from Dr.
Perrick.

"A son, my lord, small but astonishingly healthy. The
Lady Arabella has presented you with another son."

Robyn felt her body relax into a state of utter peaceful-
ness. She was almost glad that the nightmare had carried
through to the bitter end and given her the illusion of deliv-
ering a baby. For a dream, it had been quite an experience.

A son. She wondered why her subconscious had chosen to
reward the arrogant William with a son. In dreams, presumably she could chose whatever sex of offspring she desired.
She ought to have given birth to a daughter, just to annoy
him. She visualized the son she had supposedly produced: he
would have a fuzz of light golden hair, and blue eyes like
William's. Like Zach's. And he would have cute chubby
fists like the baby in the portrait in Zach's living room.

What portrait in Zach's living room? The moment she
tried to bring her memory of the picture into sharper focus,
the whole image faded. Robyn yawned and realized that her
head ached abominably. Now that the pains of her imagined
labor had stopped, she had energy to spare for feeling the
throbbing behind her eyes and the soreness on the ridge of
her scalp where the bullet must have grazed her scalp.

"I need some aspirin," she said. The curtains had been
drawn around her bed, presumably to give her some privacy
from other patients, and now that she had enough strength to
look around, there was nothing to see. Was she in a hospital?
Perhaps she had been transferred to one while she was unconscious. The bed curtains certainly suggested a hospital
room.

"Where's the nurse?" she asked sleepily. She felt euphoric
and sleepy all at once, an odd but rather pleasant combination.

"The child has been taken to her," William said, his voice gentle. "You may rest easily, Arabella, for the babe is strong, I promise you, and the nurse has plenty of milk. Her own child died but a week ago."

"I don't know what you're talking about," she said crossly. She didn't want to think about the nonsense William and the other people kept mouthing. If she thought about what they were saying, she knew she would be terrified.

"Some tincture of opium will help her to sleep," Dr. Perrick said. "And sleep at this moment is undoubtedly the best medicine for her ladyship."

"I will give the opium to her," William said. "Here, let me have the cup."

Robyn was thirsty and she drank greedily even though the mixture tasted unpleasant, both sweet and pungent at the same time. Almost at once, torpor swept over her, and she listened to the voices around her without making much effort to disentangle the strange accents.

"You should rest, my lord. Your lady wife is in no danger at this moment, you have my word on it."

"Unless she contracts a fever."

"As always, my lord, that is in God's hands. You may be assured, my lord, that you will be summoned if her ladyship succumbs to any sort of infection."

What a pompous ass the doctor was, Robyn thought drowsily. But everyone in this part of England sounded as if they'd lifted their dialogue from a musical comedy set hundreds of years in the past. Right now, she didn't even care. The ache in her head was easing blissfully . . .

She was asleep before she heard William's reply.

Her throat hurt. Her muscles ached. Her skin burned. She was so thirsty that her entire body had curled into a desiccated husk, waiting to die.

"Water!" Robyn gasped the word even before she opened her eyes. He was at her side in an instant. William. She remembered his name. Recognized the feel of him, even though she couldn't have said how he looked, whether he was short or tall, blond or dark.

"Here, drink this. It is barley water, and will help to give you strength." There was almost no light in the room, so she could barely see him, but his arm felt reassuringly strong as he lifted her up and held the glass to her mouth, helping her drink. Except it wasn't a glass, it was a metal container, and it tasted tinny. Tasted gross, in fact. The contents weren't much better—tepid, gritty, and borderline bitter. She drank anyway. Deep, satisfying gulps that eased her parched throat and cooled the fierce heat of her skin. Sweat broke out of her pores in drenching rivulets and her teeth started to chatter. She recognized the symptoms. She was vaguely aware that the same cycle of delirium, thirst, sweat, fading consciousness, and renewed delirium had been repeated over and over again. Her periods of lucidity had been brief—islands of awareness in a misty landscape of bizarre dreams.

Robyn licked her dry, cracked lips and managed to speak. "I have a raging infection," she said, recognizing the truth and hanging on to it with grim determination. "For God's sake, why doesn't somebody give me a shot? Dammit, I'd be cured in a few hours with the right shot! There must be some antibiotic that would work."

"Her ladyship be raving again," said a dour female voice. "Why does 'er keep asking to be shot?"

"I daresay she is suffering a great deal of pain. Anyway, I am not entirely sure what she is trying to say. Her words are so slurred it is almost impossible to be certain of her meaning."

"Mayhap her ladyship is speaking French, or some other foreign gibble-gabble."

"No, I am fairly sure that she is speaking English. Or trying to, at least. Just now, when she asked for water, the sound was perfectly plain."

Robyn started to say that of course she was speaking English, that these yokels were the people with the thick accents, not her, but when William ran his hand calmingly over her forehead, pushing away a hank of hair that had fallen over her eyes, she forgot all about answering him. She realized that her hair was matted with sweat and that her body smelled stale and dirty.

"I would really like to take a shower," she said, getting the request into words before it slipped away from her. "Please let me take a shower. It might help to bring down my temperature."

"A shower? Yes, you are quite right, my dear. There was a shower of rain when we found you after your accident. We feared you might contract a pleurisy of the lungs, but fortunately you have escaped with no more than a bout of birthing fever."

"Not that sort of shower. A bath. Wash my hair."

"Certainly we shall summon the hairdresser as soon as you are better. Take heart, Arabella, I do believe the fever has almost broken. This is the longest period you have been able to talk to us since your accident."

Robyn felt the inside of her head expanding. She stared dazedly at the blond, blue-eyed man seated beside her bed. "What accident?" she demanded. "Who are you? And where am I?" She closed her eyes again, not really interested in the man's answers. Her body floated upward, carried away on a hot current of air. She heard a voice speaking, calling her urgently, but it was too much trouble to respond.

"She's off again. Lookee, my lord, you've bin watching over her ladyship for more than two days. 'Tis time for you to rest and eat a good supper and us'll take care of her for a while."

"Very well. But remember that I want to be called the minute the fever finally breaks."

"Yes, m'lord. Us'll call your lordship as soon as her ladyship comes back to her senses."

The curtains around her bed had been partially drawn back and Robyn could see the sun and the bare branches of a giant oak tree through the pair of casement windows opposite the foot of her bed. She drew in a deep breath and moved cautiously. She felt weak as a rag doll, and ached in more places than she cared to enumerate, but she could remember occasions when she'd felt worse. Or at least almost as bad.

She was thirsty. Not with the raging thirst that had marked her nightmarish bouts of fever, but with the kind of thirst that could be pleasantly cured by a chilled glass of orange juice and a freshly brewed cup of steaming coffee. Robyn realized that she was hungry—starving hungry. That seemed another reassuringly healthy sign.

Levering herself upright in the bed, she looked around for

a bell to summon a nurse. The simple movement brought her up short, heart pounding and pulses racing. Good grief, where the heck was she? Surely to goodness this was no hospital bed. She swallowed hard, fighting back a surge of panic as she absorbed the strangeness of her surroundings. She had never in her entire life seen a hospital like this—or even a private bedroom. The furnishings she could see looked like expensive exhibits in a major museum.

Between the two windows, a Hepplewhite armoire flanked a chair, silk-upholstered and with the carved legs and clawed feet typical of mid-eighteenth-century furniture. A gilt-framed mirror, probably from the same period, stood next to a dressing stand cluttered with silver-backed brushes and pottery in the style of early Wedgwood. The windows were draped with the sort of stiff, fringed damask that had once been popular in English manor houses, and the pegged wooden floor was covered by carpets that appeared to be embroidered like tapestries rather than woven or dye-stamped like modern rugs.

And the bed she was lying on fitted perfectly into the overall impression of an eighteenth-century bedchamber, Robyn realized, right down to the fact that she was sunken deep into a feather mattress, reclining against a pile of lace-edged, linen-covered pillows.

Robyn tugged at the curtains obscuring her view of the full room. In the bright light of morning, with eyes not clouded by fever, she couldn't imagine how she had confused these richly embroidered silk hangings with the sort of green polyester and cotton curtains that typified hospital privacy screens. She must have been far gone in delirium not to have realized the antique oddity of her surroundings.

She wasn't sure yet if she could trust her legs to support her, but she managed to pull the curtains back without getting out of bed. The brass curtain rings clacked against the wooden rods, to reveal a young woman seated by a screened, wood-burning fire. The woman glanced up from her sewing.

"My lady, you are awake! How are you feeling?" She sprang to her feet and crossed to Robyn's side, dropping into a bobbing curtsy before hurrying back to a small table by the fire. Picking up a silver jug, she poured an almost colorless liquid into a matching beaker, then rushed back to the bed-side.

"Here you be, my lady. Fresh lemonade. The master ordered it special." She wiped her hand on a snow-white apron that covered her from shoulder to ankles. She was also wearing a frilly mobcap, set low on her forehead, which looked distinctly uncomfortable.

The woman appeared both foolish and ill at ease. No wonder, Robyn thought. Anyone would look ill at ease walking around dressed up like an escapee from the Boston Tea Party. "Who are you?" Robyn asked. "And why are you wearing a fancy dress costume?"

" 'Tis Monday morning, my lady. The housekeeper and I both has a clean pinafore every Monday." When Robyn didn't say anything, the woman continued. "I be Mary, my lady. Your ladyship's maid."

Enlightenment finally dawned on Robyn. She'd ended up in one of those olde worlde hotels that were so popular with tourists, and the maid's costume was supposed to be one of the authentic touches.

"Is this Starke Manor Hotel?" she asked. "In Dorset?"

The maid looked at her oddly. "Yes, my lady. This be Starke Manor."

That was one mystery solved, Robyn decided, although it raised a whole series of other questions. Why in the world had she been kept in a hotel, for Pete's sake? It was incredible to think that neither the doctor nor anyone in hotel management had insisted on transferring her to a proper hospital. England might not be as lawsuit happy as the United States, but surely even English hotels tried to avoid having guests die of medical neglect on their premises.

"Doesn't anyone around here worry about getting sued?" she asked the maid.

The maid curtsied and held out the silver goblet once again. "I be Mary, my lady, not Sue. Sue married Tom Footman a year last Michaelmas and you said I could be your maid. Here, my lady, drink this. 'Tis the nice fresh lemonade that you like so much, sweetened with plenty of honey."

Robyn was too thirsty to argue. She took the drink eagerly, then stopped with the silver goblet poised right at her lips. Mary was nervous, Robyn realized, and babbling utter nonsense. Why? What was there in the simple action of offering lemonade to make the woman's eyes twitch and her hands tremble? It occurred to Robyn that the drink could be drugged or even poisoned. The idea ought to have seemed insane, but she couldn't dismiss it. From the moment she got out of her car in the Starke Manor parking lot, people and events in her life had become so bizarre that she couldn't afford to take chances. In fact, the more she thought about it, the more drugs seemed to be the most likely explanation for what had been happening to her. If someone had been force-feeding her hallucinogens, it would explain why she had this confused sensation that dreams, fever, delirium, and reality were all melded into a single nightmarish whole.

Robyn thrust the beaker back into the maid's hands. "You know what, Mary? Why don't you take a sip first. Then I'll drink some."

The maid seemed to find nothing strange in Robyn's request. "I already tasted it, my lady. 'Tis plenty sweet enough, I swear. You will like it, my lady."

"Humor me. Taste it anyway."

Mary obligingly held the beaker to her mouth and swallowed. " 'Tis very good, my lady. Just to your taste, I vow." She wiped the rim of the cup with the edge of her apron and handed the drink back to Robyn. "Here, my lady, drink it down and I will send word to the master that you are awake."

"The *master?*"

Mary blanched and her hands visibly trembled. Robyn had the oddest impression that the women expected to get the beaker thrown at her head at any moment. "His lordship made me promise, my lady, to send for him the instant you regained your wits, but I will have you looking your best in a trice, never fear. We shall have time to put on your new lace peignoir before his lordship arrives."

"I'd prefer some help in getting to the shower. Right now, I'd rather be clean than elegant. I'm dying to shampoo my hair."

"Yes, my lady," the maid said, looking worried. She cleared her throat. "I don' know about your hair, my lady. Truth to tell, you will not be able to wear your wig—"

"My *wig!*" Robyn spluttered into the lemonade, which

was indeed delicious. She flopped back against the pillows, feeling totally exhausted. She drew in a couple of deep breaths and decided she had recovered just enough energy to let off some well-deserved steam.

"Look, I'm sorry to sound off at you, but this ridiculous performance has gone on long enough. I'm not in the mood for any more scenes from Country Life in Ye Olde Englande. I want to speak to the doctor in charge of my case. And maybe I'd better speak to the manager of this hotel, too. Quite frankly, I think he has some explaining to do. I should never have been kept here when I obviously had a raging fever. Clearly I should have been take to the hospital. In fact, the way I feel right now, it might be smart to transfer over to the hospital and get a quick checkup."

The maid shifted her gaze uneasily from side to side. She sank into another curtsy. "Beg pardon, my lady, but I must send for his lordship. Beggin' your pardon, my lady, but he left strict orders. As soon as you was to be awake, he must come. He says he can understand what your ladyship says, my lady."

"William!" The name came back to Robyn, surfacing from the bewildering maelstrom of her dreams. "Are you talking about a tall blond man who calls himself William? Is he the manager here?"

The maid wrung her hands nervously. "Yes, my lady. His lordship. The master. Your ladyship's husband."

"I—do—not—have—a—husband." Robyn pronounced the words slowly and carefully. "Good Lord, what is it with you people? I am *not* married, dammit!"

"Yes, my lady. I mean no, my lady. I must summon the master, my lady. With your permission, my lady." Bobbing up and down like a yo-yo, the maid finally plucked up courage to lean across the bed and tug at the bellpull, a crimson silk ribbon embroidered with flowers that Robyn hadn't noticed before among the folds of the bed hangings. As the maid lifted her arm, an odor of stale sweat and unwashed flesh wafted over Robyn, strong enough to make her gag. She turned quickly aside. Good Lord, didn't this woman watch TV? Hadn't she ever seen an advertisement for deodorants? Or even for plain, old-fashioned soap and water?

The bell was answered almost immediately by a girl who

didn't look a day over twelve. She came into the room almost at a run, and curtsied both to the maid and then—far more deeply—in the direction of Robyn's bed. She was wearing virtually the same fancy-dress uniform as the older maid, with a pinafore covering a frock fashioned from rough-woven brown woolen cloth, and shoes that were exact replicas of eighteenth-century servants' footwear. Robyn was surprised that the hotel had gone to so much trouble to maintain the illusion of authenticity, particularly since the slippery, square-toed leather shoes must have been real deterrents to employee safety. From what she had seen of the place so far, Robyn was amazed the hotel could get enough insurance coverage to operate.

"You are to fetch the master," Mary said to the young maid. "Tell his lordship that his lady wife is wide awake and . . . talking like before."

The young girl sneaked a sideways glance at Robyn. "You mean 'er wits do be gone beggin'—"

"Shh!" Mary's hiss was furious, and she cuffed the child soundly around the ear.

"Mary! Stop that!" Robyn exclaimed, utterly appalled.

"Sorry for the disturbance, my lady." Mary turned back to the little maid. "Get out," she ordered. "Hurry up and fetch his lordship"

"Yuss'm." The child ducked into a curtsy and darted from the bedroom.

"We'll have to hurry if we're going to make you pretty for the master," Mary said, smiling at Robyn and apparently feeling no need whatever to comment on her extraordinary treatment of a fellow employee. She opened a door that led into an oversize closet and returned carrying a lace-trimmed robe of a pale blue silk over her arm. "There we are. Blue. Your ladyship's favorite color. Now, my lady, we must be quick. The master will be here any minute." With an air of complete familiarity, the maid walked over to the bed and started to unbutton the white cotton gown Robyn was wearing. Startled by the unexpected intimacy, Robyn jerked away.

"Sorry, my lady. I forgot. Your breasts will be sore with the milk coming in, and all. I'll be more careful, my lady."

The maid unfastened some more buttons and began to ease the nightgown from Robyn's shoulders.

Robyn went cold with fear. Oddly enough, she realized suddenly that her breasts did feel hard and hot, although of course that couldn't possibly have anything to do with her dream of giving birth to a baby son. If her breasts felt sore, it was a perfectly logical aftermath to the infection that had ravaged her system. She pushed the maid away, closing the buttons again, and wrapping her arms around her waist in an instinctive gesture of self-protection.

"Get away from me," she ordered, her voice low and cold. "This is no longer a joke. Get out of this room and find me some clothes to put on. I'm checking out of here."

"Oh, my lady, don't be angry, but I cannot understand what you are asking me!"

"I want to leave. Is that clear enough for you? I'm going to find the bathroom and take a shower. And I want some clothes waiting for me when I get back. Otherwise I'm calling a cab and walking out of here in the gown I'm wearing. This place is giving me a first-class attack of the creeps."

Robyn pushed aside the bedclothes and had managed to swing her legs over the side of the high bed, when a man entered the room. She recognized him instantly as the man who had called himself William. The man whose orders everyone seemed to obey without question.

He took one look at Robyn and strode immediately to the bedside. He lifted her legs back onto the mattress and smoothed the covers over her before retreating to the center of the room.

"Well, this is a welcome sight! I had not expected to find you sitting up and talking to your maid." William smiled with cool courtesy. He swept a low bow, his hand resting gracefully on his heart, flowing lace cuffs tumbling in rich folds about his wrists. "My lady, it is indeed a pleasure to find you thus well recovered. My felicitations."

He should have appeared ridiculous, but he didn't. For some reason, he appeared consummately elegant and commanding. He had tied his long fair hair at the nape of his neck with a black velvet ribbon, a style that showed the strong line of his jaw to advantage. He wore silk stockings and gray brocade knee breeches, topped by a full-skirted

coat of plum velvet. His shoes were high-heeled black
leather, decorated with gleaming silver buckles, and the lace
ruffles of his shirt were adorned with two large diamond
stickpins. Looking at him, registering his perfect imitation of
an eighteenth-century nobleman, Robyn found herself teetering somewhere between panic and anger. Panic because his
choice of clothing seemed so senseless. Anger because she
was sure she was deliberately being made to feel a fool.

Anger won out. "What are you trying to do?" she demanded. "Why are you wearing those farcical clothes? For
heaven's sake, there's a time and a place for everything, and
this isn't the time for fancy dress."

William made a slight, almost imperceptible gesture with
his hand and Mary scurried from the room. Then he walked
unhurriedly toward the bed, his pleasant smile still firmly in
place. How odd, Robyn thought, that she should gain the
distinct impression that her sharp words had hurt his feelings. He paused when he was still two feet or so from her
side.

"I chose these clothes because I know how much you dislike me to come into your bedroom straight from the stables.
I am sorry if you find them too formal for this early hour of
the morning."

This man did not sound in the least like a hotel manager.
This man sounded totally crazy, in fact. Robyn pressed her
hand to her eyes, trying to ease the pounding of her headache. She could no longer delude herself that things were
even halfway normal. She was weak as a kitten and surrounded by lunatics. Not a ideal situation, even for somebody like her, blessed with a notoriously optimistic nature.

"Your head is aching," William said softly. "Allow me to
help you, my lady." He put on a darn good show of looking
worried, Robyn had to grant him that. He guided her gently
into a more restful position against the bed pillows before
drawing up a chair and sitting beside her. "You need to eat,
my dear, to regain your strength. A junket or some bread and
milk would both be easy to digest. Which do you prefer?"

What the devil was junket? Robyn didn't remember hearing the word during her previous stay in England. "I'd like
some bread and milk. And some coffee." She didn't say
please. She didn't attempt to sound pleasant. The best she

could say of these lunatics was that—so far—they didn't seem to have any plans to starve her to death. Maybe that wasn't such good news. Maybe they had some other, more horrible fate in store?

William opened the bedroom door and spoke quietly to someone who was stationed in the corridor outside. A guard? Either that, or this hotel had seriously uneconomic staffing policies. "Your breakfast will be here shortly," William said, closing the door. "Mary has gone down to the kitchens to fetch it."

"Thank you." Robyn wondered why he hadn't simply called room service, although when she looked around the room, she couldn't see any trace of a phone. Presumably all the gadgets of twentieth-century living were hidden inside the Hepplewhite armoire. If the service personnel had to hobble around in fake Georgian shoes, the hotel management presumably didn't want to destroy the antique ambience with TV screens and overhead electric light fixtures. The people in charge here had certainly allowed their enthusiasm for Ye Olde Englande to run riot.

"How are you feeling?" William asked, returning to the chair he had drawn to her bedside. "You are looking so well that it is hard to believe how fiercely the fever raged in you only a few hours since."

"I'm fine," Robyn said. "But the doctor who was here—Dr. Perrick?"

William nodded. "Yes, Dr. Perrick attended you, as always. He is your favorite physician."

"How can he be my favorite? I've never been anywhere near the man! And frankly, he sounded borderline crazy to me. Why didn't he call for an ambulance to take me to the hospital? They must have someone better on staff there—a first-year medical student would have been better than Perrick. In fact, a hospital orderly would have been more competent than Perrick."

William looked puzzled. "My dear, what is this obsession you have developed for visiting the hospital? Until you are fully recovered from your lying-in, you cannot possibly be expected to resume your charitable duties. Birthing fever is not to be treated lightly."

Robyn didn't know whether to scream with frustration or

freeze in denial. "Why do you keep insisting that I've had a baby?" she demanded. "Why? What do you hope to achieve?"

William looked sad. "Arabella, it has been a trying—"

"I'm not Arabella!" she screamed. "How many times do I have to tell you that?"

His gaze hardened. "My dear, you must stop indulging in these hysterical fits of denial. They cannot be good for you, and you are frightening the servants. I understand that the blow to your head has affected your powers of reason, but the servants are simple, ignorant people, and they are already whispering that you are possessed."

"Stop it!" she said, turning away from the false concern in his sincere blue eyes. "For heaven's sake, what are you trying to do to me? Who are you? What do you want from me, for God's sake?"

He answered her quietly. "Arabella, if you have truly forgotten so much, then I will try to help you remember. I am William Bowleigh, your husband."

She drew in a short, sharp breath. "You said that before."

"So you do remember."

"Some things." She drew in a shaky breath. "Are you claiming to be Zach's brother? Are you claiming to be *that* William Bowleigh?"

"I claim to be William Bowleigh because it is true, just as it is true that Zachary is my younger brother."

"He is your older brother."

William shook his head. "That is absurd, my dear. If Zachary were the elder brother, he would be Baron of Starke, not I." His mouth twisted wryly. "Forgive me if I point out how unflattering it is that you remember Zachary so clearly when you are having no success whatever in remembering me—your husband."

"Don't lie," Robyn begged. "You're not my husband. I've never met you. I'm in love with Zach."

"Tact, my lady, would suggest that you do not mention such feelings to your husband. Our marriage would be more tolerable to both of us if you could only learn to accept that we are neither of us likely to see Zachary ever again."

"No! Don't say that!" Robyn's voice shook with panic that she couldn't conceal. "He's coming for me! He's flying in from Paris tonight! I mean yesterday. Friday. Whenever I was shot."

"You believe my brother is *flying* here to meet you?"

"Why not? There's perfectly good plane service between Paris and London. Dozens of flights a day."

William sighed. "Never mind, my dear, you may have the right of it. We should not be discussing these subjects that distress you so. We have much that is cheerful to speak of."

"I can't think what."

"Your new son is certainly cause for rejoicing. He is thriving, eating lustily, and sleeping contentedly. Would you like me to ask the nurse to bring him here so that you may hold him for a moment? He is a handsome little fellow and you have not seen him."

"I don't have a son!" she exploded. "For God's sake, shake off your fancy dress mentality and get a grip on reality. I'd never even met you until a couple of days ago when you found me in the hotel parking lot. Dammit, I've been out of my skull with fever, and it's cruel of you to play these games with me." She felt tears welling up at the back of her throat, and she dashed the back of her hand angrily across her eyes, not wanting to display her weakness in front of a man who seemed determined to torment her.

William pulled a lace-trimmed square of cambric from his sleeve and offered it to her. "Dry your tears, my lady," he said, his voice weary but quite gentle. When she refused to accept the handkerchief, he laid it on the bed, next to her hand. "Your breakfast will be here soon, and when you have eaten something we will talk again. You will feel stronger then, and more able to accept the truth."

"No," Robyn said. "We'll talk now. Why are you keeping me here? Am I a prisoner?"

"Arabella, it is absurd to use such words to describe your plight. You have often expressed regret at your lot in life, but you enjoy all the freedoms of any other lady of your station. Indeed, you enjoy more latitude than most, for I do not question your expenditures or control your social engagements in any way."

Robyn realized that her body was covered in sweat—not the honest sweat of a fever, but the cold, clammy sweat of fear. Try as she might to find some other explanation, the longer she listened, the more she was being forced to accept that William and the other people in this crazy hotel were all pretending that they lived hundreds of years in the past. She couldn't imagine what their purpose was, but she doubted if their intentions boded well. Nobody would maintain such an elaborate masquerade for any legitimate purpose.

"Why are you trying to pretend that we're stuck in some eighteenth-century time warp?" she asked, trying hard to keep her voice under control. The less she panicked, the better she would be able to judge what she needed to do next. "Why are you determined to make me believe I'm crazy?"

"My dear, nothing could be further from the truth of my wishes—"

"Where did you get all these antiques?" she asked. "This room must have cost hundreds of thousands to furnish. Why go to such incredible lengths, just to deceive me?" She frowned. "Or maybe I'm not the person you're trying to deceive. Maybe this is connected to Zach and his problems at the Gallery. Yes, that's it, isn't it? These are antiques you've stolen from Zach, or maybe they're fakes and you're planning to pass them off through the Gallery."

"I do not understand what you ask, Arabella. What are *antiques*?"

He sounded so genuine in his puzzlement that Robyn almost found herself explaining, before she stopped short, furious with herself for falling into the trap. "Okay, enough already. Let me out of this bed," she said.

"No, I must insist that you remain where you are. You should not get out of bed—"

"Ha, now I see what you're up to!" She felt a surge of triumph. "You can't let me out of the bed because the rest of the room isn't real. I've caught you out! There's no furniture in the room, is there? The whole scene, the view from the windows, everything, it's just a hologram!"

"I do not understand. What is a hollow grim? Arabella, I beg you to repose yourself—"

"Oh, get out of my way!" she ordered angrily. "I've had enough of this farce." She swung her legs over the edge of the bed, and jumped the six inches or so to the floor. She took two steps, but got no farther. Her legs, weakened by days of fever, started to buckle under her, and only William's swift intervention prevented her from falling.

"Arabella, you must not overexert yourself," he said compassionately.

Robyn didn't answer. She was staring at her hands, transfixed with horror. "What have you done to me?" she whispered, her fingers tightening in a convulsive grip on William's sleeve. "What have you done to my hands?"

"My dear, your hands are a little scratched. They will soon recover their normal whiteness."

"These aren't *my* hands," Robyn said feverishly. She sank onto the bed and looked down at her body for the first time since she regained consciousness. On the edge of full-blown panic, she realized that not only were her hands the wrong shape, but her legs were too long, the flesh of her abdomen was limp and flaccid, and her breasts were leaking fluid from the nipples. Sick, dizzy, disoriented, she pressed her hands against her flabby belly.

"Give me a mirror," she said hoarsely.

"My dear, that is not wise—"

"Give me a mirror!" Her voice was a high-pitched wail, totally out of control, but she didn't care. She patted her hands over her face, feeling frantically for familiar contours, wincing when her fingers tangled in the matted skein of her hair.

"If you promise to lie quietly in bed, I will bring you a mirror," William said.

"Yes, yes." She lay back against the pillows, rigid with tension, but willing to say anything that would produce the desired result.

He walked across to the dressing stand and returned carrying the elegantly chased, antique silver mirror. "Here you are, but bear in mind that you have suffered an arduous lying-in—"

Robyn snatched the mirror—and confronted the reflection of a woman she had seen only once before, and never in the flesh. The immaculate blond hair was tangled, the pink-and-white complexion scratched, the gorgeous blue eyes bruised by shadows, and the full lips cracked and bleeding where she had bitten them, but the woman in the mirror was unmistakably the same woman whose portrait now hung in Zach's penthouse.

"It's a trick," Robyn whispered. "How did you make me look like this?" She flipped the mirror over. "It's some sort of electronic imaging device, right?"

"Arabella, it is your own mirror—"

"Please—stop! Don't keep calling me by that name!" Robyn glanced into the mirror again. The image was crying. She touched her face and felt the wetness of tears. "It isn't me," she said, denying the evidence of her own eyes. "*It isn't me*. I have freckles!"

She threw the offending mirror with all the strength she could muster. It hit the wall with a satisfying crash. Then she leaned back against the lace-edged pillows, and let the darkness carry her into its warm, comforting depths.

Chapter 5

THE smell of hot, fresh coffee brought her back to consciousness. Mary stood by the side of the bed, holding a heavy silver tray, loaded with silver bowls and jugs, all wafting steam. Robyn's stomach rumbled in anticipation.

William took her hand and held it lightly. "Are you ready to try and eat something, my dear?"

"Yes." Robyn was so hungry, she was prepared to postpone her confrontation with William. But when she reached out eagerly to take the bowl and spoon he offered her, she couldn't avoid noticing her long, pale fingers, and the blue-veined fragility of her hands. Her stomach churned in such violent rejection of the unfamiliar sight that she gagged.

"You need not eat very much," William said when she turned convulsively from the tray of food. "But you must try to swallow a little nourishment."

She closed her eyes, her stomach still heaving. "Go away," she said. "I want you all to go away."

"You may go about your duties, Mary. I will see that her ladyship eats something." William's voice sounded calm, even bored, as if he had dealt with her refusal to eat a dozen or more times before.

Robyn kept her eyes stubbornly shut, but she heard the maid set down the tray and leave the room. William did not attempt to spoon-feed her, as she had half expected. "I will leave the tray by your bedside," he said. "Perhaps, when you are alone, you may feel able to swallow a few mouthfuls."

"Just go away."

"As you wish. But there is no reason for you to work yourself into such a fret about the temporary impairment of your looks. The blemishes to your complexion are but minor flaws, which will soon be healed."

Robyn's eyes jerked open in astonishment. "You don't really believe I'm upset just because my face is scratched, do you?" she asked incredulously.

"Well, I understand of course that your hair doesn't look quite as you would wish. But Dr. Perrick cut only the tiniest portion in order to sew a stitch into the deepest part of your head wound. When you are recovered from your lying-in, we shall send for a hairdresser from London who will teach Mary to dress your hair so that there is not the slightest sign of your accident. And your hair will soon grow back. Reflect but a moment, Arabella, and I am confident you will see there is no rational cause for this prolonged fit of the sullens."

"The sullens? Is that what you call this?" Robyn sat up, her energy restored by anger. How dare William continue with his absurd pretense that she was some spoiled beauty who couldn't cope with the sight of a few bruises? "Gee, you're right," she said with heavy sarcasm. "Talk about a woman who gets hepped up over nothing, that's me all right. Golly gosh, I guess I'll stop worrying about the scratches on my perfect complexion and start worrying about something more worthwhile. I'm sure I can think of a few genuine problems if I concentrate *real* hard."

For the first time since she'd met him, William seemed at a loss for words. "It is good to hear you respond so reasonably," he said finally. "Now come, Arabella, for the sake of your children, and to speed the return of your normal beauty, will you not try to eat? The coffee you asked for is getting cold."

She *was* hungry, Robyn realized, and a cup of coffee sounded like a wonderful idea. The fact was, she wouldn't speed her escape from this den of lunatics by refusing to eat. On the contrary, she would need all the help she could get to rebuild her strength and sharpen her wits to avoid whatever traps they had set for her. God alone knew what their purpose was in keeping her here, but she would certainly be able to outwit them more easily if she felt stronger. Averting her eyes so that she didn't have to look at her unfamiliar hands, she reached for a bowl that appeared to contain cream of wheat cereal.

"You eat some first," she said to William, determined to

be safe rather than sorry. "Make sure you take a big bite. I have no intention of allowing myself to be poisoned or drugged."

William gave her an odd, sideways glance, but he took a spoon and scooped up a generous mouthful, grimacing as he swallowed. "Bread sopped in milk is not one of my favorite dishes," he said. "But it has been well prepared. Now it is your turn, my lady."

"This is bread soaked in milk?" Robyn said, her appetite waning rapidly as she eyed the white, pulpy concoction in the bowl. Except in fairy tales and nursery rhymes, she'd never heard of people actually eating bread and milk mixed together.

" 'Tis freshly baked bread," William said encouragingly. "And the dish is sweetened with sugar from your father's own plantation in Jamaica."

She didn't bother to point out that her father didn't have a plantation in Jamaica, and that the family farm in Virginia had been sold to real estate developers thirty years ago. She took another look at the bowl of bread and milk. She supposed there were worse mixtures, and anyway, she was too hungry to quibble any longer. Robyn dipped in her spoon and scooped up a small bite.

It tasted remarkably good, warm, creamy, with only a hint of sweetness, and the bread much less slimy than she'd expected. She finished the bowl in short order, relieved to notice that her stomach felt less queasy as soon as she had something solid inside her.

William made no comment on her sudden burst of appetite. "Do you wish for a dish of coffee?" he asked politely.

"No, thank you." She had many questions still to ask William, but the food was making her sleepy. Had the food been drugged after all? she wondered. She kept her eyes open with an effort. "Was there a sleeping pill in the bread and milk?" she asked him. "Please, William, tell me the truth."

He looked at her long and hard. "No," he said finally. "There was nothing in the bread and milk save sugar."

"I believe you," she said, her eyes drifting closed. "God knows why, but I believe you."

She felt the touch of his hand lightly against her brow. "I

will never lie to you about your health and well-being, Arabella, you have my word of honor."

He sounded so damn honest, she couldn't help believing him. Robyn wondered how many women had gone to their doom thinking William sounded trustworthy. She forced her reluctant eyelids open and stared straight into his sincere blue eyes. "So what would you lie to me about?" she asked.

She sensed rather than saw his surprise. The instant of shock in his face was immediately replaced by a courteous smile. "Nothing, my dear. There is absolutely nothing."

Robyn smiled. "That's better," she said, letting her eyes drift closed. "Now I can *hear* that you're lying."

She woke to the noise of rain pelting against the windows, and the realization that she needed to go to the bathroom—very soon. Determined to find her way without summoning the ubiquitous Mary, she eased herself carefully to the edge of the bed, relieved to find that her body felt a little more cooperative this time around. She opened the bed curtains no more than a crack and saw at once that the maid was still seated in her chair by the side of the fire, sewing a garment that looked suspiciously like an old-fashioned corset. Good heavens, didn't these people ever let up on their ludicrous pretense of being relics left over from Merrie Olde Englande?

Robyn wondered if she could make it to the bathroom unobserved. There were only three doors in the bedroom, and she already knew that one door led out into the corridor, and the other into some sort of super-sized closet, which meant that the third door probably led into the bathroom. Using one of the bedposts, she managed to get her feet firmly on the ground and her body upright before Mary noticed her.

"My lady!" The servant sprang to her feet looking, as always, slightly harassed. "My lady, how can I help you? What do you need?"

"I need the bathroom," Robyn said.

Mary wrung her hands. "My lady, the doctor would never give me leave to order you a bath."

Robyn was willing to argue the issue of when she could bathe later. Right now, she had other, more pressing needs, and she was not willing to use a bedpan.

"Don't worry, I'm not going to take a bath," she said. "At least not right at this moment." It was infuriating to realize how weak she felt, but exercise was the only cure for atrophied muscles, and Robyn walked determinedly across the room, occasionally hanging on to a piece of furniture for support. She realized as she touched the solid reality of the furnishings that her idea of a hologram had been absurd. The technology for projecting such a detailed and clear-cut appearance of an entire room of antiques didn't exist outside the movies. But it wasn't surprising that her attempts at rational thinking had been so unsuccessful these past few days. The boundaries between delirium and reality had been so fuzzy, she still wasn't sure precisely what she had dreamed and what had actually happened.

She was shaking by the time she reached her goal, the third door in the bedroom, the one she was sure gave onto a bathroom. She pushed it open with relief, but relief turned instantly to dismay.

She was in a narrow room, little larger than a broom closet, with a small window at one end. A chair, with satin armrests, a white satin seat, and a contrasting skirt of bright blue satin, was the only piece of furniture in the room. Robyn had enough experience with antiques to know exactly what she was seeing. The chair was a closestool, or commode, and this tiny dark room was an unpleasant eighteenth-century forerunner of a functioning bathroom. Good Lord, the people running this place were carrying authenticity to totally dotty lengths! Where the devil had they hidden the modern plumbing?

Mary hurried into the tiny room and rushed to the commode. She lifted the satin seat and held it to her breast like a shield. "My lady, you should have said as how you wished to use the closestool. I would have helped your ladyship."

Robyn gritted her teeth. In other circumstances she might have seen the comic side of the situation, but right now, she couldn't manage to laugh. "I suppose you're going to tell me there isn't a proper bathroom in this hotel," she said.

"No, my lady, I wusn't. I wusn't going to say no such thing."

Robyn felt a brief flare of hope. "You mean there *is* a

proper bathroom? With regular plumbing and a toilet that flushes?"

Mary shrank back behind her shield of the satin commode seat. "My lady, I know I be ignorant and don't understand how the gentry do speak, but I cannot grasp ahold of what you are asking. Don't be angry, my lady, I'm trying my best."

Robyn sighed. "Just leave me alone for a couple of minutes, Mary. I'll talk to you later."

"Yes, my lady." Mary bobbed a curtsy, her face flushed with evident relief at having understood Robyn's request. "I shall wait for your ladyship in the bedroom."

The commode was marginally better than using a bedpan, Robyn supposed. And although she would have sold her soul for a shower with hot running water, she was willing to make do with the jug of cold water she found on a shelf next to the commode.

A pretty washbasin decorated with cherubs and pink roses stood next to the water jug, and a porcelain tray, also decorated with cherubs, contained a round, rough-hewn lump of soap, scented with verbena, along with several embroidered linen towels. Despite the coldness of the water, Robyn stripped off her sweat-sodden nightgown and washed herself from head to toe. Lord, but it felt good to be even halfway clean! It was only when she realized that she was squeezing the cold water over her inflamed breasts, trying to ease the heat and hardness of them, that her pleasure faded. She ran her hands slowly over her tall, slender, slack-waisted body and confronted the terrifying, incredible truth. Not a single part of her—not a limb or a muscle—looked or felt familiar. Her skin was too white, her legs were too long, her arms were too weak. And worst of all, her belly was too limp and flaccid, with skin that hung in loose folds as if she had just given birth to a baby.

No, no! I didn't have a baby. I've never been pregnant. Robyn didn't realize she had screamed her denial aloud until Mary's worried face appeared in the closet door. "Are you all right, my lady? Are you in pain?"

Robyn snatched up her discarded nightgown and held it in front of her. The maid seemed to have no sense of how to respect another person's privacy. Robyn drew in a deep breath. "I'm okay. Look, could you please get me something clean to wear?"

"Yes, m'lady. Right away, m'lady." The maid came back almost at once with a beautiful nightdress made of soft white lawn, gathered at the wrists and throat with exquisite embroidery and fastened down the front by pale blue satin ribbons. "Would you like me to bind your breasts, my lady? To get rid of the milk, I mean."

"No!" Robyn's denial was instantaneous. To bind her breasts was to acknowledge that they were engorged with milk, and she wasn't prepared to buy into the fantasy that everyone was trying so hard to weave around her. She put on the clean nightdress, refusing Mary's help, and walked back into the bedroom. "Where is the mirror that stood over there by the windows?" she asked, suddenly noticing its absence.

"The master ordered it to be removed," Mary said, her voice nervous. "It was carried out while you were sleeping, my lady."

"I see," Robyn said, and wondered if she did. Obviously her body had not really changed its appearance since such a change was impossible. Therefore it followed that the apparent changes were some sort of an illusion, although she couldn't begin to guess how that illusion was maintained. Perhaps if she saw herself in a full-length mirror the illusion would be shattered? Why else would her supposed husband have been so anxious to remove the mirror? "Good old William certainly thinks of everything, doesn't he?" she commented.

"Yes, m'lady. His lordship is a good master," Mary said. She put her arm around Robyn's waist as they approached the bed, presumably to help her up into it. Impatient with the suggestion of weakness, Robyn shook off the maid's arm. Mary cringed back, her arm raised in an instinctive gesture of protection, as if she expected Robyn's rejection to be followed by a swift blow to the head.

Robyn was appalled. She sat down on the high bed and gestured reassuringly to the maid. "Mary, it's all right. I'm not angry with you. For heaven's sake, I'm not going to hit you."

Mary straightened and ducked into one of her endless

curtsies. "Thank you, m'lady. I will try to please your lady-ship, if I can."

Robyn looked at the woman standing in front of her. She took in the silly mobcap, the tight, uncomfortable bodice, the flowing white apron, the square-toed black leather shoes. Looking at Mary's cowering demeanor, it was difficult to believe the woman was playing a part. She looked so damned *humble*. Robyn cleared her throat. She tried to talk, but the words wouldn't come. She cleared her throat again. Finally, she managed to ask the ridiculous, terrifying question. "Mary, what date do you think it is?"

"Why, 'tis the tenth day of November, my lady."

November 10. That would be Monday—four days after she had arrived in England. That sounded reasonable enough, given her hazy memory of days and nights of fever. Robyn summoned up all her courage and asked a question she wasn't at all sure she wanted to have answered.

"Okay, so it's November 10. What year do you think we're living in, Mary?"

"Beggin' your ladyship's pardon, but what do you mean, my lady?"

"You know, what year is it? The date. Is it 1993, 1994? Whatever."

The maid looked at her pityingly. " 'Tis the year of our Lord 1746, my lady."

Robyn searched the maid's face for any trace of cunning or mockery. She could find none. "You really believe that, don't you, Mary?"

"Of course, my lady, for 'tis the truth. Why should I doubt it? My mam died the same day as the old King, the one what come from foreign parts and spoke no English. I were three years old when we lost her."

"The King from foreign parts . . . who do you mean?"

"George, my lady, the first of the kings from Hanover. That were 1727 when he died, and me mam, too. Says it on her tombstone clear as clear. And George the Second's been King of England for nigh on twenty years. 'Tis 1746 all right, my lady."

The poor woman was crazy, of course, and Robyn ought to have felt sorry for her. Unfortunately, all she could feel was fear. Deep, dark, overwhelming terror that wouldn't go away.

She lay back against the linen-covered, lavender-scented pillows and tried to control the shivers that convulsed her unfamiliar body.

"Zach," she whispered. "Where are you? For God's sake, get here soon, Zach. I need you."

Zach felt as if he had been pacing the corridors of the hospital's intensive care unit for days. A nurse hurried by and stopped to give him a sympathetic glance.

"Still haven't heard?" she asked. "Would you like me to get you a cup of tea?"

Zach tried to smile. "No, thanks." In the past, he'd always enjoyed drinking strong English tea, lightened with creamy milk, but right now, his stomach roiled at the thought of yet another cup. He wasn't sure he'd ever be able to drink tea again without remembering this hideous surgical waiting area, with its orange tweed sofas and too bright fluorescent lights.

"Shouldn't be long before you hear how she's doing." The nurse gave him another encouraging smile, and somehow Zach resisted the urge to tell her to take her professional cheer and shove it where the sun didn't shine.

"Thanks." He turned away, stuffing his hands into his pockets, not intending to say anything more, but the words burst out of him anyway. The image of Robyn lying in the car park was too vivid to be kept silent. "There was so damn much blood," he said hoarsely. "She was scarcely breathing when I got to her and the paramedics couldn't find her heartbeat. Even if the doctors manage to save her life, will she ever be her old self again?"

The nurse patted his arm comfortingly. "Head wounds bleed a lot, you know, and it doesn't necessarily mean the trauma is severe. And your girlfriend was lucky twice over. First off, the ambulance arrived right away, and second off, Dr. Forsyth was on duty here when she was brought into Emergency. He's one of the best surgeons in the country, and that's a fact, not just me praising one of our locals."

Zach allowed himself a moment of hope, then despair returned, stronger than before. "She's been in surgery for two hours."

"Surgery? In the operating theater, you mean? Two hours isn't all that long, not really."

"It feels like a lifetime. Two lifetimes."

"The waiting's the worst," the nurse agreed. "But it shouldn't be long now. Anyway, I must go. Sister'll be ranting and raving if I don't take her these dressings. But cheer up. If the bullet had killed your girlfriend, they'd have been out of the operating theater long before now. Honest. They don't waste this much time on a dead patient."

The nurse left and Zach resumed his pacing. He swung around eagerly when a male voice spoke his name. "Mr. Bowleigh?"

"Yes?" His eagerness faded when he saw that it wasn't a doctor who had spoken, but a man wearing a crumpled gray suit, carrying a raincoat over his arm. Zach slumped wearily against the wall. "Yes, I'm Zach Bowleigh."

The newcomer held out his hand. "How do you do? I'm Detective Inspector Harris, of the county CID—Criminal Investigation Department, that stands for—and I've been assigned to look into this unfortunate shooting incident. I'm very sorry that you and Miss Delaney should have had such an unpleasant welcome to England, Mr. Bowleigh. It's not what we expect in this part of the world, not what we expect at all."

Zach was tired and oversensitive. He felt his hackles rise. "I'm sure Robyn is very sorry to have disturbed the local peace. Next time I'll tell her to make sure she's shot in New York, or L.A., or some other suitably violent American city."

"Don't let's get off on the wrong foot, Mr. Bowleigh. I was trying to express concern, not to complain because Miss Delaney got shot on my turf."

Zach turned around to stare out of the small window. The overcast winter afternoon had faded into a dark, lowering night with almost no moon, presenting a scene as dank and gloomy as his mood. He drew in a deep breath. "I apologize, Inspector. My sarcasm was out of line. But this has been a rough day."

"You have all my sympathies, Mr. Bowleigh. The hospital

tells me the doctors are still operating on your friend. Any word as to how things are progressing?"

"No, nothing."

"Well, we must certainly hope for a successful outcome. In the meantime, Mr. Bowleigh, I wondered if I could ask you a few questions? In an investigation like this, the sooner we can get moving, the more likely we are to come up with results."

"Go ahead. Ask whatever you want. I'd love to put the bastard who did this behind bars. Preferably sharing a cell with a certified sadist."

"Well, we'll do what we can to accommodate your wishes, Mr. Bowleigh, at least as far as getting the gunman behind bars. Now, they told me at the hotel that you were the first person to reach Miss Delaney's side after the incident. Is that right?"

"Yes." Zach gathered his thoughts, trying to focus on the horrible scene in the parking lot and report clearly. "I'd flown in from Paris earlier that morning, and I was getting ready to go for a run. I'd caught an early flight, which meant I had time to run three or four miles and take a shower before meeting up with her."

"How long would you say it was between Miss Delaney being shot, and you calling for help?"

"A minute, maybe less. As soon as I realized what had happened, I started yelling, even before I got over to Robyn's side and saw how . . . badly she'd been wounded."

"Did you hear more than one shot, sir?"

"No, just one. The bullet seemed to have grazed the top of her scalp, ripping off the skin. I don't know if the bone was shattered, but there was blood everywhere."

The detective's voice lost some of its hard edge. "Head wounds do bleed a lot, you know. It doesn't always mean the worst."

"So everyone keeps telling me."

"It's still the truth, for all that." The detective reached into his jacket pocket and pulled out a little notebook. "Maybe we should get a few routine questions out of the way first. I understand Miss Delaney's parents are already on the way here from America?"

"Yes. My secretary's helping with their travel arrangements. They should catch an evening flight from Washington, D.C., direct to London. They'll be here early tomorrow morning."

"That was very efficient of you, sir."

"Yeah, I'm a great organizer." Zach smiled bitterly. "I organized Robyn right into a close encounter with a bullet."

"I don't see how you're responsible for this incident, sir."

The remark was more a question than a statement. Zach hesitated for a moment before answering. "I was shot at a couple of times recently in Manhattan. Robyn was with me on the second occasion. I should have realized she was in danger and taken better steps to protect her."

"I see. Do you have any idea why someone might want to take potshots at you and Miss Delaney?"

"Yes, I have an idea," Zach said, then stopped. For three months, he'd refused to report the problems at the Gallery to the police for fear of destroying his business reputation. And that stupid, high-handed reluctance on his part might have cost Robyn her life. Guilt closed up Zach's throat, making it impossible to speak.

"Sir? Would you mind sharing your ideas about the motive for this attack on Miss Delaney?" The detective's question was phrased with impeccable British courtesy, but Zach wasn't deceived. Beneath the veneer of *sirs* and fancy language, this cop was every bit as hard-nosed as his New York counterparts. Maybe even a bit tougher. Zach found that insight perversely comforting. He wanted a stubborn, seasoned cop to track down Robyn's assailant, a cop who'd get his teeth into the case and never let go.

"Someone's been working a big-money antiques scam through my Gallery," he said. "They've been passing off high-quality fakes as the real thing and making hundreds of thousands of dollars in the process. I started to investigate, called in some favors from fellow dealers. I guess I rattled a few dangerous cages, and when somebody took a shot at me, I figured it was intended as a warning to back off."

"But you ignored the warning, if that's what it was?"

"Yes. That wasn't as careless as it sounds, you know. During the first attack, the gunman fired six shots and missed every one by at least two or three feet. He was either a rank amateur, or he intended to miss. The latter seemed more likely."

"Hmm. And the second attempt? The one that occurred when Miss Delaney was with you—tell me about it."

"It happened just last weekend. I assumed it was coincidence that the attack came when Robyn was with me, and since we were both leaving on an overseas trip, it never occurred to me that she might be in real danger."

Inspector Harris wrote copiously in his notebook. "Is there an ongoing police investigation into the fraud at your Gallery?" he asked finally. "Perhaps I'll be able to get some useful leads from the detectives working on that case."

Zach felt the muscles in his jaw lock tight with tension. "There is no police investigation," he said curtly. "I was handling the investigation myself."

"And have you reached any conclusions so far, Mr. Bowleigh?"

"None that would be useful to you."

"I see."

"No, you don't see," Zach said, stung to defend himself. "You're thinking I was criminally irresponsible not to have reported those attacks—"

"My opinions don't matter much, Mr. Bowleigh. At the moment, *you* are doing a more than adequate job of blaming yourself."

The detective was infuriating, but he was right. "I shouldn't have been so damned arrogant," Zach muttered.

"Why were you so reluctant to report the fraud to the police, Mr. Bowleigh?"

"The antiques trade runs on trust. If word gets out that the Bowleigh Gallery is unable to guarantee the authenticity of its inventory, we'll be out of business in no time flat. Obviously, I made a lousy judgment call in deciding to keep quiet. I seriously underestimated the people I was up against."

"That's assuming the attack on Miss Delaney is related to the previous attacks on you, *and* to the scam being worked through your Gallery. For all we know, this could be a random shooting."

"It seems unlikely, don't you think?"

"It certainly does, but I don't like to leap to conclusions.

In police work, that can get you into a lot of trouble." Inspector Harris smiled blandly. "Perhaps you could fill me in on the answers to a few more routine questions, Mr. Bowleigh. For starters, why were you and Miss Delaney here in Dorset?"

"We were supposed to evaluate a large collection of English antique china with a view to buying it for the Gallery. Robyn is recognized as an expert in the field of antique porcelain. She wrote her master's thesis on the output of the British potteries in the eighteenth century."

"A very interesting subject, I'm sure. So you and Miss Delaney aren't personal friends, just business associates?"

"No, we're friends as well as colleagues. More than friends. This weekend was . . ." Zach cleared his throat. "This weekend I'd planned to ask Robyn to marry me."

The detective murmured something sympathetic, but he kept right on with his questions. "All right, why don't we get back to the shooting incident itself. Would you tell me exactly what you saw of this shooting incident, Mr. Bowleigh? I've been given very confused accounts from the staff at the hotel."

Shooting incident. Robyn's life hung by a thread, but to the police she was simply the victim in a *shooting incident.* Official jargon could sometimes be painfully abrasive. Zach rubbed his eyes, forcing himself to concentrate. "I spotted Robyn almost as soon as I came out of the main hotel entrance. I'm not sure if she saw me. The parking lot at Starke Manor isn't very big, as you know, but she'd parked her car at the far end of the lot, by the gates, and she was leaning into the rental car to get her suitcase. She didn't really look in my direction."

"But you saw her quite clearly before she was shot?"

"Oh, yes. I was happy to see she'd arrived safely, a little earlier than we'd expected. I waved to her, but she didn't wave back. She half turned her head toward me, and I had this fleeting impression that she'd seen me and registered the fact that I was there. Then she suddenly dived forward between the two cars parked on either side of her."

Zach fell silent, and the detective prompted him. "Go on, please, Mr. Bowleigh."

"I saw Robyn fall, but for a crucial second or two, I didn't consciously register that someone had fired a gun."

"Do you think there was a silencer on the gun?"

"There must have been, or I'd have heard the shot. It was surprisingly quiet in the parking lot, no people around, no hum of traffic."

"Did you see the gunman?"

"No. Robyn fell forward and the gunman revved up his car engine and started backing out of the parking lot almost at the same moment."

"You're saying the gunman fired from a car." Inspector Harris looked pleased at this snippet of new information. "Did you get a clear view of the car?"

"Not really. I reacted without thinking, rushing over to Robyn instead of taking ten seconds to stand still and get a good look at the person who'd shot her." Zach ran his hands through his hair, spiking it between his fingers. "Goddammit, I should have paid more attention. I should have looked at the damn car and seen who was driving."

"It was perfectly natural for you to be worried about Miss Delaney at that moment."

"Natural, maybe, but not smart," Zach said, his voice rough.

"You're a better witness than most," the inspector said. "Now think, Mr. Bowleigh. I know you've said that you didn't get a good look at the car, but try again. It's surprising what the subconscious can store away. Can you tell me anything at all about the car, or the person who was driving it? Color? Size? Anything?"

"It was blue," Zach said after a long moment of silence. "New-looking. Probably a Ford, but I couldn't swear to it. If you can show me pictures of various British models and the paint colors for those years, I may be able to take a stab at naming the year and the model."

"That's very helpful, Mr. Bowleigh, very helpful. Could you cast your mind back and think a bit about who was driving the car? How many people were in it? Male or female? Fat or thin? Young or old?"

Zach closed his eyes, trying to summon up a memory of the scene. All he could see, playing over and over again in hideous slow motion, was Robyn falling to the ground, and blood gushing over the dark asphalt of the parking lot, mingling with the rain.

"I think there was only one person in the car," he said finally. "But there's a blur in my mind where the picture of the driver ought to be."

The detective sighed. "Unfortunately, everybody on the hotel staff seems to have been too far away, and too upset, to have noticed any suspicious cars or drivers."

Zach frowned. "She'd driven off before the hotel staff came out into the parking lot, that's why."

The detective's head jerked up, and Zach stopped, stunned by the realization of what he'd just said. *"It was a woman driving the car,"* he said, his voice harsh with surprise. "She had dark hair, tumbling all over her shoulders." He felt a surge of excitement as the memory strengthened. "Middle-aged. At least forty, maybe fifty. And wearing dark glasses. Ninety-nine percent of my brain was worrying about Robyn, but one percent was registering the fact that the driver wore sunglasses, even though it was raining."

"That's very helpful, Mr. Bowleigh. Well done, sir. You're the only witness to give us something concrete to work on."

Zach smiled grimly. "Right. With a detailed description like that you can walk straight out of here and make an arrest. Female, middle-aged, dark hair, wearing sunglasses. There can't be more than ten million women in England who fit the bill."

"Not ten million, probably less than five," the detective said, allowing himself a small smile. "Statistically speaking, we've got a lot of blondes and redheads in this country."

"Robyn has red hair," Zach said. "And wonderful green eyes."

The detective cast him a sympathetic look. "She sounds a lovely young lady," he said. "Oh, look, here comes a doctor. Maybe he'll have some news for us."

"Dr. Forsyth, how is she?" Zach stepped forward, sweat beading along his spine as he waited for the doctor to reply.

"She's an extremely lucky young woman," the doctor said. "In layman's language, the bullet skimmed across the top of her head, lodging in the bone at the crown of her skull, but not actually penetrating the brain. We removed the bullet because we were afraid that it might dislodge at some point in the future and cause trouble, but in fact, at this precise moment, Miss Delaney's most serious problems are caused by the fact that she fell forward and hit her head on a concrete parking lot. She has a severe concussion."

"What does that mean? Is she going to get better?"

"It means that we have to wait for her to regain consciousness before we can tell precisely how much damage has been done. However, we've run CAT scans and we see no evidence of severe injury to the brain either on the scan or during surgery. With a little bit of luck, your girlfriend is going to be up and talking in two or three days."

The news was so good that Zach couldn't totally absorb it. "How about her mental state?" he inquired. "Is she likely to suffer from amnesia or anything like that?"

"Almost certainly," Dr. Forsyth replied. "Post-traumatic amnesia is more or less routine with this type of injury. In fact, she may never remember the events leading up to the accident. However, I wouldn't expect major long-term impairment of her mental faculties. Miss Delaney may need some therapy to regain fully normal functioning, but she isn't likely to be a vegetable, or permanently comatose, or any of those other nightmares you might associate with serious head injuries."

"Thank God!" Zach breathed. "And thank you, Doctor."

"My pleasure. I like cases with positive outcomes."

"At least I have some good news to pass on to her parents. Could I go and see Robyn now, Dr. Forsyth?"

"You'd probably better not. She's hooked up to a dozen monitors and machines, and you could only stare at her through a window. She won't regain consciousness for several hours, and when she does, she won't want to chat. Why don't you go back to your hotel and get a good night's sleep? Phone us tomorrow first thing, and we'll give you an update on her status. The receptionist will give you the number to ring."

"My God, can't I see her before then?"

"You'll be able to see her tomorrow morning," the doctor repeated. "At the moment, as I explained to you, there's nothing for you to look at but machines and bandages. You may as well go back to the hotel and get a good night's sleep."

Zach had spent enough time in England to know that there was absolutely no point in begging, pleading, or demanding to be allowed into the surgical intensive care recovery unit. The doctor might sound mild and low-key, but like the detective, his courteous manner was deceiving. Zach knew he was being ordered out of the hospital.

He gave way with as good grace as he could muster. "Thanks for everything," he said, shaking the doctor's hand. "I have it on the authority of the nurses that you're one of the best emergency surgeons in the country. I'm really grateful for what you've done."

Dr. Forsyth actually blushed. "Good heavens, what a compliment! The nursing staff are always the hardest people to impress. Now, how are you going to get home? You came with Robyn in the ambulance, didn't you?"

"I'll give him a lift," Inspector Harris said. "I'm driving back to the hotel anyway."

"Thanks," Zach said and yawned, suddenly aware that he was so tired his eyes were no longer seeing straight. Ten minutes ago he had been a jangle of live nerve endings and sleep would have been impossible. Now he felt limp and formless, like a sack of cotton batting. He yawned again.

Dr. Forsyth smiled. "When you get back to the hotel, order a nice double whiskey and a bowl of hot soup. Doctor's orders. I'll talk to you first thing tomorrow, Mr. Bowleigh. Good night."

Chapter 6

"I am going to sit in the chair by the fire," Robyn announced to the maid. "Could you please find me a robe to wear, and some slippers?" She spoke briskly. Fortified by a lunch of chicken broth and excellent crusty bread, she was determined to take charge of her life after too many days of allowing other people to control her actions.

Mary, who seemed to see her role in life as one of endless anxious protest, clucked nervously. "Ow, my lady, 'tis too soon for you to leave your bed. You'll catch your death of cold. The wind has shifted to the north, and 'tis a bitter day outside."

"Then you should tell William to turn up the thermostat," Robyn said. "Get the furnaces blowing some nice hot air."

"Yus, m'lady." Mary looked bewildered, but Robyn refused to be deceived by the maid's apparent inability to understand simple English. Of course Mary knew what the word *thermostat* meant. Earlier today, for a brief moment, Robyn had allowed herself to fall into the trap being set for her. When Mary had said so convincingly that the date was 1746, Robyn had let herself slide into the fantasy being woven around her. But now she was in control again and determined to be on her guard.

Obviously Mary didn't believe the year was really 1746. The maid gave no sign of being insane, which she would have to be in order to think she was living more than two hundred years in the past. So since Mary was lying—*must* be lying—Robyn was forced to conclude the maid was part of a deliberate conspiracy.

Which led to the question of what, exactly, the conspiracy was intended to achieve. Robyn couldn't think of any convincing reason why several people, including Zach's brother,

would want to perpetrate a massive fraud on her, but she
was confident she would come up with a credible rationale
sometime soon. The most likely explanation of her fantastic
surroundings was that William's cruel hoax had something
to do with the antiques scam being worked through the
Bowleigh Gallery. Robyn couldn't believe it was pure coincidence that William had imprisoned her in a working model
of an eighteenth-century manor house, surrounded by precisely the sort of pseudo-antique furniture that was being il-
legally sold through the Gallery.

The maid returned from her foray into the closet, an off-
white woolen gown draped over her arm. "Here be your new
winter robe, my lady. Shall I help your ladyship to put it
on?"

"I can manage, thank you." Robyn slipped her arms into
the padded, silk-lined sleeves of the robe. The deep pleats of
the skirt swirled around her knees, settling into stillness with
a smooth whisper of sound. The seams rested comfortably
along her shoulder—the perfect size. The woolen cloth was
so soft and fine Robyn couldn't resist stroking the delicate
folds of the robe. She had to hand it to William and his cro-
nies; they sure knew how to do a fabulous job of faking antique workmanship. This robe appeared hand-sewn, and the
cloth hand-woven. It would fetch a small fortune if it ever
went on sale in a New York boutique.

Realization dawned with the impact of lightning tearing
through a dark night sky. "Of course," Robyn breathed,
looking at Mary through new eyes. "Now I understand
where I am and what's going on. *This is a factory, isn't it?*
This is where you're turning out all those fabulous fake cabinets that are ending up in the Gallery, right? You're making
furniture, and maybe clothes and artifacts, too. The whole
ball of wax, in fact."

Mary bobbed her head. "Yus, my lady. Your ladyship has
the right of it. We do make furniture and wax for the candles."

"You're admitting it?" Robyn couldn't conceal her astonishment. "Just like that? No attempt at denial? What in the
world do you do about Customs, or do you ship the pieces
in as acknowledged reproductions and fake the paperwork
later?"

"I don' know, my lady. Whatever you say is very true, my lady."

Robyn clenched her fists in frustration. "If you're not going to answer me truthfully, for heaven's sake say so. Don't be so damned obsequious! You're driving me crazy!"

"No, my lady. I mean yus, my lady." Averting her gaze, Mary crouched into a kneeling position, so that she could guide Robyn's feet into a pair of white velvet slippers. Straightening, she extended her arm, but avoided touching Robyn. "Does your ladyship wish to hold on to my arm, or do you prefer to walk to the fireside alone, my lady?"

"Alone," Robyn said curtly. She felt a twinge of guilt over her curtness when she saw the maid cringe, then told herself not to be a fool. Mary was playing a role, and Robyn had nothing to feel guilty about, nothing at all. On the contrary, her rudeness was entirely justified, given the appalling way she had been denied adequate medical treatment during her illness.

Head held high, deliberately ignoring Mary, Robyn walked over to the chair by the hearth, delighted to find that she could cover the distance without needing the support of a single piece of furniture.

She sat down and glared at the maid. "Okay, if you won't talk, maybe William can tell me what's going on here. Why don't you let him know I'm up and about, and willing to hear the details of whatever nifty scam he's trying to work. I guess he wouldn't have gone to so much trouble to keep me here unless he has some deal he wants to propose to me."

"You want to speak with the master, my lady?" The maid carefully placed an embroidered footstool beneath Robyn's feet.

Robyn gritted her teeth. "All right, we'll play this by your rules. Yes, Mary, I want to speak with William. With your *master.*"

"Very good, my lady. Shall I bring a shawl for your ladyship? 'Tis drafty today, with the wind blowing so fierce."

Robyn gripped the arms of the chair and stared hard-eyed at the groveling servant. "Enough, Mary. Cut the English yokel act and just get William in here, okay?"

"Certainly, my lady. I'll fetch him instanter."

"And cut the phony slang, too. It's getting tedious."

"As you wish, m'lady." Mary scurried from the room.

William came in less than five minutes later. He bowed to Robyn, hand on heart, but didn't approach her, or touch her in any way. This afternoon, he had chosen to wear a more modest outfit than the day before: gray woolen knee breeches, gray silk stockings, and a full-skirted coat of black broadcloth, the lapels buttoned back to reveal an embroidered silver waistcoat. The lace at his cuffs and throat was as flowing and elaborate as before, but he had hidden his hair beneath a layer of white powder, so that he looked like an escaped footman from Disney's version of *Cinderella*. Robyn wanted to laugh, to throw his ridiculous appearance back in his face, but the laughter died in her throat and she found herself staring at him, heart pounding just a little too fast.

"Nifty costume," she said, hoping he wouldn't hear the catch in her voice. "Was that manufactured here on the premises, too?"

"No, these clothes were made for me the last time we were in London," William said. "I am sorry if they do not meet your high standards of sartorial elegance, but I have spent the morning closeted with my steward, and did not change before coming to see you. I offer my apologies."

"Stop it!" she commanded. "For God's sake, William, stop this absurd pretense! I'm not delirious anymore and it isn't working."

"I do not understand which pretense you refer to, Arabella. But let us not waste time in useless, mutual reproach. The children have been asking to see you, and I have ordered them to be brought here. The baby as well. You haven't yet held your new son, and it is time for you to make his acquaintance."

Robyn looked at him coldly, but inside she felt hot with anger. "You have a sick mind, William. I can't imagine how someone as honorable as Zach ended up with a brother as callous as you."

He inclined his head with a hint of weary mockery. "So you have often remarked, my dear. But do, pray, show a modicum of kindness for your children. They have been sorely worried about you and would appreciate some small display of affection from their mother."

Robyn recoiled. "Surely you haven't drawn real children into this scheme? William, that's disgusting. How can you sleep at night, knowing what terrible harm you're doing to so many innocent people?"

William turned to her, and if she hadn't known better, she would have sworn that his blue eyes darkened with genuine bewilderment. "Will you believe me if I say that I am not aware of having committed any act that merits your scorn?"

"Your treatment of me after I was shot—"

"Ah, I see." The tension in William's shoulders visibly relaxed. "Arabella," he said gently. "You were not shot. This belief that you have suffered a bullet wound is but a figment of your delirium—"

"Don't try to feed me that bullshit! What about the three-inch scar on my scalp? Is that a figment of my imagination, too?"

"Of course not. Alas, it is very real. But it is the result of your accident last Friday, not the result of a bullet wound."

Robyn's heart was pounding so fast it was becoming difficult to breath. "Tell me about my accident," she said abruptly.

"You do not remember it?"

"No, apparently not."

"Unfortunately, I cannot enlighten you as to many of the details since you told nobody where you were going. You left the house alone, in the late afternoon, perhaps forgetting how early the nights draw in at this time of year. Or perhaps you had some assignation for which you wished total privacy—"

"Are you trying to suggest I was sneaking out to meet a lover?"

"I did not say so."

"But you damn well implied it."

He looked at her coolly. "You may interpret my remarks however you please, Arabella. Suffice to say that I have no definite knowledge of why you felt it necessary to leave the house at dusk, without the escort of your groom."

"Maybe I needed some fresh air," Robyn said cynically.

"That is ... conceivable, I suppose, although you have

never been noted for your love of the outdoors. In any event, we believe the carriage horse must have bolted as you returned to the house. It seems that you did not have the strength to rein the horse in, and you were dragged beneath the overhanging branches of the hawthorn tree that stands at the entrance to the courtyard. The thorns gouged a deep and painful cut in your scalp, and you also suffered a severe blow to your temple when you were thrown from the carriage. The doctor suggests that the blow to your head is causing this strangely selective loss of your memories—"

"Give it up, William," she said tiredly. "I wasn't even here last week, much less riding a horse. You know I was in New York, working with your brother Zach—"

William spoke crisply. "My dear, you must try to remember that Zachary has been declared a traitor and that it is not wise to speak of him. Our good King George and his government have rightly set a price on my brother's head following the fiasco of the Young Pretender's rout at Culloden, and I have forbidden all mention of my brother's name in my house. We are Tories, loyal servants of the Hanoverian kings, and it is dangerous for you to forget that fact."

Robyn struggled to her feet. "Stop it!" she yelled, pummeling his chest with her fists. "Stop trying to pretend it's 1746! You can't push these horrible lies down my throa—"

William put his arm around her shoulders. Gently, but impersonally, he guided her back to the chair. "Sit down, my lady, and try not to overset your emotions. We have all been most impressed by the fortitude with which you have endured the pain of your accident, and we are certainly delighted that your premature labor resulted in the birth of another healthy child. For the moment let us concentrate on the happiness of successful motherhood and forget these painful recriminations."

The happiness of motherhood. Before she could stop herself, Robyn lifted her hands to her breasts, which ached and throbbed with the excruciating fullness of their milk. She didn't realize she was crying until William pulled a scented handkerchief from the lacy cuff of his shirt and handed it to her. "Come," he said quietly. "Dry your tears, my lady. I hear your children approaching."

"Not . . . my . . . children . . ." she whispered despairingly.

William didn't answer her. He swung around and seated himself in the chair placed at the opposite side of the fire. "Enter!" he called out at the sound of shuffling feet and a faint scratching on the panels of the door.

To Robyn's overwrought nerves, it seemed that a dozen people entered her bedroom all at once. Gradually the jostling mass of bodies straightened themselves out into two adult females dressed just like Mary, three small children, and a plump young woman garbed in drab, rusty black, who was holding a tightly swaddled bundle. Robyn turned hastily away, determined not to look too closely at that frightening bundle.

Even before the maids placed restraining hands on their shoulders, the three children all tumbled to a full stop just inside the entrance to the bedroom. They looked instinctively toward William, clearly waiting for instructions. Did they need directions for speaking their lines in a prearranged dialogue? Robyn wondered.

"Come in, children, and pay your respects to your mother," William said, smiling encouragingly. "As you can see, she is feeling very much better, but you must not shout, or you will give her the headache. George, Frederick, you first. Approach your mamma and make your very best bows."

Two boys of about five years of age, identical in appearance and presumably twins, stepped forward in unison. They swept into bows that were passable imitations of William's earlier performance. "You look very well, Mamma," one of them said as he straightened from his flourish. "And we were happy to meet our new bruvver. We are glad the angels sent him here safely."

Robyn didn't know what to say, or how to reply, so she said nothing. The twins exchanged wary glances.

"We have been out riding," said the second twin, giving up on the notion of discussing the new baby. "We rode to Uppingly Woods and Jake says we have egg ... eggsellent bottom."

"And Monsieur Petain says we will be the death of him," said the first twin.

His exasperated brother kicked him in the ankle. "But we

didn't *mean* to spill ink all over Monsieur's nightshirt," he reassured Robyn, sounding anxious. "It was a aggsident."

"The spider, too, Mamma. The spider in Monsieur's book was a aggsident as well."

Robyn astonished herself by starting to laugh. Heart pounding, she stared at the two little boys lined up in front of her. She looked at their eager, worried faces and the twinkle of mischief in their eyes and her laughter died. Her mouth went dry. She wanted to scream at them to stop play-acting, to stop participating in William's cruel deception, but something about their innocent, childish expressions cut off the angry words before they could emerge. The twins were genuinely worried, she realized. They looked at her longingly, as if they needed to be reassured that she was indeed alive and well. Even worse, from Robyn's point of view, was the distinct impression she gained that they were afraid to approach her too closely. The twins were scared of her, Robyn thought, scared of how she might react. Just like Mary.

Robyn swallowed hard, trying to grasp hold of emotions that were spiraling totally out of control. "Anyone can have an accident," she said to the twins, resisting the crazy impulse to open her arms and hug the two little boys tight against her heart. "And I'm sure the ink will wash out of Monsieur's nightgown."

The twins smiled in relief at her mild response, but William spoke sternly. "Your mama is too generous. You will come to see me in the study before dinner tonight and explain just what you were doing with Monsieur Petain's nightgown in the first place. I wish you always to remember that your tutor is a fine scholar and he is to be treated with the greatest respect."

"Yes, sir." The twins did not look in the least alarmed at this imminent interview with their supposed father, but Robyn couldn't help casting him an anxious glance. "You won't ... punish ... them. Please, William? I'm sure they meant no harm."

His gaze raked her face. For no logical reason, when his eyes met hers, she felt herself blush. His mouth tightened and he spoke abruptly. "Have no fear, my lady. With such a charming champion to plead for them, I shall not beat your sons. At least not this time."

The twins grinned at each other without even a twinge of foreboding. Despite William's threats, Robyn had the odd impression that they feared her a great deal more than their supposed father. She held out her hands, beckoning them closer, curiously anxious about these children she had never set eyes on until now.

"I hope you dressed warmly when you went out riding this morning. Mary tells me it is very windy outside today and it would be easy to catch cold."

The boys looked impatient at what they clearly considered a boring reminder, but she thought she heard William let out a tiny sigh of relief. Because she had temporarily accepted these imposters as her children? she wondered. Because she was buying into the fantasy that they had been outside, learning to ride, and getting up to mischief with their tutor? She could think of no other reason.

"We wore mufflers, Mamma," one boy said.

"And mittens and woolen stockings."

"There is ice on the pond," said the other. "Freddie and me is going sliding on the pond tomorrow."

"Jake is going to show George and me how to put sliders on our boots so that we may go faster an' faster."

"Make sure the ice is thick enough," Robyn said, feeling an alarm that was as instant as it was irrational.

The twins sighed in unison. "Yes, Mamma."

They were sturdy, good-looking little boys, and she couldn't help giving them another smile. "I know you think I'm being a boring old fusspot, but I don't want you falling into the water and coming back to me frozen into icicles."

They both giggled and would have said something more, but the little girl who had been standing behind them in the doorway lost patience and pushed forward, shaking her mop of soft, light brown curls. The charm of her chubby, unformed features was marred by a sulky expression.

"I wan' sit on you' lap," she said, clutching at Robyn's knee, her mouth pursing into a pout. "George and Fweddie is taking too long. Mamma, do you like my dwess?" She twirled around, light and surprisingly agile on plump baby feet.

"It's very pretty," Robyn managed to say, although her anger had returned with such overwhelming force that she could hardly think straight. "*You're* very pretty."

Good grief, she exploded in silent, internal rage. Where in the world had William recruited this little girl? The child was scarcely more than a toddler, certainly no more than three. How in the world had a three-year-old been trained to address a perfect stranger as *Mamma*? A child actress? Come to think of it, William lived in L.A. and might have friends working in Hollywood and the movie industry.

The little girl was squirming, trying to get comfortable on Robyn's lap. "Do not muss your mother's robe," William said quickly. "Perhaps I should hold you, Clementina."

"No, she can stay here." The way she felt about William right at this moment, Robyn couldn't bear the thought of any child coming near him, not even a well-trained child actress.

The little girl stopped squirming and looked up at Robyn, staring at her long and hard. "What have you done to your eyes?" she asked at last. "Your eyes is funny. Where is my real mamma? You is not my real mamma." She started to cry, huge gulping sobs that seemed too large for her minuscule, baby-plump frame. "I want my real mamma!"

Robyn glared at William, almost speechless with fury. "What did you tell her?" she demanded, trying to keep her voice low and calm for the sake of the child. "Surely to God you didn't pretend to a baby like this that I was really her mother?"

"You is *not* my mamma!" The little girl howled some more. Mary and William both jumped up and lunged forward. William moved faster than the maid, whisking the sobbing child away from Robyn's lap, swinging her up and over his head before nestling her in the crook of his arm. "Papa is going to take you flying. Look, you are a bird, sailing up in the sky. Flutter your wings or you will fall."

Clementina flapped her hands and laughed delightedly, forgetting her tears in an instant. "More!" she commanded. "More swings, Papa. More bird. More more!"

"Shh," he said quickly. "We must not make too much noise or your mama will not feel well. She has been very ill and you cannot climb on her lap for a little while yet, Clementina."

"My old mamma is gone away. This is a new mamma. She has new eyes." Clementina's face crumpled. "I want my proper mamma. I don' wan' my new bruvver. My new bruvver is silly."

William nodded almost imperceptibly to one of the servants, and the woman hurried forward, curtsying to Robyn. "My lady, I'm right sorry for what she is saying. I will take the child back to the nursery so that she does not disturb you. Come along, Miss Clementina, you have been a bad girl. A naughty, bad girl, and everyone is very cross with you."

"No, don't say that! She hasn't been naughty at all!" Robyn protested, horrified at the callous way in which the child was being blamed simply for speaking honestly. She held out her hand to the little girl, forcing herself to smile in a calm, friendly way. "It was really nice to see you, Clementina. Will you come back and visit me again tomorrow?"

Clementina inspected Robyn thoughtfully. "Are you going to be my new mamma for ever an' ever?"

Robyn couldn't decide how to answer. In the end, she smiled again and answered as truthfully as she could. "I will be here to look after you for a little while, Clemmie." She had no idea where the nickname came from. It simply slipped out, as natural and easy as if she had used it a hundred times before.

She saw two of the maids exchange astonished glances. The taut, hard lines of William's mouth relaxed. Robyn realized with a shock that everyone was immeasurably relieved that she hadn't lost her temper at Clementina's innocent remarks. They had obviously expected her to be furious with the child. Why? Why in the world would they expect her to behave so badly? she wondered.

"Take Miss Clementina back to the nursery," William said to the nursemaid. "And the boys should go, too. We must not tire the Lady Arabella."

"Oh, no, Papa!" The twins' response was instantaneous. "We would much rather stay here with you."

"But you will, of course, do what you have been asked," William said mildly. "Otherwise I might feel obliged to suggest to Monsieur Petain that he should give you an extra lesson in French grammar tomorrow."

"We are going, Papa," the twins said hastily. They turned to Robyn and swept deep bows. "Sleep well, Mama. We shall look forward to seeing you tomorrow."

The children and most of the maids trooped out, but when the plump servant carrying the bundle would have left with the rest of them, William held out his hand and stopped her. "Since your mistress is feeling so well, I am sure she would like to hold her new son for a little while. Annie, will you step forward so that her ladyship may see her child?"

Robyn clenched her teeth. "Don't do this to me, William."

He came and stood beside her chair, his expression implacable, although his voice sounded quite mild. "My dear, it is for your own good. I am sure you will feel easier in your own mind once you have seen what a fine healthy child your new son is. If you are worried that he is misshapen in any way as a result of your fall, you may put such fears entirely to rest."

Robyn felt her stomach lurch. She turned her head away, staring obstinately toward the window. She heard a restless, mewing little cry, followed by a shushing sound from the servant holding the baby. Beneath the rhythmic shushing of the maid, she heard the snuffling, wheezing noises of a tiny infant stirring from sleep.

She couldn't bear to look, but she couldn't bear to continue looking away. Feeling as if her head were weighted with lead, Robyn swiveled around toward the source of the sound. The plump, homespun-clad nurse held out the bundle, her expression difficult to define. Robyn thought she saw sadness and maybe a touch of resentment behind the carefully arranged features, but she couldn't be sure.

The servant dipped into a curtsy. "I been feeding him regular, my lady, and he's a healthy child, for all he's still tiny. My milk's the best, everyone around here reckons that."

Robyn's hands were shaking as she held out her arms. "Give the child to me."

The nurse placed the tiny white bundle in Robyn's arms. The baby was wrapped so tightly that only his face was visible. His eyes were screwed shut, his skin appeared red and wrinkled, and his mouth was pursed, ready to cry at a moment's notice. As Robyn closed her arms around him, he suddenly blinked and opened his eyes.

He stared up at her with a blue, unfocused gaze. Robyn stared back at him, while her heart turned somersaults inside her chest. This infant was truly newborn, no more than a few days old. *And during her delirium, she had fantasized about giving birth to a baby boy.*

The baby soon got tired of staring. His eyes squeezed shut. His mouth opened wide and he let out a loud, angry cry, a bellow that changed almost at once into a thin, high wail. The sound tore at Robyn's nerves and ate into her guts, making her frantic with the need to appease the baby's obvious discomfort. Something wet and warm spattered onto her hand and she realized it was milk, dripping out of her nipples onto the baby's swaddling bands. Without stopping to reflect on what she was doing, without a thought for William's continued presence, she pushed aside the folds of her robe and held the baby to her breast.

He felt warm and damp in the crook of her arm, a tiny weight that seemed to fill a gap the size of the universe inside her soul. He rooted around for no more than a second or two, then latched on to her nipple and sucked greedily. The release of pressure inside her breasts was so wonderful that Robyn almost cried. She leaned back, resting her head on the winged corner of the chair, stroking the transparent fuzz of silky hair on the baby's head. The strands felt soft, softer than anything she had ever felt in her life before. Unable to prevent herself, she bent over and nuzzled her cheek against the top of the baby's head, aching with the need to be close, to feel the baby's skin in contact with her own. The baby stopped sucking for a second, lost her nipple, and started to cry.

She laughed because he looked so ridiculous, so totally adorable, with milk bubbling on his lips, his eyes puzzled, and his cheeks turning scarlet with frustration. "What a fierce little fellow you are to be sure," she murmured, rubbing his back until he calmed down and let out a milky burp. "Here, try the other side and maybe we'll both feel more comfortable."

For several minutes Robyn was oblivious to everything in the room save the steady sucking of the infant at her breast, and the corresponding relaxation of tension inside her. Gradually, as the pressure of excess milk eased, she became aware of the silence in the room, and the odd, waiting tension emanating from William and the nursemaid. She ignored them both, smiling as she watched the baby suckle and reaching inside the swaddling bands to loosen them. She eased them open so that the baby's diminutive hands could poke out and curl around her fingers. She gazed at his nails, hypnotized by their minute, pink perfection, and rubbed her thumbs across the roly-poly softness of his wrists.

The baby fell asleep, breathing heavily, sated with milk. Her milk. She eased him away from her breast and held him up to her shoulder, rocking gently as she patted his back. She had half a dozen nieces and nephews, and at one time or another she had helped out by rocking every one of them to sleep. The motions she was going through with this tiny infant were familiar. The sensations rioting inside her were totally new.

A burning log split into two, tumbling into the grate with a clatter and a shower of hot orange sparks. She glanced toward the sound and saw that William had moved to stand in front of the fireplace. His booted foot rested on the fender and he was gazing at her, his eyes dark, his face wiped utterly clean of expression. Somehow, despite his outward appearance of complete self-possession, she knew that inside he was seething with a tumbling mass of unresolved emotions. She stared back at him, meeting his gaze head-on, forcing herself to look at him—really look at him—for the first time.

Like Zach, he was quite tall, she guessed more than five-ten, but less than six feet, with broad shoulders and a narrow waist. His hips were hidden by the full skirt of his coat, but his legs were long and showed to definite advantage in the silk stockings and knee breeches he was wearing. Despite his fancy getup, she had no doubt that he was truly Zach's brother. Now that she looked at him closely, she could see many similarities to Zach, not only in his straw-blond hair color and penetrating blue eyes, but especially in the strong, square thrust of his jawline, and in the narrow, aristocratic bridge of his nose. His mouth, too, was like Zach's, firmly drawn but sensuous, promising both passion and tenderness

to some lucky woman. It wasn't at all difficult to believe
that he was Zach's brother.

The baby hiccuped, and Robyn closed her arms protectively around him. William's gaze flickered to the child, then
returned to Robyn. "I did not expect you to feed the child
yourself," he said, breaking a silence that was still thick with
an odd sort of tension. "I trust that your generosity today
will not make it more difficult for you to stanch the flow of
your milk tomorrow."

"Why should I stanch the flow, as you put it? Don't you
want me to nurse the baby myself?"

She had the satisfaction of seeing that for some reason her
question had totally amazed him. He drew in a deep breath.
"I had not even considered the possibility that you would
feed the child yourself. You have never been willing to play
nursemaid to any of your other children. In fact, you said on
several occasions that the thought of a mewling infant tugging at your breasts disgusted you. It did not occur to me
that you would be willing to change such strongly held con-
victions."

His words pierced the lethargy that had suspended
Robyn's thought processes and lulled her into placidity
while she nursed the baby. Belatedly she realized that her
situation had passed over from bizarre into the realms of total and utter fantasy.

*She had just spent twenty minutes nursing a newborn in-
fant.*

For a moment she felt fear, fear so deep and enveloping
that her heart seemed to stop beating. Then, just before the
fear could consume her, she realized that there was only one
possible explanation for what was happening to her.

She was dreaming.

She half expected to wake up the moment the realization
hit her, as so often happened with dreams. But this time, for
some reason, she remained sleeping and the illusory world
of her dream remained intact.

Even so, the realization of what was happening left her
limp with relief. Robyn relaxed in the chair, settling into her
dream, willing to endure the experience now that she knew
what was happening. She stared at William, amazed at the
intriguing workings of her subconscious. Why in the world

had she conjured up such an extraordinary man? What was her subconscious trying to tell her?

"You know, you really are a strange fantasy," she said. "Why have I given you Zach's body, his brother's name, and a character that seems lifted straight out of *The Scarlet Pimpernel*? And why have I given myself a baby, for heaven's sake? If you'd asked me when I'm awake, I'd have said I wasn't all that interested in having children for at least another three or four years. I think of myself as a dedicated career woman." She gave a rueful chuckle. "Hey, maybe this dream is trying to tell me something."

The nursemaid leaned forward and snatched the baby from out of Robyn's arms. "Her ladyship's talking the devil's talk again, my lord. Please, my lord, you must send word to the parson and have him come to her, or she'll fetch trouble to us all."

Robyn yawned, then wondered why she felt so sleepy in the middle of a dream. "Honest to Pete, I don't know where all this crazy stuff is coming from. Why do you suppose I'm fantasizing about a dour nursemaid who's full of ignorant superstitions?"

"If you are asking me that question, Arabella, then I fear that I cannot answer you." William put his arm around her waist, drawing her to her feet. "Come, my dear, you must return to your bed and rest. I will bring you dinner myself and see if you are recovering your wits ... your strength ... as you should. Perhaps nursing the baby was too much for you. Women of high birth have delicate constitutions, and I should not have allowed you to overtax your resources. It could be dangerous to the equilibrium of your mind."

Robyn frowned. "William, you're a pain in the rear end, you know that? You're most definitely not behaving the way you should. Heck, this is my dream, I want to have more control over it." She chucked him under the chin. "Why don't you smile and show me what you look like when you're in a good mood? I think you might be quite sexy if I could ever get you to smile."

The nursemaid spoke low-voiced from the doorway. "Do you need me, my lord? I don' want to stay with her ladyship when she do go on so crazy like. Frightens me, 'er do."

William nodded impatiently to the maid. "I have said that

you may go. Take the child back to the nursery. I will tend to the Lady Arabella."

Robyn scowled. "I'm not Arabella, I'm Robyn."

William slipped the robe from her shoulders and lifted her into the bed. "Whoever you wish to be, my lady, you should sleep and recoup your strength."

Robyn scowled. "Dammit all, why won't you behave the way I want you to behave? Why can't I control the figments of my own imagination?" A worrying thought occurred to her. "Maybe I'm not sleeping. Maybe I'm unconscious. Big time, long-term unconscious, which is why I can't wake up. Maybe that bullet penetrated my skull and I'm hooked up to machines and everyone thinks I'm a vegetable. Maybe that's why this dream is so weird and out of control."

"I certainly don't think you're a vegetable, Arabella. I know that you are a beautiful woman."

She laughed, deciding not to fight with the vagaries of her own subconscious. "Right, that's me. A very beautiful woman. I'm blond, blue-eyed, and I have long slender legs with great thighs, just like I always wanted. You know what, Willie baby? I shouldn't complain. On second thought, this dream is getting better."

William didn't look amused. "On the contrary," he said curtly. "I fear that from my point of view it is fast turning into the most horrible of nightmares."

Chapter 7

ROBYN knotted a linen band around baby Zach's tummy and tugged at it doubtfully. Her efforts to secure a diaper around the baby's bottom without benefit of safety pins or sticky tabs were proving less than a hundred percent successful. "This is a stupid dream," she muttered. "You're not supposed to worry about loose diapers in the middle of a dream."

Baby Zach—she wasn't quite sure at what point she'd mentally given him that name—stared at her out of unwinking blue eyes for a full ten seconds, then the sound of a creaking tree bough distracted him. His gaze wavered and his hands flailed helplessly. Startled by his own movements, he began to cry.

"Ah, my lady, give him to me!" The nursemaid rushed forward. "He is moving too much, like I warned your ladyship. Look at his poor little hands beating the air, and his innards ready to fall right out of his belly if you do not wrap him more closely!"

"Nothing will fall out of his belly," Robyn said, picking up baby Zach and rocking him gently. Even though she knew she must be dreaming, the baby felt so real she couldn't help responding to him just as if he were truly there and in need of her protection. She knew she had been curt with the nurse, so she tried to make herself sound more friendly. "Annie, stop worrying and the baby will be fine, honestly. I have lots of experience with little babies. My brother and sister each have three, and I'm considered a major family resource for baby-sitting."

"Your—um—sister, m'lady?"

"Yes. My sister." Robyn spoke defiantly, although her stomach sank. She knew what was coming.

Annie shuffled her feet uncomfortably. She cleared her throat. "My lady, you don't have no sister and you never have taken care—"

"Don't argue with me," Robyn snapped. "This is an order, Annie. You're not to wrap the baby in those tight bands. It's dangerous, you'll constrict his circulation."

"My lady, I been looking after little ones for nigh on ten years, and I know as how they can't survive if you don't keep them tightly wrapped around the belly. Terrible gaping holes I've seen in a baby's belly if he ain't bandaged up right and proper."

"You're talking about infections of the umbilical cord, which baby Zach is much more likely to develop if you never let any fresh air touch his body—"

"Zach, did you say? Short for Zachary? Did the master agree as how the baby was to be called Zachary, my lady?"

"Er ... not exactly. William and I haven't yet discussed the question of the baby's name—"

"I heard the housekeeper say as how he's to be christened Arthur, in honor of his grandsire. Your father, my lady, a very good gentleman, may he rest in peace."

Robyn sighed. "I told you, Annie, his name has not yet been discussed." She heard the note of irritated authority in her voice and reflected ruefully that it was all too easy to slide into the habits of the people around her. If she wasn't careful, before long she'd be throwing hairbrushes at any servant who dared to contradict her.

The thought was so absurd, Robyn found herself smiling. What the heck, she might as well make the nursemaid happy. She took a square of soft woolen cloth, folded it into a triangle, and tucked it around baby Zach to make a neat, cream-colored papoose. "There, how's that for a compromise package? He's all tucked in, but he isn't half-strangled. That's how my sisters always wrapped their newborns. Look, he's settling down already."

Annie sniffed. Her subservience quota seemed several notches less than the rest of the servants and she watched with evident disapproval as Robyn hugged the baby, patting his back in soothing rhythm. A wonderful, peaceful lethargy settled over Robyn as she felt the baby snuggle against her and drift off to sleep.

"He's happy as a clam," she said, smiling toward the servant, anxious to make amends for the snippiness of her earlier mood. "You see, he liked having a bath after all."

Annie refused to be mollified. "Aye, m'lady, I'm sure he did. Happen that's why he screamed fit to raise the roof all the time you wus washing him."

Robyn grinned. "Well, now that the trauma is over, I'm sure he's glad to be clean and sweet-smelling. He'll get used to being bathed eventually."

"That's as maybe," the nursemaid muttered, stepping forward to claim the baby. "I will return him to the nursery, my lady, so that you can rest. 'Tisn't good for a babe to be jostled around the whole time. He needs to lie flat in his cradle and give your milk a chance to settle in his innards, otherwise he'll be screaming with the colic come nightfall."

Robyn chuckled. "Annie, I promise you, he won't get colic and I want to keep him with me. We can rest very comfortably sitting here by the fire together, enjoying each other's company. The baby likes being here, see? He's smiling."

Annie was clearly getting ready to point out that newborns never smile, when, without warning, William strode into the bedroom. He nodded to the nursemaid. "You may leave us," he said. "I will send for you when her ladyship needs you."

"Shall I take the baby, my lord?"

"Yes, of course."

Robyn's arms tightened around the baby, but she managed to speak quite calmly. "No, you will not take the baby, Annie. As I told you two minutes ago, I wish him to remain here with me. You may go."

Annie looked nervously toward William. He nodded briefly. "Of course, if the Lady Arabella wishes to keep her son with her, you may leave the baby in her care."

Annie curtsied and backed out of the room. Once William had endorsed the instruction, it seemed that she was perfectly satisfied to leave the baby, Robyn noted, feeling irritated. She was getting tired of the way the servants responded to William's slightest nod, while treating her like a moron who needed to be saved from her own folly.

"You look downright bad-tempered," she said to William, noting with perverse satisfaction that she spoke the absolute

truth. Her mood improved, and she flashed him a bright
smile. "My, my. What's happened to put you into such an
obvious temper?"

He glanced at her once, then turned away. "I understand
you were insufferably rude to Dr. Perrick this morning."

"Did he say so? Actually, in the circumstances, I thought
I was extraordinarily polite."

William frowned. "You informed him that you would not
drink his ridiculous potions and that you did not wish him to
act as physician for you or your children ever again. Is that
not so?"

"I did say that, and I'm impressed with my self-restraint,"
Robyn agreed cheerfully. "In retrospect, I've no idea how I
managed to get through our entire interview without once
telling the man that he is a pompous, incompetent idiot."

William looked at her in silence. For a moment she had
the oddest impression that he wanted to laugh. He cleared
his throat. "The doctor also told me that you plan to get
dressed tomorrow and go downstairs. I feel sure that in this,
at least, he must be mistaken."

Robyn smiled at him mockingly. "Aha, are you troubled
by the prospect of my escaping from this room, William, my
love? What will I find when I manage to get outside the bedroom door? I wonder. Electricity? Telephones? Even a fax
machine or two?"

"You will find your home," William said quietly. "Nothing more and nothing less. But please answer my question,
Arabella. I wish to know if Dr. Perrick has understood you
aright. Do you seriously contemplate leaving this bedchamber tomorrow morning?"

"Why yes, that's my plan. Do you have any objections,
my lord? Not that I plan to pay any attention to them, of
course."

"Most certainly I have objections. You are but eight days
removed from your lying-in. It would be preposterous to
speak of ending your period of confinement, even if you had
not suffered the additional injuries to your head. You are not
in a fit state to leave your sickbed, Arabella."

"This dream is becoming exceedingly tedious," Robyn
said, and even as she spoke, her stomach gave an odd little
kick of fright. When she was with William, he seemed so

real that she had to keep reminding herself that this *must* be a dream. Either that, or she was stark raving mad, and she preferred not to believe in her own madness.

This is a dream, she told herself and kissed the top of baby Zach's head. Maybe she could simply wish William away if she closed her eyes and concentrated hard.

"Arabella, what ails you? Are you in pain?" William's voice interrupted her reverie. Damn him! She'd been doing such a good job of mentally consigning him to oblivion.

She opened her eyes and glared at him. "What ails me is that I'm sick to death of being treated like an empty-headed nincompoop. I'm tired of this dream and I can't imagine a single good reason why I invented you. You're a macho nightmare, and I loathe macho men."

"Enough," William said tersely. "I cannot allow you to continually give voice to these ravings. For your own sake, if you cannot speak sensibly, you must learn not to speak at all—"

"You don't seriously believe you can order me to keep silent and expect me to obey?"

"You are my wife, Arabella, however much such a position may irk you, and you must face up to the responsibilities you assumed the day you decided to marry me."

"Wait, let me get this straight. You're saying that it's my wifely duty to lie in bed, doing nothing, preferably not speaking, despite the fact that I feel strong enough to get dressed and go downstairs?"

William looked frustrated. "No, I did not mean . . . That is to say, you mistake the degree of your strength—"

"Then let me discover my mistake for myself," she said. "I'm an adult woman, capable of making sensible decisions. I'll attempt to dress and go downstairs. If I'm exhausted, I'll come back to bed."

William looked at her, then smiled—a smile cold enough to raise goose bumps on Robyn's arms. "Ah," he said softly. "I see that I am being gauche. Forgive me for the slowness of my wits this morning."

"What the devil are you talking about now?"

He turned away and walked over to one of the windows. "Undoubtedly you have arranged an assignation with your lover and must needs go downstairs to speak with him. My clumsy concern for your health is destroying your plans."

"Oh, for heaven's sake! Of course I don't have plans for an assignation with my lover. Good grief, even a nymphomaniac wouldn't want to meet her lover a week after giving birth." Robyn stopped abruptly, alarmed at what she'd just said. In the heat of her argument with William, she'd again forgotten that this was a dream, and that his accusations were simply another figment of her overactive imagination.

William mistook the reason for her sudden silence. "You always sound most self-righteous when you are most guilty, my dear. The tactic worked for the first few years of our marriage, but the time has come for you to develop a fresh stratagem. Nowadays, your vehemence merely makes me suspicious."

Her subconscious was obviously determined to depict her as a bitchy blonde with overactive hormones—a startling contrast to her real-life, everyday personality. Why not go with the flow? Robyn thought. It was tantalizing to discover that her character within the context of this dream was so radically different from her true personality. She leaned back in the chair, instinctively shushing and cuddling the baby when he whimpered to protest her movement. Drawing in a deep breath, she asked William's back, "What makes you think I have a lover?"

He swung around, seeming momentarily transfixed by the sight of her hand, gently rubbing the baby's back. He brought his attention back to their conversation with a visible effort. "Why do I think you have a lover?" He shrugged. "Experience would suggest that it is inevitable. You always have a lover, or at least some poor potential victim caught in your toils and ready to succumb at the first friendly flash from your dazzling blue eyes."

"Is that how you were caught, William? With a flash from my dazzling blue eyes?"

"Not at all," he said coolly. "I was a far greater fool than most of my rivals. You did not have to catch me. I jumped headlong—willingly—into your claws."

"Did you get badly mauled?" she asked softly.

He kicked a log farther into the fire. "I cannot imagine what has provoked this sudden interest in the sorry history of our marriage, my lady. Suffice it to say that I am now impervious to your blandishments."

"We made a baby together less than nine months ago. Perhaps you are not quite as impervious as you would wish, my lord."

His mouth tightened. "What happened between us last April was a momentary aberration on my part. Do not count upon repeating that successful seduction scene ever again, my lady, for you will catch cold in your endeavors. Next time you find yourself carrying your lover's seed, you will not be able to conceal your indiscretion by luring me into your bed and pretending the child is mine."

Robyn was horrified. "William, you can't possibly believe I would behave so badly ... For goodness' sake, this baby is your child! Look at him, for God's sake. I've never seen a newborn who looks so much like his father!"

"Such vehemence, my lady, when we both know any resemblance to me is purely coincidental." William's voice was coolly mocking. "Change your tactics, my dear, or perhaps save them for Captain Bretton. He is your latest victim, is he not? A successful renewal of old conquests. For myself, I am no longer susceptible."

"The baby *is* your child," Robyn said tersely. She cradled Zach in her arms, rubbing her cheek against his soft skin, frightened and furious to think that his own father was rejecting him.

She felt William's gaze on her, but she refused to meet his eyes, concentrating instead on Zach's chubby cheeks and feather-soft hair. "This argument achieves little," he said finally. "If you are concerned that your son will be thrust out penniless into the world, you may set those fears at rest. I have never wished to punish your children for the sins of their mother."

"Our children," she corrected automatically. "You always call them *my* children but they are our children, not only mine but yours as well."

As soon as she spoke, she knew that she was lying. The twins looked very much like their father, but she realized with sudden, devastating certainty that Clementina was not William's child—couldn't possibly be his child.

Clementina had brown eyes.

She dropped her gaze from William to baby Zach and shook her head, feeling woozy with the absurdity of her own thoughts. What the heck was wrong with her? This was a dream, why in the world was she arguing with William about the parentage of their nonexistent children? Certainly there was no reason for her to worry about Clementina's eye color. If she wanted, she could change the child's eyes from brown to blue with a flip of her own subconscious. She could certainly ignore genetics or any other scientific fact if she chose.

"Your face is unexpectedly revealing, my lady. You are looking most unusually guilty."

There was absolutely no reason to tell him about Clementina's eyes. Even in a dream, she didn't have to confirm William's darkest suspicions. "I'm not looking guilty, my lord, merely tired. I feel very tired."

That, at least, was true. She was tired of dreaming this dream, tired of being trapped inside a fantasy world that felt too real for comfort. She wanted, desperately, to wake up.

She looked at William, annoyed to feel her heart beating faster than usual, and even more annoyed to feel her stomach clenching in a sensation close to sexual desire. It occurred to her suddenly that she would only be able to break free of her dream if she refused to accept the limits her mind was imposing. Of course! If she confronted William with the scientific truth about Clementina's genetic makeup, the fantasy of her eighteenth-century dreamworld would be shattered, and she would wake up.

"I don't have to worry about hurting your feelings," she muttered, staring at William. "You're a projection of my own imagination, so you must know as well as I do that Clementina isn't your own flesh and blood."

When she thought about it, that statement didn't altogether make sense. William was looking at her in stunned, blank silence, and she shrugged her shoulders, impatient with the dream, with herself, with him. "Dammit, William, stop staring at me like that. You must know Clemmie isn't your daughter. She has brown eyes, for God's sake!"

The fateful words were out. She waited hopefully to wake up. Nothing happened. The room didn't dissolve, to be replaced by a hospital bed, and William didn't move. "Brown eyes?" he repeated at last. "I do not believe I understand you, my lady."

"Of course you do," she snapped. "You're a projection of my subconscious, which means you know everything I know. And that means you understand simple genetic theory. You have blue eyes. I have blue eyes. Blue eyes are a recessive gene, so that it's physically impossible for two blue-eyed parents to produce children with any eye color except shades of blue. Brown-eyed parents can sometimes produce blue-eyed offspring if they both carry a recessive blue gene, but it's genetically impossible the other way around."

"Jen-eticlee?" he said, stumbling over the word.

"Yeah, genetically." Robyn could feel her nerves winding tight with fear and frustration. "William, stop looking so damn blank! You know what I'm talking about. Mendel and his experiments with pea pods, or sweet peas, or whatever the heck he studied way back in the nineteenth century. And then in the twentieth century we discovered DNA ... the chain of life ... and all that other good stuff."

William stared into the fire. "Many children do not have the same color eyes as their parents," he said.

Robyn's thin hold on her patience snapped. "Stop it!" she shouted. "I want this farcical situation to end! Give it up, William. Whoever Clemmie's father was, you can count on the fact that it wasn't you. The guy had brown eyes, and passed on his dominant brown-eyed gene to Clementina."

"So, it seems that Clementina is not my daughter." William's face gave no clue as to how this news had affected him. "Tell me, my lady, why do you feel this sudden need to confess that your daughter is no offspring of mine? I do not understand your purpose. You have sworn to me, over and over again, that you have taken no lovers since our marriage. I have never believed you, of course, but your teary-eyed pleas for my faith and trust have been one of the more frequent elements of your role as misunderstood and neglected wife. Now today, for no reason that I can discern, you choose to confess that you have been unfaithful."

"Maybe I'm tired of lying." Robyn rose to her feet, her arms tightening around the solid warmth of baby Zach's body. "Oh, God, I want this crazy charade to end! Why can't

I wake up, dammit! I'm tired of being trapped in a room with a two-hundred-year-old lunatic!"

William tugged at an embroidered bell rope that hung by the fireplace. Without saying a word, he swept Robyn into his arms, carrying both her and the baby over to the bed. "You need to sleep," he said, settling her against the pillows. "Trust me, my lady, you will feel better shortly. The blow to your head has doubtless affected your mind more than any of us had realized. Your speedy return to apparent health has deceived us as to the extent of your mental weakness. Give me the baby, Arabella, and I will send Mary to you with a sleeping draft. You must rest, and gather the strength that will allow your wits to return to you in full measure."

She was perfectly willing to sleep, because if she slept, then she could hope that she would wake up back in the real world, back in the hospital where she undoubtedly lay, surrounded by tubes, IVs, and beeping monitors. But the baby seemed so real to her that she hesitated to hand him over to William. She didn't want to wake up tomorrow and discover that her husband had murdered her baby. The emotions she felt in this dream were too vivid, too intense, to risk courting that sort of grief.

"This baby is your child," she said urgently, struggling to sit up in the enveloping softness of the feather mattress. "Don't hurt him, William, will you? Promise me you won't hurt our baby?"

"I am not a monster, Arabella. I would not seek revenge for your infidelities upon a helpless infant."

She realized that he had not accepted the baby as his, but for some reason, she believed absolutely that he wouldn't hurt the child. Relief sent her collapsing back against the pillows just as Mary came into the room, panting slightly.

"You rang for me, my lord?"

"Her ladyship is exhausted," William said. "She needs to sleep. You may give her some laudanum to help her rest."

"Yes, my lord. Do you wish me to send for Annie to take the baby, my lord?"

"I will take him to the nursery myself."

"Yes, my lord."

He walked quickly toward the bedroom door without saying another word. Robyn scarcely knew herself why she called him back. "William!"

He hesitated, then swung around. "Yes, my lady?"

"The new baby has blue eyes," she said.

William didn't respond, then he smiled bitterly. "Indeed he has. What a fortunate coincidence for all of us."

"You will catch your death, my lady." Mary had been repeating variations on the same theme for close to an hour. She had watched dourly as sweating maidservants poured copper jugs of boiling water into the porcelain tub set in front of the fire, and by now her mouth was pinched tight with disapproval.

Robyn ignored the maid's warning, just as she had ignored a dozen or so earlier ones. She smiled at the young girl who had brought up the final jug of hot water. "Thank you. Your name is Sukie, isn't it?"

The girl nodded, bobbing into a curtsy. "Yus, m'lady. I be Sukie."

"Leave the jug in the hearth near the fire, will you, Sukie? That way, it'll keep warm. I need to wash my hair."

The girl gasped and Mary paled. "My lady, the wound on your scalp—"

"Is entirely scabbed over. Mary, no more arguments. I can't stand to feel this dirty any longer. I'm taking a bath whether you approve or not. Could you please fetch me some soap?"

Mary bent and whispered something into Sukie's ear. At this precise moment, Robyn didn't much care what. Sukie nodded, and backed hurriedly from the room. Robyn sighed. Probably another story about her ladyship's insanity would soon be doing the rounds of the servants' quarters.

She pulled herself up short, frightened by the ease with which she kept falling into the trap of behaving as if her surroundings were real, and she was truly living this strange life from the past. *Watch it, kid,* she warned herself. *Remember there are no servants' quarters. Sukie has no existence once she's out of your sight.*

Imagined or not, the hot bath felt heavenly. Robyn soaped every inch of her skin, refusing to be embarrassed by Mary's hovering presence, and refusing equally to listen to the maid's litany of dire warnings about the consequences of immersing her ladyship's recently pregnant body in such unseemly quantities of hot water.

In the end, Robyn had to give up on the project of washing her hair. Mary flatly refused to help, and lacking the strength of lift the heavy copper jug, Robyn could do no more than soap the ends of her long blond hair and rinse them out in the tub water. Lathering her soft white skin and feeling the alien contours of her body beneath her fingertips was a frightening experience. Even more frightening was the realization that her slender, blue-veined hands had already become familiar to her. Too familiar. She wondered how long it would be before she totally lost her capacity to distinguish between dream and reality.

The bath tired her more than she cared to admit, and she was quite glad to submit to Mary's determination to wrap her in a huge linen sheet and pat her dry in front of the fire. She was even glad to put on her silk-lined robe and sip a cup of tea before tackling the task of getting dressed. Her spirits sank even further when a grim-faced Mary started to carry out layer upon layer of starched petticoats, bodices, underblouses, sleeves, stomachers, and satin overskirts. Robyn thought wearily that her subconscious was impressive. She'd had no idea how much information her brain had stored away about female articles of clothing, as worn in the middle of the eighteenth century in England.

"Your shift, m'lady." Mary eased the thin linen garment over Robyn's head, and shook out the heavy lace frills that hung from the sleeves, ending two or three inches above her wrists. The neckline of the shift cut off in the middle of Robyn's breasts, and the hem reached only to midthigh.

"Where are my pantalets?" she asked, scanning the pile of clothes on the bed. She willed her subconscious to make a pair of panties appear, even if in the guise of an old-fashioned, long-legged garment.

Her subconscious failed to cooperate. Mary looked utterly blank. "Panderlets, my lady? What be they?"

Robyn sighed. "Don't worry about it. My subconscious is obviously into authenticity today." She knew from a college course in historical costume that women had gone naked beneath their layers of petticoats until very late in the eigh-

teenth century. Damn! If she hadn't known that fact, would
Mary have been able to produce a pair of panties? Why was
her subconscious so fixated on the need to make this dream
totally authentic?

"Be you ready for your stockings, my lady?"

She sighed. "Yes, I am. I guess."

Mary soon had her tied into a pair of knee-high white
knitted stockings, which she covered with three layers of
stiffened, ruffled petticoats. Robyn hadn't been standing for
more than ten minutes and already her legs ached from the
weight of all the material she was carrying around. No wonder William had warned her that getting dressed was an exhausting business. This wasn't exactly the equivalent of
slipping into a pair of sweatpants, topped by a cozy sweater.

"I have your new stays, my lady. I sewed on the lace
whilst you wus laid up from birthing the babe." Mary held
out an ominous-looking white corset, and Robyn shuddered.
She had a sudden memory of talking with Zach in his apartment about the horrors of the old-fashioned corset, and she
felt a surge of such aching loneliness that her throat tightened and she knew she was only the blink of an eye away
from tears. Dear God, what did she need to do in order to escape from this nightmare and find herself back in secure, familiar surroundings, with Zach waiting to welcome her?
Cradling her arms around her waist, she faced the fear that
was growing stronger with every passing minute: maybe she
wasn't going to wake up. Maybe the bullet had damaged her
brain so badly that she was condemned to spend the rest of
her life trapped in this eerie fantasy world.

"M'lady?" Mary sounded hesitant. "M'lady? Is something
wrong? You've gone horrible pale, like."

"No, I'm fine." Robyn forced herself to smile. "But I
think I'll skip the corsets ... the stays today."

"I don't understand, m'lady. What has skipping to do with
your stays? Skipping is a game for children, m'lady."

"Right, I guess it is." Robyn drew in a deep breath.
"Okay ... I mean ... very well, tell me the worst. How tight
are you planning to tie those things?"

"Don't worry, m'lady, I'll tie 'em ever so tight." Mary
beamed, pleased to have given the right answer at last. She
hummed under her breath as she slipped the straps of the

corset over Robyn's shoulders. "Is any of the stays poking into you, m'lady?"

"Yes, all of them."

Mary fussed and fidgeted until Robyn agreed that none of the steel spines was hurting her. In truth, the corset was well padded and cupped the underside of her breasts so that it was nowhere near as uncomfortable as she'd imagined.

"You hold on to the bedpost and I'll tug and pull till you're squeezed right back to your proper shape, m'lady. We can do it, I know we can."

"Straight out of *Gone With the Wind*," Robyn murmured to herself. "Any minute now I can pretend to be Vivien Leigh playing Scarlett O'Hara and throw a temper tantrum because my waist isn't eighteen inches anymore. *Ouch!*" She let out a yell as Mary gave a final brisk tug to the corset strings.

"Stop, for heaven's sake!" Robyn protested, all thoughts of Scarlett vanishing in a gasp of pain. "Good grief, Mary, you'll crush my ribs if you tighten those laces any more."

"No, m'lady, don't worry. The ribs in these stays be made of finest steel. They won't break no matter what." She tugged again, and Robyn could feel the breath squeezing out of her lungs.

"Enough," she insisted. "Mary, no more."

The maidservant frowned. "I don't know as how you'll be able to fit into your gown, m'lady, with your stays that loose. Although you lost some flesh what with the birthing fever and all."

Loose? This corset was supposed to be loose? No wonder women in the eighteenth century had died young, Robyn thought hysterically. The effort to breathe when stuffed into their tight stays undoubtedly killed them off in short order.

Mary removed the muslin wrap from the gown lying on the bed and held it up for Robyn's inspection. "I chose the blue silk, m'lady. I know 'tis one of your favorites."

Robyn stared at the silvery-blue dress in silence. Mary rustled the peach-colored flounce anxiously, smoothing out a nonexistent crease in one of the velvet ribbons. "I can fetch another gown, should you prefer it, my lady."

Robyn swallowed hard. "No, no. That one will be fine." In truth, she didn't think she had ever seen a more stunningly beautiful gown. A tiny part of her couldn't help thinking how much fun it would be to wear such a fabulous outfit.

"Very good, my lady." Mary slipped the dress over her head. It fell in soft, shimmering folds of satin over the stiffened, starched layers of her petticoats.

"The bodice, my lady." With skillful fingers, Mary attached the tabs of the bodice to the matching tabs on the skirt, creating the illusion of a one-piece gown.

"The sleeves, my lady." Mary adjusted the blue satin sleeves over the linen sleeves of Robyn's shift, leaving the lace ruffles of the shift clearly visible beneath the outer sleeve, and fixing the outer sleeves in place with a combination of gold-tipped pins and tiny ribbons.

"Your dressing cape, my lady." Mary wrapped a full, waist-length cloak of white linen over Robyn's shoulders. "If you would sit at the dressing table, my lady, I will paint your face and dress your hair."

"I'm not going to bother with makeup ... paint ... today," Robyn said. She suspected that if she once sat down on the embroidered damask stool in front of the dressing table, she would be too exhausted to get up again and go downstairs. And she was determined to leave the bedroom before fatigue overcame her. She cherished the hope that the moment she stepped out into the corridor, the dreamworld would vanish. If not that, then at least she hoped to find another mirror. She clung to the belief that if she looked into a full-length mirror, she would see the old, redheaded Robyn she knew rather than the blond, blue-eyed Lady Arabella everyone insisted she had become. Robyn felt she had good grounds for hope—it was highly suspicious that William had ordered the mirrors removed from her room. Surely that meant he was afraid she would see her own familiar image reflected back to her instead of the alien image of Lady Arabella? And once she mentally reclaimed her own body, Robyn was confident the dream would end.

She rubbed her aching forehead, and Mary picked up one of the silver-backed brushes from the dressing table. "Does your head hurt, my lady?"

"Just a little."

"I have to pin your hair up, my lady. You cannot leave

your bedchamber with your hair hanging loose about your shoulders."

"You're right, but chose a simple style, will you? The cut on my scalp is still quite sore."

"Yes, m'lady." The maid brushed gently, her expert fingers making short work of the snarls. There was no mirror, of course, but Robyn could feel the expertise with which Mary swirled her long hair into a soft knot at the nape of her neck, and then pinned it into place.

"I be finished, my lady. I have done the best that I can. There has been no time to heat the curling irons."

Robyn heard the note of hesitation in the maid's voice, the familiar undercurrent of fear, and she hated knowing she was the cause of it. She swung around on the stool, resting her hand gently on Mary's arm. "You've done a wonderful job, I'm sure," she said. "Besides, everyone knows that my head was cut open. No one will blame you if my hair doesn't look quite as stylish as usual. Certainly not me."

Mary's eyes were watchful, uncertain. "You are very good, my lady. Thank you, my lady."

The maid's gratitude was almost as bad as her fear. "I'm not good at all," Robyn said. She stood up and shook out her skirts, mentally preparing for action. "Time to sally forth. I wonder what I'm going to find out there in the hallway?"

Chapter 8

ROBYN stepped out of the bedroom, heart pounding hard and fast with anticipation. Feeling very much like Dorothy in *The Wizard of Oz,* she squeezed her eyes tightly shut and wished with all her might to wake up in familiar surroundings. After thirty seconds or so, she opened her eyes and glanced around, slowly expelling the air from her lungs as she fought to control her disappointment.

Nothing had changed. She was still in an old-fashioned hallway, still wearing the same satin gown, still laced into stays that pinched if she moved too quickly. Robyn pressed her hand against her mouth, clamping her teeth together so that she wouldn't scream or cry out. She had been counting heavily on waking up as soon as she left Arabella's bedroom, but it seemed that escaping into the hallway hadn't broken the spellbinding power of her dream.

What if this isn't a dream?

She couldn't prevent the terrifying thought from taking shape in her mind. What if she had gone mad, and was hearing conversations that weren't really taking place, and seeing people who weren't really there?

What if the bullet shot into her brain had thrown her into some hideous time warp, and she was living the life of Lady Arabella Bowleigh, nearly two hundred and fifty years in the past?

"No!" Robyn realized she had spoken aloud at the same moment she realized she was shaking from head to toe. Good grief, if she ever started to believe she was trapped in the past, imprisoned inside another woman's body, she might as well accept that she had gone mad. "Get a grip on yourself, kid," she muttered. "Okay, so you didn't wake up when you left Arabella's room. No big deal. Just make yourself a

new plan. It's up to you to decide how to end this dream."
What should she try next? Would going downstairs break the
spell and allow her to wake up?

Robyn looked around, registering the perfect eighteenth-
century ambience of her surroundings. But, of course, that
didn't mean much. She knew enough about antique furniture
and decor that her mind was perfectly capable of providing
her with an authentic setting. The corridor looked like a
dozen other hallways she had visited in historic manor
houses, with paneled walls, a white plaster ceiling, and a
polished wooden floor covered by a center strip of patterned
carpeting. The staircase itself was an exquisite period piece,
typical of the late seventeenth century, and gorgeously decorated with painted panels of cherubs, mythical beasts, and
scenes from Greek legends. It would fetch a small fortune on
the international antiques market—except that it existed only
in her imagination.

"Mamma, Mamma! You is all pwetty again!" Clementina
hurtled down the stairs from the third floor, with Sukie running behind her. "I am pwetty, too! Look at me!"

The maid grabbed Clementina's sash just before the child
careened into her mother. "Miss Clemmie, remember your
manners!" she hissed.

Clementina pouted, but she skidded to a halt two inches
from the edge of Robyn's huge skirts and dipped into a
curtsy. "Good day, Mamma. I hope you is feeling better. I
have been a good girl. I di'n't get my dwess dirty."

Robyn laughed, delighted to have her gloomy thoughts interrupted. She bent down so that she was almost at eye level
with Clementina and gave the child a quick hug. "I'm glad
to see you," she said. "Very glad. I was just going to take a
walk around the house. Would you like to come with me?"

"Downstairs?" Clementina asked. Her hazel eyes opened
wide with wonder. "You mean I can come downstairs wiv
you?"

"I will take her back to the nursery, my lady." Sukie
bowed her head. "I'm sorry she got away from me, my lady.
Sometimes she do move so fast, I can scarce catch up with
her."

"There's no need to apologize." Robyn was heartily sick
of cringing servants and cowed children. "I'm glad to spend

some time with my daughter. I'll take care of her, so you can have a rest from chasing her for a while." She held out her hand and Clementina took it after a split second of hesitation. "All right, Clemmie, where shall we go first?"

"To the kitchens!" Clementina exclaimed. "We can play wiv Polly. She is fat."

"Is Polly the cook?" Robyn asked, and knew she had guessed wrong when she saw Sukie stare.

"Polly is a cat," Clementina explained patiently. "My old mamma—the one who was here before you—doesn't like cats, but I like Polly 'cos she is soft and furry. Do you like cats, Mamma?"

It was disconcerting to hear the casual way in which Clemmie accepted the disappearance of one mother, and the substitution of another. Perhaps she was so close to infancy that she saw with the clear-sighted vision of a soul not yet tainted by subterfuge. Robyn looked like the missing Lady Arabella, but Clementina instinctively recognized—and accepted—that a different person lived within the familiar body of her "old Mamma."

"I like cats and dogs, too," Robyn said, and felt the waves of disbelief emanating from Sukie. All right, so Lady Arabella didn't like pets, Robyn thought. Well, too bad. The woman sounded like a totally obnoxious person, who didn't deserve to have a daughter as cute as Clementina and a beautiful son like Zach.

Robyn pulled her thoughts to an abrupt full stop, afraid of the direction they were once again taking. "Come on," she said to Clementina, helping the little girl to hop down the stairs on wobbly, pudgy legs. "Let's go and meet Polly and ask her why she's so fat. Has she been eating too much of Cook's roast beef, do you think?"

Clementina giggled. "She eats mice, Mamma. That's why she lives in the kitchen. To eat up all the mice. And the rats, too, if they aren't too big."

Mice *and* rats in the kitchen? Robyn decided to change the direction of the conversation. "Let's ask cook to make us a special treat for our lunch," she said. "What would you like best of all?"

"Spun sugar swans!" Clementina jumped up and down in excitement. "Sugar swans, and custard tarts and syllabubs."

Robyn chuckled. "Whoa, steady on! If you eat all those desserts, you'll get as fat as Polly."

"My ozzer mamma said I was pudding faced. Is that the same as being fat?"

Robyn squashed an irrational impulse to find the missing Lady Arabella and inform her she was a rotten mother. "No, of course you're not fat," she told Clementina. "In my opinion, you're just right. And your face is the perfect shape for a little girl who is three."

"I is nearly four." Clementina glanced thoughtfully at Robyn. "I'm glad my old mamma went away," she confided. "You smile a lot more than my ozzer mamma."

Robyn looked down at the upturned face of the little girl, swallowing over the lump that had suddenly appeared in her throat. She bent down and put her arms around Clemmie's shoulders. Quite apart from the hazel-brown eyes, the child's features bore no resemblance to William's. So who was her father? Robyn wondered. She wished she'd taken possession of Arabella's memories as well as the wretched woman's body, then she would know who the child's father was. It was so frustrating to be thrust into a situation where she could lay claim to only a tiny fraction of the facts.

Chills feathered down Robyn's spine as she realized what she was thinking. Furious with herself, she pushed the crazy thoughts away. She might have been struck in the head by a bullet but she *wasn't* going to glide into madness. Not while she had the willpower left to prevent it.

Clementina patted her cheek. "Don't look sad, Mamma. We is going to have a lovely day."

Robyn nuzzled Clemmie's soft curls and gave up trying to understand what was happening to her. "Yes," she said. "We're going to have a lovely day. Listen! Did you hear a cat meow? I think it's time for you to introduce me to Polly."

In the space of four exhausting days, with the twins and Clementina romping happily at her heels, Robyn explored Starke Manor from attics to cellar. The twins were eager to lead her into tiny rooms under the eaves that she might otherwise have missed, and she even breached the sacrosanct precincts of William's library, but she still found no trace of a piped water supply, or electricity, or a phone, or a fridge, or a TV, or any of the other appliances that kept life functioning in the late twentieth century. In fact, the harder she looked, the more Robyn was forced to concede that there wasn't a single item anywhere in the house that looked as if it had been produced after the middle of the eighteenth century. Mary had claimed they were living in the year 1746, and Robyn could find nothing in the house that gave the lie to the servant's outrageous statement. Her subconscious, she thought with wry humor, was determined not to let her slip into anachronisms.

She did find several mirrors, however, but they provided no comfort. All of them reflected back the disquieting image of a willowy blonde, with a fragile, delicate neck, and huge, worried blue eyes. Robyn recognized the woman who appeared in the mirrors all too well—she was the Lady Arabella Bowleigh, the woman in the Gainsborough portrait hanging in Zach's living room. Seeing the fair perfection of her new features, Robyn would never have believed she could yearn with such intensity for the return of her once-despised red curls, not to mention her snub nose and freckles.

She was nursing baby Zach, and struggling to make sense of her discoveries, when Mary came into the bedroom, a burgundy satin gown draped over her arm and a note in her hand. She held out the note to Robyn. "From his lordship, my lady."

Robyn managed to unfold the heavy, cream-colored paper without causing any interruption in baby Zach's eager suckling.

My Lady, the note said in exquisite black-inked copperplate. *I wish that you will join me at dinner today so that we may celebrate your rapid return to health and strength. We shall dine at three. Ever Yr. Obedient Servant, Yr. Husband, William Bowleigh.*

"The master has ordered dinner to be put back an hour so that you may have time to complete your toilette, my lady. I finished sewing the skirt of this gown back together so as you could wear it, if you wish. It cleaned very well, and looks as good as new."

Dinner at Starke Manor seemed to be served in the early

afternoon rather than at night, but Robyn was already
hungry—nursing the baby always left her feeling
ravenous—and she squashed her instinctive impulse to refuse William's peremptory invitation. Since she couldn't
seem to wake up from this dream, why not spend an hour or
so pretending that she was dining with an eighteenth-century
aristocrat in his country manor? She laid the drowsy baby in
his cradle, which she had ordered brought from the nursery,
and smiled at the maid. "Okay ... I mean ... very well.
Baby Zach's changed and fed, so I'm ready for my bath."

"The water's being brought, my lady." Mary sounded resigned. After days of argument, the two of them had reached
an uneasy compromise. Mary no longer protested her mistress's insane obsession with soap and water. Robyn no
longer protested the layers of petticoats and the hours, literally, that it took to lace, tie, pin, and sew her into each elaborate outfit.

Their harmony survived the bath and the usual battle over
her stays, but it broke down when Robyn saw the bodice she
was supposed to wear. A splendid affair, decorated with ro-
settes of pink velvet ribbon, the neckline ended at the same
height as her shift. In other words, it cut off smack in the
middle of her breasts. A deep breath, or a too sharp turn,
would leave the neckline—a misnomer if ever Robyn had
heard one—below her nipples.

"But, my lady, you cannot put a kerchief across your
bosom!" Mary wailed. " 'Tis so ... so *provincial.*"

"I am provincial," Robyn said, with grim humor. "Posi-
tively colonial in fact. Mary, I refuse to eat dinner wondering all the time if my bosom and my dress are going to part
company! Get me a strip of lace if the idea of a kerchief of-
fends you."

Mary shook her head. "I don't understand you, my lady.
You're not the same person since your accident, and that's a
fact. You used to like wearing a low-cut bodice. You wanted
all the gentlemen to admire your breasts, nipples an' all.
Why, you used to paint your nipples carmine red, same as
your lips—" She broke off, hurrying toward the closet before Robyn could say anything. "Beggin' your ladyship's
pardon for speaking out of turn, my lady."

"You have nothing to apologize for," Robyn said, her

heart thumping against her rib cage. She laughed, but the sound was brittle even to her own ears. "Maybe I am a different person since the accident, who knows?"

"A kinder person," Mary said, "even though your wits be gorn beggin'." She stepped back, hand clapped over her mouth, eyes wide with fear.

Robyn would have laughed if she hadn't been ominously close to tears. She held out her hand. "Oh, come on, I'm not going to eat you, or even beat you, for that matter. Give me the piece of lace, Mary." The maid obliged, and Robyn tucked it into the neckline of her gown. "There. How does that look?"

"Very well, my lady. Most flattering. Here is your fan, my lady." Mary dipped into a new curtsy with every sentence.

"Thank you. And if you curtsy one more time, I really will throw a hairbrush at you."

"Yes, m'lady." Mary stopped herself in the midst of a knee bend. She straightened and ducked her head in an awkward little bob. "Sorry, m'lady," She sneaked a quick glance at Robyn. "Mayhap 'tis lucky for me I have your hairbrush in the pocket of my apron."

Robyn laughed. "Good heavens, Mary, did you actually make a joke?"

The maid flushed, but didn't answer, and Robyn decided not to push the issue. She flared open the fan, gasping when she saw it fully extended. The ivory sticks were carved into an exquisite lacy pattern, but it was the painting on the pink silk fan itself that took her breath away. She was accustomed to seeing fans that were faded by a hundred or so years of use and storage. The brilliant colors and gleaming gold decoration on this fan were all vibrantly new, and she sighed with pleasure at the sheer, frivolous appeal of its painted butterflies, strutting peacocks, and dancing ladies.

"I can get you another fan if you prefer, my lady, but that one matches the ribbons on your dress."

"This one is lovely," Robyn said. The little clock on the mantelpiece chimed the hour and she closed the fan. "Three o'clock already. I must hurry."

"Yes, my lady. Lord knows, you would never wish to keep the master waiting."

Robyn swung around. "What does that mean? Wait, let

me guess. Before the accident, Lady Arabella always kept her husband waiting, right?"

Mary stared at the pile of petticoats on the bed. "You always kept everyone waiting," she said after a long pause.

"Did I?" Robyn touched the maid lightly on her arm. "That took courage," she murmured. "Thank you."

Mary was startled into looking up. "Whatever for, my lady?"

Robyn smiled ruefully. "For telling me the truth, even though it was unpleasant."

Mary shuffled her feet. "You're welcome, my lady."

William was seated by the fire, reading a book, when Robyn entered the drawing room. He rose at once to his feet, setting the book on a small boulle table and sweeping into a bow. "My lady, what a pleasant surprise! You are not only on time, but looking ravishing as well. Indeed, I cannot recall when you appeared more splendid."

His compliments pleased Robyn more than she wanted to admit. Having spent the past half hour berating the maid for her endless curtsies, Robyn wasn't quite sure why she decided to sink into a deep, formal curtsy herself. She was surprised at how smoothly she dipped into the correct position, even more surprised to find that she instinctively waited in her kneeling position, head bowed, skirts cascading around her in a billow of rose-trimmed burgundy satin.

William crossed the room and extended his hand to raise her up. As if the muscles of her body were working to a preordained pattern, Robyn flicked open her fan, fluttered it in front of her face, and peeped flirtatiously over the silken edge. "Thank you, my lord," she murmured.

William's eyes gleamed with mocking appreciation. "Magnificent, my dear. I never fail to marvel at the perfection with which you convey that impression of blushing shyness."

Robyn snapped the fan shut. "For centuries women have been taught to simper," she said, strung by his cynicism—and the fact that it was justified. "Do you wonder if it becomes second nature to us? Look at your own children and you can see them learning the rules to perfection. George and Freddie are encouraged to romp around outside and get up to all kinds of mischief, whereas Clementina is confined to the house and taken care of by nursemaids who worry only about her clothes and how neatly her sash is tied. When she's trying to make friends with me, all she can think of to say is that I am pretty."

"She is an intelligent child," William said coolly. "She has learned well how to please you."

Robyn flushed with frustration. "Tell me something, my lord. Do you dislike me as much as it appears, or am I imagining the venomous undertones in everything you say to me?"

She was glad to see that she had startled him, even if not enough to strip away his habitual mask of ironic courtesy. He recovered quickly, and bowed low over her hand, not quite kissing the tips of her fingers. "My lady, how can you accuse me of such an ungallant emotion? You know I am a slave to your extraordinary beauty."

"Right. I can tell I'm a real favorite with you."

William looked at her, and for a moment his mask slipped and she saw puzzlement in his gaze. "Let us not destroy the pleasure of our first dinner together since your accident," he said at last. "Why do we not put the past behind us and simply agree that we are going to enjoy each other's company over the next hour or so?"

"A charming reply, my lord, except that you didn't answer my question. No matter. You may take me into dinner and entertain me with witty epigrams about the current political situation, or maybe the latest London plays, and I will flutter my fan and pretend to be lost in admiration of your superior masculine wisdom."

"Let us not strain your powers of acting," William said dryly. "You do not share my views on either plays or politics."

Robyn spoke without stopping to think. "Frankly, I'd be surprised if Arabella had any political views, other than the inalienable right of the aristocracy to behave exactly as it pleases and be damned to the consequences."

"It is the duty of all ranks, however noble, to obey the King and honor their obligations to society," William said. He looked so self-righteous that Robyn wondered if she had really heard a faint note of mockery in his voice. She

watched as he cast a swift glance toward the lackeys stationed in pairs at either end of the room, then turned back to
offer her his arm, face wiped clean of all expression.

"Are you ready to go into dinner now, my dear? I believe
that the chef has prepared several of your special favorites."
He nodded toward one of the lackeys, who immediately
flung open the double doors leading into the dining room. A
table was revealed, laden with covered silver chafing dishes
and platters of roasted meats.

No, she hadn't been imagining the subtle thread of mockery in his voice, Robyn decided, but she wondered why William felt the need to conceal his political views. Was it the
servants he worried about, or Lady Arabella? If it was the
servants, his reticence was surprising. He seemed perfectly
willing to discuss anything else, including the most intimate
details of their personal relationship.

Robyn mentally raked over her scanty knowledge of
eighteenth-century history as two white-wigged footmen as-
sisted her into a chair, and the majordomo himself began
serving the meal. If she remembered correctly, various com-
binations of European countries had been at war with each
other for most of the century. Other than the fact that England and France were always on opposite sides, and the
King of Prussia wanted to grab bits of the Austro-Hungarian
empire, Robyn couldn't remember who had fought whom, or
why. Even if she had been able to remember, foreign wars
hardly seemed a subject to set William's steel nerves jan-
gling. England in the eighteenth century enjoyed the most
liberal government of any country in Europe, and William
would have no reason to conceal his views on foreign policy
from his own servants.

"I see that you have acquired a taste for stewed calf's
brains," William remarked, interrupting her reverie. "The
chef will be pleased to learn that you have eaten so heartily."

"Stewed *what*?" Robyn—the woman who considered rare
steak an adventure in exotic dining—looked down at her
plate and realized that she had consumed several forkfuls of
a gray pulpy mound piled in the center of her plate. She
reached for her gilt wine goblet, swigged a hearty gulp of
sweet red wine, and managed to refrain from gagging.

"Could someone please take this plate away," she said

faintly, relieved when the footman hovering behind her chair instantly whisked the horrible mush away. For once, she appreciated the advantage of having swarms of servants waiting to indulge her every whim.

"Would you care for some buttered carrots?" William asked politely as the footman provided her with a clean silver plate. "I can recommend them."

Carrots seemed innocuous enough, and Robyn served herself generously. She was hungry, but she didn't want to risk more surprises of the calf-brain type. "Are there any potatoes?" she asked, deciding that the chef couldn't have done anything too dreadful to potatoes.

The well-trained servants made no sound, but she felt the electric current of shock that rippled through them, as if she had mentioned something unspeakably vulgar. William cleared his throat. "We . . . er . . . don't serve potatoes at the table, my dear."

"Why ever not?" she asked. "I distinctly remember that Sir Walter Raleigh brought them back to England from his first voyage to America. He presented a sack of them to Queen Elizabeth the First, and she died ages ago. So you know all about potatoes even if you are determined to pretend this is the year 1746."

A footman dropped a spoon, and the majordomo glared at him. Robyn saw the footman stare at her surreptitiously as he bent to pick up the spoon.

"We do, indeed, know all about potatoes," William said. He spoke soothingly, as if addressing an idiot, or the lunatic they all seemed to consider her. "I am most impressed by your knowledge of our nation's history, my dear. However, you must have forgotten that potatoes are not served at the table here in Starke Manor."

"I still don't understand why."

"Even the poorest laborers refuse to eat potatoes until their supplies of bread and cheese are completely exhausted. At Starke, we grow them only to feed the pigs during winter."

"What a waste!" Robyn took another swallow of wine that, so far, seemed far and away the best thing about dinner. "Well, at least I've found something useful to do tomorrow."

"And what is that, my dear?"

She smiled, mellow enough from the wine not to resent his patronizing tone. "I'll show the chef how to cook potatoes. He's going to be thrilled with all the wonderful new dishes he'll be able to prepare once I've given him a few lessons. Wait until you taste a baked potato topped with sour cream and chives and you'll regret all those crops that you've been wasting on the pigs."

William's eyes gleamed, whether with laughter or with alarm she wasn't quite sure. "My dear, I am thrilled by this burst of domestic enthusiasm on your part, but I must beg you to stay away from the chef. He has a very high opinion of his own dignity and would not, I fear, respond well to cooking lessons. Indeed, if you insist on entering his kitchen, he will undoubtedly return to France on the next available schooner."

Robyn shook her head. "No, he won't. Jean-Luc's threats are all Gallic hot air and no substance. Besides, he's in love with Sukie, and he has no interest whatsoever in leaving Starke."

William's blue eyes turned almost black with astonishment. "Jean-Luc is in love with Sukie?" he said. "And how, pray, did you acquire this astonishing piece of information?"

"Jean-Luc told me himself. He would like to be married at Christmas time, but there are still some problems to be worked out. Sukie wants the wedding to be in the local parish church and Jean-Luc, of course, is a Catholic."

"A definite dilemma. I am most curious to know how you advised him."

"I suggested that since there are no Catholic churches in England, and virtually no Catholic priests, there's not much point in agonizing over an abstract issue. He either marries Sukie in the local parish church, or he doesn't marry her at all. Theology doesn't really enter into the discussion."

"Dare one inquire how Jean-Luc responded to your most practical advice?"

Robyn chuckled. "He sputtered a great deal of outraged French and waved his hands a lot. But Sukie told me this morning that they're planning to meet with the vicar on Sunday to arrange for the calling of the banns."

William's gaze lingered on her smile, then his mouth tightened and he inclined his head in ironic acknowledgment. "Congratulations, my lady. It seems that your talent for persuading reluctant males to the altar has soared to new heights."

His words sliced into her, inflicting totally irrational pain. "You have no reason to sound bitter, my lord. From everything I've heard, you couldn't wait to walk down the aisle and claim me as your bride."

"You are right, my lady." William raised his glass in an ironic toast, but his eyes flashed ice-blue fire. "I claimed my hotly contested prize and have enjoyed eight years of marital bliss as my reward."

"Stop sounding so sorry for yourself," Robyn snapped. "It takes two to screw up a marriage, you know." She pushed back her chair, impatient with herself for feeling wounded by his snide comments. She wished his arrogant features didn't bear a haunting similarity to Zach's. That slight resemblance must be why she felt this crazy need to make peace with a man whose sensitivity level hovered somewhere between Neanderthal and Napoleonic.

She stormed across the room, the satisfying swish of her skirts helping to soothe her lacerated nerves. Two lackeys sprang forward to open the doors for her, but she declined their help with a quick shake of her head. "Thank you, but I really can twist a doorknob for myself." She left the dining room with a flourish.

William had been driving her to distraction, but as soon as she arrived in her bedroom she felt oddly restless. Baby Zach and Annie were both sleeping in front of the fire, and she had no desire to waken either of them. Dusk was closing in, but she wasn't tired, and the prospect of the long, empty evening yawned ahead of her. She was pacing the room when she heard the sound of footsteps marching down the hallway, and her stomach gave an odd little lurch of excitement. She swung around just as William flung open the door and strode into her bedroom.

The baby snuffled into his shawls but remained sleeping. Annie choked on a snore and woke up. "Leave us," William said to Annie, not even bothering to glance in her direction.

"Stay," Robyn said, her gaze locking defiantly with William's.

The maid, of course, obeyed her master, scuttling from the

room with her head bowed, but leaving Zach in his cradle. Robyn raised her chin defiantly, furious that she had laid herself open to Annie's snub, but she said nothing. She wouldn't demean herself by repeating her command to the nursemaid, and hell could freeze over before she would speak to William. She walked over to the window, deliberately turning her back on him.

She heard the door close, then his voice came from behind her, quiet and steady. "I owe you an apology," he said.

It was the last thing she'd expected to hear, and she turned around, staring at him in surprise. He shrugged. "Sometimes it seems that we cannot help but hurt each other, even when we do not wish to wound."

The lamps had not been lit and his face was in shadow. She wished, suddenly, that she could see his features more clearly, but the flames of the fire provided at best a fickle, flickering glow and his expression wasn't easy to decipher. He stood beside Zach's cradle, his gaze fixed on his son. She thought he looked unbearably sad, but that might have been no more than a fireside illusion.

"Did you ever love me, William?" she asked, not sure where the question sprang from but caring very much about his reply. "Truly love me, I mean, and not just lust after the beautiful, desirable body of Lady Arabella Bowleigh?"

He looked up, his eyes darkening with sudden understanding. "So that is your game," he murmured. " 'Zounds, my lady, I had not thought you would strive for so impossible a victory."

"I don't understand—"

"But I, my lady, understand you all too well."

"Great. I'm delighted to hear it. Because I've not the faintest idea what you're talking abou—"

He laughed softly. "Have you not? Then I will make my meaning absolutely clear. Do not aim so high, my lady, and your chances of success will be greater. It is just possible that you could one day inspire me with renewed lust for that delectable body of yours. But there is no chance in hell that I would ever again allow myself to crave possession of your heart."

Robyn had a temper to match her bright red hair. Her red hair had gone missing, but her temper was fully present, and in great functioning order. "Why you arrogant, self-important, macho hypocrite," she exploded. "If you didn't have such a good opinion of yourself, you might have noticed that you're not being offered my body or my heart, or any other part of me, for that matter."

William laughed mockingly. "Am I not?" He walked across the room and reached out his index finger, running it lightly from her throat to the center of her breasts. "If these luscious breasts of yours are not an offer, then I would like to know why your nipples are peeping out so enticingly from behind that veil of lace fichu. That was a clever idea, my lady. A hint of mystery is so much more appealing than a blatant display of your charms."

"That lace isn't there to entice you!" Robyn said furiously. "It's there because the neckline of this dress is too low!"

"Not too low, my lady. Let us say rather the perfect height for its purpose." Before she had any idea what he intended, William was running his fingers along the inside of her velvet-trimmed neckline, pushing gently downward. Lace and gown immediately parted company and Robyn's breasts sprang free.

For a moment neither of them moved, then William very slowly rasped his thumb across the tip of each nipple. "My compliments, my lady. As I said, the perfect height for its purpose."

Robyn wanted to tell him to go away, to stop making physical overtures that were entirely repugnant to her, but when she opened her mouth, the only sound that came out was a strangled gasp. She turned her head away, chagrined and angry, but William cupped her chin and forced her to look up at him.

"You offered, my lady, and I am taking. We neither of us have to like our bargain, but by God, you will look at me as we make the exchange. You will not fantasize that it is my brother who caresses you."

"I'm not thinking about your brother! Stop it, William! I ... want ... you ... to ... stop."

His thumb circled first one nipple, then the other, and all the time he stared deep into her eyes, watching her with cynical amusement, watching her desire intensify into full-scale arousal. "Say that again, my lady, and I may believe you, which would disappoint us both."

Robyn balled her hands into fists, as if that way she could regain her vanishing willpower. She drew in a deep breath. "I want you to stop touching me, right now this minute. Please, William."

The agonizing, wonderful caresses ceased with humiliating promptness. He stepped away from her, sweeping at once into an elaborate and ironic bow. "When next I can be of service in one of your ladyship's games, pray do not hesitate to summon me." He held up the lace fichu and smiled mockingly. "In the meantime, I believe I shall keep this, my lady. A fond memento of an evening that ended all too soon. Too soon for both of us, I'll wager."

Robyn finally regained her voice. "Go to hell," she said.

Chapter 9

DUSK was falling; the gardeners and outside laborers had long since packed away their tools. The inside servants were busy clearing away dinner or eating their own meal, and Robyn had seen William retreat to his library as soon as dinner ended. She drew in a deep breath. Time to leave. Escape from Starke Manor was never going to be easier than this.

The pretense that she was dreaming had been proving harder to maintain with every passing day. Yesterday, after William left her, Robyn had paced her bedroom for hours trying to make sense of a situation that defied reason. In the aftermath of William's kiss, her entire body had trembled with a potent mixture of frustration, fear, anger, and desire, creating a jumble of feelings too powerful to ignore. She acknowledged, finally, that she could no longer explain what was happening to her in terms of a dream. The illusion of a prosperous eighteenth-century manor house was too complete. The people of Starke—quite simply—were too real.

But if she wasn't dreaming, then what was happening to her? Robyn paced her room some more. She kicked the furniture, the shiny *new* eighteenth-century furniture. She cried, even prayed a little. In the end, she was left with no choice but to accept the impossible truth staring her in the face. If she wasn't dreaming, then she was truly *living* the life of Lady Arabella Bowleigh, wife of the Baron Starke, in the year of our Lord, 1746. And since wishing herself back into the 1990s had achieved nothing, it seemed that if she wanted to return to her own time, her own life, and her own body, she would have to take a more active role in catapulting herself back into the lost world of Robyn Delaney.

Her plan for escape was simple, and she hoped that sim-

plicity was in its favor. The transfer of her consciousness
into Lady Arabella's body seemed to have taken place right
after she was shot in the parking lot of Starke Manor. The
last thing she remembered was pitching forward onto the
hard ground in a pool of blood, a few feet from the ancient,
wrought-iron gates that marked the entrance to the Starke
Manor Hotel. By a bizarre twist of fate, it seemed that Lady
Arabella had fallen from her carriage and pitched forward
onto the ground in the same spot, at the same time—
although centuries earlier. Logically, if logic was the word to
use, Robyn could only conclude that a return to the precise
place where she and Lady Arabella had both suffered head
injuries was the course of action most likely to work a little
reverse magic. She was even willing to bang her head on the
ground again if unconsciousness was what it would take to
bring about a transfer through time into her own body.

Baby Zach presented the only major snag in her planning,
because she wasn't willing to leave him behind. Robyn had
worried about the baby all day, but she had no real choice.
Since she wasn't prepared to be separated from him, she
would have to bring him with her, and there was no point in
worrying about how his presence would affect her plans. No
point, either, in worrying about how William would feel
when he discovered that his wife and infant son had disappeared from the face of the earth.

She glanced down and checked the knots of the makeshift
linen sling that held baby Zach nestled against her ribs. Her
handiwork seemed secure, and Zach was sleeping peacefully, his fists scrunched into soft little balls against his face.
She couldn't resist giving him a quick kiss. Then, mouth
dry, heart pounding, she slid open the heavy sash window,
recoiling guiltily when the cords let out a raucous screech.

She huddled against the wall, palms pressed against the
rough plaster, waiting to be discovered. No one came. The
bustle of the house remained faint and distant, and her heartbeat slowly returned to normal. William had issued orders
that she was not to leave the house, but nobody expected her
to disobey those orders and she wasn't guarded, or even
closely watched.

She straddled the broad windowsill, hunching protectively
over Zach's tiny body. Stretching her legs to their limits left

her toes dangling at least three feet above the grassy mound outside the window. The air felt chill and dank, but the temperature hovered above freezing so the ground wasn't too hard. When she jumped, she would get muddy, but she wouldn't kill herself or the baby. Drawing another deep breath, she tightened her fur-lined cloak around Zach, hitched up her cumbersome skirts, and jumped out of the window.

She landed with more force than she'd expected and toppled onto her knees, unbalanced by the weight of the baby. The impact of the fall snatched her breath away and made Zach whimper, but neither of them was badly hurt. She scrambled to her feet and broke into a run. She was on the north side of the manor, and the entrance gates faced southeast, which meant that she needed to turn right at the first corner. The wind, salt-tanged and chill, sliced into her face with knife-edge sharpness, blowing the drizzle of misty rain against her cheeks. Her sense of urgency was so great that she scarcely felt either wind or rain. Holding her cloak over Zach's face, she fled across the grassy knoll, keeping to the shadow of trees and bushes. She was so close to freedom, she couldn't afford to have William see her now.

She had barely run three hundred yards when she had to double over to cut the stitch in her side. Her breath came in great shuddering gasps, and she felt as exhausted as if she'd attempted a ten-mile race. Her mind knew how to move her limbs and muscles in rhythmic, economical strides, but Lady Arabella's body had apparently never before been asked to move so fast or so far. Stumbling and gasping, Robyn made her way toward the shelter of a cluster of outbuildings.

She leaned against the damp stone wall, wondering if Lady Arabella's out-of-condition body was going to throw up from the minor exertion of running less than a half mile. Gradually the roaring in her ears faded and she realized she could hear horses snorting and neighing on the other side of the wall. She huddled under the thatched eaves, trying to figure out which would be the shortest and least wet route to the front gates. To her dismay, she realized that she had somehow taken a wrong turning. Instead of skirting the manor and ending up by the front gates, she had rounded a courtyard and ended up at the back of the house, near the stables.

She was on the point of unlatching the stable door and seeking a few moments of warmth and dryness when she was stopped by the sound of gruff male voices. Creeping to a lead-paned window, she peered inside. A young lad, clad in the homespun, eighteenth-century garments she'd come to expect, was sitting on an upturned keg, polishing harness. An older man lounged comfortably on a pile of hay, covered with sacking. Belching richly after a long swallow from the wooden mug he held, the older man wiped foam from his mouth with the back of his hand.

" 'Tis good news about the Dalrymples, lad, and that's a fact." His voice carried clearly through a crack in the lead pane window.

"Aye. Happen they had some gold put by that none o' us did know aught of."

The old man banged his mug against his thigh in derision. "They Dalrymples don't have a penny to scratch with. You knows that better 'n most, my lad. You'd 'a' bin in a pretty pickle if 'is lordship 'adn't taken you on last winter. Couldn't even feed you, they Dalrymples."

"That's true, I reckon. They never had no money, and what little bit o' plate and jewels they still 'ad, they gave over to the Stuarts two year an' more past. Eatin' their dinners from wooden bowls they be. Not a silver fork or plate left in the 'ouse."

The old man spat his disgust. "A curse on all princes, that's what I do say. 'Specially Stuart princes from across the water."

The stable lad stopped polishing for a moment. "They do say as 'ow he's a wonderfully 'andsome fellow, the Stuart prince. Bonnie Prince Charlie, the young master did call 'im."

"Aye, so 'e did, and that proves lords are bigger fools than the rest of us. The roof were near fallin' in round his 'ead, and what does young Dalrymple do? He ups and rides off to fight for some furrin prince what claims God wants 'im to be King o' England."

"You shouldn't speak ill o' the dead, uncle. Remember the young master got hisself killed a-fightin' for the prince."

"Hah! More fool him."

"I dunno 'bout that. I do reckon Stuarts have a better right to be kings of England than they Hanoverian upstarts. Why, the old King couldn't speak a word of plain English, only German gibble-gabble, and this new un' ain't much better. By my tellin', King George and his brood o' Germans be more furrin than the Stuart prince if you want the truth of it."

"Shh!" The old man shook his head. "Don't 'ee have the sense of a peahen, lad? If one o' Captain Bretton's men hears such talk, you'll be clapped up in jail. The sooner you learns to be a loyal servant of 'Is Majesty, King George the Second, the better. 'Tain't never worth risking your life for kings and princes. Let they kill and fight each other."

"B'ain't nobody here to listen but us," the lad said, shrugging. "Tell me, uncle, if the Dalrymples didn't 'ave the money to pay that fine theirselves, who paid it for them?"

"That's a right good question, that is."

" 'Tis my belief they was given the money by the same person what's hiding Master Zachary."

The old man snorted. "And who might that be, pray tell? 'Tain't nobody from these parts as has money to spare, 'cept mebbe Richard Farleigh, and he's King George's man from 'is arse to 'is elbow."

"True enough." The stable lad spat on a brass buckle and rubbed vigorously. "Richard Farleigh and the master here, they make a matched set, don't they? Prim as a pair o' parsons. Abide by the law. Obey the established king. Keep out o' trouble. Not like Master Zachary—"

"You watch your mouth, my lad. We should all be grateful 'is lordship don't mix and meddle in pol'ticks. Fine fettle we'd be in if 'is lordship had declared for Bonnie Prince Charlie. And as for Master Zachary, we don' even know if he do be alive, save that Captain Bretton do keep sniffin' round the Manor, makin' life difficult for 'is lordship and 'onest folks like us. I don' hold with rebellions, but I don' hold with what Captain Bretton and his dragoons is doin' neither. Vicious man that captain is, and I wish 'im out o' here."

"Do you think Master Zachary is alive, uncle?"

"Better you don't ask questions, lad. That there Dook o'

Cumberland, he's a-waiting to snatch honest folks' land at the first hint o' treason, and Captain Bretton's waitin' to help 'im. 'Is lordship could lose the Manor quick as a wink if he don't watch out for hisself. Master Zachary were seen in the thick o' battle, and that's enough to make 'is lordship suspect, they being brothers an' all."

"Aye, Master Zachary fought like ten men I did hear tell." The stable lad set aside the buckle and reached for a stirrup. "Culloden, that's where they fought their last battle. Funny old name, that is."

" 'Tis Scottish, look you. Fearful strange names you find up in they wild parts up to the north."

"Any road, wherever they fought, Master Zachary, he covered hisself with glory."

The old man snorted. "You cain't cover yourself with glory when you be fighting on the wrong side."

"Nay, uncle, the Stuart prince were never the wrong side."

"He lost the battle," the old man said dryly. "That means he were the wrong side." He pulled himself to his feet and headed toward a ladder. "Well, I'm for bed. My bones is aching in this damp. Make sure you douse the lamp, me lad, and hang up all that tack afore you dosses down for the night. 'Is lordship pays 'ee twenty pound a year. That's a right good wage. See that you earn it."

The direction of the wind changed and the rain started to blow in under the thatched eaves of the stable, soaking Robyn's hair and chilling her bones. But it wasn't the wind or the damp that made her shiver. It was the conversation she had overheard. Dear God, if ever she had wanted proof of the fact that she wasn't dreaming, this conversation had provided it. The farther she traveled from the confines of her room, the more she seemed to become trapped in an alternative reality that got progressively more vivid and more alien.

The stable lad hung up the leather girth he'd been cleaning, scratched his head and his armpits, then ambled toward the door. Afraid that she'd be seen, Robyn pulled the hood of her cloak farther over her face and hurried down the path that led away from the stables and Starke Manor toward a copse of trees.

After twenty minutes of walking, she realized that she was hopelessly lost. The trees she had seen were not part of the small ornamental copse at the front of the manor, but rather the edge of a large, dense wood. The path she was following probably skirted the wood, but she wasn't sure she had the physical strength or the mental stamina to walk around the entire perimeter of what was looking more and more like a small forest. Dusk had given way to winter dark. Clouds covered the stars and the rain had begun to fall in a steady, soaking sheet. Her cloak was sodden and the path was rapidly turning into a puddle-strewn bog that pulled at her shoes and splattered the hem of her gown with dollops of heavy mud. Sensing her discomfort, Zach stirred restlessly in her arms, giving occasional fretful cries to let her know that he wasn't enjoying his outing one bit.

"I don't know why you're complaining," she said softly, lifting her cloak and sneaking a quick look at the cozily bundled baby. "You're dry, you're warm, and you're being carried. I should be so lucky."

At the sound of her voice, Zach opened his eyes. In the shadowy light of the cloud-veiled moon, it seemed almost as if he smiled at her, his gaze full of wry sympathy. Then his mouth puckered as he realized he was awake and hungry. His anxious wriggles freed his hands from their shawl, and his flailing fists pummeled his nose. Zach was delighted by the encounter. He latched on to one of his fingers and sucked eagerly.

"You want to eat *again?*" Robyn asked, unable to resist stroking his soft cheek. "You know what, fella? I think it's time you and I had a chat about your eating habits. You don't seem to remember that it's less than two hours since your last meal."

Zach tried to turn toward the sound of his mother's voice. He lost his fist and promptly expressed his frustration with loud, angry cries.

Robyn chuckled. "Okay, no need to yell. I'm open to negotiations if you're that hungry." She saw a convenient tree stump and sat down, glad of an excuse to stop a walk that seemed to become momentarily more pointless. The thickness of her fur-lined cape kept out the dampness of the stump and her outer clothing was already so wet that sitting down couldn't possibly make her any wetter. She loosened the laces at the top of her gown and held Zach against her breast, protected under the tent of her cloak. She stroked the top of his head as he nursed hungrily.

"You and I should read Dr. Spock together," Robyn murmured. "I think it's time you learned about the pediatrician-recommended, four-hour feeding schedule." She rocked back and forth, aware of the absurdity of nursing a baby in the pouring rain, seated on a tree stump, and yet somehow feeling oddly at peace. She sighed. "Eat up, honey, and then I guess we may as well go home. We'll try our great escape plan tomorrow, when it's daylight, and we're not so likely to get lost. The grounds of this place don't look anything like the parking lot around the hotel. I'm all disoriented."

She heard the snapping of branches and rustle of undergrowth almost at the same instant as rough hands reached out and grabbed her arms.

"Don't 'ee try to run," growled a harsh voice behind her. An arm, covered in coarse serge, wrapped roughly around her throat.

"The captain's been a-waitin' for 'ee," said another voice, dragging her off the tree stump and propelling her backward into the woods.

Robyn went hot and then cold with sheer terror, not for herself but for Zach. She scarcely felt the overhanging branches that caught at her hood and tore it from her head. "Don't hurt my baby!" She tightened her hold on Zach's tiny body, and he started to cry, thin, anxious cries that ate at her soul.

"Babby?" She heard the astonishment in the first man's gruff voice, and his hold around her throat slackened as he spun her around. "'Struth, her does have a babby. What for did 'ee bring a babby?"

"Don't matter none," said the other, leaning forward to see the child. His stinking breath wafted so close to Robyn's nose that she almost threw up. "We was told to bring all marauders to the captain. She do be a marauder. 'Tain't for us to worry about babbies or no babbies."

Zach's cries had changed from fearful to a steady roar of frustration at his interrupted meal. As best she could with her neck held in a stranglehold, Robyn jiggled him up and down and made soothing noises. "Where are you taking me?" she asked, fighting back her fear. "What do you want?"

"The captain got word as 'ow a most treacherous traitor was making a run for the coast tonight. We're to bring in all persons found lurkin' outside after curfew."

"But you're trespassing on private property!" Robyn protested. "You can't impose a curfew on private land. These woods belong to the Baron of Starke!"

"Dook o' Cumberland's direct orders," the man said, sounding pleased with himself. "Signed and sealed with 'is royal seal, then delivered personal to Captain Bretton. Ain't no treacherous Stuart rebels goin' to escape to France while Captain Bretton is on duty and a-helpin' the dook."

"Captain Bretton?" Robyn said.

"Aye. Don't pretend you don't know about 'im. An important man is Captain Bretton in these parts. He's in charge of military security for the whole of Dorsetshire, the captain is."

The men didn't lead her far into the forest. After two or three minutes of dragging her along, they came to a small clearing, sheltered from the rain by the overhanging branches of a giant oak tree. The stockier and dirtier of her two captors propelled her forward and drew himself up into a smart salute. "Here you are, sir, Captain Bretton. We caught her lurkin' on the edge of the woods, just like you said."

"Her? You have brought me a woman? I trust you are not wasting my time bringing in some serving wench out on a tryst." A man stepped out from the shadowy darkness of the oak tree and glanced toward Robyn. He drew in a sharp, angry breath. "My God, unhand her ladyship this instant! That is the Lady Arabella Bowleigh, you idiots."

Her captors dropped Robyn's arms and jumped back as if they'd been scalded. The captain swept into a deep bow. "My lady, forgive these doltish soldiers, I beg. I extend my most heartfelt apologies for the behavior of the clods who dared to lay hands upon you. The troops I have serving under me are not yet as well trained as I would wish."

Robyn said nothing, but she took advantage of her renewed freedom to pull the cloak tightly across her breasts, concealing both the gaping front of her gown and baby

Zach. As the captain straightened from his bow, she saw that he was about thirty-five years old and had light brown hair tied and secured in a black velvet bag at the nape of his neck. His features were well formed but unremarkable, at least insofar as she could discern by moonlight. He was wearing a uniform consisting of scarlet, gold-frogged jacket and white leather knee breeches, topped by a swinging shoulder cape in heavy gray wool. The outfit looked as if it had been loaned straight out of a museum specializing in military costumes of the American Revolution.

"You are silent, my lady." The captain's voice was still unctuous, and Robyn wondered if she was imagining the hint of menace she detected in his body language. "I trust you have not been alarmed beyond the point of speech?"

"No."

The captain smiled and Robyn knew she hadn't imagined the threat that this man posed to her. He bent his head in another half bow. "I am relieved that your ladyship retains the power of speech, because my duty compels me to ask for an accounting of your actions this evening. Mayhap, my lady, you would be good enough to explain why you are strolling the grounds of Starke Manor on such a damp and unpleasant night?"

"No," Robyn said, deciding that she definitely didn't like the captain and anyway couldn't think of any explanation she could give that he was likely to accept.

"I beg your ladyship's pardon? I believe I have not heard you aright."

"I said that I have no desire to explain to you why I choose to walk in the grounds of my own home. By what right do you inquire?"

"I ask by right of the personal warrant of His Royal Highness, the Duke of Cumberland," the captain said. He clicked his fingers at the two gawking soldiers. "Be off about your duties, the pair of you. And next time you report back to me, make sure you bring a Stuart rebel with you, not a lady of impeccable loyalist reputation."

"Yessir!" The soldiers saluted in unison and marched smartly out of the clearing. When the sound of their footsteps had faded, the captain visibly relaxed. "Good. Now we can take our ease and speak to each other freely. You understand that I needed to keep up appearances in front of my men." He gave her a wide, warm smile that he probably intended to be reassuring. Robyn found it about as reassuring as seeing a snake slither toward her, holding a rosy red apple in its rapacious jaws.

"I trust that you are recovered from your recent ordeal in childbed," the captain continued. "The child, I heard, was a boy."

"Yes."

The captain's smile took on a faint edge of cruelty. "What a splendid gift for your husband! Blood of his blood, flesh of his flesh. The baron must be delighted that he now has three healthy sons to secure the succession to his lands and titles."

The heavy sarcasm was unmistakable and Robyn's cheeks flamed, although why she felt so angry on William's behalf she couldn't have explained. "Yes, my husband is delighted at the happy outcome. Our son is strong and healthy, and the very image of the baron."

"How wonderfully—convenient," the captain murmured, his voice still derisive. "Fortune rarely fails to smile on you, my lady. I have always said that."

"I see nothing fortunate in the fact that my son looks exactly like his father."

The captain shot her an assessing, sideways gaze. She noticed, however, that he made not the slightest move to look at the baby, even though Zach chose that moment to give a subdued cry.

"You must be fatigued, my lady, after your long walk." The captain reached out and placed his hand beneath her elbow, managing to make the simple action lascivious in the extreme. He reached inside her cloak, found her hand, and raised it to his lips. Robyn was immensely grateful for the fur-lined leather gloves separating her skin from his mouth.

The captain leaned closer. "Pray rest against me, my lady. I regret most sincerely that I cannot offer you a seat."

"I prefer to stand." Robyn disengaged her hand from his clasp with a determined tug and stepped back, feeling better once there were two or three feet of space between them.

His smile faded. "I cannot help but remark, dear Arabella, that your manner lacks much of its customary warmth and charm. I trust that your aloofness doesn't mean you have decided to renege on our bargain."

She looked at him coldly. "I cannot imagine what bargain you refer to."

The captain frowned. "I am not a man who enjoys being trifled with, my lady. My plans have been laid counting on your cooperation. I hope I have not been mistaken in believing that you are indeed my true . . . friend."

Robyn looked at the captain's saber, its blade gleaming in the moonlight, and decided this was not the best moment to tell the slithery reptile to go to hell. "I am always a true friend to people who are worthy of my friendship," she said.

The captain did not appear to suspect subtlety from her. His smile broadened. "Thank you, my dear lady, that is good to hear. Over the past few months I have appreciated the generosity of your . . . friendship, which has provided many happy hours for both of us, I do believe."

"Friendship usually brings happiness."

The captain bowed, appearing impressed by her trite remark. "How true! And of course I have been honored by your many confidences, and the opportunities you have given me to lighten the load you bear as the neglected wife of a brutal husband. As you know, I sympathize most heartily with the difficulties of your position. The harshness of your husband's treatment of you cannot help but be devastating to a soul as sensitive and delicate as yours—"

"What has my husband done that was so brutal?"

The captain stared at her. "My dear Arabella, now is perhaps not the time or the place to probe into old wounds—"

"How long have I known you, Captain Bretton?"

"Our acquaintance stretches back many years. Our . . . intimacy . . . also has a long history—"

"That figures," Robyn muttered. "I should have known Arabella's taste in men would be long-term lousy."

The captain edged away from her, his expression becoming uneasy. He cleared his throat, drumming his fingers against the shining buckle of his belt. "My lady, much as I regret the necessity, I am obliged to inform you that our . . . close . . . personal ties cannot be allowed to interfere with my duties as the Duke of Cumberland's personal representative in the shire of Dorset. I must ask that you answer me honestly and completely. Why did you leave Starke Manor tonight, knowing full well that a curfew has been imposed and that rumors continue to circulate that your brother-in-law is hidden somewhere within the grounds of Starke Manor?"

Her brother-in-law. The captain must mean Zachary, William's younger brother. And if she had correctly understood the conversation she overheard at the stables, Zachary had rebelled against King George by fighting in the army of Bonnie Prince Charlie, the Stuart pretender to the throne. Robyn knew from her college history courses that the prince had been catastrophically defeated at the battle of Culloden, and she remembered reading that King George's younger son, the Duke of Cumberland, had been given the task of cleaning up the ragtag survivors of the rebellion. The duke had set about systematically starving the Scottish highlanders who supported the Stuart cause, and executing or jailing every rebel who managed to flee Scotland and escape south. His punishments were so harsh that he quickly earned himself the nickname Butcher Cumberland, and his ruthlessness was despised even by supporters of the House of Hanover. As a nation, the eighteenth-century Britishers were already firm believers in the virtues of restraint and moderation.

Robyn thought rapidly. Everything she knew about William suggested that he was a staunch supporter of the Hanoverians, and ruthlessly indifferent to his brother's fate. In the circumstances, it seemed unlikely that Zachary would try to find refuge in the grounds of Starke Manor. He must know how his brother felt about him, and how fiercely William rejected the Stuart cause. And without William's support, who on the estate would dare to feed Zachary, or provide warm clothes as winter closed in? All in all, Robyn decided there was virtually no chance that Zachary was hiding anywhere near Starke, but on the slim chance that he was, she made her expression as vague and confused as she could. She didn't know Zachary, of course, but she had no desire to help a pompous lecher like Captain Bretton in his pursuit of hapless Stuart rebels.

Robyn shook her head, hoping she appeared somewhere between coy and bewildered. "I would certainly like us to continue as friends, Captain Bretton, but why are you questioning me about these rumors? I had no idea a curfew had been imposed. In fact, I have no idea why you would ask me about Zachary."

"Then let me make my meaning quite clear, Lady Arab—"

A familiar voice spoke from behind Robyn's shoulders, cool, courteous, and laced with subtle mockery. "Why do you harass a senseless woman with questions she cannot answer, Captain Bretton? Have you not heard that her ladyship suffered a terrible carriage accident and that her wits have entirely left her?"

"My lord!" Captain Bretton stiffened, then executed a curt bow. "My lord, I did not hear you approach."

"Did you not? I made no secret of my presence. I and many of my servants have been out searching for the Lady Arabella this past hour and more. We were extremely alarmed to discover that she and my infant son were both missing. I have ordered search parties with horses and hounds spread out in all directions."

The captain's mouth tightened with barely concealed fury. "I see you have been very clever, my lord. I should not have underestimated you."

William inclined his head. "It is never wise to underestimate an adversary, but alas, Captain, I fear I do not grasp your meaning. I see no cleverness in the tragic loss of my wife's mental powers."

"It is true, then? Your wife is not in full possession of her wits?"

"Why else would she roam the grounds of Starke Manor in a downpour of bitterly cold November rain?"

The captain turned to Robyn, his gaze speculative. "I had heard stories," he admitted. "Dr. Perrick has a tongue looser than an old woman's and he had half the village convinced that your lady wife was possessed."

"You, of course, are too sophisticated to be deceived by the ignorant superstitions of a country doctor."

"Er . . . yes. Yes, of course."

William smiled blandly. "She is not possessed, but neither is she the woman you once knew. Her memory is sadly impaired."

"Is that so?"

"Yes, alas, she cannot be relied upon to hold to any of her previous commitments. However, I have sent to London for Dr. Woolstone, who considered the leading physician in the care of head injuries such as Lady Arabella has sustained. We have exchanged letters, the doctor and I, and he is optimistic that my wife will eventually return to all her former robust health, mental as well as physical."

"It is an outcome devoutly to be wished," the captain said tightly.

"Indeed it is." William placed his arm around Robyn's waist. "It will be so—awkward—for all of us if the Lady Arabella fails to regain her wits, will it not?"

"For you, my lord, I believe it might even be— dangerous."

"No, how can you say so?" William smiled blandly at the Captain. When he received no reply, he turned back to Robyn. "Come, my lady. I believe it is time for us to return home."

His voice was mild, his touch gentle, and yet Robyn could sense that he was furiously angry. She was tired and wet enough that she didn't care. The prospect of returning to Starke Manor sounded wonderful, even if it did mean facing up to William's wrath. "Did you bring a carriage?" she asked in a small voice.

"Wait a moment!" Captain Bretton spoke peremptorily. "Before you leave, my lord, I think you should know that there are other interesting tales circulating in the village, not merely gossip about your lady wife. Only yesterday, for example, I heard that three Stuart rebels hidden on your property are hoping to make a run for Poole harbor this very night."

William looked at the captain, his gaze cold. "You should not believe every piece of idle chatter you overhear at the Dog and Kettle, sir. There can be no rebels hidden on my property without my knowledge, and as you apprehend full well, I am a faithful supporter of King George and the Hanoverians. I believe there has never been any reason to question my loyal service to His Majesty. The barons of Starke take pride in the quality of service they offer their country."

The captain's face flushed dark red. "Nobly spoken, my lord, but we have been acquainted for many years, and we both know full well that you have spent a lifetime protecting your brother from the consequences of his own folly. You would move heaven and earth to save Zachary Bowleigh from suffering the punishment he deserves. Until I see your brother's body at my feet, I will not believe he is dead, nor will I abandon my efforts to arrest him and bring him to justice."

"That is your choice, sir, but if you persist in looking for Zachary on my property, I fear you are destined to spend many more fruitless nights standing under a wet oak tree, waiting for an escape that will not take place." William's hold on Robyn's waist tightened. "Come, my lady, you are shivering with the cold. It is past time for us to leave here."

Robyn turned within William's arms, instinctively resting her head on his shoulder as she submitted to his command. For a few blissful seconds, relief flooded through her at the prospect of returning to the warmth and security of Starke Manor. Home. William had come to take her home. He would make her feel safe again. Safe from the baneful Captain Bretton.

The thought had scarcely formed when the enormity of it struck her with full force. Fear washed over her in a huge tidal wave. She tore herself out of William's arms, holding Zach crushed against her body as if he were some sort of talisman against the onrush of terror. Her muscles stiffened, then started to tremble, as the horrific, mind-blowing truth washed over her.

"Arabella, what is it?" William turned to her and she cried out, her voice high-pitched with panic.

"No, go back! Don't come near me!"

"My dear, what ails you? Come, let me assist you—" He pulled her cloak tighter around her shoulders, tucking a sodden strand of hair under the hood.

"I have to get out of this place," she said, her teeth chattering with shock. When had she started to feel that William was her protector? When had she started to think of Starke Manor as her home? She tugged at his hand, pleading with him to understand. "Take me to the gates, William. I have to get to the gates where I had my accident."

"My dear, you are overset. You should not be out in this cold and rain—"

"Take me to the front gates," she pleaded. "Otherwise I'll never get back to my own time. If I don't leave soon, I'll start to become Arabella—I can feel it happening already. I'll be trapped forever inside Arabella's body."

"You are not trapped, my dear. You are my wife—"

Laughter bubbled up in her throat, scratching and sticking as it tried to emerge. "I'm caught in a time warp," she said, speaking out loud so that she could comprehend the full absurdity of what she was thinking. "My God, I've been transported into the body of some dim-witted, two-hundred-year-old aristocrat who belongs in a Gainsborough painting and *I'm beginning to like it here.*"

Even in the moonlight, she could see William's face pale. "My dear, you are not yet well, you shouldn't trouble yourself with these irksome thoughts. We need to take you home and return you safely to your bed—"

"Because I'm mad," she said, and her lungs were squeezed so tight that her laughter squeaked out in a high-pitched cackle. "The bullet gave me an instant lobotomy, and now I belong inside a locked room with padded walls."

"Enough!" William rapped her sharply on the cheek and her laughter changed to sobs. She pressed her hand over her mouth, trying in vain to control the rising hysteria. Sobs changed back to laughter, hiccuping out through her fingers until William cupped her face in his hands, forcing her to look at him.

"Arabella, enough! For the sake of your children, if for no other reason, you must control yourself."

"Sure, for the sake of the kids. My kids. All four of them that I never knew I had." Robyn drew in a great shuddering breath. She looked at William's handsome face and his dark blue eyes, tinged now with compassion as well as worry. She shook her head, which felt as if it were spinning in ever-narrowing circles. "Hey, you know what, Willie baby? I've finally realized that I'm in major trouble. I can decide I'm mad, or I can decide I'm living two hundred and fifty years in the past. Which option would you choose? Insanity or time travel?"

William brushed his thumbs across her cheeks, wiping away her tears. "I choose to take you home where you can rest and regain your strength. You are strong, Arabella, and you will recover."

The hysteria died as suddenly as it had begun. "Don't be kind," she said. "I can't bear it when you're kind."

"You know I am never kind," William said. "Merely practical. That is my nature." He bent down and picked her up, holding her without apparent effort in his arms. "Come, my lady. Rest your head against my shoulder. You will feel much better when you are tucked up safely in your bed."

William started to walk out of the clearing, and the captain broke his lengthy silence. He spoke pityingly, his voice thick with disgust. "My lord, you have my deepest sympathy. The Lady Arabella is a sad case. A sad case indeed. What a tragic end for a beautiful woman."

Chapter 10

EXERCISING phenomenal willpower, Zach decided not to ask any questions until Dr. Forsyth had finished checking Robyn over. It seemed that he waited a lifetime, and when the doctor finally straightened from his examination, Zach couldn't tell from his expression whether the news was good or bad.

"Is she going to be all right?" The words burst out, harsh with the accumulated tension of the past twenty-four hours.

"It's a mite too early to give you a definitive answer." The doctor scrutinized a bleeping monitor and scribbled a note on one of the many charts hanging around Robyn's bed. "All in all, though, I'm optimistic that there will be a full and total return to normal health. As I explained to you last night, the operation to remove the bullet went well, and there have been no post-op complications. Have you been shown the X rays?"

"Yes. Dr. Bennings went over them this morning. He explained that the bullet hadn't actually entered Robyn's brain, just . . . ripped along the surface of her skull."

"I'm sure you understand that's very good news." Dr. Forsyth rubbed his forehead a touch wearily. "Look, Miss Delaney's recovery has been normal in every way, and the neurological tests are positive. The swelling is minimal; she's breathing on her own, and so far there's no sign of any infection."

"I can hear a *but* in your voice."

The doctor hesitated, then shook his head. "No, you can't. Now all we have to do is wait for her to wake up."

Zach looked down at the inert, bandage-swathed figure on the bed. Robyn appeared tiny, fragile, vulnerable, oddly un-familiar. Every cliché he'd ever read or heard about the diminishment of the seriously ill seemed to fit. He stroked her arm, needing the reassurance of feeling the warm pulse of life among the needles, drips, and electronic wires feeding into her skin.

"Why is she taking so long to regain consciousness?" he asked. "If everything's going so darn well, why doesn't she wake up?"

"There could be a lot of reasons, Mr. Bowleigh, not all of them bad. From the readings on the brain scan, I'd say she's likely to regain consciousness anytime now."

"Today?" Zach asked.

The doctor finally permitted himself a small smile. "Within the next couple of hours. That's what we're hoping for, anyway."

"And if she doesn't wake up soon?" Zach gave voice to the nightmare that had been haunting him ever since he arrived at the hospital that morning.

"Let's cross that bridge if we come to it, shall we? I can promise you, Mr. Bowleigh, that nobody anticipates your friend spending the rest of her life in a coma."

Dr. Forsyth no doubt intended to sound encouraging, but Zach felt his stomach lurch. "She looks a million miles away," he murmured. "In another world."

The doctor chuckled, sounding genuinely amused. "She's just resting, and in a state that's pretty close to normal sleep. The body does a wonderful job of closing down any systems that it doesn't need while it sets about healing itself. Miss Delaney is a healthy young woman, and she's likely to wake up and start talking to you sometime within the next few hours, possibly the next few minutes. Chin up, Mr. Bowleigh. She's a fighter, and she'll pull through."

A sound from the bed had the doctor swinging back just as he was about to leave the room. Zach held his breath as Robyn moved her head once, then lay completely still beneath the white hospital blanket. For a moment Zach wondered if he'd imagined hearing her try to speak.

The rumbling sound came again, an unmistakable groan. A ten-second pause and then Robyn opened her eyes. She blinked several times, and stared around, her gaze flicking dazedly from the flashing screens, to the doctor, to Zach, and back to the monitors.

"Where . . . am . . . I?"

Zach's throat squeezed tight with emotion, and he swallowed over a hard lump of pure joy. "You're in the hospital, honey, but everything's going to be all right." He spoke softly, afraid of scaring her. "How are you feeling, honey? Robyn, it's so good to see you awake."

Robyn blinked. "I am . . . awake?"

Zach laughed, drunk with relief. "You sure are, sweetheart. My God, you gave us all a terrible scare. We aren't used to seeing you lie so still and quiet, I guess!"

Robyn's green eyes skittered over Zach, not really focusing on him. She spoke to Dr. Forsyth. "My . . . head . . . pains . . . me."

The doctor quietly repositioned himself so that it would be easier for Robyn to see him without twisting her neck. "I'm afraid you're likely to suffer from a headache for a bit longer, my dear. You were shot yesterday, do you remember?"

"Shot?" Her eyes blurred. "Accident . . ." she muttered. "Carriage . . ." She closed her eyes, as if the act of remembering hurt. She muttered several more phrases, but her words were so thick and stumbling that Zach couldn't make out what she was trying to say. Her accent sounded oddly distorted and the only two words he heard clearly sounded like *horse* and *bolted,* which made no sense at all. Worried, he glanced toward the doctor.

Dr. Forsyth appeared unconcerned by Robyn's incoherence. He spoke directly to his patient. "Well, my dear, we had to remove a bullet from your head I'm afraid, but the operation went very well, and we hope you'll soon be feeling a lot better." He patted her gently on the shoulder. "You've been an excellent patient so far, young lady. We're all very pleased with you."

Robyn stared at the doctor. Her gaze dropped to his hand and her brows furrowed. "Thirsty," she said brusquely. "Give . . . me . . . water."

"Yes, of course. We can start you on some clear liquids." Dr. Forsyth nodded to a waiting nurse who hurried forward, carrying a covered cup and flexible straw. The nurse fixed the straw between Robyn's swollen lips and waited for her to suck. Robyn made awkward work of the simple task, coughing and spluttering as if she couldn't quite remember how to make a straw function.

Never mind, Zach thought. *She'll soon be good as new. I can't expect her to be a hundred percent okay the first second she opens her eyes.*

"That's enough," Dr. Forsyth said as Robyn nearly choked on an ill-timed swallow. "Thanks, nurse. She can have some more water or apple juice in an hour if she asks for it. In the meantime, the drip is keeping her hydrated." He freed her feet from the bedcovers and smiled at her encouragingly. "Could you wriggle your toes for me, Robyn? And if you can lift your foot a couple of inches off the bed, that would be marvelous."

Robyn's head was swathed in bandages, her face was drained of all color, and her lips were shockingly bruised. Maybe that was why it was so difficult to read her feelings, Zach thought. Right now, she looked more angry than anything else, but that must be a distortion caused by the bandages.

"Who ... are ... you?" she asked the doctor, and her voice sounded as cold as her expression.

"I'm Dr. Forsyth, the surgeon who operated on you."

"I know you not. Where is ... Dr. Perrick?"

"Dr. Perrick doesn't work out of this hospital, Miss Delaney ... Is he your physician in the States?"

Robyn didn't answer, simply frowned again, and the doctor tapped her lightly on the foot. "Could you wriggle these toes for me, please? Just to convince your friend Zachary that you're all right?"

"Zachary? You mean Zachary is here?" Robyn gave her first tentative smile since regaining consciousness. She levered herself onto one elbow and peered around the room.

"I'm here, honey," Zach said, relieved that she obviously wasn't paralyzed and yet worried that she hadn't registered his presence the first time she saw him. He reminded himself again that she'd just woken up from a twenty-four-hour concussion, and he couldn't expect her to get everything straight right off the bat. Following the doctor's example, he shifted toward the foot of the bed, so that it would be easier for her to see him.

Robyn stared at him, her eyes darkening in puzzlement.

"William?" she said, her voice rising into a definite question.

Why in the world was she asking him about his brother, a man she'd never even met? "Will is in L.A.," Zach said. "He spends a lot of time out on the West Coast." He reached out to clasp her hand, taking great care not to disturb the needles leading to the various IVs. "How are you feeling, honey? Do you think you could manage a small smile, just to convince me that you're not hurting all over?"

"You are not William," she said with clipped, angry precision. "Why do you wear those outrageous garments? And where is Zachary? The physician told me that Zachary is here."

Somehow, Zach forced back his fear. "Darling, I am Zachary." He leaned across the bed and took her hand, kissing the tips of her fingers in the hope that close physical contact would help her to remember.

The gesture seemed to make her annoyed rather than reassured. Scowling, Robyn tugged at her hand, pulling away from him. The movement made her IV tubes jangle and her gaze lighted on the needles, wires, and tubes taped into the back of her hand. Her peevish expression changed to one of stark fear.

"What have you done to me?" she demanded hoarsely, staring at her hand as if paralyzed with horror. Her mouth fell open and she gave a weak, terrified scream. "Take these monstrous leaches from me! I will not consent to be bled!"

"Robyn, honey, it's just the IV needles," Zach said quickly. She paid no attention. She tore her hand out of his grasp and ripped at the tape holding the IV tubes in place.

"Remove ... these ... accursed ... slugs ... from ... me!" she yelled, panting and gasping for air. "Dear God, 'tis no leach but a poisonous adder, biting into my flesh."

"Hold her still!" Dr. Forsyth commanded. He spoke into the intercom. "Bring me ten ccs of Valium right away!" He ran across the room and seized Robyn's arm, holding it out so that she couldn't grab the IVs. She continued to writhe and scream, twisting her body with amazing, demented strength.

Sick with worry, Zach forced himself to stroke her cheek

with a smooth, gentle touch. "Robyn, darling, you must try to calm down—"

Her gaze rolled toward him. Her screaming stopped on a choking, strangled gasp, and her body froze into stillness. She cringed back against the pillows, shrinking away from Zach's touch. "Sweet Jesu, now I understand what ails me! My sins have found me out! You are a demon, cast in William's form and sent to beguile me."

Zach drew in a deep breath. "Honey, listen to me, I'm Zach and I love you—"

"Get thee gone from me, spawn of Satan!" she hissed, crossing her hand in front of her face. "I am not deceived by thy looks, nor dazzled by thy beauty. Go back to the devil who vomited thee up from the bowels of hell. Thou—art—not—William—and I shall not be deceived!"

"Darling, of course I'm not William. Will is my brother." He fought to keep the fear out of his voice. "Sweetheart, I'm Zach. Zach Bowleigh—"

"Touch me not, devil's get!" Robyn jerked away, then suddenly stared down at her stomach. "My babe!" she croaked in a frantic whisper. "Dear God, what hast thou done with my babe? Sweet Jesu, hast thou stolen him out of my womb and offered him up to Satan?"

The doctor gave Zach no chance to answer, even if he had been capable of producing a reply. "Enough," Dr. Forsyth said. He flipped the intercom switch. "Am I going to get that Valium anytime soon?" He nodded to the nurse, who marched with unmistakable determination toward Zach.

"You have to leave, Mr. Bowleigh. Hurry up, please, you're disturbing the patient."

Robyn's hysterical cries pounded against Zach's ears. "No," he said. "You must let me stay with her. She'll recognize me in a minute—"

"Get out, Mr. Bowleigh." Dr. Forsyth didn't raise his voice, but his command brooked no argument. "Nurse, I need you over here. Take her other arm and hold her still. Dammit, she's not giving up! She's going to rip the IV right out! Where the hell is that Valium?"

"Here, sir." Another nurse hurried into the room, a syringe in her hand.

Zach was almost pushed from the room. He paced the cor-

ridor, wincing when a horrible, piercing shriek ended in an
abrupt and even more horrible silence. Christ, what was happening in there? Zach wasn't sure he wanted to know. Right
at this moment, he wasn't sure about anything much. Except
that if a bullet intended to wreck him and the Gallery had
ended up destroying Robyn's joyful and intelligent spirit, he
would never forgive himself.

Zach acknowledged the greetings of two or three nurses
as he walked down the corridor leading to Robyn's room.
During the past four days he'd had ample opportunity to get
to know the hospital staff, and he found them both efficient
and blessedly tactful. The questions they didn't ask were le-
gion, and he appreciated their reticence. At a time like this,
diplomatic British understatement was balm for his lacerated
soul.

He paused outside the door of Robyn's room for a few
seconds, mentally preparing himself. The sound of a high-
pitched chuckle caught him unprepared. Robyn was laughing? He pushed open the door.

Robyn didn't even glance toward him. She had the control
switch for her bed clasped in her hands. Brow furrowed in
concentration, she held the control at arm's length, eyeing it
warily, as if it were a monster needing to be tamed. Pressing
the button, she sent the bed zooming up and down, her
breathless giggles sounding almost as much scared as happy.

Mrs. Delaney gave him a strained smile, but she didn't
leave Robyn's side. Al Delaney, however, seemed glad of an
excuse to get away from watching his daughter's antics, and
he greeted Zach with a friendly hello, followed by a bewildered shaking of his head.

"She's been at it for an hour," he said, glancing over his
shoulder toward Robyn. "Up and down, first the head of the
bed, then the foot, then the whole dang mattress. Honest to
goodness, Zach, it's driving me crazy."

"Did you try asking her to stop?"

"Yeah." Al Delaney shoved his hands into the pockets of
his rumpled slacks. "She threw a tantrum."

"I'm sorry."

"Yeah. Her mother gets upset when she lets rip like that.
It's so unlike her, you know."

Al didn't need to say anything more. Zach had seen several of Robyn's post-op tantrums and they were definitely not a pretty sight. He cleared his throat. "I'm sure she'll be better when she's back in familiar surroundings." *His first lie of the morning, because he wasn't sure at all.* "Has Dr. Forsyth said anything about when she can go home?"

"Early next week, he thinks. He wants to make sure the wound in her scalp is completely healed before she risks a transatlantic plane journey."

"Did the doctor say anything about Robyn's mental—" Zach broke off, unable to put the harsh truth into words. He tried again. "Did he indicate how long it might be before Robyn gets back to her old self again?"

"They've no idea what's causing her behavior, so they won't commit themselves to any diagnosis about the future." Al sounded bleak.

"Look, I'm sure you'll see a world of difference once she's back home." *Second lie.* "With you and her mother in charge, instead of doctors and nurses, she'll start to remember her past." *Third lie.* "She'll have all her friends and familiar places to jog her memory."

Al attempted a smile. "Yeah, that's what we're hoping."

Zach tried to think of something else encouraging to say, wondering if he sounded as hypocritical as he felt. "We have to remember it's less than a week since she was shot, and physically she's doing a fantastic job of recovery."

"Yeah, physically she's doing great." Al looked glum. "Did you notice? They took out the last of the IV drips today."

"Hey, cheer up! That's good news."

"Is it?" Al avoided Zach's gaze. "Since she didn't have the drip anymore, they couldn't give her medication through the tubes. The nurse had to bring Robyn's antibiotic pills in a plastic foam cup."

Zach winced. "Let me guess what happened. She threw the pills at the nurse."

"No. She tried to eat the foam cup along with the pills." Al rubbed his eyes tiredly. "Honest to God, she stared at those dang antibiotics like she'd never seen a pill in her life. Then when the nurse told her to hurry up and swallow them down, she picked up the cup and started munching."

Zach would have laughed if he hadn't felt so damn close to crying. "Dr. Forsyth did explain that post-trauma amnesia can be selective," he said, trying to find something consoling to say, although it was damned difficult to be reassuring about a woman who ate plastic foam. "Remember he mentioned those strange cases of accident victims who couldn't recognize their immediate family, even though they remembered acquaintances? Or the story he told about a woman who came out of surgery remembering every detail of her life after April the twelfth of 1979 and nothing from before."

"Yeah, I remember. I'm not sure it makes me feel any better to know that my daughter's crazy just like a lot of other unfortunate people."

Zach sucked in a gulp of air. "Not crazy, Al. With expert therapy, she'll get back to normal." *A prayer, not a lie.*

"I sure do hope so." Al's voice thickened. "She was such a happy, friendly little girl. And so darn cute. Huge green eyes, a mop of curls, and those dang freckles across her nose. Lord, she was cute as a button. Her mother and I couldn't help spoiling her, but she never took advantage, you know what I mean?"

"Yes, I do. Robyn is a very generous person." Zach drew in another deep breath. "Well, I guess I'd better go and say hi to her, and to Muriel." He walked across to the bed and murmured greetings. Muriel Delaney gave him one of her brave, anxious smiles. Robyn ignored him.

"Al tells me Robyn can go home next week," he said to Muriel, voice rich with false cheer. "That's great." Behind him, Robyn's bed whirred and buzzed on its bizarre ride. He swallowed hard. "I'll book tickets on a flight direct to Washington, D.C., and arrange for a rental car to be waiting at Dulles for the drive to your house. The whole journey shouldn't take more than twelve hours, hospital door to your door."

"It's so good of you to take on the burden of making all these travel arrangements," Muriel said.

"Don't mention it. I fly to England so often on business I have a long-standing agreement with a travel agency in London. One call will take care of all the details."

"I'm really looking forward to being home again," Muriel

said. "I'm sure Robyn will get back to her old self again as soon as she's in familiar surroundings."

The hope had become her mantra. Since he'd made virtually the same remark to Al, Zach could only nod his agreement, although he couldn't think of any solid reason why the sight of her childhood home would trigger Robyn's return to normal when the faces of her own parents hadn't done the trick.

"Robyn's looking well, better every day." That, at least, was the truth. "The color's back in her cheeks and her face is rounding out again, not looking so thin."

"Yes, her appetite's pretty good." Muriel's voice tailed away, dispirited. "The truth is, Zach, that she doesn't seem to be improving mentally, even though she's doing just fine physically. The nurses had another huge dust-up with her this morning. They had a terrible time persuading her to get into the shower, and when she was finally undressed, she went off into hysterics." Muriel Delaney's face crumpled and tears trickled down her cheeks.

Zach handed her a tissue and she dried her eyes determinedly. He rested his hand on her shoulder. "What was upsetting Robyn this morning, did the nurses tell you?"

"Oh, yes, they told me."

"And?"

"Apparently she accused them of stealing away her body and she demanded that they bring it back. She got hysterical every time she caught a glimpse of herself in the bathroom mirror. She kept repeating, over and over, 'Where have you hidden my blond hair?' "

Zach felt sick to his stomach. Robyn's delusions certainly didn't seem to be lessening in severity as time passed. "Maybe they misunderstood," he said. "Her pronunciation isn't always easy to understand. Maybe she was talking about her baby. She accused me once of stealing her baby."

"I guess it's marginally less crazy if she thinks people are stealing her nonexistent baby rather than her body," Muriel said, her voice not quite under control.

Al give his wife's hand an encouraging squeeze. "She'll be right as rain when we get her home, sugar."

Muriel looked at her daughter, eyes sad. "I sure hope so," she said. "I sure do hope so."

* * *

Robyn sat hunched in her wheelchair, staring straight ahead, her mouth drawn into a tight, obstinate line. Zach and the nurses kept up a stream of would-be jaunty chatter. Al and Muriel Delaney followed behind their daughter's wheelchair in grim, despairing silence. Zach couldn't blame them if they had exhausted their supply of false optimism.

The weather, at least, was proving unusually kind for England in early December. A pale sun broke from behind the clouds as Robyn was wheeled out into the hospital driveway, and the icy blasts of wind died down to sharp puffs of breeze carrying a tang of salty ocean. "Nice day for a journey," the nurse said.

"Yes," Zach agreed. "We should make good time to Heathrow."

"I've always wanted to go to America," the nurse said. "I'm saving up for a trip to Disney World next winter."

"I'm sure you'll have a good time," Zach said. The limo he had ordered was waiting outside the concrete canopy and he waved to the driver, indicating that he should pull up to the main hospital entrance. The driver, a happy-go-lucky young man who clearly thought his fancy chauffeur's uniform was a bit of a lark, clicked his heels before giving a mock salute and jumping into the limo. His chirpy whistle was audible across the hundred yards or so separating him from the hospital entrance.

At least somebody was feeling cheerful, Zach thought. He glanced toward Robyn, his gloom increasing when he saw that she was hunched deeper than ever into the wheelchair, her eyes darting in furtive, nervous sweeps over the parking lot. When the limo engine hummed into life, she recoiled visibly, and her gaze fixed with almost hypnotic intensity on the approaching car.

Then she started to scream.

William's horse, a bay gelding, was tethered close to the tree stump where Robyn had sat and nursed baby Zach. "Hold tight to the child," William said curtly, then lifted her into the saddle in a single, swift movement. He swung himself up behind her without any need to use the tree stump as a mounting block and set off toward the Manor at a slow canter.

The manhandling by Captain Bretton's soldiers had left the front of her dress sopping wet, and Robyn was too cold and too tired to think or even to feel much during the brief ride back to the Manor. Fortunately, the rocking motion seemed to lull the baby into a doze, and he felt warm and comfy snuggled inside her cape.

At first she held herself rigidly upright, maintaining a careful distance between her spine and William's body, but gradually fatigue overcame resolution and she allowed herself to lean back against his chest. She thought she heard him draw in a sharp, hard breath, but he said nothing, and she decided she must have been mistaken. He felt strong and muscled behind her, his body an oddly comforting bulwark against the lashing rain. Ever since she woke up and found herself in the midst of this nightmare, William had been simultaneously the person she trusted least— and the person she most wanted to confide in. Why did he inspire such strangely mixed reactions? When he confronted Captain Bretton, she had felt as if she could entrust him with her life. And yet, two seconds later she had recognized him as a major threat to her security. Her nerve endings jangled with subliminal warning every time he came near. Even now, when she was hovering on the edge of total exhaustion, a tiny part of her body was quivering with tension, and she was aware of every movement he made.

A groom—she thought she recognized the stable lad she had overheard earlier in the evening—was waiting in the shelter of the portal covering the front entrance to the Manor. He ran out into the courtyard as soon as he spotted his master approaching, and held the horse's head while William dismounted. Robyn was so stiff and sore that she was secretly glad that William gave her no chance to get off the horse under her own steam. He simply lifted her out of the saddle and carried her across the muddy cobblestones into Starke.

It spoke volumes for her fatigued state that she scarcely noticed the bowing and curtsying servants who clustered in the hallway and lined the staircase. William, of course, paid them no heed at all and simply marched up the stairs, Robyn and baby Zach still held in his arms.

"I can walk," she muttered, not liking the confused emotions rioting inside her. "William, for heaven's sake, put me down. I'm not Scarlett, you're not Rhett, and I'm tired of playing low-budget reruns of *Gone With the Wind*."

He ignored her—what else had she expected?—and strode up the stairs at a spanking pace considering he was carrying a hundred twenty pounds of Robyn, plus fifteen pounds or so of sodden cape, as well as seven or eight pounds of baby Zach. Mary was hovering in the hallway outside Arabella's bedroom and she hurried to open the door for them. William acknowledged her action with a curt nod of the head.

"You may leave us," he said. "I will tend to the Lady Arabella."

"Yes, m'lord. Shall I send Annie to take the little un', m'lord?"

"No," Robyn said. "I will take care of Zach."

As always, Mary looked to William for confirmation. Robyn felt him hesitate for an instant before he nodded. "Very well, Mary. Her ladyship will send for the nurse later." He walked into the bedroom, slamming the door shut with the heel of his riding boot.

He set Robyn down on the rug in front of the fire, unhooking the frogs of her cloak and flinging it onto a chair. "The child is to be christened Arthur," he said, his voice hard. "The ceremony will take place on Sunday next, after matins. You will remember your son's name in the future, my lady, and you will use it."

Robyn's tentative spurt of goodwill toward William vanished in a flash. "You may christen my son whatever you please. I'm damn sure I get no say in the matter in this benighted place. But that doesn't mean you can force me to call my child by a name you've chosen without consulting me. I'm the one who delivered him after hours of labor, and as far as I'm concerned, his name is Zach, short for Zachary, and that's what I will always call him."

"Why are you determined to throw your infidelity in my face?" William asked tautly.

"You think Zach is your brother's child?" she asked incredulously. "For heaven's sake, William, don't be so damn melodramatic. I'm not throwing anything in your face and I haven't been unfaithful to you." She remembered Clemmie's brown eyes and flushed, correcting herself quickly. "Not for years, at any rate. You obviously don't want to believe me, but Zachary is our son. Yours and mine."

"But of course he is my son," William said, his voice heavy with irony. "Why else would you have staged that pitiful plea for reconciliation between us last April, if not to provide a father for your son? And if I cannot quite convince myself that a single foray into your bed resulted in instant impregnation, well then, you can prove my son's heritage jen-et-iclee, can you not?"

"Yes, and if you're too far in the past to accept genetic theory, you can prove it simply by looking at him. You can *see* he's your son if you would only open your eyes."

Robyn realized that she was near to tears, and she pointedly turned her back on William, setting Zach down on the chest of drawers she had designated as his changing stand. Much to the outrage of Mary and Annie who considered a lady's bedchamber no place for baby clothes, she kept a supply of clean garments in the top drawer, and a stack of muslin squares folded in a basket that stood between the chest and the fire. She picked up one of the makeshift diapers and pressed its softness against Zach's cheek. "See how warm it is?" she murmured, paying little heed to what she said, just wanting to soothe him with her chatter. "It's clean, too. Do you know how hard I had to fight to get the servants to wash your diapers instead of just drying them off?"

Zach gurgled and she smiled at him. "Right, I agree. That's disgusting. Gross, in fact. Now Mommy's going to make you all nice and dry. And we'll take that nasty wet nightgown off you, too. Are your toes cold from all the rain?"

Zachary's toes were toasty warm, but he let out a howl of protest as she untied his lacy bonnet and slipped the lavishly embroidered linen gown over his head. She bent down and gave him an absentminded kiss. "Sorry, poppet, did I hurt your arm? Mommy didn't mean to get rough with you but these clothes aren't exactly snap-and-go, you know."

She straightened from her task of tying and buttoning him into a clean diaper, long flannel petticoat, knitted cap, and

silk bedjacket, and found William staring at her, his expression arrested. "You need to change your own garments," he said, breaking the odd little silence that opened up between them. "You are a great deal wetter than your son."

"You're right, I am. As soon as you leave, I'll change."

"You cannot unhook your own gown," William said, not meeting her eyes. "If you will turn around, I will assist you."

Robyn laid Zachary in his cradle, glad of the excuse to avoid looking at William. "Thank you," she said, annoyed when her voice emerged sounding curiously breathless. "I would prefer to summon Mary."

"I wish to speak with you privately," William said. "And you will catch an inflammation of the lungs if you remain in those soaking wet clothes. My offer was purely practical in intent."

Robyn sat down in the chair beside Zach's cradle, leaning forward and rocking it gently. "I'm very tired," she said. "I can't imagine what you need to say to me that can't wait until tomorrow morning."

"Can you not?" William crossed to her side, pulling her to her feet. His eyes blazed with suppressed anger. "First you will change into dry clothing, then I will talk and you will discover just what I need to say to you."

"Don't be ridiculous, William. Stop playing macho man. I'm not going to get undressed with you standing around watching."

"Come, my lady, false modesty does not become you. I have seen all that you have to offer on many occasions and, believe me, there is no danger that I will fall headlong into lust because I unlace your stays."

His scorn pricked at Robyn's pride. "Will you not?" she asked sweetly. "And yet, when I was riding home with you, I could have sworn that I felt quite clear evidence of the force of your desire for me."

Color flashed for an instant in William's cheeks. Then he grabbed the hand mirror off the nearby dressing table and thrust it in front of her face.

"You have a high opinion of your charms," he said harshly. "Take a good look at yourself, my lady. Do you imagine that such a bedraggled female is likely to inspire me with an overwhelming longing to take her into my bed?"

Robyn turned white at the sight of herself in the mirror, not because she looked so wretched, but because she saw Arabella's ravaged blond beauty reflected back at her. Pushing the mirror away, she covered her eyes with her hand. "What is it that you want to know, William?" Even to her own ears, her voice sounded depressed and weary. "I will do my best to answer you although, believe me, I am not likely to have any answers for your questions."

"Very well, if you are determined to play the martyr, so be it. Here is my first question, and it would be gratifying if you attempted to answer it with a modicum of honesty. Why did you seek out Captain Bretton tonight? What did the pair of you hope to accomplish?"

"I didn't seek him out. Two of his men found me walking at the edge of the woods and they forced me to go with them. I had no idea they would take me to Captain Bretton."

William smiled without a trace of amusement. "Not one of your better stories, my lady. If you were not planning to meet with Captain Bretton, would you care to explain why you were strolling through the far reaches of Starke Manor on a freezing cold night, with a storm getting ready to blow in off the Channel?" His smile shaded from derision to outright mockery. "Please try to make your explanation a mite more convincing this time, my dear. It is so much more entertaining for both of us when you make your lies a little credible."

Robyn looked up, meeting his gaze defiantly. "I have a terrific explanation," she said.

"Then, pray, let me hear it. I am all attention."

"I was—running away."

William stared at her for a long silent moment, his expression unreadable. Finally, he got to his feet and walked over to the closet. He returned carrying a knitted shawl. "Here," he said, holding it out to her. "Since I rescued you from certain death after your carriage accident, I would prefer you not to die because you are too obstinate to change out of a wet dress."

"It's quite warm here in front of the fire," Robyn said. Nevertheless, she took the shawl.

William watched as she arranged the fleecy folds around her shoulders. "Why were you running away?" he asked.

What in the world should she say? "I . . . wanted . . . hoped to recapture the threads of my old life."

"And you felt that fleeing from your home and your family would achieve that?"

"Not . . . exactly." Robyn pleated the hem of the shawl between her fingers, avoiding William's gaze. "I needed to return to the place where I had my accident."

"If that is so, how did it come about that Captain Bretton's men found you wandering near the woods?"

"I . . . got lost."

"Ah, I see. After nine years of living at Starke, you could not orient yourself to the front gates. A most credible story."

"Credible or not, that's what happened," she said defiantly.

"It is a most odd coincidence that you should choose to return to the site of your unfortunate accident on the very night that Captain Bretton spread his dragnet of dragoons across the countryside."

Robyn choked on a gasp of laughter that was almost a sob. "Not nearly as odd as some of the other things that have been happening to me lately." She drew in a deep breath and forced her nervous fingers to lie still. "You will not like the truth, William, but the truth is that I didn't know Captain Bretton existed until two ragamuffin soldiers dragged me to the clearing and he confronted me."

William looked at her, then gave a harsh, frustrated laugh. "By God, you are a remarkable woman, Arabella. Just when I am convinced there is no trick you can employ that will deceive me, you come up with a fresh stratagem that leaves me floundering, trying to grasp the tiny acorn of truth that lurks behind your oak tree of lies."

"This time you have no need to search," she said quietly. "I'm telling you the truth as I understand it. It was obvious from my conversation with Captain Bretton that we are old acquaintances, but I swear to you, William, that I have no memory of the man. I know nothing of our past dealings with each other. When I saw him tonight, I felt as if I saw him for the first time in my life."

"You are claiming to have lost your memory, my lady?"

Robyn hesitated. Claiming amnesia as a result of the carriage accident might be the easiest way to account for her strange behavior. Certainly it sounded a lot more believable than an hysterical statement to the effect that she was trapped in a time warp, lost inside another woman's body. Pretending amnesia was a safe course and might even evoke sympathy. Telling the truth was likely to get her clapped away in the local lunatic asylum or confined to a dark turret in Starke Manor.

Decision made, she looked up and met William's eyes. "Yes," she said. "I think the blow to my head when I fell from the carriage affected my memory."

Her pause had been too long, and William misinterpreted it. His gaze became cynical. "How selective your memory is in its failures, my dove! Is it not curious that you forget the captain, but retain vivid memories of my brother Zachary? Your lovers would like to think that they receive equal attention, you know."

"They do. I don't remember your brother, either."

"Please do not insult my intelligence, my lady. Zachary was the first name you spoke when you regained consciousness after your fall from the carriage. And now you insist upon calling your son by his name."

"That's not for the reason you think. That's . . . for a different reason."

"Yes," William said, "I am sure it is." He glanced at baby Zach sleeping in the cradle, and for a moment his eyes darkened, as if with pain. Then he swung on his heel, turning his back to Robyn. "Poor Captain Bretton. He would be devastated to know that the lady who was once his affianced bride claims to have no memory of him. The captain does not like to feel ignored."

"Captain Bretton was once my fiancé?" Robyn sputtered in her shock. Whatever she'd expected to hear, it hadn't been that.

William's voice shimmered with sarcasm. "The first gentleman to win a promise of eternal fidelity from you, my lady, but certainly not the last."

"Wait!" Robyn was too confused to feel insulted. "Why didn't the captain and I get married? Did I break off the engagement?"

William rested his boot on the corner of Zach's cradle and rocked gently. "If you really cannot remember," he said at last, "mayhap 'tis better if we do not rake over past events that still carry the power to wound."

"No," she said, her throat tight with tension. "William, I have to know. I can't walk around with my own past a sealed mystery to me. Don't you see? If I had known the truth about my relationship with Captain Bretton, I would have handled our encounter differently. I need to know what happened in my past."

William studied her face in silence for several long moments. "Captain Bretton broke off his engagement to you," he said finally.

"Why?"

He met her gaze head on. "Because he discovered that you were with child."

Robyn felt the shawl slip out of her grasp and slide to the floor. She didn't bother to pick it up. "Was it the captain's child?" she asked, her throat feeling so dry that the words seemed to stick to the roof of her mouth.

"No."

"Whose child was it?" She rose to her feet. "Was it yours, William?"

"No."

"Tell me," she said, sensing the vital importance of the information he was withholding. "You must tell me. Who was the father?"

William shook back the lace of his cuffs and drew out a box of snuff, flicking open the lid with a casual expertise that was almost convincing. Almost, but not quite.

"The child was Zachary's," he said. "You were pregnant with my brother's child when Captain Bretton spurned you."

Chapter 11

BETROTHED to one man, pregnant by another, and married to somebody else. The lady sure spread her favors around. Fighting back an absurd impulse to apologize to William for having betrayed him in so many ways, Robyn decided that the more she learned about the Lady Arabella Bowleigh, the less she liked her.

"Okay, so Arabella was pregnant with Zachary's child," she said. "I still don't understand why she . . . why I ended up married to you." Uncertainty made her voice deepen, and the words came out sounding far more hostile than she'd intended.

"My dear Arabella, however faulty your memory, you can surely understand that a woman with a babe in her belly is in desperate need of a husband. Captain Bretton refused to ally himself with a fallen woman. In such straits, any willing fool who offers himself will have to do."

"And you were that willing fool?"

"Indeed I was. As willing—nay eager—as I was foolish." His bitter smile mocked the memory of his own past. "If I can recall the emotions of that overheated time, I believe I indulged in some boyish fantasy of redeeming my brother's honor."

"Hah! I expect your sense of family honor would have been a lot less acute if Arabella . . . if I . . . had been cross-eyed and buck-toothed."

"Undoubtedly." William appeared unruffled by her heated accusation. "I make no claim to nobility of conduct, my lady, merely to youthful lust and astonishing lack of judgment. Our marriage was entered into for selfish reasons on both sides and we have reaped the harvest we deserve."

"I'd still like to know why your brother didn't take responsibility for the child he'd created. Why did *you* need to restore his honor when he could have restored it quite easily himself? I may not understand much about social customs in the eighteenth century, but I'd have thought a man who took the virginity of a noblewoman—" She broke off. "Oh, is that it? Was I a peasant, or a farmer's daughter, or something socially beneath contempt until you deigned to marry me?"

William gave a short, hard laugh. "Now, my dear, you almost convince me that your wits have truly gone begging. No, you were not a commoner, as a moment's thought would tell you."

"How so? Do aristocrats come with a certificate of authentication sewn to their navels, ready for any interested party to glance down and inspect?"

William looked genuinely puzzled. "I do not understand your strange attempt at repartee. I refer to the fact that you are addressed as Lady Arabella, which, as you very well know, is itself an acknowledgment of your noble birth."

"Why?"

"Had you been a commoner before our marriage you would take my title and you would be addressed as Lady Bowleigh. As the daughter of the Earl of Marshe, you are of higher rank than I, a mere baron: a fact you normally delight in mentioning on every possible occasion."

Robyn bit back a sarcastic remark to the effect that Americans had staged a revolution in part so that they wouldn't have to waste their time worrying about the correct way to address the daughter of an earl, as opposed to the wife of a baron. She returned to her previous question, which remained unanswered. "Since I'm a genuine, blue-blooded aristocrat, that ought to have been all the more reason for your brother to marry me. Why wasn't my father pounding on Zachary's door, demanding that he make an honest woman out of me? And why would Zachary refuse? I should think the daughter of an earl was a pretty good catch for a second son with little hope of inheriting the family mansion."

"Zachary had left for France before your condition became apparent," William said, after an almost imperceptible hesitation. "We considered sending a courier in search of him, but we were not sure of his precise route through

France, and time, naturally, was of the essence. In fact, my brother never knew of your plight."

Robyn paid less attention to the hesitation than she might have done, because she was struck by the sudden realization of what William's revelation really meant. "Good grief!" she exclaimed, shocked into tactlessness. "If I was pregnant when we got married, that means the twins ... George and Freddie ... they're Zachary's sons and you've always known that!"

William shot her a narrow-eyed glance. "No," he said. "You miscarried Zachary's babe within the first month of our marriage. George and Freddie were born eleven months later." He gave a wintry smile. "Ever the optimist, I have allowed myself to believe that the twins are heirs of my flesh as well as the legal heirs to my estate."

Robyn was surprised at how relieved she felt to learn that George and Freddie were truly William's sons, although why she cared so much on his behalf she couldn't imagine. The state of her feelings was confusing, so she decided to change the subject. Lord knew, there seemed to be a fresh puzzle for every mystery William cleared up.

"How did Captain Bretton discover that Arabella was pregnant? I mean, given that Zachary was lost in the wilds of Europe and Arabella was in urgent need of a wedding ring, she seems to have handled the whole situation with incredible stupidity. Or did she get a sudden attack of conscience and confess everything to the captain? Although, heaven knows, that doesn't sound in the least like the lady. She seems to have kept her conscience pretty well tamed to suit her convenience."

William stopped his pacing, his eyes narrowing as he looked at her. "Why do you persist in referring to yourself thus impersonally, as if you never knew the Arabella of whom we speak?"

"Because I *don't* know her," Robyn said, admitting the truth with a sense of real relief. At some point during the evening's ventures it had begun to seem vitally important for William to stop disliking her. And if she wanted him to become her ally instead of her adversary she needed to find some way to persuade him that she could be trusted. "I wish I could convince you that my accident affected my memories," she said. "Honestly, William, I remember nothing about my past life with you and nothing about Arabella's thoughts and feelings in the past."

He made no effort to hide his impatience. "I find such a statement incredible. In fact, your actions since the accident give the lie to your claim. The first name you spoke on opening your eyes was my brother's."

How could she possibly respond without giving him grounds to doubt her sanity, let alone her integrity? "I don't recall the first few moments after the accident," she said finally, not comfortable with the half lie, but not sure what else she could say. "If you reflect back on the last few weeks, surely you must have noticed changes in my behavior? Changes that suggest I'm a different person from the Arabella you once knew?"

William inclined his head in mocking acknowledgment. "Indeed, my lady, the transformation of your behavior has been striking. I have wondered what new ploy you were attempting, and I believe I now stand on the brink of finding out. Enlighten me, my lady, I beg. If it was your aim to have piqued my curiosity, I confess you have been successful."

"There is no ploy, William." Robyn tried to lessen the tension stretching between the two of them by holding out her hands and meeting his gaze with frank, open appeal. "My lord"—strange how easily the formal title tripped off her tongue—"my lord, this hostility between us is exhausting, and I think unnecessary. Couldn't we try to treat each other more kindly? The truth is, the blow to my head when I had the accident affected my mind. I need your help." *God knew, that was the absolute truth.*

William said nothing. He stood, silent and unmoving, his expression swept carefully clean. Only the sardonic gleam in his eyes suggested he was even listening. In her eagerness to forge a new beginning to their relationship, she moved even closer, grasping his hands in an impulsive attempt to establish a link between the two of them.

"I know the servants think I'm crazy, but I'm not, William. I just feel—bewildered—by my situation. But I can reason logically, and function in an everyday situation, which must mean that I'm not totally out of touch with reality."

Of course, the reality she was in touch with seemed to be two hundred and fifty years out-of-date, but she wouldn't dwell on that minor problem for the moment.

William still didn't respond. She felt unnerved by his obdurate silence, but if she wanted his cooperation, she didn't see any alternative to persuading him to change his opinion of her, so she drew in a deep breath and pushed on with her plea for help. "What I'm trying to say, I guess, is that I honestly and truly have no memories of my life with you before my accident. I'm not lying, William, or trying to trick you as part of some obscure plot. Believe me when I tell you that I don't remember this house, or the servants, or the countryside around the Manor. Worst of all, I can't remember the children, and that hurts me more than all the rest." She shook her head, blinking back tears. "I need your help, William, if I am ever going to find my way out of the mess we're both in. Please let's try to make a fresh start to our relationship."

When she started speaking, she could have sworn she saw a flash of sympathy in his face, but as soon as she mentioned the children his mouth tightened angrily and all trace of sympathy vanished. He withdrew his hands from her clasp with exaggerated courtesy and swept her a deep bow. Heart sinking, she recognized the signal for one of his sarcastic diatribes, and knew that she had failed to convince him that she spoke the truth. Perhaps that wasn't surprising when she had no idea what "the truth" of her situation really was.

"You plead your case with superlative grace," William said, his hand on his heart, his posture all cool, insincere elegance. "I vow 'twould be monstrous ungentlemanly of me to let such an impassioned and eloquent plea go unanswered. I shall, of course, do my best not to disappoint your ladyship."

"Disappoint me? I don't understand—"

"Come, Arabella, do not be trite. Whatever *your* problems may be, *my* memory is not gone missing and I recognize the prelude to one of your usual invitations to seduction. When all else fails between us, you invariably promise a fresh start to our relationship and reward me with the offer of your body. 'Tis a scant nine months since we last danced and fumbled our way through this scene and I clearly remember the details of our ritual. Smile, my dear, it is now time for you to simper a little and glance suggestively toward your bed."

Robyn shivered. "Dear God, how could you imagine I want to make love with you? No such possibility crossed my mind."

"Make love? What an inappropriate way to describe our couplings, my dear." William shook his head. "The oddness of your speech since the accident can sometimes be quite diverting." He took her hands and kissed the tips of her fingers gracefully, his smile glittering with derision. "You should not strive so mightily to achieve so simple an object, my dear. I am but a normal man, with all the usual appetites. I am happy to oblige your ladyship if you feel a swift tumble between the sheets would serve to refresh your ailing memory."

"I feel no such thing—"

"Come, my lady, why do you waste time with useless denials? Make this easy for both of us and tell me what you would like me to do next. You cannot expect me to invent all the lines in this play we are enacting, despite its tedious familiarity. Do you wish me to seize you with passion? Whisper sweet poetry into your shell-like ears? Or mayhap play lady's maid and ease you slowly out of your damp clothing? Speak up, my lady, let me hear your pleasure. God knows, fornication is beyond doubt the activity which has played the most important role in our past. Why should we not make it the key that unlocks our future?"

"You are cruel," Robyn said. "Ruthless and cruel. Good grief, William, I asked for your help, not for this vicious mockery."

"You are ruthless and cruel," he repeated, seeming to savor the words. Robyn recoiled, but even through the haze of her own hurt, she recognized that William's ferocity sprang from a deep-rooted need to conceal his pain. "Ah yes, your familiar reproaches burst forth with all the old relish. It seems we have only to mention the possibility of a tumble on the bed, and your memory revives."

She turned away from him, shivering under the lash of his tongue. "No more, William. We're both tired, so you'd better leave before you say something unforgivable."

" 'Tis surely years too late for such worthy advice. We have said everything that is unforgivable many times before." He grasped her shoulders and twisted her around, crooking his forefinger under her chin so that he could tilt her face up to his inspection. "Such amazing beauty," he murmured, smoothing her hair away from her forehead. "My God, it startles me still when I see such amazing, *lying* beauty."

She grabbed his hand, shoving it aside. "William, get away. Get out of my room. This is sick behavior—"

He laughed, but she heard the harsh note of self-recrimination lurking behind the derision. "Sickness, madness, desire. Who cares what name we give to the passion since we both know that we feel it?"

"It matters a lot. We can either exploit each other—"

"Another odd but apt turn of phrase," he murmured, lowering his mouth toward hers. "Kiss me, my lady. Let us exploit each other to the full so that we may find out if we still despise each other as acutely as we remember."

His mouth came down on hers, rich with passion, hot and fierce with self-loathing. Robyn turned her head away, knowing that she moved an instant too late for the evasion to be convincing. She was surprised—but surely not disappointed?—when he drew in a shuddering breath and ended the kiss.

"Ah no," he murmured against her mouth, his body tantalizingly close yet not touching her at any point. "You will not pretend that I force myself upon you against your will, my lady. Rapist is the one role I am not willing to perform for you. If you want me to kiss you, I fear that you must ask me nicely to oblige. Come now, surely you can manage one of your usual pretty speeches so that we may both indulge our needs?"

Robyn averted her eyes, frightened by the intensity of her longing to close the tiny gap between them and move into his arms. Despite William's simmering anger, she wanted the comfort of intimate contact with another human being. She wasn't truly William's wife, but she was trapped here in this impossible situation. Why shouldn't she refresh her memories of Zach and the joy of their lovemaking? William looked like Zach, at least a little bit. On one or two occasions, she had heard William's voice take on the same mellow, laughing timbre as Zach's voice. What harm would it do if she pretended, just for a while, that he really was Zach? If she made love to him generously, with thought for his needs and feelings, wouldn't she be doing him a favor as well as herself? Arabella had probably never made love with generosity of spirit in her entire life. William would enjoy the change.

She swayed toward him. "Hold me," she whispered, stumbling over the words, cutting herself off before she made the mistake of calling him by Zach's name. "Oh, God, I'm so scared. I want you to hold me."

For a moment he went utterly still. Then she heard the quick, stifled intake of his breath and felt the explosion of his desire as he took her mouth in a kiss that seemed to speak of years of silent longing.

Her body responded with mindless, primitive urgency. Her breasts, heavy with milk, tingled with arousal and she instinctively moved closer when she felt the thrust of his erection against her. *Yes.* This was what she had needed for days, for weeks, ever since the accident. She had needed Zach, holding her close. Zach stroking his hands over her hips, ravaging her mouth with kisses. She twined her hands in his hair, pulling at the velvet ribbon that tied it in place, relishing the silkiness of the long, thick strands curling around her fingers.

"Arabella, dear God, what has happened to you? You feel so warm and responsive."

He said her name with soft, husky urgency. The syllables fell against her ears with the icy chill of a spring shower in the Arctic.

Arabella.

Good lord, she was not Arabella, and he was not Zach, and she had damn near committed the outrage of making love to one man while pretending he was another.

Trembling, her body still reluctant to admit the deception, she pulled herself out of William's arms. "William, we must stop," she said. "We cannot . . . make love. It was a mistake. I'm sorry, I didn't mean to . . . lead you on."

His face shuttered, all passion and warmth draining away in an instant. "It was a mistake, and you are sorry," he murmured. He stepped away, turning his back to her, and she saw the muscles strain beneath the serge of his riding jacket as he struggled for control. After a moment or two, he swung around to face her again, bowing in ironic salute.

"Congratulations, my lady. It seems you have proven once more that I am still the fool I had persuaded myself I was not. A month ago, I would have sworn you had entirely lost the power to make me desire you." He picked up his greatcoat from the chair where he had thrown it, and slung it around his shoulders. "Practice your new role of distraught innocent, my lady. In faith, 'tis vastly more appealing that most of your earlier roles." His voice sounded patrician, faintly bored, as it so often did. But she knew him better now, and she saw the tiny leap of the muscle in his throat, the almost imperceptible tension in the line of his jaw. William had been deeply aroused, and control was not coming easy to him.

She reached out her hand and touched him lightly on the arm. Beneath her fingers she felt his muscles bunch and then deliberately relax. His face remained impassive, so that only the closest of observers would have realized his tension.

"William," she said wistfully. "Do you think it is too late for us to learn to be friends?"

William stared at her, then laughed. "Friends? My dear Arabella, the possibility of friendship between us is so breathtakingly absurd that I cannot believe you pose the question expecting a serious answer."

"I am extremely serious. Think about it," she said coaxingly. "Our relationship causes us nothing but pain at the moment, and yet we are forced to live in the same house and share our lives, at least to a certain extent. Isn't it worth trying to make things better? We have so much to gain and so little to lose."

"True, but alas, I see no method whereby we could achieve such a desirable end. The wounds between us are old and deep."

"All the more reason for both of us to forget our past relationship. Why couldn't we pretend we've just met and are anxious to get acquainted? Couldn't we try that, William? Instead of assuming all sorts of hidden meanings and motives every time I say something to you, take my words at face value, as if everything between us is fresh and new. For my part, I would certainly be willing to try."

"A clean slate?" he asked. "Alas, my lady, past reality is not erased as easily as chalk marks on a schoolroom board."

"Then how else are we to move forward?" she asked. "If our past is an intolerable burden, we must either forget it, or be slaves to it forever."

He looked at her for a long, silent moment. "In losing your wits, my lady, it seems that you have become a philosopher."

She risked a smile. "Perhaps with all the frippery wiped out, there's finally space in my brain to accommodate a few great thoughts."

He seemed unable to look away from her smile. In the end, he shrugged and walked toward the door. "We could try a new start, I suppose. As you point out, what have we to lose? Indeed, the more time I spend with you recently, the more I feel that I truly do not know the woman you have become. To that extent, at least, there would be no pretense."

"Then let's do it," Robyn said, elated by his semi-agreement. "Let's discover all that we need to know about each other in order to become friends. Maybe you could come and have tea in the nursery with the children and me tomorrow afternoon? Clemmie would love to play hostess, and the boys would enjoy an excuse to stuff themselves with cake. We can have a good time, all of us, if we just keep our thoughts concentrated on the tea party and not on the past."

"Tea in the nursery?" William's expression became quizzical. "If I had not heard you extend the invitation with your own lips, my lady, I would refuse to believe you had made it." He shook his head, looking somewhat surprised at his own acquiescence. "Very well, my lady. We shall meet each other over tea and cakes in the nursery tomorrow. Does five of the clock sound a suitable hour?"

Robyn laughed, lighter of spirit than she had been since the accident. "It sounds great. I'm already looking forward to it. Five of the clock it shall be!"

Chapter 12

ZACH ate dinner alone, at a restaurant right around the corner from the Gallery. He ordered broiled lamb chops, most of which he left, and a bottle of California pinot noir, most of which he drank. He took a cab home, and walked unsteadily into his apartment building, wondering how much cognac he would need to swallow before he would be drunk enough to fall asleep without thinking about Robyn. One thing he knew for sure—a bottle of wine hadn't been enough.

Will.

The sight of his younger brother seated on an upholstered bench in the lobby sobered him up a bit, but not as much as he would have liked. Damn! He sure hoped he didn't look as wasted as he felt. He'd spent the past fifteen years lecturing his kid brother about how drugs and alcohol never solved a single problem in anyone's life. It was a great lecture. He should have listened to it himself.

His brother stood up and took a deep drag on his cigarette. "Hello, Zach."

"Hello, Will." On the brink of giving his brother a bear hug, Zach hesitated and held out his hand instead. He was relieved when Will took it, even more relieved when Will thumped him hard on the shoulder. Maybe there was hope yet for their tattered relationship.

Zach stood back. "Hey, it's great to see you, kid. Have you been waiting long?"

Will leaned against the wall. "Not too long. You look like hell."

Zach grinned. "Gee, thanks. You're looking terrific, all California tan and muscles."

"Yeah. Claire makes me work out. I run a lot. Taking after you, big brother."

Claire's name fell between them like a weapon. Zach avoided the challenge. "Well, like I said, it's good to see you. What brings you into Manhattan at this time of year?"

"You. The Gallery. Claire." Will shoved his hands in his pockets. "You gonna invite me up to your apartment or do we have to stand around in this god-awful lobby freezing our asses off? This place is about as cheerful as a dentist's waiting room in Moscow."

Zach chuckled. "Go easy with the sweet talk, or I'll think you want to borrow money."

He knew the instant the words were out of his mouth that he'd said the wrong thing. Will scowled at him, then ran his hands through his hair in a swift, angry gesture, tousling the arrow-straight, light brown strand that fell over his forehead. "Goddammit, Zach, you never let up, do you? One of these years, you may get it through your thick skull that I don't want your fucking money."

Zach wasn't sober enough to think smart and he lost his temper. "Hell, no, you don't want my money. You just want my ex-wife. Couldn't you find any other way to screw me over?"

Will gave a short, hard laugh, and started walking toward the door. "We never change, do we? Two minutes. That's how long it took for us to start fighting. Good-bye, Zach, see you around sometime. Claire warned me you'd never agree to talk."

Zach lunged forward and grabbed his brother's arm. "Don't go, Will. You're right, we need to talk, to straighten things out between us."

"That's a great idea in theory, but when we get together, we don't talk. We fight."

"Not always. We used to be good friends."

"Yeah. Until I dropped out of high school and started running with the wrong crowd. According to Dad and Grandfather, you were the family saint and I was the asshole who couldn't keep away from the booze."

"Let's not argue about who's to blame for the past. We both screwed up plenty." Zach drew in a deep breath, aware of the doorman busily pretending not to listen. "Look, could we start this conversation over? Come up to the apartment where it's warm, and I'll make us a pot of coffee."

"Still playing the good guy," Will sneered. "Always ready to forgive the prodigal son one more time?"

"I don't have to forgive you," Zach said. "You need to forgive yourself."

"Jesus, now we get the pop psychology."

"Nope, that was wisdom of the ancient Orient. Confucius said it a few thousand years before the psychologists."

A smile gleamed for a moment in Will's eyes. He shrugged and walked slowly toward the elevator. "You still make the same lousy coffee you always made?"

Zach felt relief surge through him as he pressed the button to open the elevator. "Yep, it's still the same lousy brew. I can defeat every coffee-making machine known to man. You coming up?"

"I guess." Will stubbed out his cigarette and followed Zach into the elevator. "Same dreary lobby, same hard bench. Same nagging brother. Same rotten coffee. Now it really feels like I've come home."

"Does it? I'm glad. It's good to have you back, Will."

"Yeah, it's great, terrific. I hope you think that way half an hour from now."

"Any special reason why I shouldn't?"

"Not one reason. Maybe a dozen or so." The elevator clanged to a halt and they stepped out into the penthouse lobby. "Let's talk about it later," Will said. "My psychiatrist advises me to face my problems one at a time. Right now, I'm facing the problem of how I'm going to swallow a cup of your battery acid disguised as coffee without lighting up a cigarette in the sacred vicinity of Grandmother's antiques."

"You can make the coffee yourself if you prefer." Zach tossed his overcoat onto a chair and walked into the kitchen. "That takes care of the first problem. And you can smoke a cigarette if it's that important to you."

"Good God, you've mellowed."

Zach grinned. "I guess some of the sharper edges are getting ground down a bit now that I'm heading toward middle age."

"You still look like the same tight-assed do-gooder to me."

"Lay off, Will. I'm feeling in the mood to punch some-body's nose, and I'd hate like hell for it to be yours."

Surprisingly, Will laughed. "I don't need to smoke in here," he said. "As a matter of fact, I'm trying to give up smoking."

"Hey, great! I wish you luck."

"Yeah. I figured that since I'm already on the wagon, I may as well make my life a total hell and give up smoking, too."

Zach sat down and stretched his legs out, his sprawling position belying the tension that curled inside him. "Gerry told me you'd been sober for a while," he said carefully. "That's great news, Will."

Will busied himself pouring water into the coffeepot. "Yeah. Nine months and counting. No booze. No coke. Not even a puff of pot. I'm not planning to backslide this time, either."

"Nine months, huh? You've never lasted that long before. That's terrific and I sure hope you keep up the good work."

He sounded so damn patronizing, Zach thought. He was sober enough to appreciate the irony of being too drunk to handle his brother's climb onto the sobriety wagon with the sensitivity the situation demanded.

Will, fortunately, didn't take offense. He opened and closed a few cupboard doors, making a lot of noise and pro-viding himself with an excuse to avoid Zach's eyes. "I'm thirty-two," he said through the clatter. "I guess I decided that was a couple of years too old to keep on playing the role of misunderstood teenager. Where the hell do you keep your coffee, anyway?"

"In the cupboard above the sink." Zach watched his brother grind the coffee beans, feeling a faint stirring of hope along with the familiar mixture of love and anxiety. Will looked less volatile, less edgy, than Zach had seen him in years. His brother was never going to be a placid, laid-back individual, but he did seem more at peace with himself and the world.

"How's the painting going?" he asked.

"Okay. Better than okay." His preparations finished, Will turned around and leaned against the counter. "Rick Bernsteen is giving me an exhibition next month. A solo."

Zach sat up. "Hey, congratulations! I'm impressed as hell. I didn't know Bernsteen handled abstract oils."

"He doesn't. The paintings he's agreed to take are a series of portraits."

"Who did you paint?"

Will paused for a moment. "Claire," he said finally. "When Claire and I moved in together . . . well, anyway, after a few months of being around her, I decided representational art still had something left to say to the world."

"I see."

"I'm sure you don't, but it doesn't matter because I know these paintings are good." Will poured out the coffee and carried a mug over to Zach. "I'm sorry about Robyn Delaney," he said, his voice a little too casual. "That shooting was a rotten deal and I heard from Mother that she isn't recuperating too well."

"No, not too well." Zach cradled his hands around the steaming mug. "Physically, the doctors can't find much wrong with her, but mentally, she isn't recovering like we all hoped."

"That's too bad." Will hesitated, then fell silent.

"She doesn't seem to recognize any of her family or her friends," Zach said. "Not even Al and Muriel. In fact, she insists her parents have been dead for years."

"I guess she doesn't recognize you, either."

Zach's smile was bitter. "I don't know whether she recognizes me or not. If she does, she sure doesn't like what she sees. The mere sight of me seems to send her off into a screaming fit."

"I'm sorry, that must be real tough on you. Gerry said you were obviously in love with each other."

"He did? He's never discussed Robyn with me."

"I guess he didn't think there was any point in rubbing salt in the wound."

Zach leaned back in his chair, stirring his coffee. "Why did you come here tonight, Will?"

"For one thing, Claire and I plan to get married on Christmas Eve. We want you to come to the wedding."

"I don't think that would be such a good idea," Zach said. "I'd like to pretend I'm happy for you both, but I'm having a hard time of it. The fact is, Claire and I got divorced because we can't stand the sight of each other."

Will shrugged. "Claire came out of her marriage convinced you're a monster, and you think she's a witch. Life would be a lot easier if both of you would accept that you're not bad guys. You were just two immature kids who should never have gotten married."

"Great advice." Zach didn't attempt to hide his sarcasm. "Don't forget to mention that you just happen to be the next sucker waiting in line to get hexed by Witch Claire. She may look like honey and sweet cream on the surface, but take it from me, she's pure poison at the center."

Will pushed back his chair and strode over to the sink to pour himself another mug of coffee. "My psychiatrist doesn't like it when I solve my problems with physical violence," he said. "Count yourself lucky, big brother, because I sure as hell resent people who talk that way about the woman I love."

Zach stared into his empty mug. "Why are you marrying her, Will? Bottom line."

"Bottom line? We're in love. Claire and I make things go right for each other. We enjoy each other's company, even when we're not in bed, which is more than could be said for the pair of you when you were married."

Will was throwing down the gauntlet with a vengeance and Zach stopped himself on the brink of hurling back an angry response. The hell of it was, Will's direct approach was the right one. They were never going to get their relationship back on track as long as they refused to acknowledge the problem of being two brothers who'd shared the bed and the sexual favors of the same woman.

"Doesn't it worry you that Claire scarcely waited for the lawyer to fax her a copy of the divorce papers before she cozied up to you? She made damn sure I knew what she was doing, too. I don't think it's just my overinflated ego that suggests she started an affair with you at least in part to get back at me."

"You're probably right," Will agreed mildly. "And my own motives in starting the affair sure as hell don't stand scrutiny. But Claire and I are different people today from the people we were a year ago. Vengeance against you plays no part in our relationship anymore." He lifted his shoulders in an embarrassed shrug. "I guess we both finally grew up."

"Fine. That's good to hear," Zach snarled, then realized to his amazement that his response was no more than the simple truth. If Claire and his brother were genuinely in love, who was he to stand in their way? He loved Robyn, had loved her for months, and Claire had no role in his life nowadays except as a figure from the distant past. He felt an enormous sense of liberation as he mentally closed the book on his youthful marriage.

He thumped his brother on the shoulder. "Hey, you know what? I've been making a total ass of myself because of some hang-up I should have grown out of years ago. I hope you and Claire will be very happy together. You have my sincere good wishes, both of you."

Will's mouth broke into a smile. "You really mean that, don't you? Are you going to attend the wedding after all?"

Zach hesitated. "If Claire won't feel uncomfortable having me around."

"Not a bit. She says you being there will give her a feeling of necessary closure."

Trust Claire to make him feel about as significant as a malfunctioning zipper, Zach thought with mild amusement. He got up and dumped his coffee mug in the sink. "Let me know when and where I have to turn up, and I'll be there. In the meantime, why don't you tell me what's really bothering you? Something's chewing you up, kid, and I don't think it's my screwed-up attitude toward Claire."

Will stopped pacing, obviously steeling himself to break bad news. "I never could deceive you worth a damn," he said at last.

"Then don't try. Tell me what's eating you."

"It's about the Gallery." Will drew in a deep breath. "Zach, word's out in the trade that the Bowleigh Gallery can't be relied on anymore. I've heard rumors all over town that the Gallery has been passing high-end fakes on a regular basis."

Zach didn't say anything for a moment. He realized that he finally felt stone-cold sober. The churning in his stomach was caused by tension, not by alcohol. "Where did you hear that?" he asked.

Will looked miserable. "The fact is, Zach, I heard it in a half-dozen different places. Rick Bernsteen even mentioned something about it, and he's three thousand miles across country, plus he has almost no contact with people in the antiques trade." Will broke off. "Jeez, Zach, you could at least look a little surprised, or worried, or something."

Zach shook his head. "I guess I'm not surprised and I passed from being worried into being numb weeks ago, when Robyn was shot."

Will shoved his hands into his pockets. "I can't believe I'm asking this, but is there even a crumb of truth to the rumors?"

"More than a crumb. I've identified at least nine fakes we've sold in the past year. The Farleigh cabinet you spotted in L.A. was just one of them."

Will's breath expelled in a hiss of surprise. "Jesus H. Christ! What the hell are you doing about the situation?"

"I have investigators working on the case, a couple of top specialists from the J. W. Grady Agency."

"They're good, the best in the business. Are they getting anywhere?"

Zach walked over to the window, parting the slats of the blind and peering out into the darkness. The J. W. Grady Agency was getting somewhere all right. That was why he'd spent most of the evening trying to make himself drunk.

"Zach?" Will stood behind him. "Have the investigators found out anything useful?"

Zach tried to shake off his black mood. "They've found out quite a lot. In fact, as far as the folks from J. W. Grady are concerned, the case is wrapped up. They're hoping for a bonus, based on the speed with which they've solved the case."

"That's all good news, so why are you looking so damn gloomy?"

Zach released the slats of the blind with a snap. "Because I'm not willing to accept their conclusions."

"Why not? What have they concluded?"

Zach felt a white-hot explosion of pain in the middle of his gut. He thought he'd gotten over the shock of the day's revelations, but apparently they still had the power to wound. He drew in an unsteady breath. "The investigators think Robyn Delaney was responsible for the scam."

Will was silent for at least a minute. "Gee, I'm sorry," he said at last. "Real sorry."

"She didn't do it," Zach said tightly. "Dammit, I know Robyn and she just isn't capable of that sort of betrayal."

Will cleared his throat. "What makes the investigators suspect her?"

"They found the design specifications for at least twenty of the Gallery's major antiques coded into her computer. They also found the address of a factory in Taiwan that made the pieces according to her specifications, and the address of a warehouse in Queens where she stored the fakes until she was ready to make the substitutions."

Will gave a low whistle. "Wouldn't you consider that pretty damning evidence?" he asked.

"On the contrary," Zach said. "Robyn wasn't a fool. Why the hell would she leave all that incriminating information on an office computer where anyone could find it?"

"Well, it was coded. And maybe she didn't have access to any other computer?"

"If she's responsible for this scam, she must have been making at least twenty thousand dollars per deal, maybe as much as two hundred thousand dollars over the past year. She's too bright not to have worked out that it would be smart to use some of her profits to buy herself a home computer."

"You're right, I guess." Will tried to look persuaded and didn't entirely succeed. "Did the investigators find any trace of the money she supposedly made working the scam?"

Zach stared at the coffeepot, resisting the totally irrational urge to pick it up and fling it against the wall. "Yes," he said, through gritted teeth, hating to make the admission. "They found an account of hers that has seventy-five thousand dollars in it."

"Wow!" Will recovered quickly. "Maybe she has rich parents," he said.

Zach shook his head. "No."

Will touched his brother on the arm. "I'm ... sorry, Zach."

"There's no reason to be sorry. I don't accept the agency's

conclusions. The investigators are missing something, somewhere. God, I wish Robyn was able to come back to work and answer all these damn questions." Zach rubbed the back of his neck, trying to ease the crick that seemed to have lodged there permanently for a week at least. "It's hard enough to imagine Robyn as a criminal," he said brusquely. "It's flat out impossible to imagine her as a *stupid* criminal."

Will seemed to think it would be tactful to change the subject. "Did the investigators say how the fakes were introduced onto the Gallery floor?" he asked. "Do they realize Robyn couldn't have done that alone? She was only a junior buyer, and her verifications would always be vetted by someone else."

"Except for the so-called Farleigh cabinet, there's no evidence that fakes were ever brought into the Gallery showrooms," Zach said. "I've realized for a while that the substitutions had to be made *after* the Gallery made a sale, not before."

Will knew enough about the antiques trade to understand at once. "My God, of course! That way the thieves avoid the problem of authentication. The genuine antique goes through all the tests, and whoever is working the scam produces a fake at the last minute."

"You've got it," Zach said grimly. "The scheme these folks worked out is so simple, it's embarrassing. A couple of the Gallery's deliverymen have been bought off. When a substitution is going to be made, the drivers take the delivery truck on a detour to the warehouse in Queens. They remove the crate with the genuine antique in it, and substitute a crate containing the fake antique—"

"And that's it!" Will exclaimed. "The buyer gets a perfect copy of the antique he's just bought, complete with all the necessary provenance documents, and the whole deal guaranteed by the highly reputable Bowleigh Gallery. He's no expert, and he doesn't suspect a thing—"

"Why would he? These fakes are good enough to fool all of us, expert or not. So the buyer pays upward of fifty thousand dollars for a well-crafted fake, and the thieves are left with a genuine antique that they can offer for sale anywhere."

Will looked stunned. "Damn, you're right, Zach. The plan's so simple, it's damn near foolproof."

Zach smiled without a trace of mirth. "It is, isn't it? So now I'm left with only one really important question."

"What's that?"

Zach's eyes hardened. "Since I know Robyn didn't organize this scam, I want to know who the hell is setting her up to take the fall? And is that the same person who tried to kill her?"

Freddie, who had stationed himself on a stool at the nursery window, stopped eating caraway seed cake long enough to inform everyone that it was snowing. George jumped up and ran to the window.

"Hooray!" He hopped from foot to foot in sheer pleasure. "It's snowing lots and lots! We can build a fort, and a castle, too! Mamma, may we go outside and play? Papa, will you come with us?"

William left his chair by the fire and strolled over to join his excited sons at the nursery window. He watched as a few snowflakes fluttered to earth, adding to the patchy coating of white already on the ground. He caught Robyn's eye and they exchanged wry smiles.

"I fear there may not yet be quite enough snow to build a fort *and* a castle," he said. "At the moment, there may not be enough snow to build even a small turret. However, the sky looks heavy with promise. Shall we wait until tomorrow when there may be enough snow for us to fashion something really superior?"

Responding to a chorus of groans from the twins, Robyn got up and joined William at the window. "Actually, I do believe the snow is starting to fall more thickly," she said. "If this keeps up, tomorrow morning you could have a snowball fight."

"A battle," Freddie agreed enthusiastically. "An 'normous battle."

"Papa shall be on my side," George said.

"And you shall be on mine, Mamma." Freddie, who was good-natured in the extreme, did not appear too crestfallen at having been left with the burden of a female teammate.

"We cannot expect your mother to play in the snow," William said quickly. "But we will find some way to make up a good game, never fear. I shall ask Jake and Aaron to send their sons."

"Hey, not so fast," Robyn interjected. "Don't count me out. I'll have you know that when I was growing up, I was considered the neighborhood champion in snowball fights. You picked a winner for your team, Freddie. We're going to whip the pants off George and your father."

"Whip the pants off?" Freddie repeated. He chuckled. "That's very good, Mamma. We shall whip the pants off you, George."

"May I play wiv you, Mamma?" Clemmie jumped up excitedly. "Me, too. I want to play battles wiv you and Fweddie."

"Very well," Freddie said, although this time he looked decidedly reluctant. "But you will have to stay back behind the line of fire. You're only little."

"She can't play. She's a *girl*," George said, appalled by his brother's lack of judgment. "She'll get her stupid petticoats wet. Besides, you know girls can't throw snowballs."

Clemmie burst into tears. "I want to play," she said between sobs. "I don't want to be a girl. Petticoats is silly. Girls is silly."

Robyn swept the child into her arms. "Shush," she said, using the corner of Clemmie's embroidered apron to wipe her eyes. "It's great to be a girl and of course you can throw snowballs tomorrow. I'm a girl, aren't I? You can be my helper, and hand me the snowballs so I can throw them faster. We'll show George and Papa who are the really tough cookies around here."

"I can play?" Clemmie's tears dried in an instant. "What is a cookie?" she asked.

"A cookie is . . . er . . ." Robyn thought hard and remembered that in England cookies were called biscuits, at least in the twentieth century. "It's another name for a biscuit," she said triumphantly.

William smiled. "If the two of you prove to be as tough as sailor's biscuits, you will surely be unconquerable. Freddie, you have acquired a formidable team. We had better look to our laurels, George."

"It's getting dark," Clemmie said, wriggling in Robyn's

arms so that she could get a better view out of the window. "Is it nearly tomorrow?"

"Very nearly." Robyn gave the squirming child a quick kiss on the nape of her neck. "And if there's enough snow, we'll start to play right after breakfast, won't we, William?"

William seemed to have difficulty in dragging his gaze away from Clemmie. Perhaps he disapproved of his daughter's disheveled hair and slightly scruffy pinafore, Robyn decided. Well, too bad. She had no intention of allowing the servants to bully the child back into her previous state of permanent doll-like neatness. She lifted her chin and repeated his name. "William? Is that all right with you?"

"What?" He blinked. "Oh ... er ... yes, certainly we'll play early in the morning."

Clemmie and her brothers cheered in unison. Not surprisingly, baby Zach woke up and immediately announced his displeasure with the boring view inside his cradle. Clemmie clung tighter to Robyn's neck at the sound of the baby's cries, and Robyn knew she was being tested. She didn't attempt to untangle herself from Clemmie's possessive hug, but smiled pleasantly at George and Freddie. "Would one of you please pick up your little brother?"

The twins stopped cheering. "Pick him up?" George sounded horrified.

"But we are boys!" Freddie looked too shocked to speak.

Robyn chuckled. "I promise you Zach doesn't bite," she said. "Not even boys." She walked over to the cradle, still holding Clemmie. Kneeling down, she gently slid Clemmie to the floor, but kept one arm around her so that the child wouldn't feel displaced by her little brother. Using her free hand, she guided George's cake-sticky fingers toward the baby, feeling relieved that Zach's fragile, newborn skin would be protected by his bonnet and long silk gown. Carefully she showed George how to support his brother's head at the same time as he cradled the baby's body.

"Very good," she said when George's hands were positioned just right. "You can lift him up now."

Clemmie, fascinated by the sight of her older brother picking up the baby, stopped clinging to Robyn and peered into the cradle instead. Gingerly, with Robyn's unobtrusive help, George lifted the baby into his arms. Zach's cries stopped abruptly when he sensed his liberation. His gaze wobbled around the room, then fixed with newborn fierceness on his older brother.

George stared down at the baby, his expression uncertain. "He is very small," he said finally.

"Yes, but he is strong and healthy, so he will soon grow bigger."

Freddie peered over his twin's shoulder. "Were we that small when we were borned?"

"Even smaller, I expect, because the two of you were born at the same time."

"That's because we are twins. Twins are always borned together." Freddie sounded pleased to deliver this piece of insider information.

"That's right, they are." Robyn noticed that George's arms were beginning to droop. "Baby Zach feels heavy even though he's so small," she said casually. "His head, especially. Would you like me to hold him now?"

George had no chance to answer. William bent down and carefully removed the shawl-wrapped bundle from his son's arms. "It is my turn to play nursemaid," he said. "Freddie, I see the box of spillikins on the shelf over there. You and George should show Clementina how to play the game. She is old enough now to learn the rules."

The children took off for the corner of the nursery happily enough and William sat down on the opposite side of the fireplace.

"This is very cozy and domestic," Robyn said, smiling.

William looked at her, then glanced down at the baby. "The children's noise does not seem to disturb you today."

Robyn laughed. "Gosh, William, this isn't noise. You should see my parents' house when all the grandchildren get together—" She broke off abruptly. "No, the noise doesn't bother me," she said.

"I am wondering ... do you understand that the children will be very disappointed if you do not join in their game tomorrow?"

"I'll be disappointed myself if there isn't enough snow," Robyn said. "From what I recall of my last stay in England—" She caught herself up short. Good grief, it was difficult not to make remarks that were calculated to provoke precisely the sort of questions she wasn't willing to answer, not even to herself. She tried again. "We must hope for the best. Snow doesn't usually last long in this part of the country, does it?"

"Not longer than a day or two," William agreed. Zach started to cry and he looked down at the baby with a consternation that was almost comical. "What's wrong? Have I hurt him?"

Robyn smiled. "No, I'm sure you haven't. Unfortunately, Zach has a very simplistic view of life. He believes that if he's awake, it must be time to eat."

William got to his feet. "I will summon the wet nurse," he said.

"There's no need. I prefer to nurse him myself."

He turned in midstride, and unaccountably, Robyn felt herself blush. "I did not realize that you were still feeding the child yourself," he said.

"You sound almost as disapproving as Annie," she said.

"Not disapproving. Merely—surprised. In the past, you always found the children so shattering to your nerves. You couldn't bear to spend time with them."

Robyn held out her hands and he gave Zach to her. "You shouldn't be surprised," she said quietly. "I've told you a dozen times that I'm not the same Lady Arabella you remember from before the accident."

William looked at her, his gaze somber. "You have almost persuaded me of the truth of that claim, my lady. Is that not an ironic testament to the triumph of hope over reason?"

Robyn smiled grimly. "Reason, my lord, seems to have very little to do with our situation. That's the one thing I'm absolutely sure about."

Chapter 13

CLEMMIE, bundled up in a pair of her older brother's cast-off pantaloons, pranced through the hallway singing a lusty, made-up song, the chorus of which consisted chiefly of "We winned, we winned, we *winned*!" Freddie, having acquired a wooden spoon and a pewter platter on his way out of the kitchens, banged an enthusiastic accompaniment, and Robyn, hair tumbling down her back, wet skirts hitched up to her knees, gave a final jubilant wave to William and shepherded her winning team in the direction of the nursery and dry clothes.

They were all three making so much noise that they totally failed to hear the stately tread of Hackett, the majordomo, and an accompanying patter of light, feminine steps. Caught up in her triumphal song, Clemmie bumped right into the portly figure of the majordomo as she skipped around the corner of the corridor and entered the main hall. Freddie and Robyn barely managed to skid to a halt behind her.

"Oops." Clemmie grinned happily when Hackett steadied her. "We winned," she informed him with a beatific smile, equally unimpressed by his severe expression and his tasseled, silver-knobbed staff of office. "Mamma and Fweddie and me winned the snowball fight. George and Papa and Tom losted. We winned."

"I am delighted for you, Miss Clementina." The servant ruffled her mop of curls. Then he caught sight of Robyn and his indulgent gaze froze into a look of sheer horror. He immediately started bowing. "My lady, I did not know ... I beg your ladyship's pardon ... I would not have permitted ... But Mistress Wilkes is ever a welcome visitor ..."

Robyn took hold of a child in each hand, which seemed to be the easiest way to stop Freddie banging his makeshift gong and Clemmie from bursting into renewed song. "What is it, Hackett? Could you please refrain from bowing and scraping long enough to explain your problem?"

"I rather believe I am the problem," said a pleasant female voice. A short, plump woman of about thirty-five stepped out from behind the shadow of a suit of armor. Her round face, incongruously rosy-cheeked and cheerful beneath a gray-powdered wig, was redeemed from plainness by a pair of fine gray-green eyes, fringed with long, dark lashes. Like Hackett, her smile froze into an expression of almost comical amazement when she saw Robyn, but she was clearly a woman of some self-possession and she soon recovered herself, dipping into a slight, formal curtsy.

"Forgive me, my lady, I see that I have—um—called at a most inconvenient moment, but I was driving back from a visit to my sister in Poole and wished to inquire how your ladyship was faring after your lying-in. Hackett was conducting me to the morning room when we encountered your—um—victory parade."

"Papa and George are with Tom in the kitchen," Freddie explained, wriggling out of Robyn's grasp in order to execute a neat bow. "How do you do, Mistress Wilkes?" He put his hand on Clementina's head and pushed her into a curtsy. Robyn smiled at him fondly, feeling oddly proud of his attempt at good manners. "We already finished our hot chocolate," Freddie said. "But the others are still drinking theirs." He smiled warmly at Mrs. Wilkes, his confiding manner suggesting that she was a frequent and popular visitor to the Manor.

"You look as if you had a very good time," she said. "Did you take a sleigh out in the snow?"

"No, we had a war, and my team won." Freddie gave his pewter platter a jubilant thump. "Mamma is the most excellent snowball thrower in the whole world. She hit Papa square on the nose, can you imagine? And when he wouldn't surrender, she ran over and tickled him until he gave up."

"Papa laughed but George was very cross," Clemmie announced. " 'Cos we winned and I am a girl. Mamma is a girl, too."

"I can see that George might feel he had grounds for complaint," Mrs. Wilkes murmured. She glanced at Robyn and her face fell into another comical expression of repressed amazement. "It is good to hear that your ladyship feels so—er—robust. I am delighted to see that the rumors of your ill health circulating in the village are greatly exaggerated."

"Village rumors are always exaggerated," Robyn said. "Think how dull they would be if they stuck strictly to the truth!"

"Quite so." Mrs. Wilkes smiled, and an endearing dimple appeared at the corner of her mouth. She didn't seem to be a naturally censorious person, but Robyn noticed that her gaze kept sliding away from the sight of Robyn's skirt. Too late, Robyn remembered that she'd tucked her skirt into her waistband to prevent its damp folds clinging to her legs. Unfortunately, this hitched-up style revealed the scandalous fact that she was wearing not petticoats, but leather boots and a pair of man's riding britches beneath the decorous woolen skirt, and from the tinge of color in Mrs. Wilkes's cheeks, it seemed that she found the sight genuinely shocking. Hackett, who was studiously looking everywhere except in his mistress's direction, was obviously equally embarrassed.

"We are just on the way upstairs to change," Robyn said, pulling her skirt back down over the offending male garments, to the evident relief of Hackett and Mrs. Wilkes.

"I am wearing Fweddie's pantaloons," Clemmie announced with a child's infallible instinct for saying the wrong thing at the wrong time. "They is wet," she said, tugging at the seat of her pants and wriggling graphically. "From the snow," she added, trying to be helpful.

Mrs. Wilkes cleared her throat. "Yes, dear, I see you are wearing . . . er . . ." Her voice died away, unable to mention the unmentionable garment. She curtsied again in Robyn's direction. "I can also see that this is a most inopportune time for your ladyship to entertain callers, so I will apologize for intruding and take my leave. Please accept my good wishes for the continued good health of the new baby. I will look forward to seeing him another day." At the mention of the baby, her voice took on a faintly wistful tone.

"Oh, but you mustn't leave without seeing my son! I would love to take you up to the nursery when he's been fed." Robyn couldn't pass up the chance to display her gorgeous Zach to someone so obviously willing to coo over his many perfections. "Besides, it's much too cold and miserable for you to drive home without having a snac—without taking some refreshments. Hackett, please show Mrs. Wilkes into the morning room and bring her something hot to drink. Coffee, tea, chocolate, whatever you would like." She smiled in what she hoped was a friendly fashion. "It won't take me a minute to make myself presentable. Please do wait, Mrs. Wilkes."

Robyn hurried upstairs, refusing to take no for an answer. When she saw herself in the dressing-table mirror, she could understand why the majordomo and Mrs. Wilkes had both appeared so shocked. Quite apart from the outrage of her boots and britches, the rest of her appearance was an unmitigated disaster. Her face was wind-chapped to a bright red— her nose, Robyn thought wryly, would have ousted Rudolf from the lead position on Santa's team of reindeers. Her hair, or perhaps she should say Lady Arabella's hair, had no natural curl whatsoever, and it had fallen in damp, blond hanks over her shoulders, without a clip or a ribbon left to show for the neat style she had given herself early this morning. She had a brown smudge of chocolate on her cheeks where Clemmie had kissed her, and her jacket had popped two buttons where her breasts refused to stay confined within the space provided by Arabella's skintight jacket. If Mrs. Wilkes was a stickler for the proprieties, confronted by such a spectacle she might decide never to set foot in Starke Manor again. Which would be a pity, because Robyn thought that she might prove a good potential friend. There had been a definite twinkle in those handsome gray eyes, despite the rigorous decorum of her manner.

It was obviously going to take her the best part of an hour to feed Zach and make herself presentable, Robyn decided, not the few minutes she had promised Mrs. Wilkes. Organizing quickly—she had found that although the Manor swarmed with servants, they rarely displayed even a smidgeon of initiative—she sent a message to William informing him of Mrs. Wilkes's arrival and asking him to entertain their guest while she changed. Then she summoned Annie and asked her to bring Zach to the bedroom. Settling into the winged chair by the fireplace, she fed the baby while Mary laid out the multitudinous layers of garments that she considered de rigueur for Lady Arabella to host a simple visit from a neighbor. For once Robyn didn't protest her maid's inflated standards of elegance. She didn't want to appear insulting to Mrs. Wilkes, and she would endure however many layers of silk and satin it took to restore herself to her neighbor's good graces.

"Does Mrs. Wilkes often come to visit?" Robyn asked, stroking Zach's head as he suckled, and watching Mary painstakingly smooth the goffered ruffles on a starched linen petticoat.

"Aye, often enough. Sometimes she just comes and spends time with the children, if you are not in the mood to receive callers. She likes children, Mistress Wilkes does, and she has none of her own."

"What a shame. Have I known her for a long time?"

"No, m'lady." Mary showed no surprise at the odd questions. She had given up trying to make sense of her mistress's behavior, and clearly found her role as lady's maid much more enjoyable now that she no longer expected her mistress to behave rationally. Working for a madwoman had definite advantages, not least the fact that Lady Arabella no longer lost her temper and ordered her maid whipped on the least provocation. Mary knew her duty, and she prayed nightly for the return of her ladyship's scattered wits, but she secretly hoped that the Good Lord would continue to ignore her prayers. The new mad Lady Arabella was a heap less trouble to deal with than the old sane one.

"Mistress Wilkes was widowed two or three years ago and came back to live with her father, Master Richard Farleigh, over at Oakridge House." The maid spoke through a mouthful of pins. "He do be a widower hisself, Richard Farleigh, and Mistress Wilkes keeps house for him."

Master Richard Farleigh. The name rang a bell, but try as she might, Robyn couldn't remember why. "Did I know Master Farleigh before I was married?" Robyn asked, almost afraid to hear the answer. From what she had learned about Lady Arabella's past, the gentleman was quite likely to have been one of her lovers. "Has he been our neighbor for long?"

"Oh, no, my lady, a real newcomer to the district is Master Farleigh. Hasn't been here more than a dozen years. He was a merchant in Bristol, with ships sailing all over the world, until he decided to set hisself up as a country gentleman. His brother handles the shipping business now, I did hear tell. A nice enough personage is Master Farleigh, but only a tradesman when all's said and done."

"You sound as if you don't approve of tradesmen. Without trade, England would be a much poorer country and its people would lead less comfortable lives. The average citizen here is better fed than in almost any other country in the world, you know."

"Average citizen, m'lady, what be that?" Mary shrugged, dismissing yet another of her ladyship's queer statements. "Don't matter none, anyway. If you say 'tis so, m'lady, I am sure you have the right of it."

Robyn's attempts to heighten Mary's social awareness never met with much success. She sighed and returned to the original topic. "Tell me more about the Farleighs."

Mary was happy to oblige. "There's no harm in Master Farleigh, and his daughter is as kind as can be, a lovely lady for all she's so plain to look at. But they aren't aristocrats, not like you and his lordship. Master Farleigh's from common stock, nothing special about his family. Why, there isn't a soul in these parts who remembers his grandsire. Which isn't surprising, since folks say he was naught but a peddler, who spent most of his time over to Poole way."

"If his grandfather was just a peddler, isn't that all the more credit to Mr. Farleigh for working so hard to make a success of his life?"

Mary seemed to find the question disconcerting. "I dunno about that, my lady. Folks is supposed to stay in the station they was born to, not keep struggling to push theirselves above their proper station."

"In America, people are encouraged to forget about their old position in life and to make the best of themselves. To branch out and flourish in new ways."

"The American Colonies is in furrin parts, and they be full o' heathens. Catholics and Puritans, and such like, not good solid Church of England, like us." Mary clearly considered American habits entirely irrelevant to the discussion. "Be you ready to start getting dressed, m'lady?"

"Not quite. Zach seems hungry today. Tell me why the Farleighs decided to buy a house in this particular neighborhood."

"Well, I expect Master Farleigh wanted to keep an eye on his business in Bristol, and his son-in-law has a warehouse in Poole, so Oakridge is right in the middle. When old Squire Babbitt died and left naught but a passel o' debts, Master Farleigh saw his chance to buy Oakridge and he snapped it up. He paid Widow Babbitt a fair price, though, when all's said and done. And Mistress Wilkes has done a right fine job of running his household, even if she weren't born to the task. Kept on all of Squire Babbitt's people, she did. Didn't turn a single one of them off, indoor servants or out. Course, Farleigh has the money to fling around, being a tradesman, like, and not proper gentry."

Poor Mrs. Wilkes and her father were going to find it tough to get accepted into the bosom of this conservative community, Robyn realized. She found Mary's class consciousness appalling, and yet she knew that order, rhythm, and the cycle of the seasons were important to farming communities even in contemporary, hyped-up, wired-in America. No wonder it seemed a crucial keystone of security to servants in eighteenth-century England.

Despite Mary's rambling account, Robyn still couldn't recall where she had heard the name Farleigh. Then Mary reached into the exquisite lacquered drawer of the dressing table in search of a ribbon and suddenly Robyn remembered.

The Farleigh cabinet. That was how the Gallery had labeled the chest of drawers, set on an elaborate gilded base, that had held pride of place in the Gallery showrooms just before Robyn's accident. The name sounded familiar because the provenance papers had contained a paragraph describing the first owner of the cabinet, and the circumstances of the original purchase.

Robyn's mood of effervescent good cheer collapsed as quickly as a pricked bubble. This linkage of Mrs. Wilkes to an object Robyn had dealt with in her twentieth-century life was spooky. What did it signify? she wondered. Had the threads of her life and Lady Arabella's begun to interweave even before the fateful moment when she had been shot and Lady Arabella had tumbled from her carriage?

Zach whimpered, returning Robyn to a realization of her surroundings. She was squeezing Zach so hard she had left finger marks on his skin. "I'm sorry, babycakes," she whispered, cradling him over her shoulder and slowly patting his back. "I wish you could talk," she murmured. "You were part of Lady Arabella when all this happened, and then you became part of me. So you probably know better than anyone else what went on. Can't you tell me?"

Zach delivered a milky burp, and Robyn gave a little laugh that was perilously close to tears. "I know. Dumb question. But you feel so real and solid, so much a part of me." She paused a minute. "Everything here seems real and solid. Does that mean your mommy's crazy, huh? What's your considered opinion?"

Zach's eyes crossed with the effort of concentrating on his mother's voice. He gave a grunt and his head flopped against her chest. Robyn laughed, loving the feel of his warm soft body against her heart. She looked up and found Mary waiting patiently, Arabella's shift held out to the fire.

"To warm it, my lady, since you have been out in the starving cold for so long. 'Twill feel good and hot when you are ready to put it on."

Robyn set Zach in his cradle, where he fell instantly asleep. "You spoil me," she said to Mary. "I'm getting so that I soon won't remember how to dress myself."

"But there's no reason for you to dress yourself when I'm here, is there, my lady?" Mary bustled around, bringing scented cloths for Robyn to wipe her face and hands, then expertly tying and lacing her into an apricot velvet outfit. She shook out the skirts, adjusted the folds individually. Not satisfied, she shook and folded and shook some more, then sighed. "It looks well enough, my lady, although if you would only allow me to tighten your stays—"

"Don't even mention my stays, Mary. I'm already half-dead from lack of oxygen ... I mean air."

"All I can say is, you look very lively, m'lady, for a woman what is claiming to be half-dead. Still, if you won't let me lace you up proper, there's nothing more I can do. You look the best I can manage, m'lady."

"It's an excellent best. You take wonderful care of my clothes, Mary, and of me."

The servant flushed. "Thank you, m'lady." She pointed to the dressing table. "Now, if you'll sit down, I can brush your hair. We could even use powder and make you look like a proper lady again. I must say, 'tis downright wonderful how quick your head has healed over. I never would have believed that wound on your scalp would close up so nice, with you insisting on washing your hair so often like you do."

Robyn smiled a touch ruefully. "Even crazy people have their flashes of wisdom, it seems."

"Right, my lady." Mary risked a smile. "But not too many of them."

Robyn chuckled. At moments like this, she allowed herself to hope that it wouldn't be long before she persuaded Mary to relax and become the lighthearted, jolly woman she was sure lay trapped somewhere behind the servant's thin lips and cowering demeanor. At other times, she was less optimistic. Even now, Robyn could sense the fear that hovered beneath every smile, the hesitation that lurked behind every vestige of initiative that Mary showed.

"What do you say, then? Shall I powder your hair, m'lady?"

"Oh, not today. It would take me hours to wash the powder out again. Just pin it up, can you? Nothing too elaborate because we haven't got time."

She did, however, allow Mary to cover the remnants of her red nose with a swish of rice powder, and paint her lips with a carmine concoction that Robyn sincerely hoped didn't contain anything deadly poisonous like lead or mercury, favorite ingredients in eighteenth-century cosmetics. Then she looped her skirts over her arm and hurried downstairs. She gave an absentminded smile to the inevitable lackeys, posted at the foot of the staircase and staring mindlessly into space. This evening, after dinner, she really would have to talk to William about the swarms of footmen who inhabited Starke. There must be some way to employ them more usefully than posted as sentinels with no function other than to look decorative in blue livery and open doors that Robyn and William could perfectly well open for themselves. With a murmured word of thanks to the bowing flunkeys, she entered the morning room.

Mrs. Wilkes was seated on the needlepoint embroidered sofa, next to William. In the split second before Mrs. Wilkes looked up and William rose to his feet, Robyn gained a vivid impression of intimacy between the two of them. Mrs. Wilkes had spread out a set of sketches and William laughed as she made some comment. Decorously separated by a foot of hooped skirt from any contact with William's body, there was nevertheless a hint of yearning in the way Mrs. Wilkes leaned toward him. And in William's eyes, Robyn could see a glow of answering admiration.

"I apologize if I have kept you waiting." Robyn was horrified at the acid note that soured her voice. Good Lord, what was the matter with her? The tightening in the pit of her stomach felt astonishingly like jealousy. She walked quickly across the room, holding out her hands to Mrs. Wilkes, her smile all the more effusive to make up for that odd, irrational moment of resentment.

"I trust my husband has been keeping you well entertained," she said. "I had to feed the baby and so took much longer to change than I would have wished."

"You have no reason to apologize, my lady. The needs of your new son must take precedence over an uninvited visitor." Mrs. Wilkes looked flushed and almost pretty, but her voice remained calm and amicable. Whatever her feelings for William, clearly she was accustomed to keeping them well under control.

"Mistress Wilkes has been showing me some sketches of furniture," William said. Robyn noticed that his easy manner disappeared as soon as he spoke to her. In fact, he appeared thoroughly disapproving as his gaze flickered over her carefully chosen dress and the swell of her breasts, inevitably displayed by the square, low-cut neckline. Tension stretched between the two of them, their camaraderie of the snowball fight already forgotten in the habitual tug and strain of their relationship. Robyn was aware of a piercing sensation of regret. The game that morning had been such *fun*.

"Do you plan to buy new furniture?" she asked Mrs. Wilkes, tearing her gaze from William's and trying to establish a neutral, friendly topic of conversation. From the silence, and the quick exchange of glances between William and the widow, she realized she had said something foolish.

Mrs. Wilkes, ever the peacemaker, tried to gloss over Robyn's error. "You have probably forgotten that we spoke just before your lying-in of my father's plans to redecorate Oakridge," she said, her voice encouraging rather than condemning. "Of course, with a new baby to fill your time, you have much more important things on your mind nowadays than the problems I am encountering in choosing a design for my father's wallpaper!"

Robyn's hands felt chilled and she held them out to the blaze of the fire. "Er . . . yes, it has been a busy time for me, with many changes in my life." She hesitated for a moment, then decided to confront the problem of the Gallery's "Farleigh cabinet" head on. "Is it possible . . . I seem to remember that we talked about a new cabinet your father has ordered," she said, with a false air of casualness. "Am I right?"

"Indeed you are," Mrs. Wilkes said warmly. "I mentioned to you that there is a talented young cabinetmaker who has just set up a temporary workshop in Bristol, and my father has decided to purchase a cabinet and several chairs from him. Master Chippendale has been most diligent in executing the commission."

"Master Chippendale!" Robyn exclaimed. "Do you mean *Thomas* Chippendale is making your new furniture?"

Mrs. Wilkes smiled at her obvious excitement. "Why yes, I believe that is his Christian name. How clever of you to remember! My father prides himself on his expert eye where cabinetry work is concerned, and he insists that this young man is destined to go far."

"Your father is evidently a man of discernment," Robyn murmured. "Are these the sketches of Chippendale's work?" She sat down on the sofa beside Mrs. Wilkes, rather pleased with the cool nonchalance of her manner. Inside, she was experiencing a riot of conflicting emotions, not least the professional excitement of actually seeing and hearing Thomas Chippendale's work discussed years before he had become an object of veneration to furniture makers around the world.

"These are the pieces my father has already decided to

buy," Mrs. Wilkes said, spreading out the drawings. "Here is the cabinet Papa is so excited about." She pointed to a well-executed sketch, delicately colored, and Robyn felt almost no surprise when she realized that the drawing was of the cabinet she had last seen displayed in the showrooms of the Bowleigh Gallery.

"Why does your father like this cabinet so much?" she asked, needing to say something to cover the disorientation she felt on seeing such a tangible point of convergence between her two lives.

"Because of the exotic decorative motif." Mrs. Wilkes smiled fondly. "My father visited India once, as I am sure he has mentioned to you on far too many occasions, and he actually saw several elephants during his stay there. He swears it is as strange a beast as the artist depicts here, and of the most enormous size, three times as tall as a man."

William chuckled. "Your father's tales of his travels are highly entertaining, Mistress Wilkes, but I must inform you that the size of the elephant increases every time Mr. Farleigh recounts the hair-raising story of his ride between the beast's giant ears. I am beginning to think that, in truth, the monster is not quite as awesome as its reputation."

"Oh, no, Mr. Farleigh isn't exaggerating, elephants are huge," Robyn said, looking up and forcing William to meet her eyes. "Perhaps not quite three times the height of a man, but they weigh as much as six tons when they are fully grown. Even in captivity, they routinely live to be sixty years old, and in the wild, there are many stories of hundred-year-old animals."

"You are remarkably well informed," William said. "I would be interested to hear the source of your information."

"My first-grade teacher," Robyn said sweetly. "And the tour guides at the Washington Zoo." Her voice tailed off into silence as she registered the look of pain in William's eyes and saw the array of embarrassed emotions crossing Mrs. Wilkes's face. The widow looked first bemused, then startled, and finally her expression softened into sympathy.

"How . . . how interesting," she said, hastily gathering up the pictures of the furniture and reaching out to lay a soothing hand on Robyn's arm. She smiled brightly. Too brightly. "Now, my dear Lady Arabella, we must not talk anymore of bizarre beasts like elephants when we have so many more important matters to discuss. Tell me how your new son fares. I trust he is as robust as his lordship has been telling me?"

"Yes, he is very strong, thank God." Robyn flushed guiltily. She had recited her information about zoos and elephants knowing that she would cause consternation. She had deliberately tossed her alien wisdom into the conversation and sat back to watch the reactions of William and the too-good-to-be-true Mrs. Wilkes. Whatever she had hoped to achieve, she had failed. She had simply confirmed that it was easy for her to cause William pain, and that Mrs. Wilkes was a genuinely kind woman who reacted to signs of Lady Arabella's "madness" with nothing but compassion.

Hoping to make amends, she smiled at Mrs. Wilkes with all the friendliness she could muster. "Zachary is in my room," she said. "Why don't you come upstairs to my bedroom and we can see if he is awake? As you can imagine, he still spends most of his time sleeping."

Mrs. Wilkes folded her hands tightly in her lap. She appeared stunned. "Z-Zachary is in your . . . bedroom?" she murmured.

"Lady Arabella has chosen to call her son by my brother's name," William said, his voice cool as a floating iceberg.

"Oh, good heavens, you mean the *baby* is in your bedroom. I had no idea you had called him Zachary. I understood he was to be christened Arthur. At this perilous time, the risks—" Mrs. Wilkes broke off abruptly. "I beg your pardon, I am becoming incoherent. No doubt I have been traveling too long and the jouncing of the carriage has rattled my wits."

Robyn's smile was tinged with bitterness. "My dear Mrs. Wilkes, pray don't apologize. Surely you realize by now that in this house, rattled wits are all the fashion."

A muffled sound from William's direction might have been a crack of laughter, but when Robyn turned to look at him, she could detect only remote, bland indifference. She held his gaze, her chin thrust upward in challenge. "Do, please, come and see the baby, Mrs. Wilkes. I want you to tell me how handsome he is, and of course, you mustn't forget to mention how much he looks like his father. William insists he cannot see the likeness."

In the end, Mrs. Wilkes not only spent half an hour admiring the baby, at William's invitation she also stayed to eat her dinner at Starke Manor, leaving just in time to complete the eight-mile drive back to Oakridge before darkness closed in completely. Robyn was grateful for the widow's tranquilizing presence at the dinner table. By sheer force of her good nature, Mrs. Wilkes kept the conversation flowing, displaying a kindly disposition, spiced with intelligence and keen powers of observation. Robyn decided she would have liked the sprightly Mrs. Wilkes even if the widow hadn't demonstrated her superb good sense by falling in love with baby Zach the moment she set eyes on him.

William was all smiles and kind solicitude as he waved good-bye to Mrs. Wilkes from the portico, but as soon as her carriage rumbled out of sight, he retreated to the library without attempting to speak to Robyn. So much for their supposed truce, Robyn thought ruefully. The evening stretched ahead, long and lonely. There was nothing for it but to retire to her sitting room and take another stab at adding a few stitches to the flawless embroidery Lady Arabella had been working on prior to the accident.

She was halfway up the stairs to her room before indignation overtook her. Why was she giving in so meekly? What was William's problem, anyway? By what right did he bestow smiles and kind words on Mrs. Wilkes, and simultaneously heap scorn and disapproval on his wife? No wonder Arabella flirted with every male specimen who came in sight if she was constantly subjected to William's freezing and irrational displeasure.

Robyn swung around and stormed down the stairs, her temper on slow simmer. She marched along the hallway and flung open the door to William's study. It banged back against the linen-fold paneling, but Robyn didn't even wince at the prospect of damage to the priceless wood carving. She glared at William. "What the devil have I done to offend your high and mighty lordship this time?" she demanded.

With careful deliberation, William set down his quill and closed the small ledger in which he had been writing. Illogically, it infuriated Robyn even more to think that he had been calm enough to sit down and tot up the estate accounts, or write business letters, or whatever he'd been doing. Why hadn't he been drowning his sorrows in after-dinner brandy, for heaven's sake? Didn't anything ever ruffle the wretched man's composure? And most infuriating of all, did he always have to look so damned *handsome*?

"Don't rush into an answer," she said with heavy sarcasm. "Take a week or so to think about it, if you need the time. Lord knows, you may have to scratch around before you can find anything remotely logical to complain about in my behavior."

"I need no time," William said, his voice sounding flat and distant. "You mistake the situation, my lady. You have not displeased me, and I am not angry."

Robyn almost snorted. "Well, if this is your way of showing warm approval, I sure as heck hope I never do anything to offend your high and mightiness. If I haven't offended you, then what's the reason for the freezing looks? The hostile silence? Come to that, what's happened to the truce I thought we'd agreed on yesterday?"

William pushed back his chair and walked across the room to the fireplace. He stared into the heart of the fire, his face in shadow, his body silhouetted against the flickering yellow glow of the flames. "I apologize," he said at last. "I have not been very good company. I did not intend to appear discourteous—"

"You weren't discourteous," Robyn said impatiently. "You were angry. Why? What have I done?"

"Nothing that I should not have expected," he said. "You cannot help yourself, Arabella, I realize that now. But Mistress Wilkes is a good woman who has extended nothing but kindness to our family. She makes no pretension to beauty and high fashion. She would laugh at the very idea that anyone might consider her your rival. Was it really necessary for you to set out with such brutal deliberation to humiliate her?"

Robyn blinked and shook her head. "Wait a minute, say that again. You're accusing me of setting out to humiliate Mrs. Wilkes? You can't possibly mean that I did something to hurt her feelings *today*?"

"Of course you did, Arabella." It was William's turn to sound impatient. "I know how angry you must have been that Mistress Wilkes encountered you when you came in from the snowball fight, wearing an old woolen gown, but that was not reason enough to wreak such a mean-spirited revenge."

Robyn's indignation dissipated in a cloud of bewilderment. "You won't believe this, but I have absolutely no idea what you're talking about."

"Have you not?" William gave a muttered exclamation and strode across the room, grabbing her shoulders and spinning her around so that she stood in front of a beveled glass mirror that adorned the space between two sets of bookshelves. "Look at yourself," he commanded. "Look at yourself and then tell me that you bore no malice toward Mistress Wilkes when you ordered your maidservant to dress you in this outfit."

Robyn stared into the mirror, her stomach jolting with shock as it always did when she confronted the alien image of Lady Arabella. She could see absolutely nothing special about her appearance, however, and she spoke stonily. "Except for flushed cheeks and a lingering trace of red nose, I see only the usual Lady Arabella," she said. "But what has my appearance to do with our discussion? I bear Mrs. Wilkes no malice, and I assure you that I did not intend to hurt her feelings in any way."

William's face darkened with a flush of renewed anger. "You are not a convincing liar, my lady. You have exquisite judgment where matters of dress and fashion are concerned. Why did you leave your hair uncurled and unpowdered, if not to contrast with the unfortunate style of Mistress Wilkes's wig? Why did you choose your most richly embroidered gown if not to emphasize that Mistress Wilkes came calling in crumpled travel clothes of gray serge and dark worsted?"

She was so stunned by the misconstruction he had put on her efforts to dress smartly in honor of their visitor that for a moment she couldn't speak. His expression turned to one of mockery, and he flicked the lace ruffles that formed a collar to her dress. "You do not answer me, my lady. Mayhap you find it difficult to explain why you chose this exquisite

foam of peach-colored lace if not to display the perfection of
your complexion. And why would you wear no jewelry if
not to remind Mistress Wilkes of how your slender neck and
generous breasts need no artificial adornment?"

The situation would be almost funny, Robyn thought, if it
didn't so painfully underscore the sort of misunderstanding
that seemed to plague every aspect of her relationship with
William. His hands rested for a moment on her shoulders,
and Robyn was surprised to feel that they were deathly cold.
She reached up, instinctively covering his icy fingers with
her own warm hands, but he jerked away from the contact as
if he could barely tolerate her touch.

"No more tricks, my lady," he said harshly. "I am not in
the mood for your blandishments."

"You have misunderstood the situation," she said. "I wore
the dress that my maid set out for me, not one that I chose
myself. I didn't powder my hair because the wound on my
scalp is not completely healed and I am afraid that powder
may cause an infection, or at the very least an irritation. As
for my lack of jewelry, I wore none because I was in a hurry
to go downstairs and I simply forgot about it."

"You have never forgotten to wear jewelry in your entire
life," he said irascibly. "You cannot expect me to believe
such an unlikely set of excuses."

"No," she said. "Of course I can't expect you to believe
the best of me when for so long we have obviously taken
pleasure in believing the worst about each other."

He didn't say anything for several seconds. Then he
reached out and touched her hair, very lightly. "Your answers these days constantly astonish me. You have changed
since your accident, Arabella. Changed greatly."

Her smile contained more than a hint of sadness. "Yes, I
have, but not in the way you most likely mean. I fear you assume that I have changed because I have gone mad."

"I am not convinced of that at all." He met her gaze in the
mirror, but his eyes appeared opaque and his precise mood
was hard to read. "The wound in your head," he said. "Does
it still pain you?"

"Hardly at all, but I think it will be some time before I
can wear a hat or a wig. I hate the thought of something
perched on top of my head all day."

A tendril of her hair had come loose, and he tucked it carefully into the knot at the nape of her neck. "It is many years since I have seen your hair without any trace of powder," he said. "It is . . . a beautiful color."

She heard the huskiness in his voice and felt the answering lethargy in her own body. She knew how easy it would be to lean back in his arms and surrender to the desire throbbing between the two of them. She could guide his hands to cup her breasts. He would lean down and kiss the hollow of her throat. She would slowly turn around to face him. Then he would bend toward her, capturing her mouth in a ravishing, passionate kiss . . .

Fortunately, he broke the silence before she could commit herself to the folly of such a kiss. "I want to thank you for organizing our snowball fight this morning," he said. "The children all had a wonderful time. They are in your debt, my lady, for a happy experience."

She turned in his arms, wanting to see him in the flesh, not a shadowy reflection in the mirror. "What about you, William? Did you have a good time?"

He smiled, the quizzical smile that always set her heart pounding. "I did indeed, although my masculine pride is severely wounded by the knowledge that my team was so ignominiously defeated."

"I cheated." She glanced up at him. "You're very ticklish."

His gaze fixed on her smile and his head bent slowly, inexorably toward her. "Somehow, at this moment, defeat does not seem so terrible. Masculine pride can be redeemed in many different ways."

Robyn swayed toward him. She felt his breath warm against her cheek, and then his mouth touched hers. His kiss was soft at first, but as soon as she parted her lips, he deepened the kiss and his tongue flicked against hers with tantalizing invitation. A shiver of response ran through her, and she reached up, clasping her hands at the back of his neck. His shoulders were hard and muscled from hours in the saddle, making her more aware of the soft yielding of her own body.

He pulled her against him and she found herself wishing that her layers of petticoats and satin overskirts could magically vanish, so that she could feel the hard thrust of his body against her thighs and the caress of his hands over her breasts.

"My God, you are so desirable, Arabella ..." He murmured his wife's name against her lips, and she closed her eyes, melting into his embrace. Heat flooded her veins, desire clouded her brain, and it took several seconds for her to realize that the thunderous noise she heard was not blood roaring in her ears, but the heavy iron door knocker pounding against the front door. With lightning speed, William moved away from her and strode across the room, flinging open the door that led into the corridor.

A hoarse shout penetrated the thick walls of the Manor. *"Open in the name of King George!"*

Robyn pressed her hands to her cheeks and discovered that they were burning hot, but whether from fear or the aftermath of William's kiss she couldn't decide. She followed William out of the library and entered the hallway just as he gave Hackett permission to open the front door. A flunky lifted the heavy iron bars and drew back the bolts. The pounding stopped and in the glow of a burning torch, Robyn saw the caped, white-wigged figure of Captain Bretton, flanked by a small troop of red-coated, white-belted soldiers. She shivered, a visceral American reaction to the sight of British redcoats.

Captain Bretton stepped into the house without waiting for an invitation. His booming, high-pitched voice echoed in the vaulted entrance hall. "Ah, my lord of Starke, I am delighted to find you at home."

"How can I help you, Captain?" William sounded bored, almost disdainful, but Robyn could see the tension that held his spine rigid and kept his shoulders tensed as if to ward off a blow.

"We have caught a traitorous Jacobite rebel," the captain said gleefully. "Caught him right slap dab in the middle of your lordship's land."

William reached into his sleeve and withdrew his snuffbox. He flicked open the lid and removed a tiny pinch. "How excessively enterprising of you, Captain. But I confess that I do not understand why it was necessary to inform me of the capture?" He inhaled the snuff and offered the box languidly to the captain. "I assume you do not wish me to shoot your captive for trespass since you, no doubt, have every intention of hanging him for treachery."

Captain Bretton was too full of malicious excitement to take time out for snuff. He waved the box away. "I inform you of the rebel's capture, my lord, because the traitor bears letters addressed to you, begging for sanctuary."

"How amazing." William stifled a yawn. "My Hanoverian sympathies are well known, so I cannot imagine who would write such an absurd letter, knowing it has no chance of success."

"Can you not?" Captain Bretton's eyes glinted with spite. "Why, it was written by your lordship's brother, of course. It came from the Honorable Zachary Bowleigh, the notorious Jacobite traitor."

Chapter 14

WILLIAM insisted on accompanying the soldiers assigned to search Starke, and Robyn took advantage of the momentary confusion surrounding his departure with the dragoons to evade Captain Bretton and slip quietly upstairs. She made her way into the night nursery where she found Annie rocking Zach's cradle, and Clemmie sitting bolt upright in bed, the counterpane and blankets clutched to her chin.

"Hello, cutie pie." Robyn gave Clementina a hug before glancing over at the nurse. "Is Zach all right?"

Annie nodded. "Aye, sleeping like an angel, he is. Doesn't seem to have heard a thing, but that's babbies for you. Sleep through a battle and wake up when you drop a pin."

"Who was banging on the door, Mamma? Is it soldiers? Annie and me think it's soldiers." Clemmie was wide-eyed with excitement and trepidation.

Robyn tried to make her smile reassuring. "Yes, it's Captain Bretton and a small detachment of dragoons. How did you guess?"

"They camed before. They was horrid." Clemmie's hand crept out from beneath the covers in search of Robyn's. "Will you stay wiv me, Mamma, until they is gone?"

"Of course I'll stay. And perhaps we should ask Freddie and George to come in here with us. Will you fetch them, Annie?"

"Certainly, my lady." The boys' bedroom opened directly off the other side of the nursery, and Annie returned a minute or two later, the twins in tow, their feet encased in lambswool slippers, nightcaps perched on top of their tousled curls, and both of them chattering nineteen to the dozen.

"Listen to the pair o' them, all overexcited and anxious.

It'll be hours before they get back to sleep." Annie sniffed. " 'Tis an outrage, that's what it is, sending soldiers to disturb honest folks at this hour o' the evening. There's no reason for it, neither, when all the world knows as how his lordship is a loyal follower o' the King."

Full of bravado, Freddie and George stuck their heads around the nursery door, and peered out into the corridor, waiting with slightly nervous relish for the soldiers to arrive on the third floor of the Manor. Robyn noticed that Clemmie was still shivering, and she wrapped one of Zach's knitted shawls around her shoulders.

"Warmer now?" she asked, encouraging Clemmie to snuggle up to her. The night air was bitterly chill, but she suspected the little girl's shivers were caused as much by fear as by cold.

"Yes, thank you, Mamma." Clemmie was silent for a moment. "What are the soldiers looking for?" she asked. "Why does they keep coming here?"

"They are looking for traitors trying to escape across the Channel to France," Freddie informed her from his post by the doorway. "They want to capture all the rebels who fought in Bonnie Prince Charlie's army."

"Are we rebels?" Clemmie asked anxiously. "Will the soldiers take us away and chop off our heads?"

"Of course not, sweetheart." Robyn gave her another reassuring squeeze. "There are no traitors in Starke."

"Then why does the soldiers keep coming back?" Clemmie persisted.

"They are looking for Uncle Zachary," George said. "I told you that before." Suddenly uncertain, he swung around. "They will not find my uncle here, will they, Mamma?"

"Most definitely not," she said. She smiled brightly, to cover her fear that their uncle was most likely dead of the wounds he had sustained during the Battle of Culloden. "Your uncle Zachary is safe in France."

Annie snorted. "That b'ain't likely to stop the soldiers a-coming," she said, her voice rich with scorn. "Captain Bretton is bound and determined that he's going to discover Master Zachary hidden somewhere in Starke. Swears up and down, black and blue, that he gave chase to Master Zachary three month ago and more, and that he shot and wounded him during the chase. Swears Master Zachary would have bin captured long since unless he was hidden in this house, protected by his lordship."

"But that's absurd!" Robyn protested. "Zachary would never have sought sanctuary here. William was totally opposed to the Stuart rebellion. Even I know that—I mean, he has said so on many occasions." She didn't add that relations between William and his brother seemed strained to the breaking point, quite apart from Zachary's foolhardy commitment to the Stuart cause.

Annie shrugged. "Mayhap, my lady, but the captain believes what he wants to believe and there's no telling him otherwise."

"But doesn't the captain understand how ridiculous he's being?" Robyn asked. "How could Zachary be hidden inside the Manor without any of the servants knowing that he's here?"

"That's easy," Freddie said. "The captain thinks Uncle Zachary is hidden in the priest's hole."

After a moment of surprise, Robyn realized that she should have expected Starke to have at least one priest's hole. The Manor had been built a hundred years earlier, when England had been torn apart by civil and religious wars. In those days, a wise homeowner made sure that he had a secure hiding place built into the carved paneling of his library or bedroom. The so-called priest's hole would be used to hide jewels and valuables from marauding armies at least as often as to secrete fugitives and Catholic priests. The prudent seventeenth-century gentleman always kept a safe bolt hole ready and waiting.

Robyn frowned. "Even so, I don't see why the issue can't be quickly resolved to Captain Bretton's satisfaction. Why doesn't he look inside the priest's hole and settle the matter once and for all?"

"Because he can't find the entrance, of course!" The twins chorused in unison.

"The entrance is a family secret," George explained. "Only the head of the family is told where the door is hidden."

"Papa is the head of the family," Freddie added. "He is the Baron of Starke."

"I still don't understand," Robyn said. "Since your father has nothing at all to hide, why doesn't he show Captain Bretton the entrance to the priest's hole and thus save the household from these repeated searches?"

"A very good question, Lady Arabella." Captain Bretton's suave voice spoke from the door of the nursery. "It is one I have posed to Lord Bowleigh myself on several occasions."

Robyn's stomach jumped with fright, but she rose to her feet, and looked steadily at the captain. "And what does my husband answer you, Captain Bretton?"

"Why, he informs me that the hole was blocked up fifty years ago, when his father was still a boy, and that he was never told where the entrance was located."

Robyn raised her chin. "If that is what my husband has told you, Captain Bretton, then I have not the slightest doubt in the world that it is true."

The captain's eyes narrowed. "Your devotion is touching, my lady. You have become a most loyal wife in recent weeks."

"Do you not approve of wifely loyalty, sir?"

"Not when it is so sadly misplaced." The captain snapped his fingers, and two burly dragoons entered the room, their bayonets held at the ready. "Search the room," the captain ordered.

The dragoons saluted in acknowledgment of the order. They didn't speak, nor did they look at Robyn or the children. Poking their bayonets into wall hangings and window coverings, their faces bore the carefully blank expression that Robyn had seen on old television news shots of East German border guards preparing to shoot a fleeing citizen. She shivered, concealing her hands in the folds of her skirt to disguise their shaking. The soldiers finished poking curtains and turned toward the fireplace. Disturbed by the clump of booted feet approaching his cradle, Zach woke up and began to cry.

Robyn moved swiftly to interpose herself between the soldiers and the baby. "Don't you dare put your filthy bayonets anywhere near my son!" she exclaimed. "Why are you frightening my children like this? Good heavens, you can see at a glance that there's nowhere in this room to hide *any-*

thing. There are no cupboards, only open shelves. No paneling, only whitewashed plaster walls."

Captain Bretton spoke brusquely. "That's as may be, my lady. Now, pray, stand aside and allow my men to continue their search."

She snatched Zach from his bed and tossed his pillow and covers onto the floor. "There, now are you satisfied?" She glared at the captain. "Hey, surprise, surprise! There wasn't a single escaped Jacobite curled up beneath my baby's blankets."

The captain said nothing. He snapped his fingers at the soldiers again. Stolidly, not once allowing their eyes to meet hers, they turned away from the cradle and moved toward the bed. Furious at her helplessness to withstand the captain's malicious stupidity, Robyn sat down on the bed, cradling Zach in one arm and hugging Clemmie with the other. Meanwhile, the soldiers stomped around the room, sticking their bayonets into the dust balls under the bed and rattling the curtains hanging from the wooden posters. Every time they passed by her, Clemmie trembled, which only made Robyn more annoyed.

"Where is my husband?" she asked the captain, her voice icy cold.

"Why, his lordship is in the stables, I do believe." Captain Bretton looked smug. "I decided it would be helpful to take him to see my prisoner."

"Why?" As soon as she had asked the question, Robyn wished that she hadn't. Captain Bretton's smile was even less pleasant than his earlier sneers.

"The foolish rebel we captured has refused to give us his name, no doubt out of some mistaken sense of loyalty to his family. But we felt sure we could persuade your husband to identify the traitor for us. I have every reason to believe the rebel is a young man from this part of the country."

His leering explanation left Robyn feeling uneasy. William supported the Hanoverian cause, but she doubted if he would be anxious to help Captain Bretton in building a case against some poor, misguided local lad who had thrown in his lot with the wrong set of royals. Still, she was probably worrying unnecessarily. If William didn't want to identify the rebel, the soldiers couldn't force him to do so. Being an aristocrat had its advantages, and refusal to cooperate with lowly troopers was presumably one of them. Robyn lapsed into a stony silence, watching as the dragoons completed their search of the nursery. They were obviously veterans at their task, and she reflected with a thrill of fear that if William had in truth been trying to hide his brother, the captain's men would certainly have found him out.

William arrived at the nursery door just as Captain Bretton gave his dragoons permission to move on to another room. William looked grim-faced and pale, but he spared a moment to greet each of the children and to bow politely in Robyn's direction. The glance he finally cast toward Captain Bretton displayed his usual cool courtesy, laid over barely concealed contempt.

Captain Bretton covered a jolt of surprise at William's arrival with a curt bow. "Lord Bowleigh, I did not expect to see you so soon."

"Did you not?" William spoke with calm indifference.

"I assume that you chose to identify the rebel," Captain Bretton said.

"You assume far too much, Captain." William strolled across the nursery and took up a position near the fire before turning around. "The Jacobite rebel has died," he said, his voice flat. "Your men wish for instructions on where they should take the body."

"You did not identify him?" The captain spoke sharply.

"Alas, he had been tortured and flayed well past the point of recognition." William drew out his snuffbox and inhaled briefly. "You should encourage the men under your command to moderate their enthusiasm for brutality, Captain. With more finesse and less savagery, you might have been able to coerce from me the identification that you apparently crave."

Robyn didn't fully understand the conversation, but she saw Captain Bretton's nostrils flare in anger, and knew he had badly wanted William to identify the prisoner. He spoke stiffly. "Bravely spoken, my lord, but I am not deceived by your pretense of indifference. I know that the presence of my troops strikes fear into the depths of your soul—"

William yawned. "Forgive me, Captain. It is late, and I am sure your ... eloquence ... has a point?"

Captain Bretton flushed. "Indeed it has. I know that your brother has not yet made good his escape to France and I offer you a warning, my lord. Do not be tempted into assisting him to a safe harbor, for he cannot succeed in escaping my grasp. And if you are caught aiding and abetting a traitor, not only will your brother lose his head, but you will risk imprisonment, and your estates will be forfeit to the Crown."

William looked up from contemplation of the design on his snuffbox. He spoke softly. "Do you dare to threaten me, Captain Bretton?"

The captain swung on his heel. "No, my lord, I make a simple statement of fact. The law is on my side, and this time, I shall win."

"Ah." William closed his snuffbox with a single, elegant flick of his left hand. "So that is what this is all about, Captain. I have long suspected as much. Alas, I believe you will discover that some battles cannot be refought. Once lost, they are lost forever."

"I do not understand you, my lord."

William's lips twisted into a small, tight smile. "The Lady Arabella is *my* wife," he said. Giving the captain no opportunity to reply, William turned to Robyn and inclined his head in a slight bow. "My lady, I will return to you shortly, as soon as I have escorted Captain Bretton and his minions off the premises."

"I will eagerly await your return, my lord." Robyn looked straight into William's eyes, offering him reassurance that she sensed he needed. He returned her gaze with apparent coolness. Then, for a moment, his composure cracked, and she saw the roiling volcano of emotions seething behind his calm facade.

She had always suspected that William was a man of tightly controlled emotions rather than a man immune to passion. Nevertheless, the glimpse behind the mask was almost shocking in the intensity of feeling it revealed. Captain Bretton would consider such intensity a weakness to be exploited, and she realized that William was desperate to get rid of the man before his composure finally unraveled.

She turned quickly to the captain and sketched a perfunctory curtsy. "Good-bye, Captain Bretton. I am sure you must be anxious to report your triumph in capturing a Jacobite rebel. What a pity you did not manage to preserve him alive, in all his ferocity."

Her sarcasm did not sit well with the captain. He swept her an elaborate bow, his cheeks mottled with suppressed anger. "Let us say au revoir rather than good-bye, my lady. We shall meet again in the very near future, I promise you."

"Shall we? Oh, dear, I do hope not." She smiled sweetly, then turned her back with ostentatious disdain, busying herself with picking up the covers from Zach's cradle. She didn't turn around again until the sounds of the captain's departure had faded completely from earshot.

Annie emerged from the dark corner where she had been cowering during the entire search. She held out her hands for the baby, shaking her head as she took him. " 'Tween't wise to taunt the captain, my lady. He do be a cruel, hard man. I'm afeared you have made yourself a right dangerous enemy."

"Perhaps. But friend or foe, I don't think Captain Bretton can be trusted."

"Mebbe not, but 'tis best not to annoy him, my lady. There's no knowing what he might do if he gets angry. Beats his own men something horrible, he does, if they doesn't jump to his orders the minute he gives 'em. And Lord knows what terrible things he does to those poor hungry Jacobites he chases up hill and down dale. Hates Jacobites does Captain Bretton, hates them something fierce."

Clemmie started to cry. "I don't want the captain to hurt my uncle Zachary. You is not a Jackbite, Mamma, is you?"

"No, sweetheart, I promise you I am not a Jacobite, nor will I ever be. Their cause is entirely lost, anyway."

"Is Uncle Zachary a Jackbite?"

"He is in France, sweetheart." Robyn spoke with spurious confidence. "We don't have to worry about Uncle Zachary."

With the lightning swiftness typical of a three-year-old, Clemmie decided to be consoled. She stopped crying and snuggled down beneath her thick wool blankets and starched linen counterpane. She wriggled around for a few minutes, then her eyes closed and she gave a few little snuffling snorts as she drifted off to sleep.

The twins, more scared by the soldiers' invasion than they cared to admit, volunteered to sleep in the nursery where they could "protect" Clemmie and baby Zach. Realizing that they wanted the comfort of Annie's presence, not to mention the reassuring light of the coal fire and the oil lamp that burned permanently on the nursery mantel, Robyn helped them to bring the feather mattress from their bed, and set up a makeshift sleeping arrangement on the floor. Burrowing into the plump mattress, the twins curled up top to tail in front of the fire.

George gave her a grateful smile as she knelt to tuck them in. "Thank you, Mamma. Freddie and me will take good care of Clemmie and Zach."

"That's wonderful news, I'm grateful for your help." Robyn patted his cheek, then leaned across to pull Freddie's nightcap down over his ears. The bitter drafts slicing in around the window and beneath the door meant that nightcaps were almost a necessity. If the fire went out during the night, the air would be cold and damp enough to give the children frostbite. Robyn was beginning to appreciate why Annie and the other servants were always so anxious to have Zach swaddled in multiple layers of silk and wool. The danger of a newborn dying of hypothermia in the vast, drafty rooms of Starke must be significant.

William returned to the nursery just as Robyn was getting up from the floor. He walked over to her side and, without speaking, extended his hands. Unaccountably self-conscious, she accepted his silent offer of help and got quickly to her feet.

"Thank you," she murmured. "With these hoops and petticoats, kneeling down is much easier than standing back up. Have the soldiers gone?"

"Yes, but I have no doubt Captain Bretton will return as soon as he can think up an acceptable excuse."

"He is a brutal, cruel man."

"You did not always think so."

"But we have agreed, haven't we, that my opinions about a lot of things have changed since the accident."

He didn't answer her directly. His gaze flicked from the twins to Clemmie to Zach and the nurse. Anywhere, in fact, save toward her. "You indicated that you wished to speak with me, my lady," he said at last.

"Yes, I think we have a lot to discuss. Shall we go to my bedroom?"

"Why not?" His gaze finally met hers. The vulnerability he had let her see earlier was entirely gone. Now she saw only cynicism, tinged with weariness.

She was frustrated by his determination to keep the barriers so firmly in place between them, and she hastened to correct any mistaken impression he might have gleaned. "I suggested my room because it will be warm. Mary always keeps the fire burning in there, and it seems especially cold tonight."

"There is a hard frost," he agreed, his voice as chilly as the temperature.

Robyn recognized that William was desperately backtracking from his moment of self-revelation, so she restrained her irritation. Nodding to Annie, she walked briskly out of the nursery. "Good night, Annie. Please bring Zach to me as soon as he wakes up in the morning."

"Aye, my lady. Like always. Good night, my lady."

William followed her into the corridor, closing the door behind him. "You must have spent more time in the nursery in the weeks since your accident than you had spent in our entire marriage prior to that time."

"You sound as if you are making an accusation," she said. "What are you condemning? The fact that I now spend too much time in the nursery, or the fact that I previously spent too little?"

There was an infinitesimal pause, and then she saw William's mouth curve into a wry, self-mocking smile. "You underestimate my perversity, my lady. In my present mood, I am quite capable of condemning you for both."

She answered his smile. "How provoking of you to be so honest. You make it absurdly difficult for me to quarrel with you."

"For tonight I believe I would be grateful not to quarrel."

Robyn looked up at him. "The soldiers . . . in the barn . . . was it very bad what they were doing?" She hadn't known what she was going to ask until the words were spoken, but she had sensed some time ago that William was being rubbed raw by the events of the night.

His reply seemed to come from a great distance. "I realized at once who it was they had captured," he said. "I recognized the crest on his signet ring." His mouth tightened. "God knows, his face had long since been beaten past recognition."

"Was it . . . was it someone you knew well?"

"Yes, an old friend." William stopped, then swung around so that they were face-to-face. "It was Harry Dalrymple."

"Harry Dalrymple?" She repeated the name, trying to place it. Then she remembered that on the night of her attempted escape from Starke she had heard the stablehands discussing the Dalrymple family and their ill-fated support of Bonnie Prince Charlie. Putting a name to the Jacobite rebel added poignancy to the horror of his end. "But how can that be?" she asked, shocked. "I thought he had already died on the battlefields of Culloden!"

William stopped in midstride. He turned and grabbed her arm, dragging her out of the hallway and into the nearest room, which she realized was his bedroom. But he gave her no chance to look around this previously forbidden stretch of territory. He frog-marched her to the fire and held her tightly by the shoulders, staring deep into her eyes. "Enough is enough, Arabella. We have played foolish games for too long. I demand that you tell me the truth. What led you to suppose that Harry Dalrymple had died at Culloden, when the rest of the world believed that he had escaped safely to the Stuart court in France?"

"There is no need for you to sound so accusatory," she said hotly. "Why do you always leap to the worst possible conclusion? I simply overheard two of the grooms talking about the Dalrymple family, that's all. They were trying to decide who had paid a fine levied on the Dalrymple family—" She broke off. "Good Lord, that was you, wasn't it? *You* paid the Dalrymples' fine."

He avoided her eyes. "That is absurd. You know I have no patience for the Stuart cause. For good or ill, the Hanoverians are in control of our government. If we do not like their manner of governing, we must compel them to change, not chase after romantic princelings who promise the moon and cannot deliver a lump of cheese."

"You're very clever at changing the subject," she said. "But your opinion of Charles Stuart has got nothing to do with paying the Dalrymples' fine. They're your friends and you consider friendship far more important than politics."

"Now it is you who leaps to conclusions," he said, but she noticed that he hadn't denied her statement. He looked down at her, his gaze opaque. "Are you going to tell Captain Bretton that his prisoner was Harry Dalrymple?"

"Of course not," she said, revolted. "Good heavens, it is insulting that you would even ask me the question."

He studied her for another long moment, then allowed his hands to drop to his side. He gave a short, grim laugh. "That is another change since the accident," he said. "I no longer know when you are lying."

"That's because I don't lie to you," Robyn said quietly, but she blushed when she spoke because her whole life as Arabella was, in essence, a colossal lie.

Either the fire concealed the flare of guilty color in her cheeks, or else William chose to make no comment. He stared deep into the flames, the brilliant blue of his eyes shadowed. "Captain Bretton's soldiers are well trained in the art of torture," he said. "They didn't dare to lay hands on me, so they asked me if I knew Harry's name, and each time I denied any knowledge of him, they broke another of his fingers."

"Oh, my God!" Robyn's stomach lurched.

"Fortunately, Harry died before I was compelled to admit that I knew him." William smiled bitterly. "Do you note what I said, my lady? I found it *fortunate* that my good friend died tonight. Fortunate because his death meant that I was no longer constrained to wrestle with the horror of watching him suffer while I refused to name him."

"You're too hard on yourself, William. Presumably you had a good and important reason for keeping silent."

He shrugged. "Perhaps. I told myself that Harry was destined to die whatever I did or did not do. By keeping his identity secret, I may—possibly—have saved his family from being forced into even greater poverty and hardship than they currently endure."

Rationally, he had done the only possible thing, but emotionally, Robyn could see that he blamed himself for Harry's death. She couldn't find any words to offer him the consolation he needed. If he had been one of the children, she would have held him close and murmured soothing nonsense until the pain eased. But her relationship with William was too fraught with strain to allow her to offer him that sort of comfort, so she touched him lightly on the arm, stroking his sleeve as she expressed her sympathy.

"Some choices are so horrible we should never be expected to make them," she said softly. "Instead of berating yourself for moral cowardice, perhaps you should simply be grateful that Harry is at peace, and his family saved from the consequences of his actions."

He looked down at her hands, then up at her, and she saw that he had allowed his protective mask to drop once again. His face revealed a confused mixture of bewilderment and longing. "Who are you?" he muttered. "Where have you learned such gentleness?" He crooked his finger under her chin and dragged her around so that her face reflected the full light of the fire. "You look the same," he said. "And yet, I sense the difference, feel it in the marrow of my bones. What manner of woman have you become since your accident?"

"A different woman," she said. "I may have Arabella's face and body, but my mind and soul have nothing in common with the woman she used to be. The accident changed everything."

William reached out his hand, touching the tips of his fingers to her cheek. "So soft, so smooth, so *familiar*," he said. "And yet, when you look at me thus sweetly I can almost believe that you speak the truth." He smiled savagely, as if mocking his own gullibility. "You have Arabella's luscious lips, but your mouth never forms one of her jaded pouts. You have Arabella's sapphire-blue eyes, but they gaze at me with fire and intelligence, instead of cold disdain. The timbre of your voice is Arabella's, and yet your speech is strange, and your conversation is threaded through with the richness of laughter." He cradled her face in his hands, gazing at her as if willing himself to find the truth hidden behind the perfection of Arabella's features.

Robyn returned his searching gaze openly, and for a moment the strength and integrity she saw in William's eyes reminded her so strongly of Zach that she was pierced by an aching, bitter sense of loss.

"What makes you sad?" William asked quietly. "Is it something I said? The light is quite gone from your eyes."

Unless she wanted to convince him that she was crazy, she couldn't tell him that she grieved for her lover, a descendant of his living two hundred fifty years in the future. And yet she was reluctant to answer him with a flat-out lie. There had obviously been far too many lies between Arabella and William in the past and she didn't want to add to them. She hesitated for a moment, then found the partial truth she was searching for.

"I was feeling regret for love lost," she said.

His expression shuttered, and he touched his forefinger to her lips. "Do not speak of love," he said. "We have used the word too freely in the past and it is debased currency between us."

"Is it? But I don't remember Arabella's past and I would like to think that we could find some . . . affection . . . for each other."

He lifted one of her luxuriant curls, artfully set by Mary, and then let it fall, watching with a brooding, heated gaze as the golden tress tumbled forward over her shoulder. "It is a beguiling fantasy that you offer," he said, his voice thickening. "A new start to our lives, the past unwritten, the stained and blotted pages of our marriage wiped clean. But then you have ever been a mistress of beguilement, have you not? What would happen, I wonder, if I showed myself willing to succumb to your lures?"

Robyn was experiencing difficulty in breathing, and for once she didn't think it had anything to do with her stays. When William's long, supple fingers played with her hair, they wreaked havoc with the functioning of her lungs.

"I wasn't casting out lures," she said. She smiled at him in what she hoped was a frank and honest fashion. "I was simply trying to find some basis for a new, friendly relationship between the two of us."

"Abandon your efforts," William said, his grip on her shoulders tightening. "*This* has always been the only real basis for our relationship." He bent his head and covered her mouth in a hard, aggressive kiss.

For a moment—a wild, passionate moment—Robyn felt herself respond to the powerful physical demand of his embrace. Blood pounded in her ears and she swayed toward him, giving a tiny sigh of pleasure when he pushed aside the sleeve of her gown. His fingers slipped inside her bodice, seeking her nipples at the same moment as his tongue thrust against her lips. His touch was tantalizing, expert—and totally lacking in any trace of emotion. As soon as she realized how empty his manipulations were, Robyn's passion died.

"William, stop!" She recoiled, tearing herself out of his arms and scrubbing her mouth with the back of her hand. "How can you demean both of us with a kiss so utterly lacking in emotion?"

"I am your husband," he said, his eyes glittering with icy blue fire. "I have the right to kiss you, if I so desire."

"That's debatable. And marriage certainly doesn't confer the right to kiss me without a shred of feeling except animal lust!"

"Ah!" he said. "I see that some things in our relationship have not changed, despite the supposedly new Arabella."

"Of course not," she said. "Why would they, since you still persist in treating me like a whore!"

He smiled coldly. "Would you prefer that I treat you like a virgin, my lady? Come, tell me your wish. In our ongoing bedroom farce, one role is as good as another, and I pride myself on being infinitely adaptable."

"I have no desire to pretend anything," she said quietly, regaining control of her temper. "Why should we assume roles, when we can be ourselves? If you want to kiss me, I'd like you to do it as if I were your good friend, which I hope I am."

His hands fell from her shoulders and he gave an odd, frustrated little laugh as he stepped away from her. "You win, my lady. You have set me the one challenge I cannot meet. To kiss you as a friend oversteps the limit of my skills."

"It wouldn't be nearly as difficult as you think," she said. Seconds earlier, she would have sworn she wasn't ready for any sort of sexual relationship with William. Now she realized how badly she wanted him to kiss her. Not with cold lust, but with the sort of warm, tender passion she instinctively knew he was capable of showing.

She put her hands on his shoulders and moved closer, until her breasts touched the velvet braiding of his jacket. She swallowed nervously. "I could show you how it's done, if you like."

"How generous of you." William's smile was sharp enough to cut flesh. "You know, I had never before considered the many benefits of being a cuckold. Now it seems I am to profit from the lessons you have learned in your lovers' arms. You will teach me how to kiss. À la Zachary? I wonder. Or is it to be à la Captain Bretton? How truly fortunate I am to benefit from their instruction!"

She flinched. "No," she said. "For God's sake, William, it's not like that."

"Then pray, my lady, do tell me precisely what it is like."

She knew there was no verbal answer that would satisfy him, so Robyn reached up and linked her hands behind his head, pulling his mouth down toward her own. He offered her no resistance, but neither did he cooperate. He simply stood, rigid and unbending, his mouth twisted into an ironic smile. The barricades he had erected against any offer of emotional warmth were so high that for a moment Robyn paused, with her body curved against William's, but her mouth still a fraction away from his.

He spoke into the silence, his voice sounding terminally bored. "So far, my lady, the embrace of the whore and the embrace of a friend seem to have much in common."

Robyn blanched at his deliberate cruelty. She was on the point of moving away from him when she glanced up and made a momentous discovery.

William was afraid. But what did he fear? She cast her mind over the picture she had built up of Arabella, and suddenly understood. William had no doubt offered friendship and affection to Arabella on dozens of occasions—and each time, his offer had been rejected, probably with vicious, cutting disdain. He had been wounded by Arabella so many times that he now felt an obligation to protect himself from the risk of further pain.

"William, you don't need to worry," she said, resting her cheek against the unyielding wall of his chest. "I promise that I will never knowingly hurt you."

"I quite fail to understand your meaning, my lad—"

"Then I will make it clear," she said, standing on tiptoe so that she could wind her fingers in the long, thick queue of his hair. "Open your mouth for me," she whispered against his lips.

For an instant longer he held himself aloof. Then she felt a shudder sweep through his body as he loosened the relentless hold he had been maintaining over his feelings. Heat suffused her veins, a glorious flood of warmth, and she arched against him, aching to show him a tenderness that would make up for Arabella's years of cold indifference.

"I want you." He looked down at her, his gaze dark. "Dear God, how have you brought me to this?" He muttered the words against her lips, but she had no chance to reply. He caught her by the waist and drew her hard against him, thrusting his tongue into her mouth with all the fierce urgency and passionate longing he had previously refused to express.

She had never intended to resist, but she wasn't prepared for the swiftness with which her body melted into his embrace. He ran his hands down her spine and her skin tingled in instant response. He teased her lips with his tongue, and her breasts swelled, nipples taut and aching as they pressed against the silk of her gown. He moved against her, and even through the layers of her starched petticoats, she could feel the strength and urgency of his desire.

His kiss went on, an endless, turbulent voyage into the heart of his desire. She kissed him back, but not with the friendship she had promised. His passion called to her with irresistible force, and she kissed him with the intensity of a hunger she had fought to keep hidden, even from herself.

She was trembling when he finally raised his head. He drew back slightly and looked down at her. His breath came in short, sharp pants, but his blue eyes still gleamed with a trace of mockery. "You have—a—singular—idea—of what—constitutes—friendship, my lady."

She fought for breath. "Friendship between a husband and wife isn't quite the same as other friendships," she said.

"Is it not?" He cradled her face in his hands, his thumbs stroking her mouth. "You know, I would really appreciate further instruction in the art of marital friendship. May I hope that you are planning to expand upon this demonstration of how a wife kisses like a friend?"

They were both shaking from the impact of their love-making, but even now he couldn't let down his guard. He persisted in defending himself by assuming an air of ironic detachment, and Robyn realized that if she was to break through his protective shield, she would have to make most of the running.

"I'm not giving you an abstract demonstration," she said softly. "I'm showing you how I truly feel."

"I know how you feel, my lady. In need of bedding. An inconvenient state of affairs when only your husband is available."

"I don't want to be bedded," she said. "I want to make love with you, William." She unfastened the buttons of his jacket as she spoke, reaching inside his shirt and laying her palm flat against his chest.

"Your heart beats very fast," she said, taking his hand and placing it beneath her breast. "As does mine. Whatever you are feeling, it seems that I'm feeling it, too."

"That, my lady, is a matter of considerable doubt."

She pressed her finger against his lips. "Hush, William, you don't have to pretend with me, not anymore."

He didn't answer. He stood, not speaking, letting the pulse of her heartbeat throb against the tips of his fingers for several seconds. Then, slowly, his hand trailed up the side of her breasts, seeking the hooks of her bodice. This time, instead of working with cool, passionless efficiency, his fingers were clumsy with need, and she had to help him with the knot of her ribbons before the hooks parted and the bodice of her gown fell open.

He drew in his breath on a tight, harsh sigh and she saw a dark flush of color stain his cheekbones. Slowly, reluctantly, he bent his head and trailed his tongue across the swollen mound of her breasts, his touch an exquisite mixture of hungry desire and teasing gentleness. She gasped, with surprise and delight, closing her eyes and clinging to his shoulders for support.

He kissed her throat, the hollow of her neck, and the slope of her shoulders, while his hands worked magic on her body. His touch burned her skin, the pleasure so fierce that she writhed with the intensity of it. The layers of clothing separating the two of them seemed an unbearable irritant, and she untied the lacings of his shirt, pushing the starched linen aside so that she could feel the muscles of his chest against her breasts and the prickle of his hair tingling against her nipples.

As soon as she started to undress him, William went utterly still. Then a small, rough sound tore from deep in his throat and he began to unhook her skirt and petticoats with frantic haste. The cumbersome layers fell at her feet in a pool of lace and satin, leaving her naked and exposed. He gave her no time to feel vulnerable. He swept her into his arms and carried her over to the bed, kicking off his buckled shoes and laying her amid the damask-covered pillows in a single, swift movement.

Outside, the wind picked up, rattling against the window in a gust of unexpected fury. Robyn heard the harsh sough and felt the chill of an icy draft ripple over her skin. For a moment, beneath the groan of the wind, she thought she heard the sound of a door opening, but before she could turn to look, William drew the curtains around the bed, shutting out the cold and wrapping them both in a warm, crimson glow. She hadn't realized how desperately alone she felt in this alien, long-ago world until William drew her into his arms and held her close, making her feel safe and loved. "Are you warm enough now?" he asked.

"As long as you stay near me." She smiled at him, and he shaped the outline of her mouth with slow, careful fingers.

"I have always dreamed of seeing you so," he said. "When you smile, you are surpassingly beautiful."

"Then I must certainly learn to smile often."

"I believe that is a lesson you have already learned." He brushed his mouth against her lips, but his eyes were shadowed with memories that she didn't want to share. Robyn guessed that only mutual passion would lift the shadows, and she turned to him on the pillows. "Hold me," she whispered. "Make love to me. Don't wait any longer, William."

The last dam of his restraint broke. He seized her mouth, thrusting his tongue deep inside, at the same moment as he parted her legs with his knee. His fingers rippled down her body, rousing her with swift, sure strokes, and Robyn arched up to meet his questing hand, already shimmering on the edge of release. Her world shrank to the crimson cocoon inside the bed curtains and the hot, ravenous taste of William's desire.

He pushed her full onto her back and moved over her, poised between her thighs. On the verge of entering her, he stopped, his forehead sheening with sweat. "The babe," he demanded hoarsely. "Your lying-in. Is it too soon for me to take you?"

It was less than six weeks since the birth of baby Zach. Yes, it was too soon, medically speaking. But, dear God, how could they stop now? She put her hands on his shoulders, pulling him back down to her, settling the weight of his body between her thighs.

"No," she said fiercely. "It will be all right."

His body vibrated with impatience, but still he didn't enter her. "Help me," he said. "Help me not to hurt you."

He waited above her, and she reached down to guide him. He held back for one final moment, then eased slowly into the slickness of her heated flesh.

The split second of pain as he entered was obliterated in a spasm of pleasure, but William tensed, instantly sensitive to her discomfort.

"I have hurt you," he said. "Sweet Jesus, Arabella, I should not be doing this to you."

She shook her head, frustrated by his willful failure to understand. "You aren't doing this *to* me. You are not taking anything I don't want to give. We are making love with *each other.*"

He didn't answer her with words, but she felt sweat break out along his spine. His flesh stirred, and he thrust deep within her. Robyn caught her breath, opening herself to him, moving beneath him in fervent, rhythmic response.

William surged within her, and her body pulsed with life. "Hold me," she gasped. "It feels as if the world is falling."

"Mayhap it is," he groaned. "My God, Arabella, I have waited so long for this."

He climaxed with a harsh cry, and Robyn heard the answering sob of release rise in her own throat. Their passion crested in a thundering wave, sweeping her away, casting her adrift.

In the heaving, formless sea there was only William. William holding her safe, pulling her back from the edges of eternity.

William—who wasn't a dream.

Chapter 15

THOMAS Gainsborough had finally left for his return journey to London, after spending three weeks painting a picture of Lady Arabella and her infant son, the Honorable Zachary Arthur Danville Bowleigh.

Robyn had frozen with shock when William, beaming like a schoolboy, had ushered the young painter into the drawing room and announced that he was ready to start work immediately on Arabella's portrait. It seemed that Master Gainsborough was a friend of Hannah Wilkes, and sorely in need of money. Unwilling to acknowledge openly the intensity of emotion developing between himself and Arabella, William pounced with alacrity on the idea of supporting Thomas Gainsborough's talent by having him paint a picture of the wife who was fast becoming his obsession.

Robyn, feeling the threads of destiny pull frighteningly tight around her, had resisted at first. Only when William pointed out to her that Master Gainsborough was sorely in need of the money had she surrendered to the inevitable and agreed to be painted.

Unfortunately, sitting on a silk sofa in the drawing room, with Zach dozing in her arms, left far too much time for contemplation. Robyn's thoughts constantly circled back to the bizarre fact that the picture of Lady Arabella in Zach's Manhattan apartment was actually a picture of herself.

William's frequent appearances in the drawing room did nothing to help calm her tumultuous spirits. His repartee made her laugh, and eased the boredom of hours of sitting, but his eyes spoke a silent and more sensual message that left her dizzy with longing and restless for the night ahead. Then she would remember the portrait in Zach's apartment and her entire body would flush with embarrassed heat.

Having seen the finished work, she knew Thomas Gainsborough had both seen her desire and skillfully recorded it for all posterity.

But at last the portrait was finished, and Robyn could put aside the confusing welter of emotions that sitting for it had aroused. A mere three days remained until Christmas, and Starke Manor vibrated with the sights, sounds, and smells of the holiday season. The children weren't expecting a visit from Santa Claus, a nineteenth-century invention, nor was there a tree to decorate, a German custom introduced into England by Queen Victoria's husband. But William and the children, aided by an army of servants, had garlanded the staircase with boughs of fir and festooned the mantels with great bunches of scarlet-berried holly. Clemmie never walked into one of the decorated rooms without sniffing the pine-scented air and giving a little skip of pure pleasure. Robyn often found herself tempted to follow the child's example.

"Lady Arabella" was on the upswing in the servants' esteem. The household had been much impressed by her creativity when she combined a swatch of cheap scarlet ribbon with strips of gold satin from a discarded ball gown and tied giant bows to all the drawing-room sconces. The servants made the flimsiest of excuses to come to the drawing room and gaze in admiration at the bright, shiny bows nestled amid the somber evergreens. Robyn discovered one of the little chambermaids surreptitiously fingering the gold satin, her face alight with pleasure. She realized, with a profound sense of shock, that the child had never before touched a piece of silken cloth.

The excitement generated by her Christmas bows was a reproach to Robyn, a humiliating reminder of how few changes she had produced in the daily life of the Manor, and how trivial those changes had been. At her behest, everyone bathed more frequently, and the servants all had warmer bedding. She'd doubled the number of pot boys to four, so that she could be sure dishes got washed and not handed to the dogs to lick clean. Her first-aid advice was sometimes followed—at least when she was in sight. For the most part, however, she knew she'd had little impact on the way life was lived at Starke.

This was not the fault of tradition-bound servants. Robyn soon realized her grasp of twentieth-century technology was humiliatingly superficial. Far from being able to revolutionize the way daily tasks were performed, she could offer William almost no useful advice. She knew crops needed to be rotated and fertilized, but she had only the vaguest idea how. She couldn't rewrite history by inventing a steam engine years before James Watts because she didn't know how a steam engine worked. As for the mysteries of more advanced technology, they were just that—mysteries. She didn't know how light appeared when people flipped electric switches and she had no idea how computers stored information, or how antibiotics promoted healing. Like many other New Yorkers in the 1990s, she had been content to behave as if food grew in Chinese take-out boxes, and electronic data retrieval was a phenomenon of nature. If she had met one of the great inventors of the eighteenth century, she doubted if she would have been able to take his researches a single step further.

The entire household's unabashed pleasure in eating had been another surprise for her. Food was seasonal, hard to store, and precious. Sweets were a rare treat, dinner the most eagerly anticipated hour of the day. When the choristers from the parish church entertained the household with a series of Christmas rounds and carols, the singers were rewarded with mugs of apple cider and a plate of hot damson tartlets. From their ecstatic expressions as they ate the pastries, Robyn concluded that damson tartlets were something looked forward to all year, and probably talked about for weeks before and after they were consumed.

The traditional plum puddings had been boiled months earlier and put into the larder to steep in brandy, but Jean-Luc still worked at frenzied speed, supervising his kitchen minions in an orgy of baking, boiling, and roasting, preparing special treats for each of the Twelve Days of Christmas, and organizing huge quantities of food for the Boxing Day feast. The day after Christmas, the dependents of Starke would come to the Manor and gorge themselves on ale, cakes, and hot ham, before collecting their Christmas boxes as a reward for another year of loyal service to the baron. Wages for the laborers on the estate amounted to about

twenty-five pounds a year—William was considered a recklessly extravagant employer—so Robyn soon realized that
the silver penny polished and wrapped for each child was a
generous gift. Excitement was guaranteed as the children
searched for their pennies, hidden in the family Christmas
box amid nuts, prunes, and fragrant dried apples from the
Manor's own orchards.

Now that she had learned not to ask the ingredients of the
dishes served to her, Robyn was finding Jean-Luc's food delicious. Mince pies, rich with suet and far less sweet than
their twentieth-century counterparts, had become Robyn's
personal nemesis. With so many servants waiting to do her
bidding, she fought a constant battle against the temptation
of ordering pies at all hours of the day and night. On this
chilly, overcast morning, she had just succumbed to temptation and was biting into the hot, flaky crust of a sample from
Jean-Luc's latest batch, when the twins and Clemmie gave a
perfunctory scratch at the door and burst into her sitting
room. They sketched the obligatory bows and curtsies and
tumbled across the room, calling out instructions as they
progressed.

"You must come now," Clemmie informed her. "You are
late."

George nodded. "Hurry up, Mamma, there is no time to
waste eating."

Robyn, who would have expected the twins to find time to
eat on their way to the Day of Judgment, abandoned her pie.
"Good heavens, what's happened? What's wrong?"

"Papa is taking us to bring home the Yule log!" Freddie
announced.

Robyn's acquaintance with Yule logs had been limited to
chocolate cakes in the supermarket freezer. "Papa is bringing home the Yule log? I'm afraid I don't quite understand
what you mean."

"Of course you do, Mamma." Freddie took her hand.
"You know that Papa always cuts down the tree three days
before Christmas."

"We must set the Yule log burning as soon as dusk falls
on Christmas Eve, and keep it burning all night long, to light
the way for the Christ child." George couldn't understand

his mother's failure to start moving. Even Clementina tugged at Robyn's skirts.

"Come quick, Mamma. Papa is waiting." She waved her muff in the air, and gave a little twirl of anticipation: "I *love* chopping down trees!"

By the time Robyn arrived downstairs with the children, a spirited knot of servants had already gathered outside the front door, mugs in hand. William was seated in one of the farm carts, holding the reins of two sturdy plow horses, strong enough to haul home the log. In honor of the occasion, the cart had been decorated with banners of bright red flannel, the manes of the horses plaited with ribbon, and the plank seats of the cart lined with thick woolen blankets. Chattering nonstop, the children clambered into the cart, impatient to be off.

William looked down at Robyn and his mouth curved into a faint smile. He swept off his hat, absurdly elegant even though he was seated at the helm of a hay cart. He inclined his head. "My lady."

She hoped the servants would attribute her bright red cheeks to the cold. She curtsied. "My lord."

He leaned down and offered her his hand to assist her into the cart. "I was not sure that you would come," he said.

"I wouldn't miss it for anything."

He looked at her, eyes gleaming. "How relieved I am that your . . . exertions . . . last night did not exhaust you."

The red in her cheeks flamed several degrees brighter. Despite three weeks of sharing William's bed, she still didn't feel relaxed in his company. She looked at him with deliberate blankness. "What exertions do you speak of, my lord? I confess that I can't recall anything special."

William's eyes gleamed darker. "Can you not? I am desolate. Tonight I must clearly strive to make more of an impression." He whipped up the horses, giving her no chance to reply, since anything she said would have been drowned in the chorus of encouraging shouts from the accompanying servants and children.

The plow horses traversed the countryside at a steady, ambling trot. In the back of the cart, the children started to sing. Clemmie's voice, although scarcely out of babyhood, was clear and true. The twins, less tuneful, sang with equal gusto, and the servants occasionally hummed the harmony or banged out the rhythm with their mugs. The words of the songs were unfamiliar, but Robyn recognized most of the melodies. It gave her a strange feeling to realize that a dozen generations into the future, children still sang the same Christmas tunes as their ancestors.

The oak tree that had been chosen as the source for this year's Yule log grew to the north of the woods where Robyn had first encountered Captain Bretton. With a disregard for safety that would have given any twentieth-century employer heart failure, two dozen of William's men had gathered to chop down the tree, which stood almost thirty feet tall, and measured close to a yard in diameter. Alternately swinging lethal-looking axes, and reinforcing themselves with something potent out of stoneware jars, the self-appointed woodsmen were clearly having a wonderful time. Robyn was relieved to see that there were some ropes looped around the upper branches, presumably ready to guide the tree to the ground, but the whole operation looked dangerous in the extreme. She ignored the children's protests and held Clemmie firmly by the hand, insisting that the twins stay close to her, out of range whichever way the tree happened to fall.

William didn't attempt to countermand her orders to the children, but he tried to reassure her. "My men know exactly what they are doing, you know. You need have no fears for the children's safety."

"How can you say that? Good Lord, William, half a dozen of those woodcutters can barely stand upright, let alone make intricate calculations about the angle of their cuts!"

"But if you watch closely, you will see that the ones who are drunk are no longer working. Those who drink are the older men who have already completed their share of the chopping."

"Well, I sure hope the tree falls down before they do. What are they imbibing with such enthusiasm?"

William smiled. "Ginger wine, made from a recipe first written down by my father's grandmother. You should taste it sometime. It does a marvelous job of keeping out the cold."

"And numbing the brain, too, I'll bet!"

He smiled again. "Don't worry, my lady. The Yule log will be cut and shaped without mishap, ready to burn for us on Christmas Eve." He strolled over to the trestle table and accepted a pewter tankard from Aaron, who seemed to be acting as impromptu foreman for the operation. Robyn couldn't hear what they said, but she was horrified to see William drink deeply, then accept an ax from Aaron and stroll toward the ominously swaying tree.

"Good heavens, what is your father going to do?" she demanded of the children.

"He is going to cut down the tree for the Yule log," George said.

"Himself? In person? But I thought aristocrats never lifted a finger in the eighteenth century! For goodness' sake, doesn't he realize that chopping down a tree that big could kill him—could hurt somebody?"

The twins looked at her blankly. "Papa is the Baron of Starke," Freddie reminded her, as if that explained everything. "It is his duty to cut down the Yule log."

"It is the tradition," George said and Freddie nodded, clearly considering this the final word on the subject.

Clemmie skipped in a small circle, clapping her hands. "Look! Papa is going to cut the tree down now!"

A great cheer rose from the assembled laborers as their lord and master strode into the chip-strewn clearing around the tree. William bowed in acknowledgment, then raised the ax and brought it down with a thundering blow at the apex of the tree trunk. The tree shuddered, but remained standing. He swung the ax twice more, and then a third time. The tree teetered, creaked, and swayed into a lumbering, graceful fall. The noise of its crash was deafening, and when the reverberations finally died away, a roar of approval went up from the crowd.

"Hurrah! The Yule log is cut! Three cheers for his lordship!"

"Four blows," George said. "That was very good of Papa."

"Last year he took six," Freddie commented.

As the cheers died away, Robyn could hear the twitter and caw of frightened wildlife, but nobody else paid any heed to the scampering squirrels and nervous rabbits. A swarm of

men descended upon the tree the instant the dust cleared.
Some worked at chopping off the upper branches, but the
largest number ranged themselves on either side of a huge
saw, supported on trestles. Four men worked in concert on
each side, sweat running off their foreheads and dripping
from their noses as they sawed through the massive trunk.
After fifteen minutes or so, the first team of cutters was replaced, and the rhythmic sawing continued with new men.
Robyn realized that cuts were being made at foot-long inter-
vals, and each man was taking possession of a giant wheel
of trunk, leaving a section about six feet long and three feet
in diameter to serve as the Yule log for the Manor.

Tired of standing on the sidelines, Clemmie and the twins
begged for permission to join the other children, who were
playing a game similar to pin the tail on the donkey, except
that a wooden peg had to be slotted into a small box. With
the tree safely felled, Robyn gave them permission to play.
The twins instantly improved the game by surrounding the
box with a wreath of holly, which meant that misjudgments
by the "blindman" were inevitably punished by a painful
scratch. The twins' innovation was much admired by the
other children, who all competed to show the most bravado
when pricked by the holly. All, that is, except Clemmie, who
showed no bravado, but won the game by the simple process
of peering under the blindfold and cheating. Robyn wasn't
sure whether to be appalled at Clemmie's lack of honor or
impressed by her ingenuity.

Shrugging back into his greatcoat, William came over to
join her as the children refreshed themselves with foaming
mugs of ginger beer and heavily spiced ginger cookies. "We
are fortunate that the ground remains frozen," he said. "Last
year we ended up slithering around in a pool of mud. You
can scarcely imagine the spectacle we presented by the end
of the morning."

"On the contrary, I can imagine it well." She smiled. "You
may have been chilled and dirty, but I'm sure none of you
felt any pain."

He frowned in puzzlement. "Why would we feel pain? We
were not wounded."

"I meant only that you would have been warmed by the

ginger wine," she said, disconcerted at the need to explain her twentieth-century idiom.

"Ah! Now I understand. But you wrong me, my lady. I was, as always, the very model of dull sobriety."

"You are never dull, William, and you know it, so stop fishing for compliments."

He smiled. "How can I, my dear, when you deliver them with such sweet tartness?"

A robin, disturbed by all the commotion, flew out of the undergrowth and perched on the branch of a young oak. Plump, tiny, with a particularly brilliant red breast, it cocked its head and looked straight at Robyn.

"Don't glare so accusingly," she told it. "I'm not the cruel person who chopped down your tree."

The bird chirruped, and Robyn laughed. "Sorry, fella. If you have a complaint, speak to the lord of the Manor, who is right here with me. He's the coldhearted villain who wrecked your home."

William stared at her, genuinely astonished. "It may have escaped your notice, but he does have an abundance of other trees in which he may pass the winter."

"How can you be so heartless? I'm sure he had a particular fondness for the one you cut down. It was the tallest in the wood, after all, and gave him a splendid view of Starke Manor."

"In that case, of course, I extend to him my deepest and most heartfelt apologies." William took off his hat and swept an exaggerated bow.

The robin flapped his wings, chirruped twice, then flew away. "I'm afraid he wasn't impressed," Robyn said. "He doubted your sincerity and with good reason, I'm sure."

"I did not mean to destroy his home—" William cut off abruptly. "This is absurd!" he exclaimed. "You're trying to make me feel guilty because a bird failed to accept my apology." He stopped again, shaking his head. "What is the matter with me? The bird didn't *refuse my apology*. All that happened is that a robin perched on a branch and then flew away."

Robyn chuckled. "Are you sure?"

"No, curse you, I'm not!" He turned to her and their laughter died away. He rested his hand lightly against her cheek. "I cannot remember a time of so much happiness," he said. "These past few weeks you have been like that robin. Your presence has brought a splash of warm color into the cold winter of our family life."

"Thank you," she said huskily. "I'm glad you feel that way. I have been happy, too." Robyn realized that she had been given an opening to make a request that had been on her mind for several days. "When I was a little girl, my mother used to call me Robyn," she said with perfect truth. "She spelled it R-o-b-y-n. I wish you would call me by that name, too. At least when we're alone."

"The Countess of Marshe called you Robyn?" William's eyes widened in surprise. "I'm amazed that your mother permitted such a plebeian name to be appended to her elegant daughter. You are much too beautiful for such a plain name. If you are to be called after a bird, it should be at least a swan or a peacock."

"Nevertheless, if you would try calling me Robyn for a while, I would be most grateful. The name has a lot of sentimental significance for me."

"Does it, indeed?" William took her hand from her muff and chaffed the tips of her chilly fingers. "How grateful might you be if I agreed to this change of name?" he inquired with suspicious smoothness.

She blushed. "Very grateful, William."

He stepped in front of her, so that she was screened from the view of the woodsmen. Then he leaned forward and brushed a quick hard kiss across her mouth. "In that case, my dear, I daresay I can be persuaded to put aside all thought of peacocks and swans in favor of the humble robin red breast." His eyes gleamed, and his smile became predatory. "I can't tell you how much I am looking forward to nightfall, and the full demonstration of your gratitude."

"That's bribery!" she protested. "William, I'm shocked. Aren't you ashamed of yourself?"

He pressed a hot, hungry kiss into her palm before tucking her hand back into the muff. "Alas," he said. "Dear Robyn, I fear not the tiniest bit."

The Delaneys had obviously decided to put on a brave show for the holidays, even if they didn't have too much to celebrate. The Douglas fir in their front yard had been festooned with colored lights, and a collection of silver bells jingled merrily when Zach pressed the doorbell. Al Delaney opened the door almost at once.

"Zach, come along in! Good of you to stop by."

"How are you doing?" Zach stepped into the little entrance hall, which was fragrant with the smell of Christmas baking. "Mmm, something smells wonderful."

"Mince pies," Muriel Delaney said, poking her head out of the kitchen. "Come on back to the family room and help yourself to some before the grandchildren wolf them all."

"Thanks, a mince pie would be great, but I mustn't stay too long. I have to catch a three o'clock flight to L.A." He felt his face break into an unexpected smile. "My brother's getting married tomorrow and I'm acting as his best man."

"How nice! Christmas is a lovely time for weddings." A shadow crossed Muriel's face. "I always teased Robyn that everyone else in the family got married in midsummer, so she'd have to oblige me with a winter wedding."

Zach cleared his throat. "Speaking of Robyn," he said, trying to sound cheerful and sounding unctuous instead. "How's she doing these days?"

Muriel and Al exchanged glances. "She's keeping busy," Al said.

Zach kept his smile fixed. "Did she start work with the occupational therapist in the end?"

"Yeah, and we think that helped some. She's doing a lot of sewing, so I guess that's an improvement."

"The therapist suggested she should do something to get her hand-eye coordination going again," Muriel said. "It was amazing. As soon as we gave her needle and thread, she turned out some beautiful embroidery. Really wonderful stuff."

"It's real nice," Al agreed. "Even I can see that. Professional standard, according to the therapist, isn't that right, Muriel?"

"She told us Robyn could sell her first piece for a lot of money, and this one she's working on now is even better." Muriel shook her head. "I can't imagine where she learned to do embroidery like this. She never told any of us that she'd been taking lessons. Maybe she took a class when she was studying at the museum over in London."

Al pushed open the door to the family room. "Ask her to show you the piece she's working on right now, Zach. She's always willing to show it off."

Mentally armoring himself against the pain of seeing Robyn's familiar face superimposed on a personality that bore no relationship to the woman he'd loved, Zach entered the family room.

Gerry Taunton was seated on the sofa, sipping a cup of eggnog.

Zach felt a surge of surprise that was out of proportion to the situation. "Gerry!" he said. "What's up? I had no idea you were going to be here."

Gerry smiled. "Well, I'm planning to spend Christmas in D.C., so it wasn't much of a drive over. Robyn and I were good friends, as well as colleagues. I keep hoping that if I pay the occasional visit, she'll remember me, maybe even wake up one day, ready to explain about those coded files on her computer." He shook his head wearily. "You know, I can't believe Robyn was behind the sale of all those fraudulent antiques, even though the sales seem to have stopped now that she's—like this . . ."

His voice tailed away unhappily, and Zach followed his gaze to the corner of the room, where Robyn was hunched on a stool, watching television, her gaze glued with hypnotic fierceness to the screen. She must have sensed people looking at her, for she suddenly jerked up her head. Her cheeks whitened, but it was a measure of how much her parents and therapists had achieved that she didn't scream the instant she saw Zach. She shrank further into herself, staring at him in hostile silence, but at least she didn't scream.

Be thankful for small mercies, Zach told himself sardonically. He gulped, feeling as gauche and uncomfortable as a teenager. Hell, he couldn't bear to accept that his relationship with Robyn was never again going to be more than this painful mishmash of her fear and his regrets.

"Hi, Robyn, merry Christmas." He held out the small, brightly wrapped package he had brought with him. She stared at him with alien eyes, and he felt as if he were being confronted by a hostile stranger masquerading behind

Robyn's familiar features. The sensation of otherness was so strong, he shivered. Then Robyn reached out to seize the box, snatching her hand away as if she feared any form of physical contact with him. Safely in possession of the box, she stroked the shiny tinsel paper for several seconds, untying the ribbon slowly, her eyes shining with almost childish anticipation as she removed the glittering gold foil bow.

Inside was a bottle of perfume, an unoriginal gift, but Zach hadn't been able to bring himself to choose something unique for a Robyn he no longer knew. Fortunately, she seemed well satisfied with his choice. She removed the stopper and sniffed cautiously, before taking a handkerchief and tipping perfume onto the corner. She waved the hankie in front of her nose, breathing in the scented wafts of air with a pleased smile. She made no effort to dab the perfume anywhere on her skin, but she was wearing a high-necked sweater, so Zach supposed that was why.

Her smile faded as she turned to Zach, but once again, she managed to control her obvious mistrust. "I thank you," she said stiffly. "It is a most pleasing scent. Although here in this country, I find it most strange. Even the servants are agreeably perfumed."

One of her quirks since the accident was the belief that ninety percent of the people she encountered were servants. Zach took the coward's way out and ignored the comment, as he ignored most of her comments that he didn't know how to deal with.

"I'm glad you like the perfume." Zach sat down, careful to leave plenty of space on the sofa. Robyn tended to get nervous if he sat too close. "Your mother tells me that you have done some beautiful embroidery," he said. "Would you show me something you've sewn?"

"My mother is dead," she said, her voice aching with resentment, as if she had already made the same remark a thousand times and had given up all hope of being listened to.

Zach glanced toward Gerry, who simply shook his head in silent warning. Zach turned back to Robyn. "I would still like to see your embroidery," he said.

"You mean that which I have stitched?"

"Yes, that's it. Your mother tells me you're doing beautiful work." *God, what a patronizing ass he sounded.*

She shrugged and got up from the sofa, walking quickly to an old-fashioned dresser that stood against the wall of the family room.

Gerry leaned over and whispered in Zach's ear. "She insists her mother was a countess. She refuses to call Mrs. Delaney anything but Muriel. Honest to God, Zach, she treats the poor lady like a slave. You could hardly believe sometimes that this is the same Robyn we both used to know and love."

"You seem to be very well up on the details of Robyn's condition," Zach said.

Gerry shrugged, clearly not wanting to take credit for the time and effort he was expending on a hopeless case. "I feel so sorry for her parents, you know? Somehow, it seems to help if I call and chat every now and then. They don't feel so abandoned."

Robyn returned and held out a piece of canvas, two feet by two feet. "It is not yet complete," she told Zach. "I trust, sir, that you find it pleasing to the eye?"

Despite the Delaneys' lavish praise, Zach hadn't expected the embroidery to be quite so wonderful. He examined Robyn's work with awe, trying to recall if he had ever seen such an exquisite piece of needlepoint outside of a museum or an art gallery.

"I find it *very* pleasing to the eye," he said, smiling at Robyn as his fingers stroked the superlative work. An eighteenth-century lady stood in a garden of flowers, her sky-blue satin skirts looped up to reveal a froth of lace, depicted in minute, almost invisible stitches of varying shades of white and cream. In the background of the tapestry, a riot of flowers bloomed, old-fashioned English flowers like flock, lily of the valley, and midnight stock. The lady's white-powdered curls fell forward over the slope of a delicately curved bosom, even her hand and fingers had been worked in flawless detail.

Captivated by the impeccable details, it took Zach a minute or two to register the precise subject of the canvas. Then he realized that this was not simply a picture of any old eighteenth-century lady.

"Good heavens," he said. "Robyn, you've done a truly outstanding job, and all from memory, too. This is a portrait of the Lady Arabella Bowleigh, isn't it?"

Robyn stared at him, her mouth slackening. She gripped her arms around her waist, shaking with fear, and he gave what he hoped was an encouraging smile. "You've remembered the portrait that hangs on the wall of my apartment, haven't you? Do you recall how we talked of Lady Arabella Bowleigh and her family the night before we flew to England to visit the Baron of Starke?"

"We . . . *flew* . . . to see the Baron of Starke? You and I?" This was the longest conversation they'd had so far, and Zach felt heartened, despite her cowering demeanor.

"Well, we didn't fly together," he said. "You flew from New York and I flew from Paris. We were supposed to meet in England, at the Starke Manor Hotel. Do you remember, sweetheart?"

Gerry leaned forward, anxious to offer encouragement but clearly not quite sure what to say. Robyn ignored him, her gaze fixated on Zach. She backed away until she was pressed to the wall and could go no farther. Her fingers clawed at the walnut paneling. "The Lord has not heard my prayers," she whispered, her gaze still locked with Zach's. "My sins have found me out. I am truly in hell, and thou art indeed the devil disguised in William's form."

His stomach lurched with sick disappointment. "Robyn, sweetheart, I'm not William. I'm Zach. Will's brother."

She stared at him, eyes dilating in pure, unadulterated terror. Then she fainted.

The lackey flung open the door. "My lady, I crave pardon. But Captain Bretton is here, my lady."

Robyn didn't bother to look up from the cat she was drawing for Clemmie. "I am not at home," she said.

Captain Bretton pushed past the servant and bowed. "This is not a social visit, my lady. I come on the King's business."

Robyn raised her head. "You come so frequently on the King's business, Captain. I trust the matter is of truly vital urgency?"

"Indeed it is. Where is your husband?"

Robyn did not invite the captain to sit. She gently lifted Clemmie from her lap, gave her a quick hug, then gestured to the lackey. "Please escort Miss Clementina to the nursery."

She waited until the servant and child had left the room before answering Captain Bretton. She eyed him coolly. "The urgency of this situation entirely escapes me, sir. I cannot imagine how the Baron of Starke's present whereabouts could be of any concern to His Majesty."

"We have been given to understand that the baron has ridden out to Poole." Captain Bretton was tight-sprung, not with nervous tension but with an unpleasant kind of suppressed glee.

Robyn refused to display her uneasiness. "And so? Even if that should be true, I believe His Majesty still grants his subjects the right of free passage." The charcoal Robyn had been holding broke with a loud snap. She laid the pieces on the table and wiped her fingers with meticulous care. "I repeat, sir, that I fail to see how my husband's presence in Poole, or his absence therefrom, could be of any interest whatsoever to the King's servants."

"Are you determined to be willfully blind?" he demanded.

"Not blind, Captain, but busy. So busy that I'm sure you will excuse me if I go about my duties." She walked over to the bell rope and closed her hand around the tasseled pull. "Now, sir, I wish you good day—"

He strode across the room, squeezing his hand so tightly around hers that the rope cut painfully into her palms. "I recommend that you summon no servants, Lady Arabella. You would not wish them to overhear our conversation."

"Sir, you can have *nothing* of a private nature to say to me—"

His mouth twisted into a jeering smile. "Well played, my lady. A man who knows you less well might have believed you as innocent as you sound. Alas, our acquaintance is too old and too intimate for such a ploy to work."

"Captain Bretton, I am asking that you leave—"

He put his hand over her mouth and leaned toward her, brown eyes gleaming. "You always did talk too much, Arabella. Now, my dear, I suggest that you shut those delectable, rosy lips and listen. For the sake of the good times we once shared—and which I believe we could share again—I take pleasure in warning you of the peril you face."

She tugged his hand away from her mouth. "Captain Bretton, I have not the faintest idea what you are talking about."

"Then let me make my meaning crystal clear. Do not aid and abet your husband in committing treason. We both know the road down which the baron is headed, and the end is inevitable ruin."

She tossed her head, genuinely impatient. "I cannot possibly aid and abet my husband in the commission of treason, sir, since he plots no treason. The Baron of Starke would not dream of betraying his oath of loyalty to the King."

"Fine-sounding words, my lady, but falsehoods nevertheless. If you wish your children to enjoy their inheritance, you will cooperate with me."

Despite her conviction that William was a true Tory, Robyn felt suddenly chilled. "In what way are my children affected by this discussion, Captain Bretton?" *Dammit, she hadn't meant to let her voice quaver.*

"Surely you do not need me to remind you that if the baron is executed for treason, his property will revert to the Crown, thus disinheriting all of your children—and at least one of mine."

Fear was subsumed in puzzlement. "What do you mean?"

As soon as she asked the question, even before she saw his derisive smirk, she knew the answer. *Clementina.* Brown-eyed, round-faced Clemmie was the captain's child. Stupid, she told herself. *Stupid, Robyn, to have laid yourself open to his taunts and to his threats.*

Almost in the same instant, she realized how she could protect Clemmie, and William, too. Everyone for miles around knew that Lady Arabella had lost her wits when she fell from her carriage. If Robyn could convince Captain Bretton that she had no memory of her affair with him, then he would lose much of his power over her. If Lady Arabella remembered no guilty, adulterous secrets, what weapon could the captain use to threaten her?

She hoped that she hadn't revealed too much of what she was thinking during her moment of silence. With a little shake of her skirts, she turned around, opening her eyes very wide and gazing at Captain Bretton with a simpering portrayal of bewildered innocence.

"You speak in riddles, Captain, riddles that I am at a loss to fathom. Can you not make your meaning plain?"

She had counted on the captain's conspiratorial instincts to keep him silent, and the gamble paid off. He stared at her, his sneering expression freezing into a frown. "Whatever you may remember or not remember, my lady, think carefully on this. Your husband is a traitor and he will be executed, along with his foolish brother. That I promise you. So if you wish your children to inherit the lands of their ancestors, you have no choice other than to marry me, and throw yourself on my mercy." His voice lowered, and he cupped her breast with insolent vulgarity. "You will discover, my dear, that I have much to recommend me as a husband."

However much might be at stake, she couldn't bear him to touch her. She threw off his hand, and whirled around to tug the bell rope. "Your loathing of my husband does not make him a traitor, Captain Bretton, except in your fevered imagination. The Duke of Cumberland may have empowered you with much authority over this region, but the Baron of Starke has powerful friends at court. Take care that you do not imperil yourself rather than my husband with these wild and groundless accusations."

She had no idea if William truly had powerful connections, but her threat seemed to have struck a chord with Captain Bretton, who continued to look furious, but suddenly less sure of himself. Like most bullies, she concluded, he had no fallback position if his victims didn't immediately surrender. Her optimism that she had controlled the situation was short-lived, however. Even as the captain hesitated in the doorway, a great shout came up from the courtyard, followed by the sound of gunshots.

Robyn ran to the window, but her sitting room overlooked a walled garden, and there was nothing to see. Before she could run out into the hallway, a footman arrived at their door, breathless, his wig askew.

"M'lady, troopers, all over the courtyard. They be a-firing o' their muskets." He poked at his wig, so agitated that he only succeeded in setting it farther over his left ear.

"Why are they shooting?" Robyn asked. "Take your time to draw breath before you answer."

"They do be a-chasin' of a Jacobite rebel, m'lady. They claim as 'ow they chased the rebel right inside o' the Manor." The footman's speech fell back to the dialect of his youth under the stress of the moment. "They do be a-swarmin' all over th'ouse, m'lady. Hackett cain't stop 'em a-comin' in."

"This is an outrage!" Robyn drew herself up, never more glad that she possessed Lady Arabella's extra inches, and glared at the captain, eyeball to eyeball. She had no need to pretend fury: her Irish blood was boiling at the helplessness of honest citizens to protect themselves from the wrath of a jealous, malevolent, jumped-up despot like Captain Bretton. It was to protect themselves from just this sort of exploitation that solid American citizens had thrown tea into Boston harbor and successfully staged a revolution.

"Call your men off," she demanded. "Or I shall see to it personally that the King is informed of how his loyal subjects are being treated by soldiers under your command."

Captain Bretton merely laughed, a laugh rich with triumph. "Straight home to roost!" he exclaimed. "Now—at last—we have him!"

"You make no sense, sir."

Captain Bretton paced the room, literally rubbing his hands in glee. "We were told that he would today attempt to escape to France from Poole harbor. We set close watch, and now we have him. *We—have—him!*"

A soldier appeared in the doorway, saluting and standing smartly to attention despite sweat dripping from his forehead and staining the underarms of his uniform. Captain Bretton lunged forward, barely able to control himself. "Yes!" he said, his voice thick with satisfaction. "Is he alive? You haven't killed him?"

"There are two rebels, sir. At least one of them wounded."

"Excellent. You chased them from Poole?"

"Yes, sir."

"At least one of them wounded . . ." The captain's voice sharpened. "What do you mean? Don't you know if they have both been shot? Do you have them under arrest? By

God, I will have you all lashed if you have allowed them to escape."

The soldier stared straight ahead. His body grew even more rigid. "Sir, I winged one of them meself, but they disappeared, sir. One minute they was there, and then they wasn't. Sir. They wasn't more than a hundred yards ahead of us at the end. We 'ad them in sight, sir, when we came through the gates of Starke. Then they went 'round the corner and they was gone. Sir."

Captain Bretton was too angry to speak. "Check the stables," he said finally. "You damn fool, if you've let them escape this time, Sergeant, I will not forgive your stupidity. Order your men to surround the house, blast you!"

The soldier paled beneath his sweat. "Yes, sir. Thank you, sir. I 'ave already so ordered, sir."

"Then get out of here and start searching the Manor. Room to room. Attics to cellars."

"Yes, sir."

Robyn turned to the still-panting lackey. "Find Monsieur Petain and ask him to take both the boys and Miss Clementina for a walk. Immediately. They are not to stay inside the house, is that clear?"

"Yes, m'lady." The lackey bowed and backed out of the room. Robyn turned to Captain Bretton not attempting to keep either the scorn or the dislike out of her voice. "I seem to be holding you back from your duties, sir. I would not like to deprive you of the pleasure of searching from room to room for whichever wretched rebels your soldiers have shot this time."

She jumped when William's voice spoke from behind her. "You mistake the captain's pleasure, my dear. He does not search with this degree of avidity for humble rebels. He searches for me, is that not so, Captain Bretton? For me, and for my brother Zachary."

Chapter 16

STARTLED to hear her husband's voice, Robyn swung around. William, still dressed in the riding clothes in which he had left her at dawn, sauntered across the room, swept off his hat, and bowed with casual gallantry. He raised her hand to his lips and brushed a kiss across the tips of her fingers. "You are especially beautiful today, my lady. Blue is undoubtedly your color."

"Thank you." Despite his nonchalant greeting, Robyn sensed an underlying tension in William. He looked pale and tautly controlled, no doubt because he was trying not to show his anger at Captain Bretton's intrusion. She wondered where he had been all morning, but she wasn't going to play into the captain's hands by asking, and William volunteered no information. With a quick squeeze of her fingers, he flung himself down in the chair by the hearth, and glanced with bored mockery at the captain.

"Do not, I pray, remain here on our account, sir. I am sure there must be many useful tasks still awaiting your attention. At least three of our housemaids have not yet fainted. Should you not fire off some more muskets and terrify them into proper submission?"

"You are pleased to jest," Captain Bretton said, his cheeks flushing with anger. "But you will soon learn that the time for ridicule is over. My men shot and wounded your brother, that is indisputable—"

"Alas, sir, I must dispute with you. Your soldiers are doubtless great warriors, but even they cannot fire their bullets from here to France. Which is where my brother resides."

The captain spoke through clenched teeth. "We shall find

your brother's hiding place today, my lord, and then *you* will not be quite so arrogant and *I* will be making the jests."

William closed his eyes, as if the prospect of Captain Bretton's jokes was too horrible to contemplate. He set his hat on his lap, then yawned. "Excuse me," he apologized. "My land agent insisted on dragging me over every turnip field in Starke this morning. He is quite determined to make me as devoted to the concept of crop rotation as he is. What is your opinion of turnips as a soil refresher, Captain Bretton?"

Except for an annoyed tsk, the captain didn't reply and William stretched out his legs, resting one elegantly booted foot on the brass fender and leaning down to admire the silver buckle. He polished it languidly with his pocket handkerchief, and straightened only when Captain Bretton spoke angrily.

"Good God, my lord, have you nothing better to do at a time like this than clean your shoe buckles?"

"There is rarely anything more important to do than insure one's boot buckles are correctly polished," William said mildly.

"You do not seem to have grasped the fact that your brother's life hangs in the balance! He has been identified by a score of rebel prisoners as the man who took possession of Charles Stuart's treasure chest after the Battle of Culloden. You are much mistaken if you believe King George will allow your brother to escape to France carrying enough money to pay for the next invasion by the Pretender's army of malcontents."

His hat held at his side, William rose slowly to his feet, his face whiter than before. With rage, Robyn assumed, since his voice was cold enough to have frosted an entire field of turnips. "I have grasped very well the hatred you hold for my brother and me, Captain Bretton, just as I am aware of your misguided conviction that Zachary is hiding Prince Charles Stuart's treasure. Fortunately, I do not have to worry either about your misinformation or about your vicious intentions, since my brother has been safely removed from your jurisdiction for many months."

"So you would have me believe, my lord. Our informants insist otherwise."

"Has it never occurred to you that torture will induce a man to say whatever his tormentor wishes to hear?" William sat down again, turning away in a clear gesture of dismissal. "I wish you all possible speed in your search, Captain. Pray do not bother to return and bid me farewell. I am willing to consider your apologies and excuses already spoken."

"You will receive no apologies from me, my lord. I do not ask pardon for acting zealously on the King's business."

William raised a quizzical eyebrow. "Lud, how admirably fierce. But I would remind you, sir, that my uncle, Lord Pevensy, bears an inexplicable fondness for me, and he is privy counsellor to His Majesty. I think King George would be annoyed to hear from Lord Pevensy of the unhealthy obsession you have developed for searching my property at all hours of the day and night."

The captain appeared momentarily taken aback by the threat. Then, remembering that he was secure in the protection of the Duke of Cumberland, the King's own son, prepared to continue the argument. He had scarcely opened his mouth, however, when a breathless young lieutenant arrived bearing a message. Captain Bretton acknowledged his subordinate's salute. "Yes, what is it?"

"We have captured the ship, sir. The *Bon Voyage* has been secured in Poole harbor."

Captain Bretton's frowns turned at once into a cruel smile. "That is good news. And the crew? They are in jail?"

The lieutenant stared straight ahead. "Er . . . no, sir. The ship was . . . um . . . abandoned when our men boarded her."

"What!" The captain let out a bellow of rage. "How can that be? Where the hell did the crew go? The ship carried a full complement of men last night, and that I know for a fact. My informant was still on board, for God's sake!"

The lieutenant flushed, not from anger or embarrassment, Robyn suspected, but from fear. "It seems that the crew was warned of your intentions, sir. It also appears that they could all swim."

"Swim? Good God, sailors can never swim! They think it is tempting destiny."

"True, sir, but this crew apparently defied tradition. They must have dived into the water from one of the lower decks whilst we were guarding the shore." The lieutenant cleared his throat, sweat beading in a line along his forehead. "We were never ordered to patrol the waters, sir, only the quayside, which we did."

"Idiots! Buffoons! I'll have you cashiered and the men whipped!" The captain stormed out of the room, yelling for his sergeant, so overwrought that he forgot to bow to Robyn. The lieutenant, clumsy with dread, snapped his heels in Robyn's direction and hurried out after the captain.

Robyn waited until all sounds of their descent down the stairs had died away. Then she walked quickly to the door of the sitting room and quietly shut it, throwing home the bolt.

"Thank you," William said, sounding somewhat stiff. "Forgive me, my dear, but I need to go to my room for a few minutes—"

Robyn interposed herself between William and the connecting door into his bedroom. The strain of the previous few minutes broke in an eruption of furious, body-shaking rage. "You're not going anywhere until you've given me some explanations," she said as soon as she could speak without screaming. "Where have you been? And don't you *dare* tell me one of your lies about turnips!"

"I went . . . for a ride," William said.

She stamped her foot. Arabella's body, she reflected ruefully, still seemed to have some built-in reactions that she couldn't control. "Did you go to Poole?" she demanded. "Is Captain Bretton right—have you been aiding and abetting the Jacobites? And is Zachary truly safe in France?"

"My dear Arabella, you know quite well that I have not been absent from your side long enough to ride to Poole and back."

"My name is Robyn, and I don't know any such thing. How in the world would I know how long it takes to get somewhere by *horse,* for heaven's sake? And I'm not entirely stupid, you know. I'm perfectly well aware of the fact that you didn't answer my question."

"Which question, my dear?"

"Any of the important ones," she retorted. She lowered her voice. "William, please tell me what's going on. If you're in trouble, let me help you."

He looked at her consideringly for several silent moments. Then, still without saying a word, he tossed his hat onto the chair. In a spot directly beneath where he had been holding the hat, his riding coat was stained with damp circles of red. Robyn blinked, momentarily unable to grasp the significance of the stains. Then she leaned forward and pulled back the concealing skirt of his riding coat.

She found herself staring at a blackened, bloody mess of ripped riding breeches and torn flesh. She gulped, swallowing several times to conquer a surge of nausea. Dear God, William had been shot! *This* was the reason for his pallor, for his rigid self-control. Not rage, as she had assumed, but pain. Excruciating pain. She pressed her hand against her mouth, forcing back an instinctive cry. It would be disastrous if she did anything to attract Captain Bretton's attention.

William gripped her hand. "Pray do not faint, my love, for if you fell, I fear 'twould be beyond my powers to pick you up again."

"I'm not going to faint." She drew in a deep, steadying breath. "Tell me what I must do."

"Bandage the wound—and quickly. We cannot count on Captain Bretton slinking away from Starke without an apology. He is likely to return any minute."

"You seem very sure that his men will find no rebels," she said.

"I am quite sure that they will not."

She looked at him steadily. "Zachary's hiding place is that good? How can you be certain none of the servants will betray you?"

"My dear, you mistake my meaning—"

"I've asked you before not to lie to me," she said, turning away in frustration. "I believe I have earned something more than your lies, William."

A pounding at the door cut short their incipient argument. With a quick glance of silent pleading, William slipped through the connecting door, out of her sitting room and into his bedroom. After a hurried check that he had left no bloodstains on the carpet, Robyn crossed to the door and unbarred it. Captain Bretton stood in the hallway, flanked by the inevitable escort of blank-faced soldiers.

"Yes?" She was getting rather good at sounding imperious when her stomach was roiling with fright.

Captain Bretton spoke curtly. "I am come to bid you farewell, my lady, and to remind you that aiding a traitor is itself an act of treason."

"Good-bye, and thank you so much for the kind warning. It is, of course, completely unnecessary."

"And yet you had chosen to lock your door," the captain pointed out. "I must ask myself why, if neither you nor Lord Bowleigh has anything to hide."

Robyn's heart thumped so hard she was actually grateful for the stays that stiffened her bodice and disguised her physical reactions. She forced her mouth into a coy smirk. "A husband and wife may have many reasons for wishing to be private, sir." She tittered, another skill of Arabella's that she seemed to have inherited. "I can assure you my husband and I were *much* too busy to waste our time discussing Jacobite traitors."

The captain scowled, then suddenly pushed past her and crossed the room, throwing open the connecting doors first to her bedroom and then to William's. Robyn noticed William's hat still lay on the floor by the hearth. She knew there hadn't been enough time for him to bandage his thigh, let alone change into fresh clothes, and panic set in. Without his concealing hat, could William position himself so that the blood on his coat wasn't visible? She followed the captain into William's bedroom, trying frantically to think of some excuse—any excuse—that they might offer for the incriminating bloodstains.

She needn't have worried. William's bedroom was empty. So were his dressing room and his closet. Robyn, far more astonished than the captain, stared at the empty rooms in disbelief.

"Where is he?" Captain Bretton demanded. "Where did he go when he left you?"

Robyn felt giddy with relief. "I believe you have already asked that question several times today, sir. As a mark of my willingness to cooperate with the King's servants, I will answer you this once, although why I should account to you for the Baron of Starke's movements I cannot imagine. Lord Bowleigh's plan was to ride out to meet again with his agent."

"Lord Bowleigh planned to meet with his agent at this hour of the day?"

The captain sounded so genuinely incredulous that Robyn realized she had invented an unlikely excuse. She took refuge in aristocratic hauteur. She swung around in a rustle of silk, satin, and velvet, posing dead center of the hearth, in such a way that the Bowleigh crest, carved in dark, solid oak, rose majestically behind her. Sometimes, she decided, there were real psychological advantages to be derived from the trappings that came with being rich and aristocratic in the eighteenth century.

"Your discourse becomes wearisome, Captain Bretton. You have searched Starke repeatedly and found nothing—"

"On the contrary, Lady Arabella. Each time I search, my men discover another rebel."

"In the grounds, Captain, never in the house. My husband's property is extensive. He cannot be held responsible for desperate men who take refuge in his woods and outbuildings under the cover of darkness. I ask that you leave Starke, and that you do not return again on these repeated wild goose chases. Whomever, or whatever, your men shot this morning, it was clearly no one from Starke."

He bowed, acknowledging defeat, fury barely contained. "This time we may have found nothing," he admitted, "but the chase is by no means over, and at the finish, I am confident I will capture my geese. You are warned, Lady Arabella."

He didn't wait for her to reply, but strode out of the room, spurs jingling. The soldiers trooped out after him.

Robyn's knees were feeling distinctly wobbly. She sank into the nearest chair. "Odious man," she muttered. "Slimy, creeping *reptile*. Right now, I can think of only one man who's worse." She raised her voice and leaned toward the paneling at the side of the fireplace. "And he will undoubtedly die of gangrene because he won't trust me, so I shall soon be a happy and contented widow." She got up and thumped her fist on the paneled wall. "Can you hear me in there? If I'd known how to get at your hiding place, I'd have let Captain Bretton find you. That's what you obviously expect me to do, isn't it? Betray you to that buffoon Captain Bretton. Why else would you refuse to confide in me?"

"My lady! Begging your ladyship's pardon, I did not know you was in here."

She swung around and found William's valet hovering in the bedroom doorway, a burgundy velvet jacket draped over his arm. He eyed Robyn with evident wariness, which wasn't surprising considering that he had found her talking to the walls. He coughed delicately. "Er ... is there something I could bring for your ladyship? Mayhap Mary could prepare your ladyship a soothing tisane ..."

She could feel a blush flame all the way from her neck to the roots of her hair. Good grief, the valet was going to have a field day reporting this latest example of her ladyship's craziness back in the servants' quarters. But maybe it was better to be called crazy, she realized. Much better than having the servants wondering if Captain Bretton was right, and Zachary Bowleigh truly was hidden in a half-forgotten priest's hole.

"No, thank you, I don't need Mary or a tisane," she said, trying to look dignified, or at least like a lunatic who was only intermittently mad. She stood up and fixed herself center hearth, once again making sure the Bowleigh crest soared above her head in flamboyant splendor. "You may put his lordship's coat in the dressing room, Jackson. That is all. You may go."

"Yes, my lady." The valet crept on silent feet into the dressing room and emerged minus the jacket. He hesitated, clearly not sure if he dared to speak. Robyn gave him another glacial stare, which she hated to do since he seemed a well-meaning man. "Yes, Jackson, what is it now?"

"Humbly begging your ladyship's pardon, but it is past time for his lordship to dress for dinner. Does your ladyship know if his lordship is at home?"

Robyn sent the valet a withering glance. "He will send for you when he needs you," she said loftily. "You may tell Jean-Luc that we shall be eating dinner an hour later this afternoon."

"Yes, my lady." Head bent almost to his knees, the valet bowed himself out of the room. Robyn barely restrained herself from running after him and apologizing. Now she had another complaint to lay at William's door, she reflected ruefully. Being rude and arrogant with Captain Bretton was one thing, intimidating hapless servants quite another.

But she had no time to indulge her grouchy mood. There were three different entrances to William's bedroom, one connecting through his dressing room, another through Robyn's sitting room, and the last directly from the upstairs hallway. Robyn swiftly barred all the entrances, except the one leading into her sitting room. From there, she was able to retrieve several of baby Zach's stomach binders—ideal thigh bandages—and a kettle of hot water that was simmering on the hob. At least she would be able to sterilize the cloths she used to clean William's wounds, although she was afraid that so much time had passed since he was shot, infection could well have set in already.

Hanging the kettle over the fire in William's bedroom, she locked the door to her sitting room and softly called his name.

Nothing happened. She walked around the bedroom, stopping every yard or so to press her mouth to the wall and say his name. She received not a glimmer of response.

Baffled, she completed the circle. Why was William refusing to acknowledge her? Surely he must be able to see what was going on in the bedroom? The priest's hole—and she was certain that was where he must be hiding—had been built during a time of bitter civil war, when Cromwell's self-righteous fanatics had imposed their own harsh brand of religious salvation on an unwilling British populace. Citizens who refused to conform often ended up as fugitives from the law. Hidden in the tiny cubbyholes, their lives literally depended on knowing when enemies were in the outer rooms. As a consequence, almost all priest's holes were equipped with peepholes. Sometimes an exquisitely carved flower would have a petal that glided to one side. Sometimes exotic animals would have eyes that slid away, to be replaced by a human eye, peering out at its hostile pursuers. The priest's hole at Starke was likely to follow the traditional pattern. So the question remained. If William could see that Robyn was alone, why didn't he come out and let her tend his wound?

The answer came with frightening certainty. *He didn't acknowledge her calls because he was unconscious.*

Robyn tried hard not to panic. The walls of William's

bedroom were covered in elaborately carved paneling, a holdover from the previous century. Looking around the room, she guessed there might be three hundred flowers and five hundred scrolls of leaves, interspersed with carved bunches of grapes and exotic birds. Working systematically, pressing every flower, leaf, bird, and grape to find a hidden spring mechanism, she reckoned it would take her an entire day to discover the entrance to the priest's hole. And that was assuming the mechanism didn't work on a coded sequence, so that the lock sprang only when, say, the third rose from the left was pressed immediately after the fifth grape from the right. In which case, she might work at pressing flowers and leaves for a lifetime without ever finding the correct sequence.

William would die from loss of blood before she managed to find him.

"Dammit," she muttered. "You're not going to die until I've told you what a total pain in the ass you are. I'm going to find this stupid door and open it in the next ten minutes, okay?"

From her experience studying the layout of other manor houses, Robyn knew that the priest's hole was most likely to be built into the space next to the chimneypiece, where a hollow wall was harder to detect. She knew the locking mechanism was usually built into the door itself, since seventeenth-century engineering skills didn't run to fail-safe long-distance levers. And since the lock often needed to be sprung in a hurry, with soldiers in hot pursuit, the spring-lock device was likely to be located in a carving at, or near, eye level.

So far, so good. Her graduate-school courses in the history of architecture had provided her with a veritable mine of useful information, Robyn thought wryly. The theory was great, but the trouble was, the Starke priest's hole could easily be an exception to every one of these general rules.

Resisting the impulse to dash wildly from one likely spot to the next, Robyn took the panel to the right of the hearth and started a methodical search. On close examination, so many of the marguerites seemed to have oddly raised centers—ideal for concealing a lock—that she decided they had been deliberately carved to disguise and confuse possible searchers. Checking the left-hand panel, she found the same pattern, a tempting hint that the lock was hidden under the heart of one such flower. For a moment she debated concentrating her search only on the marguerites, then decided that was too risky. They were such an obvious lure that they might be a double-blind, with the lock concealed behind something far less obviously suitable.

In the end, all shortcuts seemed too chancy, and methodical plodding the only safe course. She pressed bumps and notches until her thumbs ached, but no doors sprung open and William still didn't appear. The clock on the dressing table checked off the seconds, its loud and relentless ticking making Robyn's palms turn slick with sweat.

In the distance, she heard the sound of Mary's voice, calling worriedly from the hallway. "My lady, be you well? My lady, 'tis long past time to dress for dinner."

Robyn ignored the maid, chiefly because she couldn't think of any conceivable answer that would send Mary away without increasing her curiosity. The clock chimed three-quarters past two o'clock. In fifteen minutes, Jean-Luc would expect to serve the dinner that had already been delayed for an hour, and the absence of master and mistress would become glaringly apparent. From past experience, she doubted if any of the servants would show any immediate initiative, but when dusk turned to darkness Hackett would become sufficiently worried to retrieve his keys of office and march ceremonially upstairs to unlock her door. In other words, unless she wanted to have the entire household alive with gossip, she had less than half an hour in which to find William, dress his wound, and make him comfortable until she could return.

Robyn was tired, exhausted in fact, and for a moment she allowed herself the luxury of leaning her forehead against the paneled wall and giving way to tears. After twenty seconds of weeping, she realized William didn't have time for her to indulge in useless bouts of self-pity. She pulled her lace handkerchief from her pocket, wiped her eyes, drew in a determined breath, and prepared to resume pressing flowers, grapes, and vines, the only course open to her.

The dove with the olive branch in its break was staring at her.

Robyn's stomach lurched. For a split second, she was paralyzed with shock, then anger overwhelmed her. She banged her fists on the wall, not caring if she made enough noise to attract the servants.

"Get out of there!" she yelled. "Dammit all, how could you do this to me? You and Captain Bretton deserve each other! You're both lower than snakes!"

The bird's eye winked, then closed. The wall panel to the left of the hearth swung in on a pivot and a man stepped out of the dark, cavernous recess concealed alongside the chimney. Shorter and more slender than William, he smiled crookedly, inclining his head in an offhand, quizzing acknowledgment.

"Hello, Bella," he said. "No need for you to get yourself in such a taking. William is going to be all right, you know. I dressed his wound myself."

She stared at him, guessing the answer to her question as soon as she asked it. "Who are you?"

His face assumed an expression of exaggerated hurt. "Come now, Bella, you can't have forgotten me, however far your wits have gone begging. I am Zachary, of course. Your much maligned, oft misunderstood brother-in-law."

"Mr. Bowleigh? This is Inspector Harris of the Dorset police." The detective's voice came smoothly across the transatlantic cables, with only the faintest of echoes to suggest that he was calling from several thousand miles away and not from the next office. "I have some news regarding the shooting of Ms. Delaney to share with you, if you have a moment."

Zach's hand tightened around the phone. "I always have time to hear how your investigation is progressing, Inspector. What have you found out?"

"We had a bit of good luck." The detective couldn't conceal his satisfaction. "We've found the gun that was used in the attack on Ms. Delaney."

"My God, that's great news!" Zach exclaimed. "How did you manage that, Inspector?"

"Like I said, a bit of good luck and a lot of routine hard work. We arrested a burglar last week in Poole. When we searched his apartment, we found a stash of stolen articles in his flat, including a handgun, a Swiss-made 9mm pistol. We don't have many incidents involving guns and shooting in a small town like Poole, not even one a year, so we checked the gun against the bullet that was fired at Ms. Delaney. Turned out to be a perfect match. We're sure we've got the gun that was used to shoot your friend, no question about it."

"Are you charging the burglar with the shooting?" Zach asked. "Does he have any possible motive?"

"None that we can find so far. Besides, he swears he's innocent, at least as far as shooting Ms. Delaney is concerned. He claims he stole the gun barely a week before we arrested him, and he's never taken it outside his flat. Hasn't even tried to fence it because the shop he goes to doesn't deal in guns."

"Was the burglar willing to identify the house he stole the gun from?"

"He was indeed," Inspector Harris said. "Led us right to it, and we know he's telling the truth because guns in this country have to be licensed, so it didn't take us more than a few hours to trace the name and address of the gun's legal owner. Turned out to be a woman, a lady called Gloria Hasskins, resident in the very house our chappie said he burglarized."

"A woman!" Zach interjected. "My God! Then maybe I was right, after all. It *was* a woman who shot Robyn. Have you arrested . . . what did you say her name was?"

"Hasskins. And no, we haven't arrested her, nor even spoken to her. That's the bad news. Unfortunately she wasn't at home when we went calling. According to her neighbors, she left the country a couple of weeks ago. Went to visit her family in America."

"She's here? In the States?"

"Seems so."

The back of Zach's neck started to prickle. He rubbed it absentmindedly. "So she's got some sort of a connection over here," he muttered. "Is she involved in the antiques trade, do you know?"

"Not professionally. She was an English teacher until last year, when she had a nervous breakdown."

"Can the U.S. Immigration people help you to track her

down? They have computerized records of all foreigners coming into the country."

"We've asked for their help, Mr. Bowleigh, and we're running a background check on her from this end. As a matter of fact, I was hoping her name might ring a few bells with you, that's why I called."

"Hasskins . . . Gloria Hasskins," Zach murmured, trying to attach a face to the name. Absolutely nothing clicked. "Is she married?" he asked. "Maybe I knew her by her maiden name."

"Married and divorced, that much we already know. Her husband ran off with a woman barely out of her teens and Gloria reverted to her maiden name. She had a nervous breakdown after the divorce, according to her neighbors, and was in and out of mental hospitals for a couple of years. That's why she gave up teaching. Her husband's name was Britten if that's any help."

Gloria Britten sounded no more familiar than Gloria Hasskins. Zach sighed. "Something's connecting, Inspector, but I can't put the pieces together. I'll call you at once, if I remember anything. Did you try the Delaneys? I guess it's possible she's some sort of relation of theirs."

"Yes, I spoke to them both. I'm afraid they couldn't give me any help at all. The Delaneys came across from Ireland a hundred years ago, and they don't have any family connections in England. I understand Miss Delaney spent a year or so living in London, but of course her parents don't know the names of all the friends she made while she was over here."

"Something's nagging at me," Zach said, frowning in frustration. "Dammit! I can't catch hold of it."

"Stop pushing so hard and maybe it will come." The detective spoke briskly. "Keep me posted, Mr. Bowleigh. If you have any bright ideas, call me anytime, day or night. I don't want this woman to get away."

"Neither do I."

The detective hesitated for a moment. "Is there any change in Miss Delaney's condition? Her father told me she has good days and bad."

Zach stared out of his office window. The sky was gray and snow-laden, but the view wasn't anywhere near as bleak as his mood. "No," he said quietly. "Robyn's condition hasn't improved very much. She has a lot more bad days than good ones."

"I'm sorry to hear that," the detective said. "Very sorry."

"Yeah," Zach said bitterly. "So am I."

Chapter 17

AT another time, Robyn might have been interested in talking to Zachary. She would have liked to find out why William's younger brother had been prepared to risk his life—and his family's safety—fighting for Bonnie Prince Charlie's doomed quest to regain his inheritance. But right now, all she could think of was William and his injuries, injuries he'd acquired trying to save Zachary from the consequences of his reckless gallantry.

"Where is my husband?" she demanded, scarcely noticing the ease with which she claimed the relationship. "I need to take care of his wounds at once or he'll develop an infection."

"Now, Bella, there's no point in trying to be brave when you know you cannot abide the sight of blood. Besides, the wound is already taken care of. The bullet, thank God, had not lodged in the bone. All William needs now is a little rest."

"How can his wound be taken care of when you didn't even have any hot water," Robyn muttered, unfastening her satin skirt and stepping out of it as she spoke. "I hope to God you at least used some alcohol."

"Yes, I poured brandy on his ..." Zachary's voice collapsed into a strangled gasp. "Bella, have a care! What in the world are you thinking of? My God, what are you doing?"

"Taking off my hoops, of course." She let her skirt and steel-girded underdress drop to the floor. She patted her remaining petticoats, trying to get them flat enough for her to squeeze through the narrow entrance to the priest's hole. The builder hadn't designed his door to accommodate people who were either fat or wearing fashionable female clothes.

"For God's sake, Bella, show some discretion." Zachary was flushed with embarrassment. "William is only dozing, you know. He's not in a deep swoon, so he could wake up at any minute."

She whirled around, shaking with anger at his not-so-subtle implication. "Are you suggesting that if he were unconscious one of us might choose to take advantage of the situation to indulge in a little romantic dalliance?"

"Good Lord no! Naturally I meant no such thing . . ."

"Right, I'm sure you didn't. *Damn* Arabella and her miserable gaggle of lovers." Robyn pushed into the dark, shallow cubbyhole, not waiting to hear Zachary's spluttered explanations and apologies. Once inside the door, a single quick glance around was enough to ascertain that the cubicle opened out into a space no more than three feet deep by two feet wide, and William was nowhere inside it. Which must mean that the hidey-hole had been built with a doubly secret inner room, to offer more space and greater safety from pursuing enemies. Robyn could barely contain her frustration.

"Where is he?" she demanded. "Zachary, we don't have time for you to procrastinate any longer. Show me his hiding place, for God's sake."

Zachary hesitated. "Bella, you know how loose your tongue is, I dare not confide in you. At the moment you know the hiding place exists, but you cannot reveal how to open the outer door, because you do not know where the locking mechanism is concealed. And that is best for you, as you will realize if you reflect for just a moment. If you ever revealed the secret to Captain Bretton, you would put William's life at risk, as well as mine."

She gritted her teeth, forcing herself not to lose control of her temper. "Zachary, listen to me carefully, because I have no time to argue my case more than once. I'm not going to waste time trying to persuade you that I can be trusted. I'm simply going to point out a few indisputable facts, the most important of which is that William and I have already aroused the suspicions of every servant in the house by our prolonged seclusion. If we are not downstairs, ready to eat dinner, in fifteen minutes from now, one of Captain Bretton's spies—and I am sure this household contains several—will have carried the news of our disappearance to the captain before nightfall."

"Let the miserable captain do his worst," Zachary said, with what Robyn considered excessive bravado. "He has never yet found my hiding place in a half-dozen tries."

With supreme difficulty, Robyn managed to refrain from pointing out that the "miserable captain" had, however, terrorized Clementina and the twins, imprisoned several rebels, and tortured poor Harry Dalrymple to death. What's more, she had no doubt that his failure to find Zachary's hiding place had been bought at the cost of enormous effort on William's part, culminating in the chase today when William had taken a bullet in the thigh in order to save his brother.

"The captain is no fool," she said with remarkable restraint. "He knows the priest's hole exists, and he must know that its most likely entrance is either in the library or in this bedroom. He will eventually decide to concentrate his search on those two rooms, and he won't waste time pressing flower petals and bird beaks like I did. He will simply take an ax to the paneling and chop until he finds what he is looking for. In the circumstances, it seems to me that turning Captain Bretton loose on yet another search of Starke Manor is a far greater risk than revealing to me the secret of how this inner door opens."

"Even Captain Bretton would not dare to destroy the property of the Baron of Starke!" Zachary protested.

"You're wrong," Robyn said. "He carries letters from the Duke of Cumberland authorizing him to take *all necessary steps* to secure King George's realm from Jacobite traitors. He is hovering right on the brink of deciding that an all-out attack on Starke Manor is a *necessary step*. Now, are you going to show me how the lock works, or are you going to keep talking and condemn yourself and your brother to almost certain discovery by Captain Bretton?"

"William is right," Zachary muttered. "You are not the same woman I used to know." He didn't sound as if he considered the changes an improvement.

"No, I'm not the same woman," Robyn agreed, nearly frantic with impatience. "Trust me, I don't suffer from a loose tongue and I won't reveal the secret of the mechanism, I swear it. For God's sake, Zachary, open the door."

Looking distinctly uneasy, Zachary stepped into the priest's hole and pressed the top right-hand corner of the dark walnut panel that formed the back wall. Simultaneously, his left hand sought a knot in the wood at waist level. Robyn heard only a faint whirring noise, before the inner wall twisted inward, revealing William standing on the other side, leaning against the wall of a dark but spacious room.

"She insisted that I open the door, William." Zachary sounded apologetic.

"I know. I heard the tail end of your argument." William's voice was husky with fatigue, but he managed a wry smile. "Do not feel dashed, Zachary, because you lost your argument with my wife. She wins all her disputes with me, too. I have learned simply to surrender with grace and save myself a great deal of humiliation." Smiling to take the sting out of his words, William raised Robyn's hand to his lips and kissed the tips of her fingers. His eyes were shadowed with the pain from his wound, but Robyn saw the warmth of affection and pride deep in their blue depths. Her heart turned over with an unexpected leap of joy.

"H-how are you feeling?" she asked.

"Disastrously likely to fall flat on my face at the first puff of wind, but I must hurry up and change for dinner." He stepped out into the bedroom, walking with no more than a slight limp. Ever the consummate aristocrat, he bowed to indicate that she should precede him to the dressing closet. "Fortunately, Zachary proved to be a tolerable needlewoman. He has sewn me up quite neatly, and the blood has stopped flowing, thank God."

How many bacteria had been breeding on the needle Zachary used? Robyn wondered despairingly, and what would she do if William developed a raging fever? She had never thought it would be possible to yearn with such intensity for a supply of twentieth-century antibiotics.

"Let me see Zachary's handiwork," she said.

William had no time either to protest or to oblige. A scratching came at the bedroom door, soft but insistent. "My lord? Are you there? 'Tis Jackson, my lord. 'Tis way past the hour for your lordship to ready yourself for dinner."

Robyn, William, and Zachary exchanged horrified glances. Robyn acted almost on instinct. Pressing her finger to her lips in a gesture that she fervently hoped indicated silence to people living in the eighteenth century, she seized Zachary's arm and propelled him back into the priest's hole.

"Close the doors," she whispered in his ear, her words no more than a breath of sound. "Don't come out until William summons you."

She was untying her bodice even as she spoke, gesturing to William that he should remove his riding jacket, which he was still wearing, presumably to keep out the bitter chill of the unheated room behind the priest's hole.

"My lord?" Jackson's voice came again from the corridor outside the bedroom door. "We are worried about you, my lord. Are you sick, my lord?"

Why was he being so persistent, Robyn wondered, when most of the servants at Starke were remarkable for their stolid lack of initiative? There was no time to worry about possible reasons. Shaking her head in a frantic signal to William not to answer his valet, Robyn grabbed his jacket and tossed it onto the floor, where it landed a couple of feet away from her discarded skirt. On tiptoe, she ran to the connected door that led to her bedroom suite. Beckoning to William to follow, she tugged and pulled at her remaining petticoats, not bothering with pins or tapes, or buttons, simply stripping off her clothes in urgent, silent haste. She dropped the petticoats behind her in a trail leading directly to her bed.

William, thank heaven, understood what she was trying to do. He tore off his shirt and tossed it down close to her bodice. He had to keep his breeches on, because they were torn and stained with blood, but he pointed to his boots, miming a request for Robyn's help in pulling them off.

"My lord?" Jackson's voice was louder now, although still extremely deferential. "My lord, Hackett is with me, my lord, and we are coming in, begging your lordship's pardon."

The majordomo had been persuaded to use his keys much earlier than Robyn would have expected. Was that Jackson's influence? Or had she simply miscalculated? Robyn leaned over and whispered in William's ear. "Leave your boots on. Too late for anything else."

He grimaced, but climbed booted into her bed and

stretched out his arm in rueful invitation. "You look so entic-
ing," he murmured as she pillowed her head on his shoulder.
"What a shame that I am too exhausted to take advantage of
your quite spectacular state of dishevelment."

"When they come in, I will pretend to wake up and be angry," she whispered. "Can you pretend to be embarrassed?"

"Somehow I do not think I will have any difficulty in being entirely convincing," he said dryly.

"Hush, here they come."

The heavy iron key grated loudly in the lock. They heard
the door to William's bedroom open with a creak, followed
by the muted sound of the servants' voices, floating through
the open, connecting door.

"Well I never—they aren't here!" Jackson said. Robyn
wondered if she was imagining the faint note of disappointment in his voice.

"Well, where are they?" Hackett sounded genuinely bewildered. "Nobody has seen hide nor hair of them since
Captain Bretton left, and that's nigh on two hours ago."

"They were here in this room, I saw them, and there do
be clothes all over the floor." The rustle of garments being
picked up drifted through the door. "Lord love us, her ladyship's petticoats do be scattered clear across the room."

"But where is her ladyship?" Hackett asked querulously.
"And what about the master? Why have they not come
downstairs to eat their dinners?"

"Something fearful strange has happened," Jackson declared. "Vanished, they has, like Jonah, swallowed down
into the belly of a whale."

"There are no whales in Starke," Hackett said dourly.
"Look, the door to her ladyship's bedroom is open, and
her—ahem—her . . ."

"Her stays!" Jackson exclaimed. "Her stays is lying in the
doorway. Lord love us, Mr. Hackett, do you think her ladyship was felled by a Jacobite murderer, crazed with cold and
hunger?"

Hackett snorted. "You do be obsessed with Jacobite murderers, Jackson, and that's a fact. You and Captain Bretton
make a matched pair, seeing Jacobites under every bed. You
know the master supports King George. There are no more
Jacobites in Starke than there are whales."

The voices were coming nearer, approaching the connecting door to her bedroom. Robyn closed her eyes as she heard two pairs of feet creep cautiously toward the bed.

"Good Lord alive, they are in bed!" Jackson broke a moment of breathless silence.

"What are they doing in bed at this hour of the day? Be they dead?" Hackett's voice quivered with anxiety.

"No, they b'ain't dead. I think they do be sleeping after they've . . . you know. See how her ladyship's breasts do rise and fall?"

"You should not be a-looking at her ladyship's breasts," Hackett said sternly. Robyn tried not to blush as she felt the majordomo edge even closer to the bed. "Lordie, lordie. They be stark naked under those covers, can you imagine it? Catch their death of cold they will." He sounded torn between awe at such lustful, wicked abandon and disapproval at the foolhardiness of it.

Robyn could feel a blush starting at her toes. William's body was beginning to shake and she had a dreadful conviction that he was trying not to laugh. Good grief! Did the man have no sense of self-preservation? Didn't he realize the danger they were in? She decided it was past time to start her portrayal of a sultry, bad-tempered Lady Arabella waking up after two hours of passionate sex.

She stirred sleepily against the linen pillows, yawned, stretched, and finally opened her eyes. With languid movements, she pulled herself into a sitting position, hugging the sheet close to her body. She didn't want Jackson's prying eyes observing her nakedness, but more importantly, she didn't want him to glimpse William's boots and breeches. Some powerful primitive instinct was warning her not to trust Jackson.

She rubbed her eyes and allowed her gaze to wander drowsily around the room before focusing on the two servants. With more acting skill than she'd ever known she possessed, she fluttered her eyelashes in mock amazement, before giving a little shriek of outrage.

"Hackett, Jackson! What are you doing in my bedchamber? How dare you enter my rooms when you have not been summoned!"

Bowing and backing toward the door, the two servants both tried to apologize at once.

She threw a pillow at them, taking care to miss. "Be quiet," she commanded. "Where is Mary? How dare you awaken me when I was feeling so tired and sleepy? Why did you enter the room without permission?"

"We tried to awaken you, my lady. When there was no response we became worried, my lady."

"Why did you wish to wake me, when clearly I wished to sleep?"

Hackett bowed, picking up the pillow and simultaneously retrieving some of his natural dignity. " 'Tis past three of the clock, my lady, and dinner is ready to be served."

"And so?" Robyn gave an arrogant toss of her head. "Am I now to adjust my life to suit the whims of my cook? No wonder my poor nerves are quite shredded to pieces. First that dreadful Captain Bretton marches through my bedroom, and now my own servants plague me. I should not be in the least surprised if I developed a case of the vapors."

William gave a muffled snort that he managed to turn into a yawn. He sat up, giving a fair imitation of a man, exhausted by sexual exertions, trying to gather his wits. His gaze flicked from the servants to Robyn and settled into an expression somewhere between embarrassment and outrage. "What has happened, my dear? Why are the servants in your bedchamber? Did you summon them?"

"Of course not." Robyn leaned back against the pillows, pouting. "Your servants tell me that I must get up for dinner because it is three of the clock. But I do not wish to get up for dinner. I wish to eat dinner in my room. With you."

"Come now," William said coaxingly. "Remember that you have your new blue silk gown to wear. Would you not prefer to eat downstairs?"

"There is nobody to see my new dress," Robyn said pettishly, renewing her pout. "I am tired and I am bored. You never invite guests to dine with us. We are always dining alone."

"My dear, we have scarce recovered from twelve days of Christmas feasting when we were never without company."

"Yes, and I am quite exhausted by all the rich food. I want you to eat with me in my sitting room. I am much too tired to get dressed." Robyn turned to the two servants, who hovered in the doorway, uncertain whether to go or stay. "You may tell Jean-Luc to prepare a meal to be served upstairs tonight. His lordship will join me."

"Yes, my lady. I will deliver the message myself." Hackett bowed deeply.

"And you may tell Mary that her ladyship will not be needing her services for another hour or so," William said. "Jackson, I will require hot water for washing. See to it immediately."

"Yes, my lord."

The servants left the bedroom, closing the door quietly behind them. Robyn got out of bed and crept across the room, pulling the door open a crack and peering around to make sure they had truly left.

"All clear," she said, returning to the bed. "Was it wise to ask for hot water? How can you bathe in front of Jackson without revealing your wound?"

"I won't bathe, I will simply ask him to shave me," William said. "I needed a convincing excuse to send Jackson from the room."

"Do you think we persuaded them we had spent the past two hours making mad, passionate love?"

"For the moment they are too embarrassed even to consider questioning the scene we presented for them." William eased himself out of the bed, wincing as he straightened his leg and stripped off his breeches. "Unfortunately, their embarrassment will soon fade and they will begin to wonder why we were suddenly consumed by a lust so overwhelming that we chased each other through an entire suite of rooms, and ended up in a state of such mutual exhaustion that we slept through three separate attempts to rouse us."

"Perhaps we could pretend that since my accident I've woven a spell over you," Robyn said. "For the next few days, whenever we are together, try to appear as if you are driven half-mad with longing and desire."

William paused in the act of rolling his bloodstained breeches into a bundle. He looked away, giving an odd, harsh laugh. "That would be no pretense," he said. "Do you really not know how desperately I want to make love to you? Have you not realized that I spend my days pretending to work, but in reality counting the hours until nightfall, when we can be together? Since the accident, I burn for you, Arabella."

He stood by the hearth, his shoulders tensed, the strength of his body all the more apparent in the glow of the firelight. His hair, still streaked with the gray of that morning's powder, hung to his shoulders in a thick, unruly mass. When he swung around to look at her, Robyn was reminded so strongly of Zach that her heart squeezed tight with despair.

Not now, she thought hopelessly. *Don't make me think of Zach when you and I are literally fighting for our lives, and there is no time to straighten out the muddle of my feelings for each of you.*

But even as she remembered Zach, her pulses raced and her body swayed toward William. She ached to be held in his arms, to feel the warmth and security of his love surrounding her. It was William she desired at this moment. And yet—she still loved Zach.

"My dear, you must not look so sad." William's hand closed around her wrist, and he pulled her into his arms, kissing her gently on the forehead. "Forgive me for burdening you with my nonsense. There is no reason for you to listen to me."

"Yes, yes there is, and what you said wasn't nonsense. It was wonderful." She hung her head, afraid to look at him, afraid of what she was going to say. "I think I've fallen in love with you," she said, and her body convulsed in shivers. "My God, how is it possible? What am I going to do?"

William crooked his finger under her chin, tilting her face upward. His eyes met hers, dark with passion and a hint of wry, sympathetic laughter. "Listen to the pair of us," he said. "You would think that falling in love was a terminal affliction."

She smiled tremulously. "Not an affliction, but terminally confusing, at least for me."

"Take heart, my love." He brushed his thumb tenderly across her mouth. "Since we are both victims of the same disease, perhaps we can discover together how to survive it. I have heard tell that there is no cure for what ails us, so we can only hope to endure the symptoms as best we can."

"I didn't mean to love you," she said, more to herself than

to William. "I knew I was beginning to love the children, but I thought it would be all right to love them."

"And I most assuredly did not mean to love you." He carried her hand to his lips and pressed a kiss into the center of his palm. "Robyn," he said softly, "is it so very bad that we should love each other?"

"No. Yes." She shook her head. "I don't know. I can't think straight anymore."

"Sometimes we can think too much. I know I have spent far too much of my life trying to be calm, rational, and logical." He slid her hand down between their bodies, closing her fingers over the rigid thrust of his erection. "This is what you do to me, Robyn, every time you come near. And this surely has nothing to do with reason and logic." He gazed down at her with one of his wry, self-mocking smiles. "Is it not absurd that with so much at stake, I am holding you in my arms and thinking not of the risk of discovery, but only of how much I want to make love to you?"

"Yes, it is totally absurd," she said, but she didn't move away. Instead she nestled closer, rubbing her face against his chest. His muscles rippled beneath her cheek, and she flushed with heat, longing to drown out the clamor of her confusion in a session of passionate, stormy lovemaking. When he kissed her, when he caressed her, when he thrust deep inside her, doubts disappeared. When they made love, she could forget everything that had happened before her accident and simply *feel*.

He cupped her face between his hands and looked at her searchingly. "Do not tempt me with your softness," he whispered. "My God, Robyn, we must be sensible. We have only minutes to prepare ourselves for the return of the servants."

"Yes." But still she didn't move.

"Tonight," he said. "Tonight we can be together."

With a shuddering sigh, Robyn turned away. William stepped forward, as if to take her back into his arms, then stopped abruptly. "I must put on some clothes before Jackson returns."

"Take care how you hide your breeches," Robyn said, finding her robe and wrapping herself gratefully in its swansdown warmth. "Something in Jackson's manner today made me uneasy."

"I owe Oliver Cromwell and his Puritan fanatics a debt of gratitude," William said. "My bedchamber is a treasure trove of hiding places." He twisted the center of a carved rose by the window in his bedroom. A small panel swung out, to reveal a space about one foot square beneath the windowsill. He shoved the bloody breeches inside the hole. "Easy enough to dispose of them," he said. "Less easy to imagine what I should say to Jackson to explain their disappearance."

"Make it a convincing story," Robyn said, sitting down in front of the dressing table. "Perhaps you will think I am seeing problems where none exist, but have you ever wondered if Jackson could be an informant for Captain Bretton?"

William smiled grimly. "My dear, I do not *wonder* if Jackson is an informant, I am quite *sure* he is in the captain's pay. In fact, I have frequently counted on Jackson to carry false information from Starke to the captain's encampment. He has never yet failed me in his treachery."

Robyn stopped in the middle of brushing her hair. She recognized in William's voice the forced calmness of a man who had grown accustomed to living on the knife edge of danger. "Dear God," she whispered, the brush falling unheeded from her hand. "You are a supporter of Bonnie Prince Charlie! You haven't just helped a few rebels who happened to be old and close friends of the family. You've been a leader of the Jacobite movement all along, haven't you?"

For a moment she thought that he wasn't going to answer her. When he finally spoke, he did not look at her. "I have always believed the Hanoverians are usurpers," he said. "In my opinion, the Stuart cause is just, although appallingly disorganized, as rebellions usually are. Bonnie Prince Charlie appealed not only to the downtrodden and the malcontent, but also to those of us who believe that freedom of worship and political representation for Catholics has been too long delayed."

Her heart thudded with fear. "The prince's cause may have been just, but it is irretrievably lost," she said. "William, you must believe me. The Stuarts will never regain the throne of England, and Bonnie Prince Charlie will die in exile. It will be a hundred years before Catholics are given the right to hold public office in England."

Fortunately, he assumed that she was making a political prophecy rather than stating an historical fact. "I am neither fool enough nor sentimental enough to believe that Charles Stuart will be granted a second chance to reclaim his kingdom," he said bleakly. "The prince's failure is the more complete because he came within a hairbreadth of achieving success. You do not need to warn me that the Hanoverians and their Teutonic hangers-on have become too strong to be forced out of England. All I strive for now is to salvage a few wretched Jacobite lives from the wreckage of a thousand romantic dreams."

"Very well. And please don't forget that the first life you must save is your own."

"No," he said, "the first life I must save is my brother's."

Chapter 18

THE clock in the bleak and chilly room behind the priest's hole showed that it was past midnight, but Zachary and William still argued, their voices harsh from the strain of being kept constantly low. Most of Zachary's plans for escape were wild to the point of utter recklessness, and Robyn could understand why William was hard put to control his impatience. But she could also see that her brother-in-law was fast approaching the point of frustration where he would prefer capture and execution to the torment of continuing to live in a windowless, six-by-eight-foot cell.

He had been confined to the room behind the priest's hole for over five months, and he showed the effects of his captivity physically as well as mentally. His face was pale and his features—more classically handsome than his brother's—were fine drawn to the point of emaciation. His body, still wire-thin from the bout with septic fever caused by his battle wounds, seemed ready to explode with thwarted energy. Robyn suspected that only the realization that his capture would condemn the entire Bowleigh family to prosecution kept him locked into his self-imposed prison.

"Wait," she said softly, breaking into a particularly heated exchange. The tension between the brothers seemed all the greater for being expressed in whispers. "Let me be sure that I have fully understood the difficulties we are facing. Captain Bretton has the harbor at Poole surrounded. He also has roadblocks set up on each and every road between Starke and Poole. Why is that such a formidable barrier? Can't you simply ride across country and escape his net?"

"He has dragoons posted at lookout points around the entire estate," Zachary explained curtly.

"And dogs," William said. "Literally dozens of hunting and tracking dogs."

"Why is he so obsessed with capturing Zachary?" Robyn asked. "Even though he dislikes both of you for personal reasons, surely that isn't justification for such a massive expenditure of men and effort. How long will his superiors support him in such a costly effort?"

Zachary shrugged. "The captain has convinced his colonel that when he captures me, he will also capture the valuable remains of Prince Charles Edward's treasure. The combination of my head, the Bowleigh estates, and Stuart gold is irresistible to everyone on the Duke of Cumberland's staff."

"And is their belief true?" Robyn asked. "Do you have the Jacobite treasure?"

Zachary's fingers drummed on the table. "No longer," he said tautly. "My brother has chosen to hide the treasure and refuses to tell me where."

Robyn looked up, but William stopped her before she could ask. "No, my dear, I will not tell you where the treasure is hidden. The fewer people who bear the burden of that dangerous knowledge, the better. What's more, Zachary already knows that I have not the slightest intention of wasting any more gallant lives trying to ship the prince's treasure chest to France. The Stuart cause is lost, and no amount of gold would now buy victory, so I shall use the prince's money to bribe jailers, to pay fines, and to support families whose lives have been ruined by the aid they offered to the Stuart cause. There could be no more useful way to spend Jacobite gold than the rescue of suffering Jacobites."

Zachary's jaw clenched. "I promised Prince Charles Edward to see that the treasure was shipped to France."

"And you fulfilled your promise to the point of near-death," William said tersely. " 'Tis I who refuse to honor the prince's request, and I take full responsibility for my refusal."

The discussion was clearly old and painful, and Robyn intervened quickly. "All right, now I understand why the captain is pursuing you with such fervor, but I still don't understand why Zachary must go to Poole in order to make good his escape. The south coast is full of natural coves and harbors. Surely there's some stretch of deserted beach somewhere that the captain hasn't the manpower to guard?"

"There are plenty of unguarded beaches, but no unguarded access to those beaches," William said. "The captain has us in a vise. The Isle of Wight lies to the southeast of Starke, and half the British navy would be on our heels if we tried to escape in that direction. To the southwest, the captain has been strengthening his dragnet around Poole for weeks. In my opinion, we have no hope of evading his patrols and reaching safe harbor by traveling anywhere to the southwest. We have made three attempts to breach his defenses in that direction, and we have failed each time."

"Well, then, since you can go neither southwest, nor southeast, obviously you must go north," Robyn said.

William smiled with determined patience. "Impossible, my dear. If we go north, the closest seaport would be Bristol, and by the most direct post road, that is a distance of almost sixty miles. Discovery would be inevitable over so great a distance."

So great a distance. An hour by car, Robyn thought, even if you obeyed all the speed limits. "How long does it take to travel sixty miles?" she asked.

Zachary squinted at her, puzzled by the need to ask such a question. "At this season of the year? Possibly seven hours if the frost holds firm and the roads are not mired in mud or buried in snow. But time and distance are not the obstacles. William himself is now under suspicion, which he was not five months ago, and that makes everything more difficult. Before I can make a run for freedom, I must have a horse, and William cannot hope to saddle two horses late at night without raising a hundred questions—and bringing a dozen soldiers in instant pursuit."

"It seems to me that if you can't travel secretly at night, then you must travel openly by day," Robyn said, once again applying her version of Sherlock Holmes's law that when everything impossible has been discarded, what remains, however unpromising, must be the solution.

It was late, William's leg was obviously hurting him a great deal more than he wanted to admit, and his patience snapped. "Arabella, I know you mean well, but I beg you to refrain from making silly suggestions. If Captain Bretton is able to detect a lone rider on horseback, clearly he would have no difficulty in spotting a coach and pair, complete with driver and outriders, within minutes of our leaving Starke."

"That's the whole point," Robyn said. "Instead of trying to sneak past the captain's guards at the dead of night, I am suggesting that we set off in broad daylight, on a harmless shopping expedition to Bristol, with all the servants standing in the front yard waving good-bye."

William and Zachary stared at each other, their bodies stiff with sudden excitement. Then Zachary's shoulders slumped. "That is a deuced fine suggestion, Bella, but it would not work in the end. How could I enter the carriage unnoticed? The servants would all recognize me instantly."

"Not if you were disguised," Robyn said. "Couldn't we fire Jackson and have William hire you in his place?"

"Fire Jackson?" William sounded appalled. "My dear, I know the man has betrayed me, but I could never approve of setting him alight. Burning is a barbaric punishment, even for murderers."

"No, no, I didn't mean you to burn him!" Robyn was horrified. "I used the wrong word. I just meant that you should dismiss him from your service, and hire Zachary in his place."

William looked thoughtful, then shook his head. "It is an intriguing suggestion, but a position as my valet would not provide Zachary with a sufficient disguise."

Zachary nodded in reluctant agreement. "Too many of the servants have known me since I was in leading strings. Wearing servants' livery isn't going to deceive them for a moment."

"Even if they recognized you, would they betray you to Captain Bretton?" Robyn asked.

"Probably not," William said. "But we cannot impose the burden of keeping silent on our servants. The Duke of Cumberland is so crazed with hatred for the Jacobites that aiding my brother is tantamount to signing your own death warrant. Such a choice must be made freely, not imposed by me."

"Then we must think of a disguise for Zachary that is so effective the servants can't penetrate it," Robyn said crisply. "That shouldn't be impossible if we give the servants very little time or opportunity to see him up close." She eyed him assessingly. "Fortunately, he isn't nearly as tall as you, William, so we should be able to pass him off as a woman. Could we find him some skirts and petticoats in the attics that would fit him? Mary takes such scrupulous care of my clothes that she would notice at once if some were missing."

"Disguise me as a woman!" Zachary exclaimed. "Deuce take it, Bella, I could never dress up as a woman!"

"Why not?" Robyn asked. "What's so dreadful about pretending to be a woman? That's how Bonnie Prince Charlie managed to escape to France."

William stopped his pacing and stood very still. "What do you mean?" he asked. "What is this about Prince Charles Edward?"

In her eagerness to convince them both, she didn't pay any attention to the curious note of tension in William's voice.

She smiled at him sunnily. "You, of all people, must know the story of how the prince escaped his pursuers after the Battle of Culloden. He hid out for months in crofts and villages all over the Highlands, until finally a woman called Flora Macdonald gave him some of her own clothes, and with his head wrapped in a plaid shawl to disguise his russet curls, the pair of them managed to make the sea crossing from the Scottish mainland to the island of Skye. By a stroke of good fortune, a mist came down and blanketed the whole area for days, so that the British naval patrols couldn't see anything, and the prince was able to board a frigate and escape to France. It's a very romantic tale."

"It is, indeed," William said, and for the first time in weeks his voice was chilled with the ice of bitter mistrust. "And perhaps you would now be good enough to enlighten us as to how you came to be familiar with this 'romantic' tale."

Because I saw a rerun of the movie on late night TV, she wanted to say, but of course she couldn't. Too late, she realized she had recounted facts that Lady Arabella couldn't possibly have known in January of 1747, when the prince's whereabouts were still shrouded in secrecy, and news from the Jacobite court in France traveled along closely guarded routes to the faithful in England. She sought frantically for a credible explanation of her knowledge, aware that every second ticking by made her appear less truthful, less worthy of trust.

"I can't remember where I heard the story," she said when the silence had stretched out to distressing lengths. The excuse was so feeble, she winced. "Perhaps from one of the servants—"

"Enough," William said, leaning forward and gripping her wrist with painful force. "Do not compound your lies, Arabella. The story of the prince's safe arrival in France is known to almost no one, and certainly not to any of the servants here in Starke."

She tried again to gloss over her mistake, hoping that communications between the defeated prince and his supporters were erratic enough that William wouldn't know how accurate her account had been. "Well, you know, that was only my version of how the prince managed to escape. Probably I was mistaken in many of the details—"

"On the contrary, my lady, you recounted the details with remarkable precision. The story of the prince's escape is a closely guarded secret, and only someone intimately connected with the Jacobite cause—or deeply involved with the Duke of Cumberland's high command—could have known such particulars." William looked across the table at her, his gaze hard, cold, and condemning. "Many people have entrusted me not only with their own lives but also with the safety of their families," he said. "I cannot afford betrayal. Heed me well, my lady. I will lock you in this room, bound hand and foot, gagged and blindfolded, before I will allow you to go free and reveal what you have heard tonight to Captain Bretton."

"Dammit, William, I told you she couldn't be trusted," Zachary muttered.

With supreme effort, Robyn managed to ignore Zachary's remark. She got up and walked swiftly around the table to kneel beside William. "Look at me," she commanded, covering his hands with her own. "Look at me, William, and tell me that you believe I am preparing to betray you and your brother to Captain Bretton."

William's eyes were shadowed with doubt, but he looked away without speaking. Robyn wasn't sure she could count that as a victory. She drew in a deep breath. "If I am planning to betray you, why have I not done so already?"

William's voice was remote, and he didn't turn to look at her. "Mayhap you wait to charm from me the location of Prince Charles Edward's treasure. That information would indeed be a prize to carry to Captain Bretton."

"Damn the treasure," she said, her voice husky. "And damn you, too, William Bowleigh, for being a blind fool." She was tired to the point of exhaustion, and tears gathered in the corners of her eyes. She dashed them away, angry with herself for betraying weakness in front of William. She would not weep for a man who scorned her, still less for a love too shallow to survive its first test. She rose to her feet.

"I'm going to bed," she said. "I need to sleep for an hour or two before Annie brings me the baby to nurse in the morning."

She walked quickly to the narrow entrance to the priest's hole, but Zachary was there before her, barring her exit. "You cannot believe that we will let you simply turn tail and walk out of here!" he exclaimed.

"What else are you planning to do?" she asked wearily. "For heaven's sake, Zachary, stop and think for a moment. If I disappear, Captain Bretton will be at Starke before nightfall, and his troops will be tearing the paneling from these walls before daybreak. You have no choice other than to let me go free."

"Arabella is right, Zachary." William rose to his feet. "We cannot keep her locked away. My threats were idle, and she has called my bluff."

"Then what are we to do with her?"

William finally looked at her, his gaze diamond-hard. "We shall have to trust her," he said. "We have no other choice."

Zachary leaned against the wall, his face deathly white in the candlelight. "My God," he said, "then we are doomed."

Robyn was energized by a sudden urge to deliver Zachary a swift kick in the pants. "Try not to be such a horse's ass," she said to him, and squeezed through the doorway into William's bedroom.

Zach woke up in the middle of the night, his body slick with sweat and his breath coming in tearing, heaving gasps.

He knew Robyn was in deadly danger and it was his job to protect her. He had been running as fast as he could to get to her side, but he was too late. She was going to be shot and it was his fault. He couldn't remember what he'd done, but he knew it was his willful stupidity that had led her straight into deadly danger.

The nightmare was so powerful that it took him almost a full minute to realize that he was sitting up in his own bed, waking from a dream, and not racing across the parking lot of the Starke Manor Hotel in a vain effort to rescue Robyn. The shadowy outlines of his bedroom furniture took on solid shape and he got out of bed, adrenaline still pumping so fast that he was shaking.

He walked to the bathroom and poured himself a glass of water, drinking thirstily. Even though he was now aware that he was awake, the threads of the nightmare wouldn't let go. His pulses thrummed with the knowledge that he had somehow put Robyn in danger, not months ago, but recently.

He pulled on a pair of boxers and a cotton sweater and walked into his living room, flicking on the lights as he went. Right now, he didn't want darkness, or shadows where obscure demons could lurk.

He flung himself onto the sofa, the place where he and Robyn had first made love. Lady Arabella stared down at him, her gaze curiously direct, as if she were seeing him and not the artist.

Looking at the portrait, Zach was impressed all over again with the skill Robyn had shown in designing her piece of needlepoint. She hadn't copied the portrait precisely. Instead, she'd set herself the more difficult artistic task of depicting the same woman, wearing the same dress, but posed in a much more formal position, surrounded by a border of stylized flowers.

The portrait of Lady Arabella had obviously made a deep impression on Robyn's subconscious. He wondered what would happen if he made arrangements to bring Robyn to New York so that she could see the portrait again. Given her hysterical fear of him, he couldn't decide if a visit to his apartment would jog loose important memories, or topple her over the edge into outright insanity. He jotted down a note to have her parents bring the question up with the psychologist at Robyn's next visit.

Despite the fact that the portrait was an original Gainsborough, it was so much a part of his daily life that Zach hadn't looked at it closely in years. Now he scrutinized Lady Arabella with an intensity that seemed as much a lingering effect of his nightmare as a wish to view the portrait anew. The beads of sweat on his skin cooled, leaving goose bumps in their place.

How damned odd, he thought. He'd never noticed before that Lady Arabella's eyes bore a haunting similarity to Robyn's, although the two women were dissimilar in every other aspect of their appearance. Looking at the portrait, it was almost as if he could see Robyn again. Smiling, good-humored, intelligent Robyn as she had looked before some woman in England took aim at her skull and left her gaze haunted with the shadows of madness.

The gun that had been used to shoot Robyn was owned by a woman named Gloria. Gloria Hasskins was a teacher who had relatives she visited in the United States.

Gerry Taunton had a sister who was called Gloria. A sister who lived in England, somewhere not too far from Starke, and taught at the local school.

Zach's hands were suddenly shaking. Jesus Christ, where had his brain cells been hiding when Inspector Harris told him that the gun belonged to a woman called Gloria? He found the detective's phone number, and dialed, totally oblivious to the fact that it was three-thirty in the morning.

For once, luck was on his side. In Dorset, it was already eight-thirty and Inspector Harris was at his desk. The switchboard operator connected Zach immediately.

"This is Inspector Harris."

Zach didn't bother with any preliminaries. "Gerry Taunton, one of my senior managers at the Gallery, has a sister," he said. "Her name's Gloria and I know she lives somewhere near Starke. I believe Gerry mentioned to me a couple of years ago that she was going through a difficult divorce and had spent time in a mental hospital. Something about her husband having an affair with a much younger woman. Do you think Gerry's sister could be the woman you're looking for?"

"Good Lord, I certainly do." For once Inspector Harris sounded almost excited. "I'll start making inquiries at this end right away. It's so much easier to find information when you know more or less what you're looking for. Any idea why Gerry Taunton might have chosen to change his name from Hasskins?"

"I've no idea," Zach said. "He's been Taunton ever since he arrived in the States, and that must be at least twenty-five years ago."

"Do you have any clue as to why he might be involved in a scheme to fake antiques? Does he gamble? Live the high life?"

"None of those things," Zach said, and his stomach lurched. "My God, it makes no sense for Gerry to be involved in the faking of those antiques. He's one of America's foremost experts on eighteenth-century furniture. He knows, better than most, that what he was doing would destroy the Gallery."

"Hmm, interesting. Do you have any reason to think that this Gerry Taunton might have cause to dislike you, Mr. Bowleigh?"

"Gerry's almost one of the family," Zach said. "He's not only my right-hand man, he was a good friend of my grandfather's from the first moment he arrived in New York."

"That's interesting. And how did your grandfather meet him?" the detective asked.

Zach thought a moment. "I don't know," he said at last. "Gerry was just always around."

"Make sure he stays that way," the detective said. "The last thing we want him to do is get wind of our investigation and start running."

The thought of Gerry on the run because he and Gloria had shot Robyn Delaney was even more absurd than the thought of Gerry as the criminal who had faked a dozen or more valuable antiques and almost destroyed the reputation of the Bowleigh Gallery in the process. Zach tried to orient himself to a world that seemed to have shifted its perspective to a new and almost unrecognizable angle. "I'll take care not to give Gerry any hint of what we suspect," he said.

"You'd better be sure you mean that," Inspector Harris said curtly. "If this man was involved with the antiques

scam at your Gallery *and* with the shooting attack on Miss
Delaney, there's one thing that's clear."

"What's that?" Zach asked.

"Gerry Taunton doesn't like you very much," the inspector said. "He doesn't like you very much at all."

The inspector, Zach thought wryly, had a terrific gift for
understatement.

Chapter 19

SHE knew the instant William came into her bedroom, although he moved so quietly that she sensed rather than heard his presence. Her pulse started to race, the inevitable consequence of his nearness, but she kept her eyes closed and gave no sign that she was aware of him. After what had happened earlier, she needed him to speak first, if not to explain his lack of trust, then at least to apologize for it.

But he neither explained nor apologized. He stood at the side of the bed, silent and unmoving, although she could feel his gaze roaming restlessly over her face and body. After two or three minutes the tension was coiled so tight inside her that she thought she would explode if he didn't speak, especially when he reached out to caress her cheek with exquisite, aching gentleness. The pretense of sleeping became impossible to maintain, but just as she opened her eyes, he turned to leave, his departure as silent as his arrival.

Despite her anger at him, she found that she couldn't let him go. "William," she said softly, pushing herself up against the pillows. "I'm awake. What do you want?"

"You," he said, his voice low and harsh. "What else? It seems that I always want you."

"Is it such a disaster to desire your wife?" Robyn asked.

He swung around, his eyes a fierce, glittering blue in a face white with fatigue and stress. "I wish that I knew," he said. "Is that not the ultimate triumph for you, Arabella?"

"I feel no sense of triumph," she said.

"How can you not? 'Tis more than three years since Clementina's birth, and in all that time, I visited your bed but once. And yet, in the past few weeks, you have woven a spell of such potent magic that I can no longer even pretend indifference, much less feel it. I want you to the point of insanity, and so I ignore the feeble protests of my conscience, just as I ignore the warnings from my brother that you will betray me. Tonight, when you spoke of Prince Charles Edward's escape, every instinct I possess cried out in warning that I must not trust you. But to no avail. I want you still, and my body craves the release that only you can provide."

"Zachary doesn't know me," Robyn said quietly. "And you mistake your own feelings. It is your reason and not your instinct that warns you against me. In your heart of hearts you know full well that I will never betray you, or your brother. And in matters of trust, the heart is a much more reliable guide to truth than the intellect."

He laughed, a grating, mirthless sound. "My compliments, Arabella. You have just given me the one answer guaranteed to ensure my total confusion—and thus the continuation of your spell."

"I don't weave spells," she said. "If I could, I would weave one to stop you using the name Arabella. Why are you so unwilling to call me Robyn?"

He shrugged. "Once I told you that you were too beautiful to be called by the name of such a common little bird. Now I know you are not only too beautiful, you are also too dangerous."

She stared at him, genuinely shocked. "Dangerous? Me?"

"But of course *you*. Before the accident you used your beauty as a cold, destructive weapon. Now you use it as a soothing, welcoming lure." He walked over to the window, drawing back the heavy draperies and staring out at the frosty, moonlit landscape. "You have become frighteningly clever since your accident. Somehow, during those days and nights of raging fever, you learned that tenderness and warmth are far more potent weapons than mere physical beauty."

"But, William, I don't even like the way I look—"

"I'm not the only fool to have fallen prey to your charms," he interrupted. "I have seen how the servants all run to do your bidding instead of cowering in fear as you walk by. The twins hide from their tutor so that they can spend time playing with you. Clementina laughs all day in-

stead of whining, and even the baby has learned to smile the
minute he hears your voice."

"Surely you don't regret that the children and I take pleasure in each other's company?" she asked, joining him at the
window. "Or that baby Zach is contented and thriving?"

"I feel not regret but fear. Fear that you will revert to your
old ways and our children will suffer all the more for having
known what it's like to have a mother who is kind and
cheerful and interested in their daily concerns."

"If I behave with tenderness toward the children, it's because I feel tenderness toward them, not because I'm working on some dastardly, secret plan to betray them."

"And toward me?" he asked, his words clipped. "What do
you feel toward me, Arabella?"

She looked up at him, her heart pounding as she acknowledged the truth. "I love you," she said. "Although I don't
expect you to believe me."

He swung around, his eyes dark and mocking in the
moon-silvered darkness. He took her hand, circling her wrist
with strong, slender fingers. "You are become a mistress of
pretty words, my dove, but I am not yet willing to surrender
every last vestige of my common sense. Your trap is well
baited, but I am not quite besotted enough to walk in."

"William, for heaven's sake, I'm not setting traps—"

"Are you not? You whisper to me of love, and my heart
races with joy. You offer up your hands to my caress, and I
shudder with need. You cradle your head on my shoulder
and I am undone." Smiling cynically, he carried her wrist to
his mouth and pressed his lips against the throbbing beat of
her pulse, but when he raised his head, he was no longer
smiling.

"I want you beyond bearing," he said. "And so I gaze
deep into your eyes and tell myself that yes, you can be
trusted, and no, you will never betray me."

"Then you tell yourself nothing but the truth," she said.

William's mouth twisted in wry self-mockery. "Truth,
trust, honor, duty—what are they? In the end, it seems that
my lust for you is stronger than any of them."

"You know, I'm getting a bit tired of hearing you wallow
in self-pity simply because you want to take me to bed,"
Robyn snapped. "Self-pity is a very boring emotion."

He swept into a bow. " 'Zounds, my lady, I offer my apologies. God forbid that I should be boring. I see that I must take a leaf from your book and instead of complaining, whisper only the sweetest of rose-scented compliments." He unfastened the buttons of her nightgown as he spoke, parting the lacy collar and trailing expert, titillating kisses along the slope of her shoulders and the hollow of her neck.

Robyn turned away. "Don't," she said. "William, I can't bear it when you kiss me like that."

"How so, my lady? With finesse? With elegance?"

"No," she said. "With disdain."

He looked at her blankly, and she realized she had shocked him into silence. She jerked her hand out of his grasp and was halfway across the room when his voice came from behind her, low and strained. "Arabella, don't go."

She closed her ears to the reluctant note of pleading and kept on walking. He spoke again. "Robyn ... please don't go."

She paused, but she didn't turn around. She heard him draw in a deep breath. "Robyn," he said coaxingly, "you cannot abandon me now. Have you forgotten that I am a wounded man in sore need of your mercy? My injured thigh is aching so badly that I can scarcely hobble. Have you no pity for my sufferings?"

Damn him, was his injury really hurting? She whirled around in a flurry of silk, lace, and muslin. "Does the dressing on your wound need attention?" she asked. "Show me your leg."

He smiled wickedly. "With the greatest of pleasure, my lady." He dropped his breeches.

Robyn blushed bright scarlet, simultaneously hiding a treacherous gurgle of laughter. One swift glance at William was sufficient to reveal that any problems he might have at this moment were visibly not related to his wound. "You're not a wounded hero," she said, trying to sound angry rather than weak with longing. "You're a dishonorable scoundrel, prepared to resort to any tactic, however despicable, to gain my sympathy."

He seized her hand, pulling her into his arms, his eyes gleaming with rueful laughter. "Robyn, I am everything that you say, and worse, but don't banish me from your bed. Not tonight. Perhaps, with a little care, you can reform me."

"Why should I bother?" she asked, determined to ignore the near-irresistible attraction of his smile.

"Because I am your husband?"

"Hah! That's no reason to waste time and energy on a wastrel."

"Then, because—you love me," he said.

She closed her eyes. "Damn you, William, that was a low blow."

"Is it? Tonight it seems that I am not in the mood to play fair." His hands grasped the curve of her waist, pulling her high and hard against his body. He bent his head, ravaging her mouth with a kiss that left her hot and shaking. Then he leaned back and looked at her, eyes glittering with satisfaction when he saw how quickly he had aroused her.

So much for his promised sweet talk, Robyn thought acidly. But then, why would he waste time seducing her with honeyed words when night after night she offered him indisputable evidence that he had only to take her into his arms, and she was helpless to resist him?

But it seemed he had told the truth about at least one thing. He might not be ready to trust her, but he could no longer pretend he was indifferent. His hands trembled as he reached for her, and he fumbled as he eased her nightgown down over her shoulders. It fell to her waist, exposing her swollen, milk-filled breasts. He rasped his thumbs across her nipples and tension vibrated between them: erotic, carnal, unbearably exciting.

He drew in a shaky, ragged breath. "I am envious of my son," he said thickly, and bent his head to her breast.

At the touch of his tongue, desire arrowed through her, so swift and so fierce that she cried out, the air forced from her lungs as she clung to him for support. Her body was so sensitized that when his long hair fell forward and brushed against her skin, she shivered.

"Come to bed and I will warm you," he said.

She could have told him that she didn't need to be warmed because her blood already raced hot and fast in her veins, but she said nothing because she wanted him to lie beside her, to thrust into her with passionate, fierce possession, to shudder helplessly as he climaxed into her. She gave him her hand and he led her across the room to the bed, holding her wrists captive as he pushed her into a sitting position on the edge of the mattress. He parted her legs and stood between her thighs, kissing her with a ravenous hunger that drove her backward into the tumbled sheets.

He positioned himself over her and she folded her arms around his neck, arching her body beneath his. He was already fully erect and throbbing with need. She was soft and wet with longing. He reclaimed her lips in a dark, seeking kiss, his tongue thrusting into her mouth with deep, questing strokes. Then his hand was over her, his fingers inside her, and she was gasping out a mindless, incoherent plea for release.

For a moment longer she felt him strain to withhold his climax, but control was spinning away from both of them, and when she tilted her hips upward he plunged into her, sending them both tumbling over the edge. The night exploded in a shower of burning starlight. The dazzling flame consumed her.

William collapsed on top of her, his face pillowed in the valley between her breasts. His voice came low and muffled. "God in heaven, Robyn, I love you so much."

Pleasure washed over her in a pounding, surging wave. She touched his cheek, too exhausted and too replete for anything more. "I love you, too," she whispered. "Whatever happens, I will always love you, William."

It wasn't until she woke up and found herself alone in the bed that the warm afterglow of her delight faded. In the clear gray light of dawn she wondered if it had been lust or truth that prompted him to speak the longed-for words of love.

She doubted if even William himself knew for sure.

Hannah Wilkes made the cold and uncomfortable drive from Oakridge to Starke especially to inform the baron and Lady Arabella that she was planning a shopping expedition to Bristol. She would be visiting many of the shops, warehouses, and merchants in order to supervise the final purchases for her father's refurbished drawing room, and she offered to run any errands on behalf of the baron and his lady that they cared to entrust to her.

William was out with his steward when she called, and she made her offer in the children's day nursery, where Robyn had impulsively suggested that they should go to drink dishes of afternoon tea and eat almond macaroons. Mrs. Wilkes had barely been able to conceal her astonishment at the suggestion, but she had agreed with alacrity. They had now been in the nursery for well over an hour, and Robyn suspected that Hannah Wilkes would be willing to stay there forever. Having bestowed a box of Christmas marzipane on the twins, thus earning their eternal gratitude, she had taken Clementina onto her lap and was showing her the illustrations in a book designed to acquaint children with the blissful rewards awaiting good little boys and girls in heaven. Children's literature in the eighteenth century, Robyn had discovered, tended to be long on sermons and very short on entertainment.

Despite her homely, down-to-earth appearance, Robyn soon realized that Mrs. Wilkes possessed a vivid imagination. Instead of reading the pious and boring text, she was inventing exciting adventures for the insipid-looking children and the languid angels who graced alternate pages in the book. Clemmie was entranced.

"You tells betterer stories even than my mama," she said.

Mrs. Wilkes smiled, closing the book. "I am sure that is high praise. Thank you, my dear."

"Thank you for bringing me the book," Clemmie said. She slid off Mrs. Wilkes's lap, bobbed a curtsy, and immediately transferred herself to her mother's lap. Robyn, preoccupied with admiring baby Zach's stunning new accomplishment of sucking his toes, gave Clemmie an absentminded hug in praise of her good manners, and simultaneously warned the twins that they were going to be sick if they ate another single piece of candy.

A child clutched in each arm, her silk gown crumpled and damp from the baby, she looked up from her exchange with the twins to find Mrs. Wilkes staring at her in openmouthed wonder. Robyn blushed, realizing that she had vastly overstepped the level of informality her guest was likely to find acceptable. Eighteenth-century etiquette was still so alien to her that she was never confident of behaving correctly. Mrs. Wilkes had seemed happy to come upstairs with the children, but perhaps she was simply too polite to say that she preferred chilly formality in the drawing room to cozy familiarity in the nursery.

"I'm so sorry," Robyn said, remembering how angry William had been with her behavior the last time Hannah Wilkes came to call. Her relationship with William was so problematic these days she didn't want to give him cause for another complaint. "Would you like to return to the drawing room? Please forgive me for bringing you upstairs to the nursery. It's just that you seem to enjoy the children's company so much that I forgot how improper it is to inflict one's children on one's visitors."

"On the contrary, my lady, I beg that you will not apologize. I cannot remember a visit to Starke when I have enjoyed myself so much. It is a great pleasure for me to spend time with your children, and it's wonderful to see them all looking so happy."

Robyn gave her a shrewd glance. "I think, perhaps, that in the past you have provided the children with far more affection than their natural mother."

Hannah Wilkes's cheeks darkened with an embarrassed blush, but she skillfully evaded a direct answer. "I have always enjoyed playing with your children, Lady Arabella. The fact that I am childless is a source of great regret to me."

"You would make a wonderful mother," Robyn said. "Fortunately, there is still time for you to marry again and make some lucky man happy."

Mrs. Wilkes smiled wryly. "You are more sanguine than I, my lady. Certainly, I cannot imagine why the suitors are not already lined up three deep at my door. A plump, plain widow of four-and-thirty, without a drop of aristocratic blood in her veins—surely that is just what most men are looking for."

"If they are men of sense, who want to be comfortable in their marriage, then most certainly they should be looking for you," Robyn said.

Mrs. Wilkes gave another wry smile. "Alas, I must inform you, Lady Arabella, that I can only conclude the world is sadly lacking in men of sense."

Robyn laughed. Zach looked up at the sound of her voice,

and his mouth curved into a smile that set his entire body wiggling. But Clemmie, bored with listening to the grown-ups talk, decided to change the subject. "Mamma, is we coming to Bristol wiv you and Papa?" she asked.

"Your papa and I are not going to Bristol," Robyn started to explain. "Only Mrs. Wilkes is making the jour ..." Her voice died away, and she felt her stomach knot tight with a mixture of excitement and anticipation. Good grief, how had she nearly missed the wonderful opportunity presented by Hannah Wilkes's trip? She had tried to persuade William that Bristol offered Zachary his best chance of escape, and now Hannah Wilkes was unknowingly offering them the perfect cover for his flight.

Robyn looked across the tea tray at Hannah Wilkes and knew that she had no right to involve such a good, kind woman in Zachary's escape. On the other hand, she consoled herself, if she acted her part properly, there would be no need to tell the widow anything about their secret mission. Heart beating fast, she tried to convey the impression of an overindulged woman who has suddenly thought of an interesting way to alleviate the boredom of a too long winter.

"My dear Mrs. Wilkes, I have just had the most delightful notion," she said. "We are in desperate need of new silk to cover the drawing-room walls. William has been talking about making a special trip to London, but perhaps we could come with you to Bristol and visit the warehouses there instead. That way I wouldn't have to be away from the children for so long and you could avoid the discomforts of a solitary winter journey. Isn't that a splendid idea?"

"It would certainly be a pleasure to lighten the tedium of travel with your company," Mrs. Wilkes said, looking genuinely pleased. She shot Robyn a puzzled, sideways glance. "Are you quite sure, however, that you wish to give up the prospect of a trip to London in exchange for a week in *Bristol*?"

Robyn realized that Arabella would never even have contemplated a visit to a provincial town in preference to a stay in London, the largest and most entertaining city in Europe. She invented the best excuse she could on the spur of the moment.

"I haven't left Starke in two months except to go to

church," she said. "I am going to tell William that he must take me to Bristol *and* London or I shall rot away like a frozen turnip root."

It seemed that she had hit the right note. "Then I am entirely delighted to have the honor of your company," Mrs. Wilkes said. She cleared her throat. "And Lord Bowleigh's, too, if he can spare the time to escort us."

Poor Hannah, Robyn thought with a flash of unexpected sympathy, *she struggles so valiantly to disguise the fact that she's in love with William.* She rose to her feet, pretending not to have noticed the catch in Hannah's voice when she spoke William's name. "My husband should be back from his appointments by now. Shall we go and find him? Perhaps together we can persuade him that he will be a cruel and unreasonable husband if he doesn't agree to come with us."

Mary was still combing her hair when William came into her bedroom. The maid bobbed an immediate curtsy and looked up at him. He pointed to the door in silent command and she backed hurriedly from the room.

At moments like these, Robyn was forced to confront the realization that there was an unbridgeable barrier between her and the rest of the people at Starke, including William. William cared about the well-being of his servants. By the standards of his day, Robyn didn't doubt that he was the most caring and enlightened of employers. But he was The Master and she doubted if he had ever stopped to question his inalienable right to command. William's arrogance was not blatant, she decided, chiefly because he had so much power he rarely bothered to display it.

He crossed over to her dressing table and picked up the hairbrush. "I have much to thank you for, my lady," he said quietly. "I do believe you may have found the solution to Zachary's escape that I have sought in vain for five months."

She looked at him in the mirror. "You worked out all the details of the plan. I only provided a means of transportation."

"That was probably the most valuable contribution."

Robyn frowned at her reflection. "I'm uncomfortable with the fact that Mary will have to be drugged in order for the plan to work."

He shrugged. "She will come to no lasting harm, and it is better by far for her that she should be a victim rather than a fellow conspirator."

"Yes, I know." Robyn shivered. "We only have three days. Can we make all the necessary preparations in three days?"

"An hour in the attics and one visit to the Dalrymples should take care of almost everything. Then what happens is in the hands of fate."

She turned around on the stool, looking at him with a troubled, searching gaze. "Two nights ago, you suspected me of being a spy for Captain Bretton. Now you're willing to accept my plan for Zachary's escape almost in its entirety. How do you know I'm not setting a trap? How can you be sure that the captain won't be waiting for us at the first crossroads?"

He smoothed the hair from her forehead and kissed her softly on the top of her head. "My wife, who is a very wise woman, told me that in matters of trust, the heart is a much more reliable guide than reason. And my heart tells me that you can be trusted. Am I wrong?"

"No, you are not wrong," she said. "I will never betray you, William."

Chapter 20

M ARY doused the candles on the dressing table and touched a spill to the fire so that she could light the lamp that was kept burning all night. Then she crossed her hands neatly in front of her stomach, and gave Robyn a sunny smile. Nowadays, Mary smiled quite often. "There you be, my lady. I can't hardly imagine as how tomorrow we shall both be sleeping over to Bristol way. Gives me a queer turn just thinking how far we shall be traveling."

"Sixty miles," Robyn said. "That's a hard day's travel."

"Not so hard since the rain and snow do look likely to hold off. Traveling in mud is what I cannot abide. Well, if your ladyship won't be needing anything else tonight, I'll away to mend the rent in your traveling cloak."

"First I need you to come into my sitting room, please." Robyn couldn't look at her maid as she issued the order. She was sure her guilt would show in her face.

Mary might smile more these days, but she didn't even consider requesting an explanation for Robyn's peremptory command. She followed her mistress into the sitting room and waited meekly to receive her orders. The maid's passive obedience increased Robyn's guilt a hundredfold, which might have been why she felt a sudden, irrational premonition of disaster. Logically speaking, what could go wrong? How could Mary come to harm, tucked away with warm blankets and plenty of food in the Dalrymples' attic? But logic didn't prove comforting, and Robyn felt oppressed by the fear that she would never see Mary again. As they walked into the sitting room, she took hold of the maid's hand and squeezed it tightly, longing to apologize for what was about to happen, and knowing that she couldn't say any-

thing, unless she wanted to put all their lives at risk—
including Mary's.

Mary patted her hand. "My lady, be you feeling quite
well?" she asked, her voice genuinely solicitous.

"Yes . . . yes, I'm fine." Robyn saw William come into the
room, moving silent and unobserved toward the maid's back,
a tightly woven black linen cloth stretched between his
hands.

Robyn swallowed convulsively, then forced a smile. "I'm
feeling very well, thanks to you, Mary. These past few
weeks you have worked so hard to make me comfortable
and I'm truly grateful."

" 'Twere naught but my job, my lady." Mary shuffled her
feet, embarrassed but pleased, and at that moment, William
stepped up behind her. He threw the linen cloth over her
head with his right hand, and simultaneously clapped his left
hand over her mouth to muffle her screaming.

The poor woman was momentarily paralyzed with fear,
then she started to claw at William's hands, struggling to
free herself from the all-enveloping blindfold, moaning behind the gag of his hand. Robyn looked pleadingly at William, begging for permission to explain to Mary what was
happening, but he shook his head in a fierce negative. They
had already agreed that Mary would be set free the instant
they returned from Bristol, by which time Zachary would be
safely in France and Robyn could make as many apologies
and explanations as she wished. Until Zachary was out of
the house, however, it was imperative that Mary should
know nothing of their plans.

"Walk!" he said to the maid, disguising his voice into a
hoarse whisper. "Nobody will hurt you. Do you understand
what I am saying? You are not going to be harmed in any
way."

Not surprisingly, Mary's only answer was a groan of
fright. William, less sentimental and a great deal more efficient than Robyn, ignored the groan. He nodded curtly to
Robyn, and with great reluctance, she took the strips of linen
she had prepared in readiness and used them to tie the blindfold over Mary's head, anchoring the cloth just above the
maid's elbows and blinding her wrists into a loose handcuff
behind her back. As soon as she tied the final knot, William

propelled Mary into his bedroom, toward the priest's hole, which he had left open in readiness.

The scratching at his bedroom door shocked both Robyn and William into a split second of total stillness. "My lord, 'tis Jackson, come with the brandy you asked for."

Robyn flashed a silent, inquiring glance at William. Surely he hadn't encouraged disaster by requesting brandy at this crucial point in their plans? He gave a quick shake of the head, which she took to mean that he had made no such order. Mary was squirming and kicking out with her feet, making a real effort to escape now that she had heard Jackson's voice. Her struggles sounded appallingly loud to Robyn, and when the maid pressed back with her buttocks, she banged the bullet wound in William's thigh. His face turned sheet-white and he groaned in pain before he clamped his mouth shut, biting off the sound.

"My lord?" The door handle rattled. "My lord, what is happening? Why is your door locked? Be you well, my lord?"

At the renewed press of questions from his valet, William gave up on any attempt to secure Mary's cooperation. Minimizing the noise of her scuffling as best he could, he dragged her to the priest's hole and shoved her inside. Unfortunately, at Robyn's insistence, they had elected not to gag her, so he was forced to accompany the maid into the hole in order to keep her silent. A loud scream from her would betray not only her plight, but the existence of the priest's hole. With a final swift glance in Robyn's direction, William pulled the lever and the entrance to the priest's hole whirred shut. Alone in the bedroom, Robyn realized that deflecting Jackson's justifiable suspicions was now entirely up to her.

With feverish speed, she closed the curtains around William's bed, marched to the bedroom door, and flung it open. "What do you want?" she demanded, reflecting ruefully that her role as the imperious Lady Arabella was being used far too often in recent days.

The valet bowed, tray balanced on one hand. "I understood his lordship required brandy, my lady."

"We ordered no brandy," she said, scowling at him. "Get out! His lordship is sleeping. Do not disturb us again tonight." She banged the door shut, but not before she had seen the avid curiosity with which Jackson's gaze flew around the bedroom. The man would cause trouble if he could, Robyn was quite certain. But with nothing to report to his paymaster but vague suspicions, how much damage could he do between now and dawn tomorrow morning?

More than enough, she thought grimly, pacing the bedroom. Undoubtedly Jackson guessed that Zachary was hidden in the priest's hole, and that he had evaded Captain Bretton's pursuit by ducking into the hidden entrance of an ancient tunnel. Would the valet be smart enough to make a connection between Zachary's need to escape from the priest's hole and their sudden plans for a trip to Bristol?

Two hours went by before William rejoined her in the bedroom, and she was still pacing. "Jackson," he said at once. "Did you manage to get rid of him without arousing his suspicions?"

"I hope so, William, but I'm worried. Why did he choose tonight of all nights to come up to your bedroom on such an obviously trumped-up excuse?"

William pushed the hair off his forehead impatiently. "He came because he suspects that Zachary is about to make another dash for freedom. Fortunately for us, he has no way to convert those suspicions into certainties."

"What if he tells Captain Bretton that another escape attempt is being planned? Won't the captain increase his surveillance of Starke?"

"Yes, he would, but I have kept Jackson under close watch these past few days. He has spoken with none of his messengers, and he himself has not left Starke."

"How can we be sure? What about at night, when we're all asleep? Jackson could easily slip out of the house."

"You know that the doors are locked and barred, and the windows, too. Moreover, he would need to evade the other servants, some of whom are late to bed and others early to rise."

She shook her head. "William, in a house this size, there will always be one window that nobody has remembered to shutter. Have you forgotten that I myself found an open window the night I ran away? If I managed to find a way out of the house, you can be sure that Jackson could do so with even less difficulty."

William frowned, considering the point, then shrugged. "My dear, you are very right to remind me that we mustn't be overconfident. But even if Jackson has managed to slip out of the house, what can he have said to Captain Bretton? Only that we are going to Bristol in order to buy wall hangings. Captain Bretton is unlikely to authorize the search of our carriages on such a flimsy pretext. After the setbacks he has experienced recently, the captain is wary. He knows my uncle has the ear of King George, and he must fear that I will make a formal protest to His Majesty. A peer of the realm cannot be harassed with impunity, even by the Duke of Cumberland's most favored minion."

She ought to have felt reassured, but the worry still nagged at her. "What about Mary?" she asked, trying to pin down the root cause of her anxiety. "Did everything go as planned?"

"Precisely as planned," he said. "The Dalrymples were waiting for us as agreed. Mary has been given milk laced with laudanum and she is sleeping peacefully. Tomorrow, when she wakes, she will be given food, and the supplies to make herself a new dress. Other than the fact that she is locked in, I'm sure she will find her situation quite comfortable. The Dalrymples are good, kind people, and since they are now too poor to keep more than two servants, both of whom would die before they betrayed the family's secrets, Mary will be safely out of harms' way. You need not worry that your maid will receive harsh treatment at the hands of our neighbors, far from it."

Perhaps it was Zachary's reluctance to dress up as a woman that was bothering her. "What about your brother?" she asked. "Has he shaved really closely? Does he know how to use the face powder I gave him? And will he be ready to leave before daybreak tomorrow?"

William chuckled. "Ready? My dear, he is in a fair way to grinding a hole in the floor with his pacing, so eager is he to be gone. But enough. We have discussed all this many times before." He drew her close, linking his arms lightly around her waist. "You are seeing problems where none exist, my love, and that is most unlike you. Are you tired?"

"A little, I suppose."

"Then you should rest. The journey tomorrow will be exhausting in and of itself, quite apart from the nervous tension we will inevitably feel. Come to bed, my love, and I will try to make you forget this sudden attack of the jitters."

She went with him willingly, eager to lose her growing sense of dread in the sweetness of his lovemaking. He gathered her into his arms, and his passion seemed more eloquent, his tenderness more profound than ever before. When she reached her peak, she felt a moment of pure joy, followed by a sense of loss so sharp that her throat ached with tears.

For once William didn't sense her volatile mood. Exhausted by three long nights of secret consultation with Zachary and the Dalrymples, William soon fell asleep. His hair tumbled across the pillow, a blond, thick frame for the strongly etched masculinity of his features. Too strung out to sleep, Robyn ran her hands lightly over his face, needing the physical contact. He smiled at her touch, but continued sleeping. Beneath her fingertips, the contours of his face felt hauntingly familiar, the cheekbones clearly defined, the chin square, the nose straight and narrow-bridged. Seven generations into the future, Zach still carried the unmistakable imprint of his ancestor's genes.

It was unbearably painful to think of Zach, separated from her by two hundred fifty years of future history, so instead she thought of her son, the child she had given birth to, but never conceived. And as had happened to her more often of late, she found herself remembering what she had been told about Lady Arabella during her brief conversation with Zach. According to the family records in Zach's possession, his ancestor the Honorable Zachary Bowleigh grew up an orphan, because his mother died when he was still a baby.

There was no point in dwelling on the possibility that her own death was imminent, but her need to see her baby was suddenly so acute that her stomach cramped in pain. She eased herself quietly out of the bed, burrowing deep into her thickest dressing robe in an effort to shut out the bitter chill

of Starke's unheated corridors. She climbed the steep stairs
to the third floor of the Manor, unable to shake her sense of
urgency. But once upstairs, all seemed peaceful, and she
opened the door quietly, not wanting to disturb the sleeping
children.

As soon as she entered the nursery she could hear Zach
whimpering, although Annie was rocking him and crooning
a lullaby. "My lady, I'm right pleased that you're here," the
nurse said. "The baby just can't seem to settle tonight."

"Perhaps he's hungry."

Annie shook her head. "No, my lady, I fed him an hour
ago, just like I always do at night. 'Tis almost as if he do
know that you be going away tomorrow."

"But only for a week," Robyn said, as much to reassure
herself as to remind the nurse. She bent down and scooped
the baby into her arms. His crying stopped as if by magic,
and he turned toward her, snuffling and patting the air with
his tiny fists. She held her cheek against his fragile baby
skin, and his hands reached for her hair, tugging gleefully.
When she gave a little yelp, he seemed to look straight at her
and smile.

"You're supposed to be learning to sleep through the
night," she said with mock severity. "Not learning how to
rip out your mother's hair."

Zach gurgled.

"Yes, well, I can see that you find the concept of an un-
interrupted night's sleep highly amusing. But these midnight
snacks can't continue forever, you know." She sat down and
rocked him gently. His thumb found his mouth. He sucked
sleepily, already drowsy from the rocking. His wriggles
slowed; his eyelids drooped and in five minutes he was
asleep.

"You have the touch with him, my lady, and no mistake,"
Annie said. A couple of weeks earlier, she had decided to
stop arguing with her mistress over the baby's care, and instead take credit for the chubby, lively robustness of the new
baby. So complete was her conversion that she could often
be heard haranguing the under-nursemaid to unwrap Master
Zachary's shawls and leave his legs free to kick. And having
seen how remarkably free of rashes Zach's bottom remained,

she had even become a convert to the idea of regularly changing his diapers.

Unwilling to put the baby down, Robyn cradled him in the crook of her arm, and walked over to Clementina's bed. Staring down at the sleeping child, she wished with all her might that she had never told William that Clemmie was not his child, even though she was sure she had spoken the truth. Thank God she had never mentioned her belief that Captain Bretton was the girl's father. Clemmie would grow up never having to bear the burden of that particular piece of information.

Of all the many reasons she admired William, Robyn thought that his unfailing kindness to Clementina was one of the most compelling. Few men in any time period would have been capable of showing such easy, loving affection to a child who was the product of their wife's adultery.

Compelled by an urge to see all the children who had become so dear to her, she went into the twins' bedroom, bending down to give them both hugs and kisses that they would have resisted fiercely if they had been awake. She ruffled their blond hair, and finally felt the sleepiness that had eluded her for most of the night catch up with her. Yawning, she returned to the nursery and put Zach gently in his cradle. Annie was already half asleep in her seat by the fire, feet tucked up onto a little stool, lap covered by a thick shawl. "Don't get up," Robyn said, putting her hand on the nurse's shoulder. "Good night, Annie."

"Good night, my lady." Despite Robyn's request, Annie got up and bobbed a curtsy. "Don't you worry none about the children," she said. "I will take good care of them whilst you are gone, and Master Zachary will be fatter than ever by the time you get back."

"Thank you, Annie. I know they're in good hands with you." Robyn left the nursery, wondering if she would still be able to nurse the baby when she returned from Bristol. After a week away, it might take a while to reestablish her milk supply. Still, getting Zachary to safety in France was more important than anything else, because until he was out of the country, the lives of everyone at Starke were at risk.

The hallway on the third floor was particularly damp and drafty. She shivered, crossing her arms and tucking her hands into the sleeves of her robe in an effort to keep them warm. She hadn't thought to bring a candle with her, and she moved cautiously, keeping close to the wall. When she saw a shadow, darker than the surrounding gloom, creep up the stairs, she was momentarily paralyzed with fright.

The shadow took on gray physical form and she realized it was Jackson, fully dressed, and wearing a heavy cloak. The valet seemed to become aware of her presence almost at the same moment that she recognized him.

He gave a start. "My lady!"

She looked at him, ice-cold with certainty of his treachery. "Where have you been?" she asked. "Why were you out of the house at this hour of the night?"

"It lacks but two hours until dawn, my lady."

"That is no explanation."

He bowed. "Beggin' your ladyship's pardon, I took his lordship's boxes downstairs to the courtyard so that they can be loaded into the baggage cart. I understood from his lordship that you wished everything to be ready so that you could set off for Bristol at the first crack of light."

Such a reasonable explanation, and so easy to check up on that it was probably true. Still, Robyn couldn't shake the conviction that the valet had been doing more than packing bandboxes and leather portmanteaus while he was out of the house. But to accuse him of running to Captain Bretton would warn him that his role as a spy had been uncovered, so she simply nodded. "I hope all goes well with the preparations for our departure," she said.

Jackson smiled. "Never fear, my lady. My preparations go very well."

He gave another unctuous bow but she didn't answer—couldn't answer—because her teeth were chattering and she would not let him see her fright. She brushed past him and walked on without once looking back.

She dozed fitfully for an hour until William came into her room to wake her. Since none of the servants could be told that Mary wasn't available, Robyn had to dress herself in the circle of warmth cast by the fast-fading fire. The task wasn't easy and she was still struggling with the lacing on her bodice when William returned to her bedroom half an hour later, now fully dressed.

"Are you ready?" he asked quietly. "If we can get downstairs before dawn breaks, Zachary's disguise will be less easy to penetrate."

"I'm ready," she said, tying the final knot on her bodice and throwing a heavy, beaver-lined cloak over her shoulders. Her jitters of the previous night had vanished, and she felt calm and purposeful. "Have you managed to get rid of Jackson?"

"I have sent him on an errand to the kitchens," William said. "Shall I tell Zachary that we are ready for him to come out and join us?"

She drew in a deep breath. "Yes, we're ready."

William was gone less than a minute. He was actually smiling as he entered her bedroom, followed by a caped and hooded figure. "Mary wishes to know how she can serve you, my dear." He stood aside with a flourish, and she had her first clear view of Zachary in his disguise.

The caped figure curtsied, face modestly hidden beneath the frill of its voluminous hood. "My lady," it lisped in a high-pitched, feminine murmur. "What is your command?"

"No command, just congratulations," Robyn said slowly. "You have worked a near-miraculous transformation. If I did not know that Mary was locked up in the Dalrymples' attic, you might even manage to deceive me for a few minutes."

"Thank you, my lady." Zachary dipped into another curtsy, but forgot to hold out his skirts as he straightened. His heel caught in the hem of his cape and he would have fallen over if William hadn't caught him.

Zachary disentangled his shoe. "Deuce take it," he said in his normal voice. "I've been practicing all night, but these cursed skirts will drive me to Bedlam before the morning is out."

"Speak in such terms and in such a voice once we leave this room, and you will find yourself not in Bedlam but in Captain Bretton's custody," William pointed out acerbically.

"Yes, your lordship," Zachary squeaked, mincing across the room. "I am sorry, your lordship."

"The sun is beginning to break through the clouds," Robyn said. "Let's give ourselves every possible advantage and get into the carriage while daylight is still in short supply." She drew on her own hood and tied the ribbons under her chin, so that she looked as bundled up as "Mary." Fortunately for their plans, the morning air was nipped with hard frost and nobody would question why maid and mistress chose to huddle beneath multiple layers of clothing and concealing bonnets.

When the three of them arrived downstairs, dawn was still no more than a hint of sun-warmed silver far to the east, but all was in readiness for the departure of the baron and his lady. Grooms and stable lads milled around the courtyard, their breath misting in the predawn air. Of the indoor servants, only Hackett and a half-dozen lackeys waited in the doorway to bid their master and mistress an official farewell. Robyn looked around anxiously in search of Jackson, but he was nowhere in sight. She hoped that his absence was a good omen.

Hackett bowed very low as she and William stepped out into the courtyard but "Mary" didn't merit so much as a glance. At a nod from Hackett, two of the footmen fell into formation on either side of the baron and baroness, for no discernible reason other than to provide a suitably impressive escort. The little party arrived at the carriage. A groom swept open the carriage door, kept closed until now to preserve the heat of hot bricks, wrapped in lamb's wool and strewn across the floor. Another groom steadied the portable steps. A footman extended his gloved hands to assist Robyn as she climbed in; another footman awaited his chance to offer the same service to William. Once settled inside the carriage, Robyn exercised extreme willpower and refrained from looking back to reassure herself that "Mary" was still with them. Spreading her skirts, she leaned against the down pillows that had been tucked across the seats to provide her with greater comfort.

This was the way to travel, she decided. No more crowded flights on cramped planes, but instead, a pampered departure, followed by a dignified canter through attractive countryside, cocooned in soft, warm luxury.

"Mary" climbed into the coach and trod on Robyn's foot. "You are very clumsy this morning," Robyn said languidly,

all too aware of the listening servants. "Take care that you
do not disturb me again, Mary."

With a silent bob of her head, "Mary" scuttled to her assigned seat, the inferior position with her back to the horses.
The footman took up the steps and Robyn exchanged a
swift, triumphant glance with William, before looking away,
afraid of revealing too much. William released the window
strap and let down the glass, leaning out to toss halfpennies
to each of the stable lads.

"Stand clear of the horses," he said. He waited for the servants to obey, then pulled the leather communications strap
to let Aaron know they were ready to leave. Amid applause
and a chorus of good wishes, the carriage lumbered forward,
iron wheels rattling noisily on the cobblestones.

The sun poked through a distant cloud just as the carriage
rolled through the gates of Starke, bathing the scarlet interior
in clear morning light. Robyn realized she had been holding
her breath. She let it out on a rush of excited laughter.

"We did it!" she exclaimed. "We're away from the house
and safely on our way!"

William took her hand and kissed it in silent tribute.
"Mary" watched them, grinning merrily. "I propose a toast,"
he said, raising his hand in a mock salute. "Here's to the
glorious city of Bristol. Bristol—and freedom."

Shirley, Zach's secretary, buzzed the intercom. "Inspector
Harris is on the line for you. He says it's urgent."

"Put him through." Zach pushed the sheets of monthly
sales figures aside and picked up the phone. "Inspector, this
is Zach Bowleigh. Do you have news for me about Gerry or
Gloria?"

"I do, indeed, Mr. Bowleigh. Startling news, in fact. It
turns out that Gloria and Gerry's mother was a woman
called Violet Taunton, and Violet worked as a nanny for the
Baron of Starke's children during the Second World War."

So Gerry's mother had worked for the English branch of
the Bowleigh family. The circle of coincidence was growing
tighter and tighter. "Go on," Zach said.

"My next piece of news may come as a shock to you, Mr.
Bowleigh. When I found out that Violet Taunton had worked
at Starke, I arranged an interview with the current Lord

Bowleigh—he was one of the children Violet looked after—and he told me a surprising story. Gerald was born in 1945, and his father was an American soldier. It seems there were several hundred American soldiers based in Dorset, waiting to be shipped out to the front lines in France and Germany. This soldier had an affair with Violet, got her pregnant, and then wouldn't marry her."

"That's a sad story, Inspector, but unfortunately I don't see why you find it so surprising. There must have been thousands of women in Europe who could tell a similar tale."

"I wasn't shocked by the fact that Violet Taunton found herself pregnant, Mr. Bowleigh. What shocked me was the name of Gerald Taunton's father."

Zach found that he was sweating. "Who is ... was ... Gerry's father?" he asked.

"A fine young American officer by the name of William Bowleigh."

"William Bowleigh? You mean the baron? But he wasn't an American soldier, he was as English as they come."

"No, sir, I don't mean the Baron. The father of Gerry Taunton was William Bowleigh the Fourth, of New York City." The inspector cleared his throat. "I believe that would be your grandfather, known as Bill Bowleigh."

"My grandfather!" Zach's sweat froze into an icy chill. "My God, how can that be? He was the most uptight, honorable man I've ever met."

"You have to put yourself back to that time and place," Inspector Harris said. "Your grandpa was due to ship out to a major battlefront. Each morning when he woke up, he knew it might be the last day he'd be alive. People do funny things in wartime. Things they would never do in normal circumstances."

"But why didn't my grandfather marry Violet—" Zach broke off. "Oh, of course. He was already married to my grandmother, and they had two young children."

"And that, according to Lord Bowleigh, is why Gerry Taunton's birth was kept such a deep secret. Your grandmother, apparently, wasn't the sort of woman to forgive and forget."

"She certainly wasn't, but why didn't my grandfather admit the truth when my grandmother died!" Zach exclaimed. "My God, he owed Gerry some sort of an acknowledgment after all those years."

"Obviously Gerry felt that way, too," the detective said dryly.

"How does Gloria fit into this picture?" Zach asked.

"Violet Taunton married a carpenter called Hasskins when Gerry was still a toddler. Gloria is their child."

"Gerry's half sister," Zach muttered.

"That's right. It seems your grandfather did the best he could for Violet and Gerry. According to the baron, he set Violet up in a little flat in Poole and sent them money regularly. Gerry Taunton went to good schools, and when he graduated from university, it seems like your grandpa sponsored his immigration to the States and gave him a job."

"But he never acknowledged that Gerry was his son," Zach said. "Not even in his will. There were no special bequests to Gerry, no deathbed acknowledgment of what he'd done."

The detective grunted. "It sounds like your grandfather never came to terms with what he'd done, doesn't it?"

"And Gerry suffered for my grandfather's moral cowardice."

"You could say that. But at least we have a darn good motive for the scam being worked at your Gallery, don't we? From what you've told me, it sounds as if Gerry Taunton must have commissioned that first fake not too long after your grandfather died. Got pissed off at being ignored and decided to get back at you, the legitimate son and heir."

"I'm having trouble absorbing all the implications of this," Zach said. "Where do we go from here?"

"You don't go anywhere," the detective said. "And you don't do anything that might make Gerry Taunton suspicious. I need to coordinate my investigation with the New York City police and I can tell you the paperwork is already proving a nightmare. Don't do anything that would trigger Gerry's suspicions until I can get an extradition warrant prepared for Gloria Hasskins."

"Are you telling me I just have to sit here and do nothing? Even though Gerry Taunton probably spent two years doing his best to destroy my Gallery, and his sister practiced her sharpshooting on the woman I was hoping to marry?"

"That's exactly what I'm telling you, Mr. Bowleigh. And you'd better listen to me if you want any arrests to be made in this case. Sit still, keep your head down, and make damn sure Gerry Taunton never has any reason to doubt your friendship."

Chapter 21

TWENTY minutes after leaving Starke, Robyn had already begun to feel sick. By the time an hour had passed, she was wondering what sadistic fiend had first invented the torment of travel by horse-drawn, iron-wheeled carriage. She wished she knew, so that she could seek him out in hell and personally shovel a few extra coals onto the fire that doubtless burned beneath him. She felt sure he was already in hell. Even God's mercy could not be sufficient to allow such a monster to escape his well-deserved punishment.

Ever solicitous, William waved smelling salts under her nose, which revived her just sufficiently to remind her that she was undoubtedly going to throw up some time within the next thirty seconds. She vaguely remembered that at dawn this morning she had rejoiced in the prospect of traveling in the comfort of her own private carriage. Right now—a *much* wiser woman—she would willingly have swapped her seat among the velvet pillows for a dog kennel in the baggage compartment of any jet plane flying the friendly skies.

"What ails you, my dear?" William tried to chafe some warmth into her freezing hands. "I have never known you to suffer such discomfort on a short carriage ride."

"Short?" she said faintly. "How far have we gone?"

"Fourteen miles and it has taken us less than two hours. We are most fortunate to have such clement weather at this time of year."

Over the past weeks, Robyn had learned that it was not only twentieth-century Britishers who insisted that anything short of a howling gale was good weather. Their eighteenth-century ancestors had the same strange standards. She was too busy trying not to throw up to point out that it looked likely to sleet at any moment. Forty-six miles to go. Seven more hours of incessant jolting and swaying. Robyn wondered if anybody else had ever died of motion sickness or if she was going to be the first.

"How long until we meet up with Mrs. Wilkes's party?" she asked.

Zachary spoke up. "Another five or six minutes, no more. We have passed the milestone for the Hare and Hounds."

Hallelujah! Less than a mile to the inn where they had arranged to rendezvous with Hannah Wilkes. Robyn closed her eyes and held her head completely still. If she didn't move and didn't look out of the window, she might possibly make it to the inn without disaster. When she heard the thunder of galloping horses and cries of "Halt!" and "Whoa!" she was momentarily delighted. They had arrived at their rendezvous quicker than she could have hoped. She sat up and opened her eyes.

One look at William's grim face warned her that they hadn't arrived at the inn and that the noise of galloping hoofbeats was not merely the bustle of a busy stable yard but something much more ominous. William leaned forward and peered out of the carriage window while Zachary hastily retied the strings on his hood and slipped his too masculine hands into a pair of knitted woolen gloves. Robyn breathed deeply, swallowing over the dreadful sickness roiling in her stomach. She absolutely could *not* throw up now.

"Is it soldiers?" she asked.

"Yes," William said, his voice crisp. "Captain Bretton's dragoons." He turned swiftly to his brother. "Zachary, for God's sake stay as much in the shadows as you can, and remember to act like a servant. Fuss over Arabella and cringe every time an officer looks in your direction." He turned back to the window. "Here comes Captain Bretton."

A gunshot exploded, obscenely loud in the pastoral peace of the countryside. "Halt in the name of His Majesty King George!" Even muted by the walls of the carriage, the bellowed command was harsh with menace. The coachman reined in and the canter of the carriage horses slowed to a trot before coming to a rocking, shuddering stop.

"I cannot put you all in danger," Zachary said. "I will jump out of the carriage and make a run for it."

"No!" William's denial was low-pitched but absolute. "The carriage has been surrounded by dragoons. You will be bayoneted the instant you open the door, and we will be thrown into jail as traitors who aided your escape. Stay where you are."

Zachary's face was pale. "I wish I could tell you both how bitterly I regret the trouble I have brought to our family. Bella, William, I beg you to believe that I would never have come to Starke if I had guessed the problems my return would cause."

"Where else would you have gone but to your home?" William asked. "Besides, don't give up before you must. Take heart, Zachary, your disguise is good and the captain, I trust, is acting on false information I have supplied him."

There was no time to ask what he meant. The jingling of harness and spurs grew louder, vying with the stomp and snort of the horses. Surprisingly, despite her extreme nausea, Robyn's senses seemed exceptionally acute, and she could hear each sound with distinct, threatening clarity. She heard the soldiers dismount, heard the thud of their footsteps on the frozen mud road as they walked toward the carriage and banged on the door panels.

"Open in the name of the King!"

William let down the window. "What is the meaning of this outrage? Have you run mad, stopping a peer of the realm as he proceeds about his lawful business? Who authorizes this criminal interference?"

"I authorize it, my lord, with the explicit permission of the Duke of Cumberland." Captain Bretton rode up, his bay gelding foam-flecked from the speed of his travel. "My orders are here." He leaned down and handed a sealed letter through the carriage window, which William broke open and read in silence.

When he had finished reading, he took his time refolding the flaps of the letter. "You have been very busy, Captain," was all he said.

"Indeed." Captain Bretton inclined his head in a mocking bow, then leapt from his horse and unlatched the carriage door. "Now, out of the carriage, my lord, and the Lady

Arabella, also." He noticed the third figure in the carriage. "And you, woman, whatever your name is, out of the carriage."

With deceptively languid movements, William positioned himself in the doorway, blocking the captain's view of the carriage interior. "In the interests of bringing this absurd search to a speedy conclusion, I am willing to accede to your demands." William stepped down from the carriage. "However, my wife does not feel well—"

"Alas, she would feel even less well locked up in Poole jail. Move aside, my lord." Captain Bretton pointed to the seemingly cringing maidservant. "You, didn't you hear what I said, woman? Out of the carriage, and look sharp about it."

Head hanging, face averted as if equally afraid to meet the gaze either of her mistress or of the captain, "Mary" climbed down from the carriage and scuttled away, ducking under the captain's outstretched arm. Captain Bretton spared the maid no more than a single scornful glance before turning his attention back to Robyn. For her, he swept his hat from his head and held it to his heart in a parody of formal etiquette.

"Now, my lady, it is your turn. Descend from the carriage, I pray you, so that my men may locate the secret compartment in which you carry the Jacobite traitor. Unless, of course, you would prefer to save us all some time and tell me where your husband has hidden his brother?"

"I would prefer never to see you or speak to you again," Robyn said.

The captain's pretense of courtesy vanished, to be replaced by a look of sheer hatred. He leaned inside the carriage and grabbed Robyn's arm, clearly intending to drag her outside.

William was between them in an instant, hand on the hilt of his sword, eyes glittering. "Unhand my wife, sir." He spoke with deadly, icy calm, indifferent to the fact that twenty dragoons had leveled their muskets at him the instant he approached their captain.

Captain Bretton flushed, but he realized that he was within seconds of being run through by William's sword, dragoons or no dragoons. He dropped his hand and ostentatiously moved himself and his horse a foot or so from the carriage.

"Do not touch my wife again, Captain Bretton." William pushed his sword back into its scabbard with a resounding click. He turned to Robyn, stretching out his arms. "My lady?"

She placed her hands in his and jumped down, landing shakily because the nausea made her feel weak-kneed. William smiled at her as if they were alone, rather than surrounded by a platoon of armed soldiers. "At least you have a few moments respite from the jolting of the carriage. Are you warm enough, my dear lady?"

She forced her voice steady. "Yes, thank you, quite warm."

"Good." Confident that she was in command of herself, William turned and bowed ironically to the captain. "Search my coach, sirrah, but a word of warning. Damage it or destroy so much as a single cushion, and I will personally ride to London to lodge a complaint with His Majesty."

"Brave words," the captain sneered. "But the King does not listen to the complaints of traitors."

"You are more arrogant than usual, Captain Bretton. May one inquire why?"

The captain smiled. "Certainly, my lord. I have firm information that your treacherous brother left Starke Manor this morning concealed behind a secret panel in your traveling coach."

William looked astonished. "I can assure you, Captain, that your information is false."

"I believe not."

William yawned. "It would, I suppose, be quite useless to tell you that you will find nobody concealed anywhere in my carriage, much less behind a secret panel."

"Quite useless," Captain Bretton agreed. He beckoned to his lieutenant. "Look beneath the seats. I have been told that one of them is hinged and that there is a space hollowed out fully large enough to hide a man. The lock is probably a spring, concealed within a decorative carving. Take one of the men inside with you and work systematically. The carriage is no great size. You should require no more than a few minutes to find the hiding place."

Somewhat relieved that Captain Bretton's attention was so securely focused on the wrong thing, Robyn sneaked a look at William. To most people, his expression might have seemed no more than a mixture of boredom, outrage, and irritation. Robyn detected a faint hint of satisfaction along with the inevitable tension, and she began to realize that the captain had been deliberately duped. William had seemed almost cavalier when she had suggested that Jackson might prove troublesome. Was it possible that he had once again used his valet to set Captain Bretton hunting along a false trail?

Two minutes later a gleeful shout came from inside the carriage, followed by thirty seconds or so of intense silence. Then the lieutenant appeared in the doorway, jumped down, and saluted smartly. He did not look a happy man.

"Well?" Captain Bretton demanded. "Have you found the traitor?"

"We have found the secret compartment, sir." The lieutenant swallowed. "The seat bench is hollow, sir, as you suggested. However, there was nobody hidden inside the compartment, sir. It was empty, except for a small chest."

"Empty?" Captain Bretton was slack-jawed with astonishment. "What do you mean, it was empty?"

The dragoon came out of the coach, a studded, tooled leather chest in his arms. He shifted the chest to his left arm and managed an awkward salute. "This is what we found in the secret compartment, sir. No traitors, sir, nary a one."

"Open the chest!" Captain Bretton bellowed, beside himself with rage.

"I think not, Captain." William stepped forward and took the chest from the corporal. "As you can plainly see, this box is scarcely large enough to contain a kitten, much less a full-grown man. My lady wife and I are making a shopping expedition to Bristol. Naturally, I require money to pay for our purchases. That chest was hidden away from the marauding hands of thieves and highway robbers in the secret compartment I designed especially for that purpose. I do not intend to give your men access to the monies I would not give to highwaymen."

The captain swung around, his eyes black with loathing. "You deliberately misled me," he said, spluttering with the force of his rage. "You had your estate carpenters working for three days on that secret compartment—"

William's gaze was bland. "How in the world do you know that, Captain Bretton? I expressly ordered them to keep their work secret. There is no point in having a hiding place for one's valuables if all the neighborhood riffraff knows the hiding place exists."

The captain looked as if he might choke on his own anger. "You *expected* me to come chasing after you," he blustered. "You made sure that I knew of the secret compartment you were having built." He suddenly stopped, horror momentarily depriving him of breath and speech. "Oh, my God!" he said and swung himself onto his horse. "Follow me!" he yelled to his men. "We have to get back to Starke before his brother escapes!"

The dragoons sprang into their saddles in an impressive display of speed and horsemanship. Captain Bretton might not have much success in capturing traitors, but his men could certainly ride. They flicked spurs to the flanks of their mounts and galloped off down the road, a brilliant cavalcade of scarlet, white, and gleaming brass.

Robyn watched their departure in silence for a moment or two, almost too relieved to speak. She was joined by Zachary, who hung his head and shuffled his feet in a convincing portrayal of a maid who knows she deserted her mistress in a time of need.

When the thunder of hooves had faded to a muffled thud, William held out his hand. "Shall we return to the carriage, my lady? Mistress Wilkes will be wondering why we are so delayed."

"Certainly, my lord." Robyn laid her hand on his arm and stepped up into the carriage. Outside, she could hear the coachmen and the postilions scrambling to get back into position. William pulled the cord and the coach lumbered into motion.

"I'm delighted the captain and his troops have gone," she said, once they were safely under way. "But why was he seized by a frantic desire to get back to Starke?"

William smiled. "That's easy to explain, my love. He suddenly feared that this trip to Bristol might be no more than a clever diversionary tactic. He thinks I have drawn him here to the Hare and Hounds, whilst Zachary is making a dash for freedom back at Starke."

Robyn chuckled, her sickness momentarily conquered. "That's such an ingenious escape plan, it's almost a shame we didn't think of it."

"With all due modesty, my love, I must point out that I *did* think of it. I merely decided we would be a lot safer if we worked a double deception upon the too eager Captain. He was so busy searching for that secret compartment, he barely glanced at your maid."

Robyn was impressed and said so. "I wonder how long the captain will spend scouring the countryside around Starke before he realizes that he has made a dreadful mistake?" she asked.

William's smile sobered. "Long enough, I trust, to see all three of us safely to Bristol."

"And me on board ship for France," Zachary said.

The seven hours of travel between the Hare and Hounds and the city of Bristol were seven hours of unredeemed torment for Robyn. The nausea that had vanished during their brief encounter with Captain Bretton soon returned with renewed force. She had thrown up so many times that when they finally arrived in Bristol she was too exhausted to feel triumph or even lingering anxiety. Zachary and William would have to make their trip to the harbor alone because walking was temporarily beyond her. She got out of the coach with William's assistance and waited in numb misery for someone to direct her to the blissful, *immobile* comfort of her bed.

The brothers jointly escorted her up the stairs to the inn's best bedroom, and Hannah Wilkes went off to the kitchens in search of weak tea and dry toast. Robyn was so absorbed in her own wretchedness that it took her a moment or two to realize that Hannah Wilkes was supposed to be spending the night with her uncle, a Bristol merchant. It took another few minutes for her to realize that Hannah's presence at the inn was a major calamity. Zachary and William would never be able to slip off to the harbor if Hannah was in the room, observing their every movement. What excuse could a husband and a personal maid give for deserting a woman who was prostrate with nausea?

When Hannah returned from the kitchens bearing a

wooden tray, laden with all the trappings for tea, Robyn forced herself to sit upright in the chair and take command of the situation. She accepted a cup of tea and even managed to choke down a bite of bread. Then she smiled at the kindly widow, thinking that in normal circumstances, her amiable, restful presence would have been very welcome.

Hannah Wilkes took the cup from her. "Tea seems to cure a multitude of ills, does it not? You look much refreshed, my lady."

"And I feel much better," Robyn said. And that was true, thank heaven. Her stomach no longer seemed determined to practice skydiving every time she moved her head. "Mrs. Wilkes, I am most truly grateful for all your help, but you mustn't deprive your uncle of the pleasure of your company. Please go to him before it gets dark. I shall be more than adequately taken care of with William and my maid to see to my needs."

"Lady Arabella is entirely right," William chimed in. "You may rely on me, Mistress Wilkes, to see that my wife is given the most tender care."

"My lord, I know why you wish me to leave." Hannah turned an agitated fiery red. With the Bowleighs watching in astonishment, she tiptoed to the door and checked to see if anyone lurked outside in the corridor. When she was sure the four of them were alone, she shut the bedroom door and drew in a determined breath.

"Lord Bowleigh, my dear Lady Arabella, I wish you both nothing but success in your attempt to outrun Captain Bretton and his overzealous troops. Believe me, my lord, you can count upon my absolute discretion if you and ... er ... the maid wish to depart from the inn sometime soon on an urgent errand. However, Lady Arabella should not be left alone. I am sure that her sickness is definitely not part of your plan, and she needs help."

William looked worried. "Mistress Wilkes, I beg you to reconsider. This is a time for you to be safely at home with your uncle, not here with us. Please accept that Mary and I will be able to provide my wife with all the comfort she needs."

Hannah Wilkes never raised her voice, but she didn't move, either. "My lord, I have known Mary for ten years, and your brother equally as long. I beg you will not insult my intelligence by asking me to believe that the person in this room wearing Mary's clothes is truly your servant. Now go, both of you, and leave me to tend to Lady Arabella's needs."

William could see that it was useless to waste time in further protestations. "Very well, Mistress Wilkes, the plain, unvarnished truth is that the tide turns in less than two hours. My brother and I should leave now if he is to be out of England by tonight."

"Then do not waste time talking, my lord, but make haste and be gone," Hannah said.

Zachary retired behind a screen and emerged five minutes later, bewigged, hatted, and wearing the clothing of a merchant, typical enough to be inconspicuous in a city dedicated to international trade. He bowed to Hannah, taking her hand and raising it to his lips. "Since the Battle of Culloden, my life has been saved by the sacrifices of many people," he said. "I appreciate your kindness, Mistress Wilkes, and I want you to know that the second half of my life will be dedicated to more useful purposes than the first."

"In that case, I have double reason to wish you Godspeed," Hannah said quietly. "My prayers will be with you, sir."

Zachary bowed, then came swiftly to kneel at Robyn's side. "Bella, I thank you for all that you have done. Without your quick wit, I would at best be pacing my prison inside the walls of Starke. At worst, I would be dead at the hands of Captain Bretton. I have always believed that my brother deserved the best wife in the world, and now I can rejoice in the knowledge that he has found her."

Robyn smiled. "I have been told you were always a consummate flatterer, Zachary. It seems that rumor scarcely does you justice." She touched her hand briefly to his cheek, feeling her eyes blur with tears. "Go with God," she said. "May you live long and happily."

William strode across the room. "Mistress Wilkes . . . Hannah . . . I ought to insist on sending you to the safety of your uncle's house. Instead, I offer you my most heartfelt thanks for your help. The house of Bowleigh will be eternally in your debt."

Hannah blushed. "Nonsense, my lord. It is my pleasure to be of assistance."

"If we had more time, I would wait to argue the point. Instead, I merely renew my expressions of gratitude." William raised her hand and kissed it. Robyn, despite her continuing nausea, couldn't help but notice the hot color that flared in Hannah's cheeks. William saw nothing amiss, probably because he turned away almost at once and crossed hastily to the fire, bending down to kiss Robyn on the cheek. "I will return as soon as the boat has sailed," he said. "You can expect to see me in less than two hours."

Robyn didn't—couldn't reply.

Hannah Wilkes bowed her head. "God willing," she said.

Chapter 22

ZACH knew.

He knew who had faked the antiques sold through the Gallery, and he knew the truth about his grandfather's wartime fling. Zach had tried to hide his knowledge, but Gerry had seen it in his eyes. Somehow Zach had discovered that Gerry Taunton was Bill Bowleigh's bastard son.

Gerry walked along Park Avenue toward his apartment, sweating despite the cold. His plans to throw Zach off the scent by setting up Robyn Delaney as the villain behind the fake antiques hadn't worked. Zach—damn him—had refused to believe in Robyn's guilt. So he had kept on poking about, delving into secrets that shouldn't have concerned him. Gerry couldn't understand how the truth about Bill Bowleigh's wartime fling had come to light, but the precise mechanism didn't matter much right now. The game was up. Gerry accepted that it was time to make his getaway, but he wasn't willing to cut and run without one last attempt to punish Zach. Goddammit! What had Zach ever done to deserve the golden ease of his life? Why shouldn't he suffer as Gerry had suffered from the moment he was born?

Gerry unlocked the door to his apartment and strode into the vestibule. Gloria heard his key turn in the lock and came out of the kitchen, hands twisting nervously in her apron. These days, ever since her precipitous arrival from England two weeks earlier, she seemed to live in a perpetual fog of nervous agitation. "What's the matter?" she asked. "Why are you home so early?"

Gerry was beginning to find his sister's constant fear irritating. He brushed past her into the living room. "I'm home because Zach Bowleigh has discovered that his late, unlamented grandfather couldn't keep his fly zipped."

"What do you mean?"

"Isn't it obvious? I mean he knows Bill Bowleigh is my father, and he knows Robyn Delaney wasn't responsible for faking any antiques."

"My God!" Gloria's hand went to her throat. "Are you sure? What else does he know? Has he guessed that we shot Robyn Delaney?"

"*We* didn't shoot Robyn," Gerry said. "*You* did. And yes, I think Zach suspects we were involved."

Gloria was gray with fright. "But how could he? Why would he link either of us to a random shooting in England?"

Gerry shrugged. "Easily. The police found that damn gun of yours. What more would he need?"

Gloria darted toward the guest room. "I'm going to start packing. We have to get out of here while we can." Her voice was thin with panic. "We can start again in Brazil, like we've talked about. Say you'll come, Gerry. Today. Tonight. The police can't touch us there."

"I don't want to live in a damn jungle," Gerry said bitterly.

"Rio is a civilized city. Or we could try Buenos Aires. We could lead a good life there—"

"Good life or not, we don't have any other choice," Gerry interrupted, his anger at his sister intensifying. "Once that gun of yours was stolen, it was only a matter of time before the police got onto us—"

"I wish you wouldn't keep nagging about the gun," Gloria said. "I've told you I'm sorry." She laid her hand on his arm. "Life won't be so bad. We can have servants, nice clothes ... You made enough money selling those fake antiques for both of us to live in luxury for the rest of our lives."

Gerry shook off her hand. "But Zach Bowleigh still has the Gallery, damn him. Despite everything, despite all our fancy plans, we didn't bring him down."

Gloria wrapped her arms around her waist and rocked back and forth. "Why can't you forget your obsession with Zach Bowleigh, for heaven's sake?"

"Because he's too happy," Gerry snarled. "I worked my ass off building up the reputation of the Gallery, and how does my father reward me? He hands over control of the business to Zach—a thirty-year-old know-nothing, fresh out of grad school!"

"Well, Zach wasn't exactly a know-nothing, was he? He had a doctoral degree in fine arts, and he spent all those summers in Paris, studying with the curator at the Louvre—"

"Good God, are you apologizing for Bill Bowleigh's failure to acknowledge me? For his decision to cut me out of my share of the Gallery? I was his *son,* dammit!"

"No, of course not. Of course he should have made you a partner in the Gallery. But it doesn't matter anymore, does it? You've had your revenge. Zach hasn't had an easy time of it these past two years since Bill Bowleigh died."

Gerry shook his head angrily. "The bottom line is that the Gallery is going to survive the scandal we created."

"But Zach has still suffered. He wanted to marry Robyn Delaney. He was desperately in love with her, and we took care of that."

Gerry's face hardened into bitterness. "Robyn isn't dead, and while there's life, Zach can always hope she'll get better. We can't even be sure that she won't regain her wits and say something that incriminates both of us."

Gloria rubbed one chilled hand against the other. "God, I wish she'd died like she was supposed to. We're neither of us safe with her around."

Gerry's mood began to lighten. "Perhaps it's time for us to take care of Robyn once and for all," he murmured.

"How? We can't just walk into her parents' house and shoot her."

"You have a simplistic mind, my love. Guns aren't always the answer. There are better ways to take care of Robyn than that." Gerry chuckled, feeling more cheerful by the moment. "You know, I do believe that poor deluded Robyn has just decided to commit suicide."

Gloria's head jerked up, her eyes gleaming with sudden interest. "How can you make her do that?"

"With planning," Gerry said. "Are you willing to help?"

Gloria hesitated for less than a second. She had always followed where her handsome, clever brother chose to lead. "Yes," she said. "I'm willing to help. Let's kill Robyn Delaney."

"There's a sentence that has a nice ring to it," Gerry murmured. "Yes, let's kill her. And this time, I'll be in charge, so we'll do it right."

Until Zach Bowleigh called, Thursday had been one of those days when Muriel Delaney felt really low. Her husband was out of town for a reunion with his navy buddies, and Robyn seemed to be sinking into ever deeper depression. Therapy had produced no improvement in her grip on reality; she had spent all last night pleading to be taken to see William and her children and begging for reassurance that "the true Zachary" was safely in France. Her delusion that she was a wife and mother had been so compelling that if William Bowleigh had happened to live in Virginia rather than California, Muriel thought she might have been tempted to drive over and pay him a visit. As it was, she had simply sat up half the night, comforting Robyn as best she could, and praying disjointed prayers for God to make everything come right again with her daughter.

When Zach called, as he did at least twice a week, Muriel embarrassed herself no end by bursting into tears. Between sobs, she assured him that she was fine, and that she would soon snap out of her doldrums, but when Zach heard about the rough night she'd had, and the fact that Al was out of town, he'd insisted that he would catch the noon shuttle to Washington, D.C., and pay her a quick visit. Muriel protested that it was the middle of the week, and he didn't have time to come visiting, but her protests were less vehement than they might have been, and she was secretly grateful when Zach ignored them all and said that he was looking forward to spending a couple of hours in her company. He was a charming liar, but Muriel felt a lot more cheerful when she hung up the phone.

And then, just an hour ago, Gerry Taunton had phoned from National Airport to say that he was touring Washington with his sister from England, and they would both love to stop by and visit. He was in such a rush that he gave her no time to explain that Zach Bowleigh was also going to be there.

Well, no harm done, Muriel thought. She always loved to entertain company and Zach and Gerry were good friends. They wouldn't mind spending an unexpected hour together.

She put her coffee mug in the dishwasher and watched Robyn, who was making a complete hash of dropping cookie dough onto a baking tray. Muriel took her daughter's hand and helped her to score the top of each cookie with the tines of a fork. Robyn actually smiled as she saw the row of lines appear in the soft dough. Muriel smiled back. She knew baking cookies wouldn't chase away all of Robyn's demons, but nothing else seemed to be working, so maybe baking was as successful as any other form of therapy.

"Set the timer on the oven, dear." Muriel helped Robyn to twist the dials, then gave her a hug when the task was done. "Now we have to wait ten minutes for the cookies to bake," she said. "Oops, there's the doorbell. I expect that's Gerry."

"Gerry Taunton?" Robyn asked.

"Yes, dear, I'm so pleased you remembered him." Muriel beamed as she walked to the front door. This day was turning out a whole lot better than she had dared to hope when dawn broke and Robyn had been sobbing in her arms. "Gerry's bringing his sister for a visit. Her name is Gloria. You'll like meeting her, won't you?"

Robyn didn't seem interested in Gerry's sister. "Mr. Taunton is a most handsome gentleman," she said, patting her hair and adjusting the collar of her sweater.

"He is good-looking, isn't he?" Muriel was still smiling as she flung open the door. "Gerry," she said. "Come in, and Gloria, too. We've been looking forward so much to seeing you."

Muriel Delaney was delighted to have them pay Robyn a visit. The poor woman was such a nice old bird, Gerry could almost find it in his heart to be sorry for her. He quickly smothered his inconvenient twinge of guilt. Hell, Robyn's brains were so scrambled he was doing the old trout a favor in putting her daughter peacefully to rest. Much better for the Delaneys to mourn a child sleeping in the graveyard than to have to cope with her crazy fits and starts on a daily basis.

He was looking at Gloria, signaling to her to get ready to put the first stage of their plan into action, when Muriel obliged them both by jumping to her feet and giving a little agitated murmur. "Oh, heavens, the cookies! They'll be baked to a crisp if I don't rescue them right away. Excuse me, please."

"Certainly." Gerry rose to his feet and pulled back Muriel's chair. He'd learned as a teenager that nothing earned a young boy more rewards than perfect manners. As an adult, he'd developed courtesy and deprecating British charm into the perfect cover for villainy. He turned to his sister, warning her with a glance to get her ass in gear. "Gloria, luvvy, perhaps you could help Muriel while I have a chat with Robyn."

"Yes, I'd like that," Gloria said, reaching into her bag to extract the present they'd chosen together. "We brought you a canister of Earl Grey tea, Mrs. Delaney. Perhaps I could brew a pot, English style, to go with your American cookies."

"That would be very nice, my dear, but you must call me Muriel."

Their voices faded as they hurried into the kitchen. Gloria knew better than to let Muriel out again for the next ten minutes, but Gerry didn't waste a second. He immediately reached for the inside pocket of his jacket and pulled out the flask of ethylene glycol, otherwise known as antifreeze. *The New York Times* had very helpfully printed an article only a couple of weeks earlier pointing out that more children poisoned themselves with sweet-smelling, sweet-tasting antifreeze than any other substance. He'd poured it into a flask with a special lip, so that it would be easy to squirt into Robyn's throat even if she resisted. But she was such a dumb-ass these days, he wasn't expecting her to protest.

Gerry was particularly pleased with himself for thinking of this way to finish her off. He knew Robyn had already tried to eat a plastic foam cup, and once she'd drunken laundry detergent. Nobody had been quite sure whether she'd been trying to kill herself, or whether she no longer understood that some things in bottles were poisonous. Gerry planned to pass this incident off as suicide, and he had the scenario all worked out. He just needed to be damn sure Robyn was too far gone for a stomach pump to work when he yelled for help and they rushed her to the hospital.

Robyn was waiting to show him her embroidery. "Will

you come and sit beside me, Mr. Taunton?" She patted the
sofa, and the smile she gave him was damn near flirtatious.

Gerry palmed the flask of ethylene glycol and answered
her smile. "With pleasure, my dear." He sat down next to
her, thigh pressed against thigh. She made no attempt to
move away. "What a pretty sweater you're wearing," Gerry
murmured.

She touched the collar. "You call this brown knitted garment a sweater? Does it please you?"

He put his arm around her shoulders, clamping her arms
to her sides. "Yes, my dear. That brown knitted garment
pleases me." *Jesus,* he thought, *what a fruitcake she's become.* "I have brought you a special cordial to drink," he
said, holding up the flask of antifreeze. "You'll really like
it."

"It is a most pleasing color," she said. "Most bright and
strange."

He leaned across her, capturing her chin in his left hand and
uncapping the flask with his right. She lifted her chin willingly,
and her eyelids fluttered closed. Gerry frowned. She was offering even less resistance than he'd expected. God Almighty, she
surely didn't think he wanted to kiss her?

It seemed that she did. Grimacing in distaste, he obliged
with a quick brush of his lips over her mouth. She opened
her eyes and giggled. "Mr. Taunton, pray remember that I
am a married woman."

"Right, luvvy. If you say so." He held up the flask. "Open
wide," he said. "Take a nice big swallow, luvvy."

She obeyed without question. Still smiling, he tipped the
warm, sweet liquid between her teeth. She began to swallow,
but after only a couple of sips, she unexpectedly resisted,
grimacing with distaste.

Gerry shook her impatiently. "Come on, Robyn, luvvy,
this is very good for you. It's medicine to make you feel all
better." He poured the deadly sweet drink into her mouth in
an unrelenting trickle, forcing her to swallow. She shook her
head forward, gagging, and bright fluorescent green liquid
spouted onto her lap. She tried to twist away out of Gerry's
grasp, but he dived forward, holding her captive against the
scratchy tweed cushions of the living-room sofa.

He had never expected to encounter this much resistance.

He tipped up the bottle again and thrust it between her lips. "Come on!" he said. "Drink up, damn you! What's your problem, don't you like this nice new cordial I brought for you?"

A bell chimed, and Gerry recognized the sound of the front doorbell. He cursed as voices sounded in the corridor. A woman and a man. Muriel's voice. And Zach's voice, damn him to hell.

With a throttled yelp of rage, Gerry stopped trying to ram the bottle into Robyn's mouth and pressed it into her hand instead. "Get in here quickly!" he yelled. "Muriel, for God's sake help! Robyn's trying to kill herself!"

"Oh, my God!" That was Muriel, and then Zach's voice came, harsh with the urgency of his command. "Get away from her, Gerry. Move away from her right now, or I swear I'll kill you myself."

The clatter of footsteps on the wooden stairs of the inn came without warning. Robyn's eye lit up with pleasure. "William!" she exclaimed. "He's back already!"

Almost as she spoke, she realized she was rejoicing too soon. Above the thump of booted feet racing up the stairs, she heard the flustered protests of the innkeeper. "Sir, you cannot go in there! Sir! The chamber is bespoken for the night!"

"Open the door or I will batter it down! And by God I will have you arrested for obstructing justice!"

Robyn and Hannah exchanged glances. "Captain Bretton," Robyn whispered.

"Thank heaven he has arrived too late," Hannah whispered back.

Too late to find Zachary, but not too late to cause major turmoil. Robyn and Hannah instinctively clasped hands as the door shuddered under the force of a blow directed at the lock. They heard the innkeeper and his wife protesting, but the protests were unavailing. The wife's horrified wails broke into sobs as the captain issued his ultimatum. "Unlock the door or you will both be in chains before the hour is out."

"We must let him in," Robyn said. "We cannot allow the innkeeper's family to suffer for our actions."

"Very well." Hannah started to walk toward the door, but Robyn arrived there first. "This is my battle," she said.

"Are you feeling strong enough to wage it?" Hannah asked.

"More than strong enough, thanks to your kind attentions. Two hours of sitting in a chair that doesn't move has worked miracles." Robyn flung open the door as she spoke and the captain practically catapulted into her room.

"Captain Bretton," she said. "I suppose I should have known that the oaf disturbing my peace would turn out to be you."

"Where is he? Tell me where he is!" The captain had unsheathed his sword, and he waved it wildly in the air. His usually immaculate uniform was splattered with mud. He stank of horse sweat and his face was streaked with the dust and grit of hours in the saddle. He pushed Robyn aside and hurtled across the room, sword slashing, eyes glittering with the fever of his obsession. "I will find the treacherous knave and kill him if 'tis the last thing I do on this earth!"

Hannah, horrified by such an unbridled display of temper, tried to calm him. "Sir ... Captain Bretton ... I beg you to compose yourself and behave with the decorum appropriate to your station. There is nobody here save the Lady Arabella and I."

Captain Bretton was beyond reason, enraged well past the point of registering the good sense of what she said. "Out of my way!" He pushed her so hard that she staggered and would have fallen if Robyn had not caught her. The captain began to pull covers from the bed with lunatic haste. The wails of the innkeeper and his wife rose to a piercing crescendo as the captain tore the hangings from the window, slitting them with his sword as if he expected Zachary to be somehow concealed within the folds of linen cretonne. Thwarted in his efforts to discover his quarry secreted behind the draperies, he pushed over the chairs and tore open the drawers of the chifforobe. When he knocked over the screen, he saw the pile of maid's clothing still on the footstool and a gleam of enlightenment pierced the enveloping fog of his rage.

Body shaking, he swung around. "Your maid," he said hoarsely. "Where is she?"

"Gone," Robyn said.

For a moment the captain neither moved nor spoke. Then he gave a great bellow of frustrated rage. "Goddammit, how did you make the substitution? How did you smuggle him out of Starke?"

This was not a moment to gloat. Robyn tried to answer the captain slowly and calmly, so as not to enrage him further. Hannah and the innkeeper were both cowering in the doorway, overwhelmed by his truly insane display of temper. "If you refer to my brother-in-law, sir, please remember that you have no proof Zachary was ever at Starke, much less that my husband and I smuggled him out of the Manor today. For your own sake, I wish you would abandon your obsessive belief that my husband is sympathetic to the Jacobite cause. The baron has never by word or deed suggested that he is anything other than a loyal supporter of Hanoverian rule."

"And I know that his appearance is deceptive! He is the region's most clever liar!" The captain's frustration was so strong that it had reached a point of simmering rage no words could appease, however conciliatory. He paced the room, a captive tiger deprived of his prey and still starving for red meat. His gaze darted from corner to corner, and then finally settled on Robyn. With a yowl, half of anguish and half of pleasure, he grabbed her arm and started dragging her toward the door of the bedchamber.

Hannah Wilkes recovered her courage and stepped forward at once. "Sir, are you run quite mad? Remove your hands from the Lady Arabella or 'tis you who will find yourself in jail tonight, not this poor innkeeper, nor anyone else."

The captain's eyes rolled upward. "I have every right to touch the Lady Arabella. I take her prisoner in the name of King George!" His words emerged as gasping grunts. "She will be freed when the Baron of Starke surrenders his treacherous Jacobite brother to my custody!"

The innkeeper, with great courage, spoke up. "Sir, 'tis not lawful to lay hands on a baroness what was resting peacefully in her chamber, sir. Beggin' your pardon, sir, but you must not take her."

"Your defense of my wife is appreciated but unnecessary." William's voice spoke coolly from outside the bedroom door. The innkeeper and his wife exchanged worried looks, not sure whether to be relieved that the baron had returned in time to rescue his wife, or fearful at the mayhem now certain to ensue. They retreated into the corridor, wringing their hands. Hannah moved to stand by the fire and William stepped into the bedroom. Hand resting lightly on the hilt of his sword, he issued his command in a voice that was quiet, controlled, and utterly implacable.

"You, Captain, will unhand my wife. I believe I warned you earlier today never to touch her again. I do not plan to warn you a third time."

"You are bold for a traitor," Captain Bretton snarled. Spittle frothed at the corner of his mouth, but he released his hold on Robyn's arm and shoved her aside. "Where is your brother?" he demanded. "God damn you to the darkest pit of hell, where is he? Have you put him on board ship?"

William made no attempt to answer the captain's questions. He turned to Robyn. "Are you all right, my dear? I trust this extraordinary display has not totally overset you and Mistress Wilkes?"

The calm, everyday courtesy of William's behavior did not soothe Captain Bretton back into reason. Instead, it seemed to precipitate the final break in his tenuous self-control. With a growl of thwarted rage, he lunged forward, clearly intent on murder.

Somehow, William managed to react to the flash of the captain's upraised sword. He swung around, simultaneously pulling his own sword from its sheath and parrying the captain's blow.

"Stand back!" William ordered and Robyn leapt out of the way. Captain Bretton was obviously in a state of such fury that his actions could neither be predicted nor controlled, except by force.

The two men fought in deadly, terrifying silence. At first the captain's thrusts were wild, and his defense was so poor that even Robyn recognized that William could have killed him on at least three occasions. But the rhythm of the fight seemed to calm the captain as words had not, and his fighting soon became focused, and thus twice as deadly.

William fought now in earnest, not simply to disarm the captain, but to save his own life. Captain Bretton was a skillful fighter, not surprising given his profession, but fortunately he was tired after fourteen hours in the saddle and his rage was still not fully under control.

William, by contrast, was entirely in command of his emotions. He fought with concentrated, disciplined energy. He was stronger, less tired, and more naturally agile than the captain, but he was not a professional swordsman and could hope to win only by dogged determination as opposed to a sudden flash of brilliant swordplay.

Steel clanged on steel. The innkeeper's silence had given way to low moans of despair. Robyn stood still as a pillar of stone, afraid that the slightest movement on her part might distract William's attention from the quicksilver flash of the captain's sword. She thought that William was gaining the upper hand, but she didn't know enough about fencing to be sure.

Gradually, her hope turned to certainty. Captain Bretton was nearing exhaustion. Sweat ran from his forehead, blurring his sight, and he no longer offered any attack. Parrying William's thrusts and lunges was the extent of his capability.

Robyn allowed herself a quick sigh of relief, but she still didn't dare to move. The innkeeper's moans faded as the end drew palpably near, and the innkeeper's wife stopped her praying in order to watch.

With inexorable power, William pushed the captain back toward the wall, leaving him less and less room to maneuver. The captain realized that all was very nearly lost and he lurched forward in a last, desperate effort to attack. But William was waiting. The blade of his sword crossed with the captain's, flashed under, then over his opponent's weapon. With sheer physical force, William bore down on the captain's right arm until his sword clattered onto the floor.

Quick as lightning, William touched the point of his sword to the captain's throat. "Must . . . I . . . kill . . . you?" he asked, panting.

Captain Bretton seemed too exhausted to respond. His hands hung slackly at his sides, his mouth gaped open, and his breath came in great shuddering heaves. His gaze skittered frenziedly around the room. Suddenly he stiffened.

"You—shall—not—win—it—all—" he rasped. "Zachary—but—not—her—" Quicker than thought, he pulled a dagger from his sleeve and lashed out with deadly intent, not toward William, but toward Robyn.

Caught totally unprepared by the direction of the captain's move, William's blade sank deep into his opponent's throat. Blood spurted out in a hideous, gurgling rush. Simultaneously, pain exploded in Robyn's rib cage. Bewildered, she watched the captain's blood trickle along William's sword and besmirch his hands with gleaming scarlet. She wondered why she felt such dreadful pain when it was the captain who was dying. She swayed, wanting to reach William, but unable to make her wobbly legs obey her mental command.

"Oh, dear God in heaven, the captain has stabbed Lady Arabella! His dagger is in her heart!" *Hannah's voice. Anguished, distraught.*

Robyn looked at the captain, who had fallen to the floor. Yes, he was dead, but the sword had pierced his throat, not his heart. What was Hannah talking about? William turned to her and she tried to smile, but the hideous throbbing pain didn't go away. She closed her eyes. Her knees buckled, and she fell forward into William's arms.

"My darling Arabella, you cannot die." She felt him ripping at the lacings of her gown, tearing it open. A pillow was placed beneath her head. Hannah took her hands and chafed them gently.

"Bring me bandages," William said, his voice shaking. "Get me water! And for God's sake send for the surgeon!"

The surgeon. Robyn realized then that Captain Bretton had indeed stabbed her, and she knew instinctively that her wound was mortal. Grief, so intense that it engulfed even the pain of the dagger in her heart, welled up from deep inside her. She wasn't ready to die. How could she die when her body . . . part of herself . . . still lingered somewhere, hundreds of years into the future?

She had to communicate at least part of the truth to William. "I am . . . not Arabella," she whispered. "I . . . am . . . Robyn. The accident . . . changed me—"

"Yes, yes, my dearest love, I understand. You are my beloved Robyn. But hush, conserve your strength. You will need it all."

She had accused William so many times of lack of trust, and yet she realized now—too late—that she was the one who had failed to have faith in the power of his love. Why had she never told him the truth about who she was and where she had come from? Now her laboring lungs wouldn't draw sufficient breath to allow her to give complicated explanations about a fantastic situation. The pain came again, squeezing her chest tight and hard with agony.

Dear God, there was so much of life she still wanted to explore! It seemed unfair that she should lose William as well as Zach, two loves snatched from her in the space of a few short months. And her poor baby! He would grow up without knowing his mother, just as Zach had warned her, months ago, two hundred fifty years into the future.

Tears splashed onto her hand and she realized that Hannah was crying. Such a good, kind woman, Robyn thought hazily, a perfect mother for baby Zach. She turned toward William, desperate for a last glimpse of his beloved face.

"You must marry Hannah," she said. She had no strength for tact, no energy for prevarication. "She loves you ... always has ... and the children. She ... will be ... good wife."

William's face was white with anguish. "My heart, you are my wife and I can take no other."

She couldn't waste time in arguing. There was too much still to say. Her thoughts no longer came in coherent sequence, and she frowned, trying to sort them out. "Write to me." She clung to his hand, consumed with the need to make him agree. "Tell me what happens to my children ... baby Zach ... Hannah ... I will find your letter ... when I am Robyn ... in the future."

Tears made the blue of William's eyes more brilliant. "My love, you could not receive my letter—"

"Yes, yes, I will find it ... Promise me you will write." But how would she ever read his letter in the future, even if it survived, when she was dying here in the past, imprisoned in Arabella's wounded and bleeding body? The question faded in a shuddering gasp of pain, and when she could speak again, she clutched at his hand. "Promise me, William."

"Of course." He pressed his lips against the tips of her fingers. "I shall write to you, my heart, if that is your wish.

But why do we speak of communicating by letter, when it is my intention to grow old and crotchety beside you?"

"Not crotchety. You . . . will be . . . old and . . . wonderful."

"If you are there beside me, indeed I shall be wonderful." He rested his hand against her shoulder. "Courage, my heart, the surgeon will be here in but an instant."

She didn't waste precious words in telling him what he already knew—that the surgeon couldn't work miracles and that her wound was fatal.

"Zachary, your brother. He . . . is . . . safe?"

"Yes, securely on board ship for France, thanks to you. He sends his most heartfelt thanks."

"I'm glad." She was tired, and the urge to sleep was nearly overwhelming, but she still had important things to say. She looked deep into William's eyes and told him what she most wanted him to remember. "I love you, William, with—all—my—heart."

He carried her hand to his face, curling her fingers against his cheek. "I love you, too, Robyn." His voice was harsh, but she knew the harshness sprang from emotion, and the struggle to hold back his tears.

"Tell the children I love them. And send baby Zach to America when he grows up. He will . . . flourish . . . there . . . and raise a fine family."

"You will be able to send him yourself," he said, but his voice shook and they both knew that he lied.

"My lord, the surgeon is here! Make way for the surgeon!"

Hope lightened William's face. Robyn wished that she could sustain that hope. With phenomenal effort, she moved her hand and pressed the tips of her fingers tenderly against his lips.

"I . . . will . . . always . . . love . . . you . . . dearest . . . William."

"No, Robyn, you must not die! Dear God in heaven, do not take her from me!"

"I . . . am . . . so . . . sorry," she said.

She heard his heartbroken cry as the red-tinged darkness came. Pain blurred her vision and her eyes drifted closed. She smiled, glad of the darkness, because she could see William more clearly in her mind's eye than she had been able to see him in reality. He reached out to her, his hands strong and secure, his face warm with love. At the touch of his hand, her pain vanished. Bathed in happiness, she felt herself slip softly, almost imperceptibly, into sleep.

She was exhausted, but he wouldn't let her rest. He grabbed her by the shoulders, shaking her awake. She sat up with a start, heart pounding, stomach tense with fear. But as soon as she saw that William was still there, standing right beside her, she calmed down. She glanced at her wound, but the bleeding had stopped, and the dagger no longer stuck out from between her ribs. She wanted to ask William how the surgeon had achieved such a miracle, but she was racked by a spasm of coughing and couldn't speak.

When the bout of coughing ended, she turned to William, but his features had become blurred and difficult to recognize. The fear surged back.

"What's the matter?" she asked him. "What's happened to me? Why can't I see your face?"

"Robyn!" She heard a mixture of fear and joy in his voice, and his hand reached out to smooth her hair away from her brow. The tension radiating from his body buffeted her with almost physical force. She plummeted back and forth into the darkness, ebbing and flowing like a wave struggling to reach a certain point on the sand.

He spoke again. "Robyn." His voice pulled her higher onto the shore. "Can you hear me, honey?"

"I can hear you, but your voice sounds—strange." As soon as she spoke, the mist parted and she understood why he sounded different. It was Zach who was calling her, not William, just as it was Zach pleading with her to open her eyes . . .

"Zach!" She smiled, overjoyed to see him again. "Why do you keep asking me to open my eyes? Look, they're open already."

He didn't reply, and she glanced around anxiously, seeing only mist—and Zach. "Where are we? What happened to me? Where is William? I must go to him, tell him I'm alive—"

"Robyn, give me your hand." Zach reached out to her, but the gap between them was too wide and their hands didn't connect. She could see his face more clearly now, and she realized he was frantic with worry. "Why do you look so worried?" she asked. "The surgeon William summoned has healed me." She pointed to her chest. "See? No dagger. No wound."

He didn't seem to hear, although he was standing less than three feet away from her. His emotions overwhelmed her, so strong that she turned her back, hiding from their power.

"Robyn, where are you going? Look at me, damn you!" His features blurred again, and he called to her, more frenzied than before, pleading with her to come back. Robyn didn't want to listen. She covered her ears with her hands, blocking out the sound, as she decided what to do. If she stepped forward, she knew she would be able to see Zach more clearly—maybe even touch him—but what about William? In her heart of hearts, she was sure William still called to her, even though she could no longer hear him. Was there any way to step into the mist swirling behind her and find William?

Robyn looked back over her shoulder, straining to detect even the slightest hint of William's presence. The mist thickened as she looked, and however hard she peered into its gray depths, she saw nothing. Refusing to accept defeat, she tried to walk into the mist, but it congealed into a solid barrier that froze her muscles and left her incapable of movement. She knew then, without reason but with absolute certainty, that to walk farther into the foggy darkness was to invite death, and that if she persisted in exploring the icy blackness, William and Zach would both be lost to her forever.

For a moment the enormity of her loss kept her immobilized. Then she heard Zach calling her name, his voice soft, compelling, and aching with regret. She turned, responding instinctively to his need. He saw her turn, and his face broke into a huge smile.

"Robyn, sweetheart, I knew you'd come back one day." He stretched out his hands in welcome, waiting for her to come back to him. Belatedly she understood that he couldn't move any closer to her. If she wanted to take his hand, if she wanted to rejoin him, she would have to choose to walk forward into his arms.

The choice suddenly didn't seem hard at all. Her feet were weighted with lead, but Robyn stepped forward, determined to reach Zach. The light brightened steadily, and the mist drifted away, re-forming into solid shapes. Her feet were lighter now, and with each step, movement became easier. Robyn ran toward Zach, hands outstretched. She was almost touching him now. Almost . . .

The darkness pulsated with flashes of scarlet and purple. Robyn clawed at the hands squeezing her neck, coughing and spluttering to stop the sickly sweet sludge from trickling down her throat.

"Get away from her, Gerry." The stranglehold around her neck eased and the weight lifted from on top of her. Gasping, lungs screaming out with the pain of drawing breath, Robyn collapsed against the sofa cushions.

"Tell me what you fed her, damn you!"

"N-nothing. I don't know! She did it herself, I swear. I tried to stop her, but she was uncontrollable."

"What were you afraid of, Gerry? It wasn't enough that she's out of her mind since your sister shot her? You had to make sure she was dead, is that it?"

"Have you gone crazy, old chap? I've no idea what you're talking about."

"Save your protests for the judge and jury. I'm not willing to be suckered anymore."

Could that really be Zach speaking? Robyn struggled to orient herself. Was she delirious from being stabbed and simply fantasizing? Or else . . . was it possible that she had come back to her own time?

Robyn realized that she'd drawn in at least a half-dozen breaths without feeling as if her lungs would explode. Stomach still churning with nausea, she pushed herself up on her elbow, finally ready to open her eyes.

She sat up and looked around. She was in her mother's living room, lying on the tweed-covered sofa that had been bought the year she left home to go away to college. Zach knelt beside her, fists clenched, jaw rigid with tension, brows drawn together in a ferocious frown. He looked so much like William in one of his more belligerent moods that she didn't know whether to laugh in tender recognition or cry with bittersweet regret.

In the end she did neither, because her body felt too disconnected from her brain to obey the simplest command. She tried to say hello, but the only sound that came out of her parched throat was a rasping grunt, and even that puny effort left her stomach clenching with nausea.

"Robyn? I won't hurt you, my dear, I just want to find out what happened."

"Don't know." The words came out sounding more like the croakings of an amorous frog than a coherent effort at human speech.

Zach hesitated, almost as if expecting her to protest, then sat down on the sofa and put his arm around her protectively, the gesture of a kindly mentor with a not-too-bright protégée. Robyn looked up at him and smiled, all she was capable of until her throat smoothed out a little.

Zach returned her smile cautiously, as if he expected rejection—or worse—at any moment. "Does your stomach ache?" he asked, his voice low and carefully mild. "Can you point to where it hurts you, Robyn?"

Her sluggish, muddled brain finally produced the words she'd been trying to say minutes earlier in the conversation. "Hi, Zach. It's me, Robyn. I'm home."

Her voice sounded scratchy, but at least this time it was comprehensible. Zach drew in a patient breath. "Hi, Robyn. I know you're at home, my dear. Do you think you could tell me what happened here?"

Gerry spoke while she was still trying to make her mouth say the words inside her brain. "I've told you what happened, for God's sake! She was going to drink that stuff," he said, pointing to the vial on the floor that still contained a trace of fluid. His face crumpled into an expression of anxious concern. "God, I'm glad you arrived right in the nick of time, Zach. It was an absolute nightmare. She went berserk when I tried to take the flask away from her. God knows what she had in it."

Muriel Delaney came into the sitting room and Robyn's heart gave a jump of happiness. "Mother!"

"Hi, sweetheart." Muriel Delaney answered absently. White-faced, she bent down and picked up the empty bottle.

"Good grief, it smells like gasoline. What happened? Where did it come from?"

"I don't know how much she drank," Gerry said. "I took her embroidery over to the light to get a better look and when I turned around, she was slugging the stuff in that bottle. It looked such a weird color, I knew she shouldn't be drinking it. I rushed over and made a grab for it. We spilled quite a bit while we were tussling. I hope I haven't ruined your sofa cushions, Muriel."

Muriel burst into tears. "Oh, lord, when is this going to end? I thought Robyn learned her lesson when she tried to drink dishwashing liquid and we had to give her an emetic. But this is worse, much worse."

Robyn wanted to get up and comfort her mother, but her knees buckled when she tried to stand. Zach was staring at Gerry, looking suddenly uncertain. A brown-haired woman Robyn had never seen came in from the hallway and took Muriel's hand. "Everything's going to be all right," the woman said. "How lucky we are that Gerry was here to stop her before any real damage was done."

"I'll drive her to the hospital emergency room," Gerry said. "That's better than waiting for the paramedics. Muriel, could you get her coat?"

Zach stepped forward, his expression belligerent. "I'll drive her," he said.

"All right, old man, no need to sound so aggressive. We'll follow you." Gerry turned to the brown-haired woman. "Coming, Gloria?"

Robyn noticed that everybody talked around her, as if she were blind, or deaf, or mentally incapable of taking part in handling her own life. But that was a puzzle to be explained later. First things first. She shook off the dreadful nausea and the mind-numbing lethargy that made her want to lean against Zach and let the world go rambling by. "Stop him," she croaked. "Stop Gerry. Don't let him leave."

Everyone stared at her. She forced her thick, clumsy tongue to pronounce the necessary words. "Gerry . . . tried to . . . kill me."

"Oh, heavens, I'm so sorry, Gerry." Muriel's face was flushed with embarrassment. "She doesn't understand what she's saying, of course."

Gerry gave a kind, understanding smile. "I know—"

Robyn broke in. "I understand exactly what I'm saying, Mother. You tried to kill me, Gerry. Why? What have I ever done to you?"

Gerry spoke quickly. "Look, she's obviously confused. What we need to do right now is get her to the hospital. I'll get my car—"

"Don't let him go!" Robyn croaked, dragging herself to her feet and tottering toward the door. "He pinned me into the corner of the sofa, shoved that flask into my mouth, and forced me to swallow. He tried to poison me!"

Gerry and Gloria didn't wait to argue. They made a simultaneous dash for the door, but Zach was there first. He knocked Gerry down with an uppercut to the jaw, followed by a two-handed blow to the back of his neck, and when Gloria looked all set to scramble over her brother's body and make a separate run for it, he grabbed her by the hair and socked her hard in the gut.

Muriel gasped. "Oh, my, Zach, don't hurt her! She seems like such a nice lady."

"Yeah," he said grimly. "So nice that I'm pretty damn certain she's the woman who tried to shoot Robyn."

"The woman who shot me had long black curly hair," Robyn said. "This woman has short brown hair."

"I expect she wore a wig when she attacked you," Zach said, busily engaged in using his belt to tie Gerry's hands securely behind his back. "There, that should keep them under control until the police get here. Muriel, could you call the police at the same time as you call the doc—"

He broke off in midsentence and strode across the room. He grabbed Robyn's shoulders and swung her around to face him. "What did you say?" he demanded, shaking her in his desperate eagerness to hear confirmation of his hopes.

"I said the woman who shot me had black hair. But I expect you're right. She probably wore a wig."

Zach stared down at her, struggling to find words. "My God, Robyn, you've come back! You're here, really here, aren't you?"

"Yes," she said. "I'm really here. And I'd better warn you that if you keep on shaking me like that, there's a strong probability I'll prove I'm here by throwing up all over my mother's favorite Oriental rug. My stomach doesn't approve of that green stuff Gerry tried to force down me."

Hugging her daughter, Muriel gave a laugh that was one part disbelief, three parts joyful tears. "That sounds like the daughter I've been longing to hear for the past three months. Hang in there, honey, I'm going to call the paramedics. Can you give me a better description of whatever it was that dreadful man tried to make you drink?"

"It was bright green, very sweet, and it tasted sort of warm in my mouth," she said.

"The paramedics may recognize what it is. Presumably it's a common household item since Gerry was planning to pass your death off as either an accident or suicide." Muriel gave her daughter a final hug. "I'll go and call right away. Zach, you'll take care of her for me?"

"You betcha." He glanced across the room to make sure that Gerry and Gloria were still safely tied together, then sat down in a chair by the fire and pulled Robyn onto his lap, cradling her head against his shoulder and running his hands over her face with yearning tenderness.

"I thought I knew how much I missed you," he said. "But I was wrong. God, Robyn, you have a smile in your eyes again and it looks *wonderful.*" He bent his head and kissed her softly on the forehead. "I don't know where you've been for the past three months, but welcome home, my love."

"It's good to be back." She realized as she spoke that it was true. Her separation from William was still an aching wound, but Zach's presence soothed the pain of her loss. His love reached out to her, folding her in its warmth, and she felt the stir of complex emotions she had deliberately kept buried during her exile in the past. She placed her hand over Zach's and gazed deep into the glowing heart of the fire. "One day, when we're both old and gray, I'll have to tell you where I went."

He carried her hand to his lips and pressed a kiss into the softness of her palm. "Just so long as you never go back. I don't think I could bear to lose you a second time."

She glanced toward Gerry and Gloria, captive and unable to wreak further harm. She remembered Captain Bretton as she had last seen him, brought to death by the violence of his own hatred. "I don't think there's any danger of my going back," she said. "The villains have all been taken care of. I'm here to stay."

Zach traced a circle around her palm, his touch tender with longing. "I missed you, Robyn."

"I missed you, too." She looked into his eyes, eyes that were a brilliant, achingly familiar blue and felt a surge of emotion so strong that her whole body shook with it. Her love for William, still fraught with the pain of their parting, fused with her feelings for Zach. The delicate bud of a new, stronger love began to grow deep inside her soul. Hesitantly, she reached up and cupped Zach's face between her hands.

He kissed her, then linked his arms around her waist. "*I love you, Zach.* Those were the last words you said to me before I left to catch my plane for Paris. Do you remember, Robyn?"

"I remember."

His voice had gained confidence, and he was beginning to smile. He leaned down, drawing her close. "One day soon, you'll say them again."

"Yes," she said softly. "I'm sure I will." Loving Zach, she realized, was how it was meant to be.

Epilogue

A full moon hung in the velvet darkness of the August sky. Robyn threw open the old-fashioned casement window and leaned out, breathing in the softness of summer night air. A warm breeze, scented with honeysuckle, blew her hair into her face and ruffled the satin ribbons on her nightgown.

Zach came up behind her, circling his arms around her waist and dropping a kiss into the hollow of her collarbone. "Happy, Mrs. Bowleigh?" he asked.

"Blissful, thank you, Mr. Bowleigh."

"You look very fetching in black lace." His hands trailed up from her waist to cup her breasts. "But I seem to recall you look even better out of black lace."

She leaned back into his arms, smiling to herself. After three days of marriage, she had decided that honeymoons were a great invention. "I'm glad the weather is so gorgeous," she said. "I'm looking forward to exploring the countryside tomorrow. Everywhere looked smothered in wildflowers as we drove down from the airport."

He turned her around in his arms, gazing down at her with sudden seriousness. "You don't have any regrets?" he asked. "No nightmares? Coming here to Starke hasn't brought back too many unpleasant memories of the shooting?"

"It's brought back memories," she said. "But that isn't necessarily bad. Gerry and Gloria are in prison, so I have no real fears anymore. And sometimes nightmares are worse if you refuse to confront them." She touched his cheek in a fleeting caress. "I needed to come, Zach, to lay a lot of old ghosts to rest."

He held her close for a moment, and she rested gratefully against him. "On a happier subject," he said. "We have another wedding present. This came for us from the baron while you were in the shower. Do you want to open it now?" He walked over to the desk and picked up a well-padded package that looked as if it might contain a picture or a small painting.

Robyn's heart gave an odd little jump of anticipation. "Yes, please, I'd like to open it now."

Zach slit open the bubble wrap. Inside was a framed sheet of vellum, covered in copper-plate script, and a note from the baron. He read the covering note, then handed it to her.

Robyn and Zach: This letter has always been a treasured item in our family archive. When I noticed the surprising similarity of names, I decided it would make an intriguing gift to celebrate the happy occasion of your wedding. It comes to you with every good wish from the Bowleighs of Starke, to the Bowleighs of the United States of America.

Robyn put the baron's note aside and picked up the framed vellum letter, which was dated January 14, 1749, and signed William Bowleigh. Pulses racing, she began to read.

Dearest Robyn, wife of my heart, I write to you from the fullness of a spirit overflowing with love and bittersweet joy. Today Hannah, my wife, in defiance of all our expectations, gave birth to a healthy daughter. She had feared herself too old to conceive, and her happiness at this safe delivery is a source of great pleasure to both of us.

You told me, on that dreadful day, exactly three years ago, when you were taken from me, that Hannah was a good woman, and you were entirely right. She is kind, affectionate, and a woman of excellent intellect. Our children—yours and mine—love her dearly, and she returns their love in equal measure. I owe her my gratitude, my respect, and my affection, and this she has in full measure. But my dearest Robyn, she can never possess my heart. That belongs only and for ever to you.

Our family thrives in all its branches. My brother Zachary has adopted the Catholic faith of the Stuart princes he admires so much. He plans, if you can believe this, to take the vows for entry into the priesthood. Like many reformed sinners, it seems he is determined to carry his penance to the ultimate lengths.

Your infant son Zachary is an infant no longer. He runs all

*over the house, rivaling even his older brothers in the mis-
chief he can accomplish in one short day. Clementina grows
ever sweeter in the kindly care of her stepmother, and our
new baby daughter seems set to startle the world with her
bright red curls. Hannah wishes her to be called Elizabeth
Arabella, in your honor, and I am delighted to agree.*

*Beloved Robyn, I write this letter in accordance with the
promise I made you on that dreadful day in Bristol.
Strangely, the act of writing seems to bring you closer and
the ache of my loss feels less. I wish with all my heart that
I could write this letter knowing that you were alive somewhere in the world to read it. Instead I console myself with
the hope that you wait to welcome me into Paradise, where
I shall remain forever and eternity, your most loving husband, William Bowleigh.*

Zach brushed his hands over her cheeks. "You're crying."

She reached for a tissue. "It's a moving letter."

"Yes, it is. He sounds like quite a guy. He must have
loved his Lady Arabella almost as much as I love you."

Robyn smiled at him through her tears. "Yes," she said
tenderly. "I think he did."